MW01469845

The Air

George Michael Sullivan

THE AIR

George Michael Sullivan

iUniverse, Inc.
New York Lincoln Shanghai

The Air

iUniverse books may be ordered through booksellers or by contacting:

iUniverse
2021 Pine Lake Road, Suite 100
Lincoln, NE 68512
www.iuniverse.com
1-800-Authors (1-800-288-4677)

ISBN-13: 978-0-595-37250-8 (pbk)
ISBN-13: 978-0-595-81647-7 (ebk)
ISBN-10: 0-595-37250-3 (pbk)
ISBN-10: 0-595-81647-9 (ebk)

Printed in the United States of America

CHAPTER 1

Morning broke early at the country club golf course as Schuyler Ballantine practiced his golf swing. As a slender young man, he was finishing his senior year at high school and was currently on the school's golf team. He measured only 69 inches and 150 pounds, but could hit a golf ball seemingly a short country mile. His distance was good, but he often lacked accuracy and his talented short golf game kept him in most of his competitions, since he often relied on his ability to get up-and-down to save par. An unusual putting style was subjective to criticism due to an excessive opening in his putting stance. He developed this open putting stance as a boy that resembled his baseball-hitting stance, allowing more opportunity to hit a volatile fastball. This open stance was always his trademark and it was continued throughout high school.

The golf course had invited young Schuyler early that morning. It was a school holiday, from spring break, and he arrived even earlier than the dawn patrol. The dawn patrol was a foursome of retired gentlemen whom regularly teed off before any other members arrived at the course. Club members claimed they could set their watches to their schedule, since they routinely teed off at 0630 hours. Schuyler, alone, started his play even earlier and was about to complete his eighteen holes in a little over three hours.

Approaching the final hole, primed for breakfast, the sun has just started to strengthen. The eighteen-hole round took a lot out of him and he slowly ventured closer to the green. The final put sank into the hole giving an estimated score of ninety. This was the norm for a golfer of his level.

Proceeding to the clubhouse, he spotted Mr. Jenkins, an elderly man practicing his putting.

"Good morning Schuyler," spoke Mr. Jenkins.

"Good morning sir."

"How did you shoot?" asked Mr. Jenkins.

"About ninety!" Schuyler marched to the clubhouse.

Mr. Jenkins was an elderly man that knew Schuyler's father. He had worked, before retiring, at the same research facility as Schuyler's father and frequently spoke to him as an extended family member. He returned to practice putting and thought out loud, "*Young Ballantine is an excellent young man, a credit to his school, but could not control his excessive thinking.*"

Schuyler received his transmission, but could not understand why excessive thinking warranted scrutiny. He has always thought to himself throughout his entire life. As far as he could remember, he communicates with himself routinely throughout the entire course of the day. Also not comprehending how Mr. Jenkins knew he thought too much caused him to feel suddenly uneasy. Since Mr. Jenkins only saw him at the golf course for short periods of time, it caused him to feel more and more uncomfortable as he tried to comprehend Mr. Jenkins' reasoning.

The clubhouse consisted of the nineteenth hole, an age of twenty-one and over establishment, serving alcoholic beverages. The clubhouse also contained a small cafe. Since he was only seventeen, he could only enter the cafe section of the clubhouse.

Walking into the cafe, removing his Cubs' hat, he spoke to fellow golfers from his high school team, "Hey, what are you'll doing?"

Mark, from the high school golf team, asked, "How did you shoot?"

"I shot about bogey for eighteen holes. I played about as good as I usually do this early in the morning."

"You didn't record your score nor did you just not take the time to write it down," asked Mark.

"Not officially," hunting through his pockets to locate his scorecard.

Kent, another team member, directed, "you need to practice for improvement to achieve expectations greater than the number six spot on the high school golf team." He looked at Mark for agreement, but he really wasn't paying much attention to him, and added, "Eventually you will have to pull your own weight."

"I'm content with being the sixth man; at least I'm in the line-up, and get to play during the match."

As Mark received his Pepsi from the waitress, he said to Schuyler. "You are good enough for the team as the sixth man and will have the opportunity to prove your ability on the course."

Drinking his root beer, Kent was sitting down waiting for Doug, another player of their school team, to arrive. They had a tee off time soon and were waiting to play. "Schuyler, you need more confidence in yourself to become an accomplished over-achiever."

Mark, selecting his golf balls for play, turned his head toward Schuyler, "don't worry, you will do alright. You have always performed well under pressure ever since I have known you."

"I do play well with my partner, and I will strive to not let the team down." He ordered breakfast from Ms. Hurt at the cafe with a voice of uncertainty, not really sure what he wished to order or knowing the proper words to say. Anyway, he eventually got the point through and ordered his breakfast.

"*You are a sweet fellow, but I can tell that you're inexperienced at certain facets of life,*" thought Ms. Hurt.

He received her transmitted thoughts with some fear, mostly because he was not sure what she meant and how she could vision his life. He sat down at the table, waiting for his breakfast, communicating to himself about his schedule for the rest of the day.

Doug entered the clubhouse, wearing a Cubs' shirt, and asked, "Can you play another nine?"

"Sorry I can't due to a medical appointment. My father scheduled an appointment for me today." Schuyler informed Doug.

"I understand, remember we have a match against Central next week and we need you prepared, both physically and mentally, for the match," responded Doug as he exited the clubhouse.

Watching the threesome tee off on the first hole and drinking his orange juice, he could tell they were having a conversation. He overheard the trio communicating to each other about him.

Kent, the tallest player of the threesome, thought, "*I'm worried about him, his progress is moving in that direction very slowly. I don't believe he will be able to adapt.*"

Mark, a short, stocky, and aggressive high school senior, shook his head and responded to Kent by thinking, "*He can handle the pressure of playing golf, can't he? Allow him to be as he is.*"

Doug, the youngest of the trio, glared at the sky and thought, "*Schuyler is a fine example of senior leadership and if he continues to be a sterling impression for others to follow, then his constant self communication is part of his character.*"

Kent ended the conversation by thinking to Mark and Doug, "*yes, but I'm worried due to the fact that he may be considered different, instead of unique. Critical opinions could harm him in the future.*"

He was shocked to hear them giving their opinions of him in that way. He could hear them thinking among themselves from quite a distance. He had detected people thinking among themselves within his presence, but never recognized communicative thinking from such a distance. He could not understand this communicative process, but eventually settled down as the threesome walked down the fairway to the green.

Schuyler finished eating his breakfast with a puzzled expression on his face. As Ms. Hurt wondered back into the kitchen, he rose from his chair and left the clubhouse. Pigeons were actively nibbling on breadcrumbs near the vicinity of his vehicle. Carefully walking around them, he entered his car.

Driving home from the country club was a pleasant drive. The clouds in the sky stimulated his thought process, enhancing his questioning of the today's earlier discussion at the clubhouse. The mental communication of Mr. Jenkins, Ms. Hurt, Mark, Kent, and Doug bothered him more and more. Why were they concerned? What can be administered to solve the problem?

Arrival time to his home was at least two hours prior to his medical appointment. His hometown, located on a highway midway between Richmond and Lexington, was a small town bearing newly developed housing and industrial parks. The city boomed from being enriched from culture influenced from both Richmond and Lexington. The two cities served as employment sources utilized vastly by his hometown, and both parents possessed technical occupations at a Richmond-based research plant. They were research analysts at a relatively high security institution. His father had worked there ever since Schuyler was two years of age, and his mother eventually got on with the plant a few years later. Together the couple earned enough money to support both their sons, Duncan and Schuyler. The Ballantine family lived in a fine house and belonged to the local country club. The Ballantine children were given much opportunity to benefit from what life had to offer. The high school was highly rated. Sure it suffered through some drug involvement, but overall it was a striving learning institution. The teacher-student ratio was low, enhancing class participation, and student-led activities grew every year, developing career strategies. The Ballantine children greatly benefited from their parent's efforts.

Duncan was a year older than Schuyler, and had already graduated from high school. He elected to enlist into the United States Army. It was his choice; thus the family was confident he would succeed as a soldier. Currently, he was stationed at a post located along the Kentucky/Tennessee border. It was an infantry post providing large soldiering motivation. Also, it was close enough to home to visit his parents a few times a year. Everybody admired him for his decision to serve his country.

Schuyler reported to his medical appointment fifteen minutes early only to learn his doctor was a psychologist. Yes, he had been referred to mental health without his knowledge. He wondered about the encounter. Why is this necessary?

"Hello Schuyler, I am Dr. Walton," he said. "I'm going to talk to you about your mental capacity."

"Doctor, uh sir, I'm only a B-level student in my senior year of high school. How could I be of any significance?"

"Yes, but your potential is stronger than you think," he responded.

"I have potential?"

"Schuyler, do you know why you are at this appointment," he questioned.

"No, I only know that I'm confused."

"No need to be confused," he said. "You are being evaluated in order to find avenues to enhance your mental thinking."

"I don't understand" as he shifted back and forth in his chair. Suddenly placing his head in his hands, freezing in midstream of thought, he was even more puzzled than before and did not know how to respond back to the doctor.

"You will be given three tests, or evaluations, that will give me some feedback of your mental ability," directed the doctor.

The fear of the tests made him sweat and the way the tall psychologist looked at him made him more nervous. He realized the tests, or evaluations, were to be used for the doctor's benefit, not his own.

Doctor Walton marched him into another room and had him sit down at a small table. As he gave the first test, he checked his watch and commanded, "Identify these shapes."

"Doc, what do you want me to do?"

"Write down, from one to ten, your feelings about these ten objects. Just use your imagination, Schuyler," he responded.

He looked at the ten objects; he reviewed what he saw, and eventually made his final decision. He believed the objects to resemble sand traps on a golf course, or a likeness of home plate on a baseball diamond. He did report that two of the figures made him think of star constellations, and later discovered the doctor had a very strong interest in his star constellation responses.

He was relieved after finishing the object test. He stretched his arms, letting out stressful inhibitions, preparing him for the next test. He incurred some fear because the following test may be more difficult than the previous one.

"Schuyler, the next test will be word identification," as the doctor paced back and forth throughout the room. "This evaluation will exhibit your capability to learn foreign languages."

Examining the words, he mentioned, "I don't understand any of the words, they have no meaning."

"It is not an actual language, the words are prefabricated. They are designed for you to construct your own dialogue," he directed.

Stressed already from the previous test and getting more puzzled every minute, he began the task to choose among four choices for the current definition of each word. The words were a major challenge; it was like the creation of a whole new language, tailored for him. He struggled through the entire test, but finally completed it. He set his pencil aside and gleamed at the doctor.

"Are you finished?" he asked.

"I guess so."

"Are you certain?" he responded.

"I have done as well as possible, sir"

"Well done Schuyler, you will be given a thirty minute break in preparation for the final examination," he spoke.

His nerves were on edge, and he detected the doc surely recognized his nervous state. He suspected the thirty-minute break was to ensure he would do his best on the final exam, in order to benefit Doctor Walton and not just himself.

Doctor Walton restored the evaluation process, assembling materials required for the final test. "Schuyler, this is your final evaluation."

"I am ready."

"You will use your highest degree of mental ability during the final phase of this examination," he encouraged. "You have a binary numbering system, solve the following twenty equations."

"I really am confused, I need more detailed directions."

"This is your real test of your ability, "responded the doctor. "The equations before you are simplified math problems requiring comprehensive analysis."

"I j-just choose among the four choices?"

"Affirmative," he commanded.

Schuyler evaluated every question, attempting some reasoning, to justify his answer for each question. He used every avenue of approach, every way possible, to conclude his final answers.

The doctor noticed he had terminated his test, "congratulations, you have succeeded in a very challenging experience."

Schuyler was so excited about finishing the tests. He breathed a big relief in conclusion of a two-hour period of torment. This was not a friendly place for him and he did not wish a return engagement. Too bad he had another appointment in two weeks.

CHAPTER 2

The Jupiter, a think tank located in Lexington, was a research analysis center, focusing on human intelligence enhancement. Don Morrison and John Boyd, Jupiter employees, concentrated on an exclusive independent study of a young boy. This study had been ongoing for almost fifteen years with the tracking of significant events of the young boy's life. A multitude of studies concerning this boy developed from his unique ability to maintain a thought. Sensed by other individuals, this thought characteristic not just affected only the boy. It was a phenomena referred by Morrison and Boyd as "The Air" or "The Vision." This young boy possessing this phenomenon was Schuyler Ballantine.

Don Morrison, a Jupiter veteran of twenty years, stated "Boyd, we have tracked all major events of The Air for almost fifteen years."

"I prefer to call him The Vision," responded Boyd as he quickly looked at Morrison for an immediate response.

"Why," asked Morrison?

Boyd stood up and walked closer to Morrison, "We only not hear him think or speak, but we also see what he sees."

Morrison looked back at Boyd and agreed, "Yes, it appears that everybody sees and hears what the boy does."

Boyd wondered around the room, "due to the phenomena, I believe the entire world may be visioning his life."

"How can we tell if these phenomena can be detected throughout all four corners of the world," asked Morrison.

Boyd gleamed at Morrison, "you can fly around the entire world to evaluate the boy's capability."

Morrison started laughing at Boyd's response and accidentally spilt his coffee all over his newspaper on his desk. He looked back at Boyd, "that's one far-fetched idea."

"Not really," returned Boyd.

Morrison shockingly raised his eyebrows at Boyd, "What do you have planned for me to do?"

"Maybe, you could travel to Seoul and monitor The Vision's phenomena range throughout the whole trip," responded Boyd.

Morrison nodded his head, "it would be almost half way around the world, providing a good benchmark for future study."

Boyd was satisfied with the conclusion, "this trip could easily reveal the true capacity of The Vision."

Morrison directed his attention to Boyd; "I will make plans to fly to Seoul immediately."

Boyd got very nervous about the future progress. And when he got nervous, he liked to eat. His favorite lunch meal was Big K Pizza, located only a few miles down the road. Grabbing the phone quickly, he ordered a ham with pineapple pizza for delivery. Also, he added an order of wings for Morrison. His partner was the only person he knew who drank coffee while he ate chicken wings.

Morrison poured himself another cup of coffee and started planning his trip. He knew the venture could provide viable information benefiting their research. He had started this project several years before Boyd. He had the initial interest in The Air, or The Vision as Boyd preferred. Every significant event from Schuyler's life was documented for continuous evaluation.

Schuyler's entire life, or as early as remembered, was viewed by not only The Jupiter, but by others. The complete listing of others is unknown, but suspected to be a large spectrum. He lives his life on "air." This means others sense his presence. Whatever he hears, feels, or sees is detected by this unknown spectrum of individuals. Also every thought in his head can be received, and every move that he plans to make can be anticipated. His life is a vision in the public's mind and the Seoul trip might provide valuable data to determine public spectrum broadness.

Boyd went outside to receive the pizza. He rendered a delivery tip and brought the pizza inside into their office. He gave Morrison the wings and a strong slice of pizza before he sat down at his desk to enjoy his favorite dish. It was routine to order pizza for lunch. It was convenient and satisfied their appetite. Repositioning his pineapple on his pizza slice, he asked Morrison, "after lunch can you brief me on your study of The Vision's early years?"

"Yes," replied Morrison as he quickly consumed his pizza slice and rinsed it down with a gulp of coffee. As he finished his lunch, he planned his briefing. He was concerned about The Air, since he was getting close to his eighteenth birthday. The research could take a paradigm shift, due to a possible drastic change of the boy's lifestyle.

Boyd consumed his ham and pineapple pizza and was eager to get back to work. He opened his personal file of The Vision, preparing himself to pay much attention to his partner's brief.

As Morrison sorted his files, he began speaking, "the past fifteen years have come and gone very quickly." He adjusted his files, separating the first five years from the rest, and followed, "during the initial five years, I've discovered that whenever The Air was in presence of other children, they acted like him. The children listen to his thinking and often would think back at him, providing their own communication mode. In my documentation, the children only returned mental thinking to Schuyler within their immediate presence of him."

Boyd directed to Morrison, "and it seems to be still that way today. It appears common for individuals, within immediate range to communicate with him through these phenomena of mental thinking, or airing, as you and I wish to call it."

"I have no documentation of airing occurring with anyone else but with him. I tracked the following five years with similar results," reported Morrison.

Boyd replied, "you mean only Schuyler, and individuals within his locality, executed airing."

"To my knowledge," said Morrison.

Boyd sighed, "I wish I had paid more attention to him. I must have gotten complacent with The Vision thinking continuously to himself throughout the day."

Morrison sat down at his desk, "I guess the whole world has gotten used to this behavior and did not really pay much attention to The Air. He seems to be a part of everybody, and everybody has grown to accept him."

Boyd looked at Morrison, shaking his head in disappointment, "I never really thought about it, I just accepted him as he was. I never realized any cause-and-effect relationship."

Morrison began his second phase of briefing, "during the second five years, I evaluated significant events that could project periods of success and failure. I learned those emotional aspects of The Air's life traveled in cycles, and the young boy's emotional life was very stressful. Frequently at major events, he appeared to be the focal point of activity. During little league baseball, bowling, or even school, he attracted specific attention to himself for some odd reason. It seemed he was the benchmark for all others to be evaluated. The adults would often direct themselves to him, expecting the young boy to take the lead. This derived attention, from being the air, created a mystique among his presence. This mystique, or indirect responsibility, indoctrinated a whole new leadership concept. This concept, never seen before, published much critical research data."

Amazed at what Morrison had said, Boyd asked, "what about his golfing experiences? I feel his golfing caused him to gain self-composure, to obtain entertainment in a less stressful environment. Golf has always provided an avenue to avoid public pressure, and still be participating actively in a sporting activity. He was skilled in baseball and bowling, but eventually found golf as his niche."

Morrison agreed, "golf made his character to the degree it is today. His initial golf experience provided him the attributes, values, and beliefs he utilizes today. He will do well in life; he has innovative ideas to progress through future stages of his life."

"I agree" responded Boyd, looking puzzled in the face.

"What is wrong?" asked Morrison.

Boyd stood up, glanced out the window, and suggested, "Maybe golf is not what he needs to prevent anxiety."

"True, he cannot play golf forever," cringed Morrison shaking his head.

Both of them agreed golf was only a quick fix now, but adulthood would accommodate potential battlegrounds providing ample opportunities for social integration.

The past five years have given the senior staff at Jupiter an increasing interest in the phenomena. The Jupiter had added John Boyd to its staff augmenting Don Morrison. The Morrison and Boyd era provided The Jupiter with even more research data than in the prior ten years.

Morrison and Boyd surveyed specific settings such as school, home, and social activities. They concluded his home environment had stabilized throughout the years. The household virtually ignored his airing. They received his transmitted air without scrutiny, but elected to not respond back with air transmission. His parents responded only to his verbal statements, being careful to stay consistent and not confuse him. They wished to judge him only from his spoken words, not any thoughts.

The brother, Duncan, refrained from airing with him at all accounts. He was very skilled at speaking to his younger brother, free of air. He was actually the best at communicating with his brother due to their unique relationship.

Morrison and Boyd concluded that the more an individual had contact with The Air, the more likely their conversation was free of air. His family proved this; they had little difficulty speaking to him without use of air.

Classroom-setting environments offered mixed reviews. Some classmates returned air extensively while others aired very little, or even at all. Several variables were evaluated such as class size, subject area, grade level, location, and time. Extensive analysis determined no variable emerging as a favorite. After little luck with the current variables, another area was considered. Every individual classmate's tenure was categorized by seniority. Thus, students were divided upon length of time spent as his classmate. By a landslide, the students with greater experience as his classmate aired much less. Hence, a strong inverse relationship was discovered between classmate tenure and classroom airing. Actually Schuyler's closest classmates seemed to ignore his airing much like his family did, while the rookie classmates showed the highest degree of return air. Morrison and Boyd believed the rookie classmates were more eager to seize a window of opportunity to experiment with the air phenomena, causing a sharp rise in the amount of their air feedback.

Both classroom and home studies resulted in viable data. His social activities complicated the research progress since public reaction could not be predicted easily. Every individual social activity possessed its own uniqueness, resulting in skewed data. Cause and effect relationships produced no certain pattern, and variables became so numerous that it misdirected analysis. Routine activities such as playing golf, watching television, and driving a car generated stable data warranting credible analysis. But less frequent activities such as movies, concerts, and vacations exhibited inconsistent information being not suitable for evaluation. The activities often had little in common, preventing variables to be compared, presenting obstacles in data research.

The surveys produced a multitude of analytical evaluation, providing correlation among variables. It discovered reasons for increases and decreases of airing, along with Schuyler's responses and reactions from this communicative form.

The most important analysis formulated was that air phenomena did occur during his association with others. Morrison and Boyd believed new relationships would surely stimulate an increase of airing. They prepared for the future because young Schuyler will venture into the world very shortly. Associates, not previously known to him, would experience a whole new life style. The Jupiter expected to be very involved with this incurring venture, since it could affect the lives of such a wide range of people.

CHAPTER 3

Schuyler returned to the country club pending a golf match with Central. School dismissed him early in preparation for the match. Arriving at the golf course almost a whole hour prior to the beginning of the match, gave him ample opportunity to practice his driving and putting. Before every match he liked to drive a bucket of practice balls and putt on the practice putting green, deploying utmost readiness in match preparation.

A golf match consisted of each team challenging six players against the other side. Positioned as sixth man, from coach's decision, he would ultimately play against Central's number six man. The number one golfer is always the team's best player; thus Schuyler was the sixth best golfer on the team, as so was his opponent. Also he would partner up with Doug, the fifth man, in best ball competition. The match schedule presented individual and best ball competitions. Schuyler would play against his opponent, Doug would play against his opponent, and together they would play best ball against both opponents. Each twosome was worth three total points.

Fellow team members consisted of Mark, number one, and Kent, number two, playing together. The two remaining players were Tony, number three, and Richard, number four. The team could earn nine total points overall, requiring only a majority of the nine total points for a victory.

Fortunately, the coach had Doug paired with him for a reason. Even though Doug was younger, his personality provided comfort during tight matches. The coach perceived the sixth position, along with Doug's mentorship, would allow Schuyler's performance to pinnacle. He had a comfort zone when playing with

Doug. They seemed to play well together, helping each other out in tight situations, allowing Schuyler to fit soundly as the sixth man.

Wondering around the putting green area, he saw Mr. Jenkins preparing to practice putt.

"Hello young man, how are you doing?" asked Mr. Jenkins.

"Fine," adjusting his golf glove and walking away from him as quickly as possible without appearing rude. Suddenly he was spooked, because Mr. Jenkins seemed to be at the course every time he was. He continued marching to the clubhouse to order something to drink. He liked Mountain Dew and felt that it offered him luck due to the energy it gave him.

"Here is the Mountain Dew you ordered," spoke Ms. Hurt. "*You are following your routine well.*"

After understanding her comments, he hurriedly exited her area of operation in the direction of the tee of the first hole. Speaking to Mr. Jenkins and Ms. Hurt had bewildered him, and venturing onto the first tee delivered some much-needed comfort.

The Central match featured six strong golfers from both schools in stiff competition. Mark and Kent began the match, teeing off first. They expected trouble since Central's top two golfers were highly experienced. Tony and Richard followed them, teeing off next. Tony had been playing real well lately, shining light upon the team's chances.

Teeing off last, Doug and Schuyler were expected to handle their opponents. They had performed well together during play at their home course. After watching the others begin play on number one, Doug informed him, "you hit first and I will follow."

"Sounds good to me, I'd rather lead off if possible." After a few practice swings, he hit his drive wide to the right of the fairway into the ruff. The first hole was a par five with a left dogleg. He, indeed, was a long way from the green. His drive had distance, but lacked accuracy. As he waited for the others to hit, he planned his proceeding shot. His four-iron lag was close enough to the hole to allow for a following nine-iron shot into the green.

His partner Doug had cut the dogleg and was in excellent shape to par the hole. Doug's superb play made him feel better, especially after he scuffed his third shot into the sand trap. He disliked sand, frequently surrendering strokes due to faulty sand play.

His poor sand play led to a double bogey seven on the first hole. Although he lost against his opponent, Doug scored a birdie four to win both individually and for the team.

Apologizing for his double bogey, "don't worry Doug, I'll hold up my side of the team on this next hole."

Doug reassured him, as he walked with his partner to the second tee, "a lot of golf left to play."

Schuyler aimed his driver down the center of the second fairway and teed off with a strong, burly swing. His drive sliced again, but was playable. The par-four second hole had a lot of room to the right side of the fairway. In the ruff again, his approach shot to the green fell short.

Doug struggled on this hole, eventually scoring a bogey five. His partner knew he had to pick up the slack. Schuyler, an excellent chipper, got up-and-down to save par tying the hole with the Central twosome. Doug's bogey, and the remaining three pars, evened the team score.

As Doug walked to the next tee, he patted his partner on the back, "you saved us two big points there with your par."

Number three, a par three, featured a big gulch between the tee and the green. Schuyler in the past had played this hole well. An eight-iron placed his tee shot onto the green; unfortunately he was a long way from the hole.

"Good shot, but a lot of green," said Doug. He took a couple of practice swings and stroked his ball onto the green.

The two Central players watched their opponents hit two good shots and accepted the challenge by following with two more green shots.

Putting determined the outcome of the third hole. Doug and the two Central players all two-putted for par. Schuyler, using his open putting stance, suffered a three-putt bogey four. He had lost his side of the hole, but Doug halved the others with his par.

After the first three holes, Doug and Schuyler were ahead by one hole during team play. Individually, Doug was even with his opponent and Schuyler was down two holes to his challenger.

Doug was worried about his partner's play. He was so worried that he aired to him, *"Schuyler try not to hit the ball so far. Maybe shorten your back swing and strive for accuracy."*

Schuyler ignored his advice and sliced another drive into the right ruff of the fourth hole. Consistently he was driving the ball deep, but with little accuracy. His approach shot to the green misfired, and was forced to salvage bogey. Doug was disappointed in his partner's play and would later try to get through to him.

The fourth hole was unkind to Doug and the Central players alike. They all too scored bogeys, resulting in an overall tie for the hole.

Doug walked over to his partner on the route to the fifth tee and asked. "Are you nervous about your tee shots?"

"No, I just can't seem to get in the groove." He approached the tee, washed his ball, and got ready to hit.

Doug looked into his eyes, airing to him again. *"Easy on the back swing."*

Calmly he drove his shot down the middle of the fifth fairway. The result of a reduced back swing helped his accuracy. "I believe I hit straighter, but not as far."

"Good shot my partner," said Doug.

"Nice," aired his opponent. He felt it was an appropriate situation to provide encouragement via air.

The fifth hole was a short par four. The green was stationed at the top of a hill challenging any shot to the green. After his accurate drive, a careful six-iron onto the green led to a par four. His strategy paid quick dividends; he recorded a par.

Doug failed to par number five. He three-putted for a bogey five, while both Central golfers shot par. Schuyler's par waged even larger since it halved his opponents and kept them in the match.

"Way to go partner!" Doug moved in the direction of the sixth tee. After his three-putt, he now trailed his opponent by one hole.

"I really needed it; remember I am down by two holes."

Doug and Schuyler knew they needed to get busy soon since they were both sucking wind.

The sixth hole was a dogleg par four. It was a long par four with a green surrounded by sand. Since Doug and Schuyler still had honors, Schuyler hit first again. He laced a smooth, straight drive down the center of the fairway. Doug followed with an even better drive. The twosome responded well to their challenge by hitting two good tee shots.

Capitalizing on their drives, they both hit the sixth green in regulation resulting in excellent shape for pars. "I think we'll both par." Schuyler suggested.

"Maybe birdie," responded Doug walking to the green to repair his ball mark.

"I'm away, so I'll secure a two-putt in order to give you a good chance at a needed birdie." Schuyler observed the slope of the green.

Watching the Central players both miss the green in regulation, Doug moved closer to his partner, "if we can both get down in two, we stand a good chance in getting back into the match."

Fortunately for the home team, both Central golfers bogeyed the hole. Although Schuyler bogeyed, Doug's par was enough to win the hole.

After six holes of play, Doug and Schuyler had a commanding team lead. They were up two holes with only three left to play. In individual play Doug was even with his man, as Schuyler trailed his man still by two holes.

As the foursome reached the seventh tee, Doug's opponent asked. "Is this a par four or five?"

Doug faced him and responded, "par four; it is our longest par four on the course."

Schuyler quickly mentioned, "and the hardest hole on the course."

Schuyler's opponent checked his scorecard to verify actual distance, "it sure is long."

Doug assured them, "usually if we bogey, we are happy. Only the long-knockers reach the green in two."

Schuyler hit first again and drove his ball about 200 yards down the right side of the fairway. He was satisfied with his drive; at least it was in the fairway.

The remaining three golfers hit excellent drives also within the friendly parameters of the fairway.

As Doug walked with his partner down the fairway he told him, "a bogey here might be worth something, remember to play safe."

"I plan to; I figure a good up-and-down hole should be near."

They hit both second shots in front of the green allowing excellent shape for proceeding shots. Their opponents tried another strategy. They went for the green on their second shots and both hooked to the left. The Central players had left themselves in trouble for their next shot. They failed to get up-and-down to save par and settled for bogeys.

During Schuyler's attempt on his third shot, he could not decide on his choice of club. He pondered between a nine-iron and a wedge. The pin placement was deep allowing much room for the ball to roll. He had chosen the wedge, when suddenly he heard a strange, distant voice advise him to use the nine-iron. Reconsidering his selection, he used the nine-iron and hit his ball on the green with plenty of room for it to roll near the pin. His ball bounced a few times and crept up to the pin about two feet away from the cup. The nine-iron strategy synthesized a winning par.

Doug failing to par, "good job! Why did you switch clubs?"

"I had a strange feeling that my nine-iron would be kind to me."

"Well it was a good selection," responded Doug.

"Now I'm only one hole down."

Doug proudly walked with him to the eighth tee, "your par secured our best ball victory."

"I wonder how the others did."

The Central players understood their position in the match and prepared themselves for a comeback. Even though they had lost the best ball portion, the individual events were still up for grabs.

The par-three eighth hole featured a small green guarded by sand. The hole was relatively short, but the tiny green among the sand traps, created a lot of havoc for numerous golfers.

"Lead off again partner," shouted Doug.

His six-iron fell off short of the green into a sand trap. Doug's shot was hit nicely, landing smack in the middle of the green. Both Central players joined Schuyler in the sand and all three of them bogeyed the eighth hole, while Doug retrieved par.

"Good par Doug." Schuyler walked with him off the green.

Doug winked at him demonstrating self-confidence, "it put me one hole up with the final hole to play."

"I'm still down a hole," as he walked along Doug's side.

Doug ensured him, "this will be your hole!"

The final hole, number nine, was a long par five. It was Doug's haven for a birdie possibility. He had recorded more birdies on this particular hole than any other hole on the course.

"You're up," Doug addressed his partner.

"I'm ready," as he teed off with a sweet drive down the center of the fairway. "Your turn Doug."

Doug drove a fine first shot and returned fire with another good second shot. He would later par the hole, as would his opponent. Thus, Doug won his individual match one hole up. The remaining match featured Schuyler and his opponent. Earlier, he hit his second shot within 175 yards of the green. He was in very good shape to par the hole; but would a par be good enough?

After his opponent hit his third shot into the center of the green, he evaluated which iron to use for his third shot. He selected a seven-iron, but heard the same distant voice again he had previous heard on the seventh hole. *"Schuyler don't use the seven, use the six. You have come up short the past few times with your irons. Go for the pin, not just the green."* After standing alone in the fairway for several minutes, trying to decide on what club to use, he hit a high six-iron directly into the heart of the green within two feet of the pin.

After his third shot, Doug quickly approached him, "you know if you birdie this hole you will halve your opponent."

"Not if he sinks his birdie putt too."

Doug agreed, "just make your birdie putt, don't worry about his."

His opponent two-putted giving him a par five. Carefully examining his birdie putt, he took his usual open stance. After exhaling from a deep breath, he stroked his ball dead into the center of the cup. Raising his arms in celebration, he enjoyed his birdie accomplishment.

Doug and Kent had already conversed prior to Schuyler's birdie, thus Doug was fully aware of the other team members' results. "Schuyler do you know your birdie putt just didn't win the hole, but won the entire match!"

"Really, how did the others do?"

Doug broke down the entire results," Mark and Kent both lost individually, but halved in best ball. Tony won easily, Richard lost, and they also won best ball. Thus, we were actually behind in the match, minus our results. Since we won as a team, along with my victory, and your tie, the total match score was five to four."

"Great, we defeated Central five points to four points!"

Mark asked, "why did it take you so long to choose an iron on your third shot?"

"I could not decide between the seven or the six."

Mark smiled, shaking his hand, "well the whole team is sure glad that you picked the right club; it was one spectacular shot."

After the team congratulated Central's team for sportsmanship, the coach briefed the team. He praised Tony and Doug for winning their matches. Also, the remaining team members received due recognition.

Schuyler bought a Mountain Dew from Ms. Hurt prior to heading home. She aired, *"found someone new?"*

Not understanding what Ms. Hurt had earlier informed him, he drove home questioning what she really meant.

He felt good about himself, his golf game made a remarkable turn around. He shot a score of 41 for the nine holes. Only two strokes behind Doug, he assured himself his accomplishment was huge. This accomplishment made the drive home even more relaxing.

Chapter 4

The homestead was comfortable; as his mom prepared supper for the family, he assembled his homework. School was little problem, balancing his other activities. After supper, he calculated his math homework. Math was a subject that presented a problem for him. For some reason he struggled in this particular subject. If he didn't dedicate himself toward success, he would surely fall way behind the rest of the class. His problem calculations fatigued his mind, causing him to prepare himself for bed a bit earlier than usual.

As he lay in bed gazing at the ceiling, he heard that distant voice again. "*Hi Schuyler, my name is Julie.*"

How can I hear you?

"You hear me think."

Where are you?

"I'm in Louisiana watching you get ready to fall asleep so I can watch you dream as I do every night."

How do you know that I'm in bed and how can you think to me when I'm here and you are there?

"Because I watch you in my mind. Your entire life is telegraphed into my mind. Thus, I watch you!"

Explain yourself again. Please Julie.

"Schuyler, I see, hear, and feel every move you make. I hear every word you speak and every thought you think. I vision everything you see. Your dreams are even telegraphed."

Getting out of bed, he dashed to the window to inspect outside.

"Why did you get up out of bed? Please trust me; I want to communicate with you."

Getting back into bed, much confused, he asked her if she watched him all the time.

"I believe everybody is forced to watch you live. You have some special thought process that telepathically transmits your expressions."

Who else reads me like a book?

"I don't know, but I do, and I'm interested in your life."

Tell me more about Julie.

"My name is Julie Crystal; I'm a senior at a small high school in Louisiana. I was the one watching you play golf and providing the club selection advice on the seventh and ninth hole."

Thank you Julie, you helped me secure the match. His anxiety then caused him to roll over onto his side.

"Much welcome, I wanted to help. At first I was afraid to think to you, but I could not hold it back any longer."

Did you hear Mr. Jenkins and Ms. Hurt think to me today?

"Sure did; they were practicing a form of telepathy."

So that explains a lot of strange happenings that keeps me bewildered.

"I'm so glad I have been some help to you. Please relax and fall asleep. I will talk to you tomorrow." She telepathically placed a kiss on his forehead assuring him that she would return.

After a long, deep sleep he awoke feeling like a new person. He went through his usual daily routines with newly discovered energy. Daydreaming about Julie, he quietly sat through his morning classes. When he wasn't thinking about her, he stayed preoccupied with his math assignment. He worried much about his math class; luckily it was after lunch allowing extra time for preparation.

Julie was at her Louisiana school, *"Schuyler, I take the same level of math at my school. Do you want me to help you with yours?"*

As he walked to his math class, he asked her for assistance. She seemed to be always helpful and he really did need a lot of help. Sitting in the front row of his math class, he noticed the rest of the class showing interest in him. It seemed that the others also wanted to learn more about his telepathic friend. Struggling with his teacher's assignment, he failed to solve about 30% of the algebra problems. He was forced to ask for her expertise.

"In my class, we are a little ahead in the syllabus. I recognize some of your material. Read the questions requiring help again, so I can follow along."

He carefully read the problems to her allowing her ample opportunity for comprehension. Any input concerning the algebra would be an improvement; he depended upon her feedback to complete the assignment.

"I hope I have helped you in your assignment?"

Turning in his assignment, he thanked her. The teacher and the other students ignored the telepathic communication. What could anybody say? The norm was to never discuss the phenomena, only acknowledge its existence.

At the Jupiter, Morrison and Boyd were very excited about the telepathic relationship. Morrison's future trip to Korea and Julie's influence upon The Air strengthened their project studies.

Morrison prepared a cup of coffee and addressed Boyd, "my trip to Korea tomorrow will be a very long flight, but very rewarding."

Boyd was eager to learn about the range of The Vision, but felt Julie's influence was much more important. He asked, "what about the girl?"

"We may obtain results from her activity. She might overhaul our whole project analysis," responded Morrison.

Boyd nodded his head in agreement, "the phenomena of the telepathic relationship could be much more powerful than expected!"

Morrison sat back in his chair, sipping his coffee, and dreamed about numerous rewards stimulating from his subject, The Air. Boyd nervously paced about the office, knowing The Vision's future was bright. They both agreed this new development expanded their research toward a brand new frontier.

As the final school bell rang, Schuyler darted off to the country club to play a quick five holes of golf. He had quite a busy day, but still wanted to squeeze out five holes. Exhibiting much relief from math assignment success, motivated by recent golf accomplishments, he quickly drove to the club and claimed a spot on the first tee. He was in such as good mood he didn't even get upset when he shanked his initial tee shot. His poor play continued all the way to the green. It took him five strokes to reach the putting surface; eventually he two-putted for a double-bogey seven. Approaching the next hole, he sensed someone watching him.

"You seem to be enjoying yourself, even though you had a terrible hole."

Is that your Julie?

"Of course, who else could it be?"

His play improved throughout the next couple of holes, mostly from increasing confidence derived from her presence. He recorded par on the second hole and a bogey on the third hole. His drive on the fourth hole was a dandy. As he marched down the fairway to hit his second shot, he listened to Julie communicate with him.

"I had an exciting day at school! Do you want me to tell you about it?"

He hit his second shot on the edge of the green and told her he was very interested in what she had to say.

"I got an offer to play basketball at a college near my hometown!"

You play basketball well?

"I'm pretty good. At least I'm good enough for South Eastern State to offer me a full scholarship."

"I've never heard of South Eastern State, but I'm sure you will do well there. Your personality alone should escalate your chances at the campus.

"It's located in Louisiana and they have a real good coach there. Her name is Cheryl Jackson and she's interested in my talent."

Familiarizing himself with her future basketball potential, he two-putted from the edge of the green saving par. Since his double bogey first hole, his improvement increased steadily. As he walked to the number-five tee, he asked Julie if she was going to help him with his math homework later that evening.

"Of course, I'll look forward to it."

Thanks a million! You have been a great help. After his drive, he accidentally hit his second shot over the green into a parking lot. He could not control his strength as his approach shot sailed among parked cars, fortunately rendering no collateral damage. After the muffed shot, they agreed to end the game and hurry home to tackle the math homework.

At home his parents went own with their business, totally ignoring Julie's intervention. In their minds they recognized the relationship, but continued to be status quo with their lives. They had adapted well to Schuyler and to the phenomena he carried with him.

He organized his homework prior to supper. At the supper table, he inquired about his brother. His parents spoke very highly of Duncan, satisfied greatly with his military service. After supper, he quickly assembled his math homework awaiting help from his telepathic teacher.

"Start doing your math and I'll help when you get into trouble."

Motivated by Julie, he tactfully prioritized his assignment. Developing strategy for his math homework, he initiated process actions. Installing a three-tier plan, his objective was to complete the easier work first and follow with more difficult material. The third tier was reserved for the math requiring Julie's expertise. The telepathic couple agreed strategic planning could identify strengths and weaknesses in study processes, allowing maximum use of resources to achieve both short-term and long-term success.

"I like the strategy; the outcome measures can be evaluated at milestone points to verify the strategy's progress."

You bet, whatever you just said, as her technical language went right through his head.

Julie's factor generated progress in his organizational skills. These skills restructured his study habits, fostering growth in algebra comprehension. The tactful utilization of his abilities facilitated prompt execution of his homework, yielding more free time to spend at the end of the day with his newly discovered friend.

His bed awaited his tired body. After dressing himself into his sleep clothes, he crawled into bed. Gazing up at the ceiling, he detected his telepathic friend's voice. It seemed so near to him; a feeling he could not comprehend.

"Are you ready for me to get you prepared for a relaxing night of sleep?"

What do you have planned? He turned to his side and anticipated her response.

"Lie on your stomach and allow me to massage your back. This should offer the relaxation required for a sound night's rest."

He positioned himself as she requested. Within a short moment, he felt impulses being transmitted up and down his back, from her. This presence illustrated similar affects as if he was actually receiving a caressing massage. After her sense of touch stimulated his torso, he rolled back over onto his back.

"Did you enjoy?"

Very much, you have pleased me much. He laid in bed with feeling he had never had before. Julie had caused a paradigm shift in his thought process. He wondered if it was her knowledgeable advice, her caressing sense of touch, her attentiveness toward him, or some other gratification she offered that he could not comprehend. Anyway, he knew he was blessed to have Julie with him. A telepathic kiss on the lips signaled the closing of their communication and the beginning of his restful sleep.

CHAPTER 5

Schuyler's week grew short due to excessive activities in concert with Julie. She kept him so busy with her dialogue he began to look forward to particular activities such as his math assignments. The math work was as an excellent opportunity for him to spend quality time with her. At night, after math completion, they engaged into telepathic dating. Julie's intriguing character elevated sensual sensations that increased his desire for her as a girlfriend. He could not hide his inner feelings from her causing his coy behavior to slowly disappear.

The last two days of the week were allocated with his medical appointment and a golf match against Westlake. He was anxious to play against Westlake since it would be the last match of the regular season. After the Westlake match, he was scheduled to play in the District Tournament.

Schuyler's medical appointment was slated after school delaying golf practice about an hour. As he drove to the clinic, he and Julie prepared their strategy. He arrived early to his appointment allowing plenty of time for him to get more nervous about his appointment. Dr. Walton greeted him with a smile and directed him into an interviewing room. The doctor had him wait at least ten minutes before he actually started the session. Every extra minute he waited, his heart pounded harder.

Dr. Walton entered the room. "Schuyler, you did quite well on your tests. The language results showed excellent potential."

"How was my math comprehension," he inquired.

The doctor sat down and focused his attention to Schuyler. "Your math potential will never match your language-reasoning capability. Your formulation of sentence structures, from unknown language forms, revealed good sound opportunities to excel in foreign language comprehension."

Schuyler nodded at him, "I guess I am better in language concepts than algebra equations."

"I believe a hidden talent inhibits your mind and I wish to capture its potential thrust," directed Dr. Walton.

Schuyler attempted to hide in his chair. He really didn't want to be some mental experiment for Dr. Walton or anybody else.

Dr. Walton paced a little bit around the room and dismissed him from the session. He informed Schuyler of a return visit with him in two weeks and at that time would present another language examination.

Schuyler anxiously booked his next appointment with the receptionist and darted out the door heading in the direction of the golf course. As he drove to the country club, he conversed with Julie about his appointment.

She informed him of his success with his appointment. *"The doctor appeared interested in your mental ability. It was a little strange, but not near as bad as I had feared."*

I was worried at first; but satisfied with the short session. I'm just glad to be out of there.

"Lets not worry about it now; you have a golf match tomorrow!" she advised.

Schuyler spent a few hours at the golf course fine tuning his driving and putting. Julie agreed to encounter with him later during the evening for their usual discussions.

After dinner with his family, he quickly got prepared for rest. He did not have any homework assignments, thus he had plenty of time to spend with Julie.

Julie entertained him for almost an hour. Her intriguing dialogue coaxed him into a feeling of euphoria. After she discussed golf and math, she performed a very relaxing back rub for his delight. He appreciated the rub and tried to return the favor. His telepathic massage stimulated her, but was not near as realistic as hers. At conclusion of the encounter, Julie kissed him vigorously causing a surge of blood to flow through selected arteries transmitting stimulating impulses throughout his body.

Schuyler had early school dismissal the following day due to his golf match with Westlake. The six-member team had to travel over forty miles to Westlake's golf course. The team was optimistic about the match even though the Westlake team possessed a superb winning record. Their line-up would be the same with Mark and Kent playing together as number one and two, Tony and Richard positioned as number three and four, and Doug with Schuyler as the final twosome.

Arriving at the course, the coach had already registered them into the match. All they had to do was to retrieve their clubs and begin playing.

Mark was interested in his putting. "Kent, I will be over at the putting green for the next ten minutes. Please get me a Pepsi."

Kent returned with a Pepsi for Mark and a root beer for himself. The two of them moved toward the first tee to prepare for competition. After two successful drives, Mark and Kent slowly walked down the fairway of the first hole.

Both Tony and Richard enjoyed some free time to practice putting. They were to hit next; they had some extra time since the foursome ahead played deliberately. Tony had been winning lately earning great expectations from the team, thus he offered encouragement to his partner. "Richard, today will be your day to have your best nine-hole score of the season!" They hit successful drives, much alike Mark and Kent, and together quietly marched down the fairway of the first hole.

Teeing off last, Doug and Schuyler had enough time to buy a hot dog and a pop. Schuyler added relish to his dog and proceeded to watch Tony and Richard play number one. Enjoying his Mountain Dew, he asked Doug, "how difficult is this course?"

Doug finished his dog and studied the course structure from the scorecard. "The course appears hilly with a few hazards along the way. We shouldn't have too much trouble with it."

Schuyler agreed with him. "If we play our best game, then we won't be worried."

The final twosome approached the first tee with confidence of challenging their opponents to the fullest extent.

"You hit first for our team," directed Doug.

"I will lead off and we'll do fine." He addressed the ball with a strong drive down the middle of the fairway.

Doug and the two Westlake golfers also hit good tee shots on this par-five first hole.

The first hole at Westlake's home course measured less than 500 yards, but featured water guarding the green. Even though the hole was a short par five, it still played long. The entire foursome lagged short of the water positioning them for an easy chip shot into the green. Doug and his partner both shot par on the first hole as well did their opponents halving the first hole.

"Good par, keep it up," Doug assured his partner.

"Do you want me to lead off again?"

"Go ahead Schuyler," responded Doug.

The par-four second hole contained a few traps surrounding the green. Both Schuyler and his partner drove good tee shots allowing comfortable approach shots into the green. Unfortunately they both missed the green on their second shots, granting two bogeys for the both of them. With their bogeys, they were at the mercy of the putting talent of the Westlake opponents. Luckily, both Westlake opponents three-putted the hole resorting to a complete halve of the second hole.

As Doug walked with Schuyler to the third tee, "we blew a huge opportunity there."

Walking straight to the ball washer, Schuyler replied, "you better believe it."

The Westlake golfers were disappointed with their three-putt bogeys. Even though the score was still tied, they were not satisfied.

The third hole was another par four. It was almost entirely uphill presenting a blind second shot at the pin. The strategy was to hit the tee shot on top of the first hill allowing as much vision of the green as possible. Both Doug and his partner hit good drives providing ample opportunity to reach the green in regulation. Their opponents followed with two better drives landing in the middle of the fairway. Schuyler's second shot fell short of the green, but in good shape for an up-and-down par. Doug followed with a four-iron off the right side of the green, leaving the number three green wide open for the Westlake golfers.

"We have the ball in our court now," claimed Doug's opponent as he bladed his second shot short of the green.

Schuyler's opponent reached the green easily with his second shot applying pressure toward Doug and his partner.

Walking with his partner toward the green, Doug praised Schuyler, "you still are in excellent shape for an up-and-down!"

Examining his third shot, Schuyler decided to use his wedge on his third shot. With the rest of the foursome watching, he gracefully chipped his ball onto the green rolling directly toward the hole; the two Westlake golfers' heads turned when Schuyler's ball dropped into the cup for a birdie three.

"Great shot," shouted Doug.

"Thanks!"

His opponent mumbled to his partner. "He's one lucky S.O.B."

Doug and his opponent both failed to save par, recording bogeys.

Schuyler's opponent was still upset with the dramatic birdie chip shot; he carefully measured his birdie putt, but missed his putt badly suffering a par and losing the hole to Schuyler.

After the first three holes of the match, Doug was even with his opponent, Schuyler was ahead by one hole, and their team was also up by one hole.

Schuyler was very excited about his chip shot. He inquired of Julie concerning the shot.

She informed him, *"you were great; I'm so proud of you; if I was there I would kiss you."*

Schuyler acknowledged her comments and went about his own business. As he approached the forth tee, Doug congratulated him again. "You put us on top. I'll win the next one."

Schuyler held his driver in his hand preparing to tee off. He could feel his opponent gleaming at him as he set up to drive. As he took his swing, he heard his opponent air; *"I hope the sissy slices the heck out of his drive!"*

The unsportsmanship of his opponent's distraction was instrumental in causing him to miss his drive. The right ruff engulfed his ball resulting in poor shape for his proceeding shot.

"Partner, don't worry about the ruff. You can still adapt to overcome the situation," said Doug.

"I must have taken my eye off the ball?"

Doug had trouble hitting his drive also on the par-four fourth hole. The Westlake golfer's unsportsmanship behavior had affected him once again.

Both Schuyler and Doug eventually scored bogey-five on the forth hole losing to both of their Westlake opponents.

Doug and his partner regrouped before they hit their drives on the fifth hole. Doug did not know what to say to him concerning the behavior of his opponent, but Julie did!

She lectured, *"Schuyler, please listen to me. You cannot do anything about his behavior. You can expect a lot of friction during competitive events."*

Yes Julie, I will try to ignore him.

The fifth hole was another par four with a dogleg to the left. The Westlake golfers, pumped from winning the last hole, hit excellent drives. Doug and his partner responded with two dandy drives of their own.

After the other three golfers hit their shots near the green, Schuyler was expected to follow with a playable shot of his own. During his swing, once again his opponent distracted him by airing, *"don't be afraid of making a big divot."*

Schuyler was discouraged when his shot traveled wide right, bouncing down a steep incline, far away from the green. He eventually lost the hole with a double bogey. His partner Doug did earn a victory on his side when his opponent suffered poor sand play. Overall the team was still tied during the match, but he was down one hole to his impolite competition.

Doug walked with him in route to the sixth tee. He was worried about his partner's composure since the last two holes had been trouble. He did not know what to do about the distractions during his partner's swing, but reassured him that he was supporting him 100%.

Schuyler was so upset with his play that he asked Julie for assistance.

"You can compete with him; he is nothing; he's only jealous of your talent." Julie's advice persuaded him to overcome his obstacles and succeed as a true winner.

The short par-three sixth hole provided opportunity for Doug and his partner to place iron-shots into the heart of the green. After their Westlake opponents missed the green with their tee shots, both Doug and his partner placed precise iron shots within ten feet of the cup.

He joined Doug on the putting surface, waiting to putt for his birdie along with his partner. The Westlake couple struggled on the par-three sixth hole recording a pair of bogeys creating a huge window of opportunity for victories to be earned with two-putt pars from either Doug or Schuyler. They succeeded in winning the number six hole with a pair of pars.

Julie praised him as he ventured beyond the sixth hole. The Westlake team was experiencing mild depression, after dropping the short par-three hole. The match got tight after the two recent pars; the results after six holes were good news for Schuyler and Doug. Doug was ahead of his opponent by one hole; Schuyler was tied with his; the team was up one hole on the Westlake couple.

Before they teed off on the par-four seventh hole, Doug gave advice to Schuyler. "We are in the driver's seat. Don't let your opponent's rudeness bother you. Your side of the match is crucial."

"How far is this next hole? It looks short to me, especially for a par four."

Doug checked the distance in his scorecard. "It measures less than 400 yards."

"Even with the tee markers back on the tee, the hole appears very short. I predict that you birdie."

"I hope you are correct. I could sure use a birdie; only you have shot a birdie so far today," claimed Doug.

The Westlake golfers hit big drives down the seventh fairway. Schuyler was shy about his drive. He was anticipating confusion created by his opponent that led to a weak drive, resulting in a long iron shot into the green. Just the thought alone influenced his golf game resulting in a disappointing performance. His drive had much less distance than the one hit by his partner Doug. Doug laced a smooth drive into excellent position for his second shot to reach the green.

Since he had the most distance from the hole, Schuyler was the first to hit his second shot. As he addressed the ball, he noticed his opponent taking practice swings in order to distract his swing. As before, he missed his shot and suffered throughout the entire hole scoring a bogey five. Luckily, his opponent could not take advantage of his poor play as he three-putted for a bogey five. Schuyler had halved the hole versus his opponent even with a poor performance.

Before Doug putted for a par to tie the hole, he told Schuyler, "I'll sink this putt, and we'll strengthen our stand on the next hole."

Doug confused about Schuyler's performance, offered comfort, "your match is still tied, and he can't beat you! You can only beat yourself!"

"Schuyler, you are doing so well under the unique circumstances. I'm behind you all the way. Just think of me when you swing, and you will always succeed," aired Julie.

The eighth hole was an uphill par three. It was a very difficult green to hit, and still be close enough to the cup to easily two-putt. The Westlake golfers hit superb initial shots of the number eight hole. Their superb tee shots put pressure upon Schuyler resulting in a wild iron shot at the green. He landed very wide right of the green presenting a problem for his second shot. The probability of an up-and-down for par was very slim.

Doug held up his spot on the team as he hit his iron shot into the green increasing his chances of earning par. He spoke with his partner along the way to the green, "don't worry about the past, and look toward the future by hitting this next shot near the pin."

He pulled his wedge out of his bag and smacked his ball onto the green; but he could not keep the ball from rolling off the back edge of the green. He savaged a bogey, but it was not enough because his opponent two-putted for a par to go one hole up on him with one hole left to play. He could only tie his match play; he had no chance to win individually against his Westlake opponent.

With his opponent recording par, Doug's birdie putt grew immensely more important. As he carefully examined it, all eyes watched him prepare for his birdie putt that could win two points for the team. Schuyler's opponent attempted to distract him by coughing continuously prior to his putt. Ignoring the rudeness of the coughing, Doug made his birdie putt providing victory over his individual opponent. Doug and his partner also earned victory in best-ball competition over the Westland twosome. They had already earned two crucial points, with Schuyler's individual match still open.

The Westlake golfers congratulated Doug for his outstanding play and Schuyler praised him, "I'm so proud of your birdie; you are much credit to the team; the coach will be very happy with the results."

The par-five ninth hole possessed much distance. Doug reported to Schuyler the ninth hole was well over 500 yards.

With the other matches already decided, Schuyler prepared for his final hole. Since he was already down one hole, he was forced to win this hole in order to tie his individual match. After a brief talk with Doug, he removed his driver from his bag and aligned himself on the tee in position to keep his drive down the left side of the fairway.

Just before he addressed the ball, he detected his opponent airing, *"don't shank your shot too bad!"*

In response to the distraction, he popped his shot up into the air with little distance behind it. The drive was only a little over hundred yards, much shorter than his normal drives.

Doug was shocked. He tried to settle him but it was too late. His partner was furious with the current situation.

Schuyler's following second shot fell short again leaving him still a four-wood shot into the green and his ball was still located in the fairway, but a long way from the hole. As he was about the hit his third shot, he was interrupted by a familiar voice.

Julie greeted him with a pleasant tone of voice, *"Schuyler, please listen to me. I do not know much about golf, but it appears that you can still par the hole. If your four-wood comes near to the green, you can still try for an up-and-down par."*

Calmly, he lined up his shot and aimed for the center of the fairway in front of the green. His hands were sweaty, but secured the club enough to allow a straight, lofty four-wood shot to be in excellent shape for an up-and-down par attempt. He had accepted the challenge and achieved success.

"Good lay-up partner," said Doug.

"Thanks!"

"The short game is your best aspect of golf, don't hesitate to go after the pin," added Doug.

"I plan to go all out for the par."

Schuyler's opposition had landed on the green on his third shot, but he was a long way from the cup. He could easily three-putt that could provide strong opportunity for a par to defeat him.

Schuyler walked to his ball, as it lay on the ground about twenty yards shy of the ninth green. He trusted his wedge to generate an easy par putt to follow.

"*Don't you dare let him bother you,*" warned Julie.

He carefully took his time during his approach shot. He paused a few moments before actually addressing the ball. During the short pause he detected transmission from his opponent.

"*Don't choke!*" aired his opponent.

But the distraction didn't work this time and Schuyler chipped his ball within a foot of the cup. He had practically a tap-in for a par.

After he marked his ball, his Westlake opponent was now challenged to putt close enough to tie with a par. With Schuyler's ball mark within a foot of the cup, his next putt was crucial. The Westlake number six man was under immense pressure to get down in two putts. He carefully stroked his ball toward the hole allowing plenty of room for the downhill slope of the green. Unfortunately for him he left his putt very short of the cup, resulting in another long putt just to save par. His frustration escalated, causing him to miss his following putt that prevented him to earn a par on his final hole. He finally completed the ninth hole, scoring a bogey six.

Needing a simple par to win the hole and tie his opponent for the match, Schuyler tapped his putt into the cup for a winning par. He had gotten up-and-down once again to save par. This par was special since it halved his individual match. Julie, in her own way, congratulated him as he ventured toward the clubhouse. The rest of the team awaited him as he entered to clubhouse area.

"I saw you almost chip that ball in the hole; great shot!" Mark told him.

Kent met him with a handshake and told him. "Good job, it looks like we won again."

Doug broke the news to him the team outscored Westlake 5–3. Mark and Kent lost all three of their points to a couple of excellent golfers. The two top players for Westlake were among some of the favorites during the upcoming District Tournament. While Mark and Kent lost, Tony and Richard won. They swept all three points during their match. Tony's 38 was the team's best round for the day setting the standard for next week's tournament. With Doug's victory, his tie, and their best-ball win, the entire team was victorious 5 points to 3 points.

It was a hard-fought win since Westlake had two of the best golfers in the district. After congratulating the Westlake team for hosting the match, Schuyler and the rest of the team conversed with their coach. He was satisfied with the match. He didn't speak of any unsportsmanship activity, but in the back of his mind he was very much aware of what had happen. The coach sponsored the team's supper on the way back home. He spoke well of Tony's 38 and Doug's 39. They had the two lowest scores of the team with Kent, Mark, and Richard all shooting 40. Schuyler brought up the rear with a very respectful 41. Since it was Friday evening, the team took their sweet time returning home. Mark requested the team stop by the baseball field, and view the rest of the high school baseball game. The team thought it was a good idea, especially since Tony might know some girls that were at the game. Of the team, he seemed to know the most girls and the others were anxious to hang out with him on a Friday night.

After an evening with the others, Schuyler was ready for rest. Between the golf match and the baseball game, he was very fatigued. As he prepared for bed, Julie joined him for a little bit of telepathic enjoyment. Also, they planned to spend most of the upcoming weekend together.

CHAPTER 6

Schuyler learned a few lessons from the Westlake match. The behavior displayed by the Westlake golfer represented just one of many haunting contradictions existing throughout his phenomena. He was vulnerable toward negative transmission that revealed his character weakness. His Westlake opponent's rude airing demonstrated destructive power generating from improper usage of air phenomena. Unsportsmanship should never be tolerated, but this type of occurrence cannot be controlled. The negative comments aired during the golf match created a mystique upon The Air developing haunting potential affecting him throughout his entire life.

Julie's role in air phenomena governed a wide range of events. She guarded against mystique-oriented activity and proposed strategies to avoid negative transmitted feedback. Her special attention formulated Schuyler's daily schedule. She indoctrinated attributes into his character that strengthened defense systems against negative airing. Her dedicated facilitation counseled his daily activities to establish principles and guidelines in benefit of his unique capability of air phenomena.

After the Westlake golf match, Julie encouraged him to face his challenges at full trust and to never allow negative airing present obstacles toward him. She reinforced the concept of he was "The Think" and all others were just poor imitations. His destiny was his phenomena and it belonged to him. Her mentorship and guidance promotes strategic avenues enhancing his gift. She serves as his master of ceremony, observing his actions, and assisting in his daily events. Julie, with her respected advice, responds promptly to any situation upon his request.

At the Jupiter, Morrison's trip to Korea had rendered much benefit, verifying Schuyler's air phenomena gift to be present even as far away as Korea. Both of them were aggressively following the golf incidents. They were very interested in the airing actions of the Westlake golfer. Morrison felt the golfer's comments were strong indicators of retaliation toward The Air. Boyd's concern focused upon The Vision's grief and Julie's actions to aid him.

"The golfer's unsportsmanship conduct acquires a whole new facet of the study of The Air," said Morrison.

"Yes, but at the cost of the boy and others. If it wasn't for Julie's intervention, The Vision would have lost his match affecting not just him but the entire team," responded Boyd.

Morrison was more interested in the project aspect of the incident. He looked at Boyd and informed him, "if negative airing increases throughout his life, then his entire character could be altered."

"His character is already affected; the boy's gift is being challenged and others may follow suit? Julie is the strongest link to keep him strong," added Boyd.

Relaxing in his chair, Morrison spoke of all of the recent achievements. The trip to Korea and the golf controversy fortified their studies. "The Air is powerful and will overcome diversity to accomplish his objectives."

Boyd agreed, "The Vision will prevail, but he is greatest with Julie's expertise. As long as he has her, he will succeed."

Both of them understood the situation well. The collaborative between The Air and Julie needed to be tight in order to defend against corrupt air feedback.

Schuyler spent most of his week attending school and practicing his golf game. His study strategies improved his math grades and his putting game steadily improved every day. Julie's frequent communication supported his efforts in both of these activities. The District Tournament scheduled for Saturday was getting near. It was an eighteen-hole competition with the top sixteen scores advancing to the Regional Tournament. Usually, the team played nine holes of match play; but this tournament was different since only individual scores counted. Schuyler knew the competition would be tough since seven schools would be competing.

Seven schools, including Central and Westlake, would be competing in a very rigid tournament. Out of 42 possible candidates, only sixteen of them would advance to the next level. He knew the odds; but he knew with Julie's inspiration he could do almost anything.

Friday night, the evening before The District Tournament, Schuyler and Julie had an extensive telepathic session. In the seclusion of his room after the close of business, he lay comfortably in his bed with only the thought of Julie on his mind. Even though he had a major golf tournament the next morning, he could only think of the warm generous touch only she could offer. She was the spirit of inspiration for him to live his life. Courses of action opened widely for him allowing his true self to meld into a growing young man; she initiated confidence and generated self-esteem in productive directions. She truly was the key to any desire he wished.

Julie initiated contact with him by telepathically massaging his shoulders. She began stimulation he had never experienced before.

I like the way you touch me!

"Sugar, have you ever been with a girl like me before?" She spoke with a sexy Louisiana accent.

Your voice sounds different than before?

"No girl has ever spoken to you like this before!" She kissed his neck causing him to get excited.

He asked her how she knew this information.

"I know your romantic life is cherry." She slowly kissed down to his chest causing him to become more excited.

He nervously squirmed in bed and told her of his lack of readiness for that type of relationship.

"You are ready Sugar; let me show you!" She slowly licked down his abdomen causing him to reveal his readiness.

He looked down at his enlargement, informing her of the fact of his near state to experience something new.

She assured her cherry was still intact and she was acting purely on instinct. She clutched his enlargement, referring to it as her "boy", and began massaging his muscle. *"How does it feel?"*

I can feel your presence, but I don't know what to do?

"As I touch you, you do the same."

What! You are requesting me to fondle myself.

"Yes and I want to watch!"

As he reached for her boy, he asked her for permission to stimulate it.

"Sugar, turn me on!"

You are my master! He began experiencing feelings he never had before. Her boy beckoned for more and more attention. He was so stimulated he caused his bed to shake.

She telepathically repositioned her body's presence and engulfed her boy causing him to increase exertion. She continued to provide service until he cried with tears of enjoyment. *"Go get a towel,"* she ordered.

He paused and searched for a towel, but could locate one. He quickly grabbed a cotton shirt and continued sexual therapy.

"Do you want to do it?"

What does it mean to do it?

"I'll show you." She mounted her boy as he lay flat on his back. The sexual fantasy injected impulses throughout his entire body. He exclaimed much joy, after about thirty seconds of doing it, by telling his telepathic lover, "Oh Julie, I'm here!"

Julie showed signs of excitement also. Even though her entire encounter was purely telepathic, her sexual feelings expressed great satisfaction toward her telepathic lover. *"Does my boy feel better now?"*

I could never imagine the feeling that I'm experiencing. Your presence felt so good! Your erotic touch can only be conceptualized by your sensual delivery of your Louisiana accent. Your voice charges my circulatory system, flushing blood throughout my body, energizing parts of my body never affected before. You treat me as no one has ever had and you are not even here physically; you exist only through the parameters of my mind.

"I'm very glad you are satisfied with me. I have waited some time for the opportunity to satisfy you. I'm willing to help you make the best of your life. Just give me the chance!"

After cleaning himself, he rolled over onto his side and prepared for the most relaxing rest he had ever experienced. His body was blessed by her presence and he began reaping the benefits.

Tomorrow, indeed, would be a brand new experience for both Schuyler Ballantine and Julie Crystal.

Schuyler woke the morning of his district golf match feeling like a new man. Prior to breakfast, he showered and dressed himself for the afternoon eighteen-hole tournament. Since he would be playing during the heat of the day, he donned a pair of khaki shorts and a Cubs' polo shirt. Being a true fan of the Chicago Cubs, he wore his polo shirt with pride.

Mrs. Ballantine had prepared a huge breakfast in preparation for the long day ahead. She went about her usual routine pretending not to know anything about her son's telepathic romance. But within her own self, she approved greatly of their relationship. She knew her baby would be developing into manhood soon and she was preparing herself for future transformation.

Mrs. Ballantine greeted her son with a kiss on the cheek. "Good morning son; eat well because you will need as much energy as possible."

He thanked his mother for the hearty breakfast.

She began washing some dishes and turned about and asked, "how do you feel this morning?"

He expressed of his feeling being the best he has felt in a long time.

Mrs. Ballantine looked into his eyes and told him, "I am very proud of you and your father asked me to wish you good luck at the tournament."

He said he would try to do his best as he proceeded to finish his breakfast before Mark arrived to give him a ride to the golf course.

Mark had offered to drive to the tournament with both Doug and him as passengers. Mark drove his parents' station wagon allowing ample room for themselves and their golf equipment.

Arrival at the golf course was prompt, providing plenty of time to encounter with their coach. Since the tournament was well represented, tee times were staggered throughout most of the morning. Fourteen threesomes would begin play from 0900 hours until 1115 hours. Schuyler was fortunate; he was in the third group and would tee-off about 0920 hours on the front side. The rest of the team drew later starting times and would have to wait an extra hour before beginning play.

The coach gave him a little lecture before he approached the first tee. He told the coach he was confident that his game would be on.

As he sipped a Mountain Dew, he selected his club and ball for the initial drive. The first hole was a 340-yard par four with a few sand traps along the way. His two playing partners were both from Central High School. Justin, Central's number one golfer, and Shannon, Central's number three golfer, joined him on the first tee.

Schuyler began his tournament with an easy-swing shot down the middle of the fairway.

"Schuyler, remember to strive for accuracy, not distance, on your shots," Julie reminded him.

As he walked to his ball to hit his second shot, he informed Julie he would not have Doug with him to give him advice.

"Don't worry, I will provide the encouragement needed for success!" She tried to ease his nerves.

He picked a six-iron for his second shot. Julie suggested he hit his ball just prior to the green and bounce it up toward the hole. Straddling the ball, aiming at the front of the green, he stroked his shot just shy of the green. He breathed a big relief, leaving him a distant two-putt in order to par.

Julie encouraged him. *"You are in good shape for a par; relax!"*

Justin and Shannon followed him with two nice approach shots to the green. The entire threesome earned pars on the first hole, an outstanding beginning for all three of them, especially Schuyler.

Julie praised him for his effort. *"That par was easy. Just keep on playing your game and you will do fine."*

He reported his score of four to Justin, the official scorekeeper for the threesome.

"Good four," Justin told him.

He responded by telling Justin and Shannon they made their putts look pretty easy.

The second hole was very short, a par three, with water to the right of the green. Since the distance was only 127 yards, he used his nine-iron to hit; his shot landed safely on the green in excellent shape. In route to the green, he complemented Justin on his tee shot. Justin had hit his shot inside of ten feet of the pin, resulting in excellent conditions for a birdie.

Julie reminded him to take a deep breath, just prior to putting, to exhibit stress relief.

Once on the green, he studied his putt. His strategy was to play safe and record a two-putt par. As he stroked his putt, his putter stumbled and misdirected the ball to the right of the cup leaving him with a difficult par putt. He then slowly walked to the ball and spotted it to allow Shannon and Justin to putt freely.

"Why didn't you putt again to secure the par?" Julie inquired.

He told her that he should allow the others to putt next since it was their turn.

Shannon and he watched Justin prepare to putt. It was almost a clinic to watch him putt. As expected, he easily made his birdie putt as the spectators just gazed at him with envy.

Schuyler's par putt was stout! It was no easy putt and he knew it. But with his open putting stance, he rolled his ball right into the cup for a three. Joyfully, he reported a score of three to scorekeeper Justin and immediately received a telepathic hug from Julie. Exiting the green, his confidence level peaked after experiencing her soothing touch.

"You are the man with the birdie," exclaimed Shannon to Justin.

Schuyler agreed, "you are the master of the putter."

As the threesome approached the third tee, he explained to Julie that Justin would be hitting first due to the fact that his birdie rendered him the honor to be the first to tee-off.

The par-five third hole was 460 yards long. After his par on the last hole, Schuyler was pumped to crush his drive. But before he hit, Julie reminded him to play smart and don't over-swing on the drive. He responded by driving an easy, safe shot within the friendly parameters of the fairway.

Both Justin and Shannon hit drives farther than him and were in good position to threaten the green on their second shots.

"Don't try to show off, just play it safe," Julie warned him.

He thanked her for her concern as he selected a four-iron for second-shot use. Shading his eyes due to the sunlight, his four-iron flew upward into the sky and landed safely about 90 yards short of the green. He was satisfied with the shot since he was still in excellent shape for par.

The other two golfers tried for the green on their second shots. Justin was almost successful with his shot falling only about twenty yards shy. But Shannon failed critically as he sliced his second shot into the deep rough eventually resulting in a bogey-six on the hole.

Schuyler placed his third shot slightly off the green, but he did manage to get up-and-down to save par. His score of five matched Justin's par and kept him even par through the initial three holes.

Julie was very impressed with his composure. *"You are playing so good today. I'm proud to be watching!"*

Justin approached Schuyler and congratulated him for his effort. "Clutch up-and-down!"

The fourth hole was a long par-four measuring 390 yards. He felt the pressure as he peered down a long fairway leading to a distant green.

After Justin's sweet drive, Schuyler answered with a playable shot of his own. His lie was about twenty yards shy of Justin's, but he had an open view to the pin. He had second thoughts about this upcoming shot; he selected his four-iron and aimed at the heart of the green. His aim was on target, but the excessive height of the shot caused the ball to fall short of the green. Depressed about the shot, he quickly marched toward the ball with a wedge in hand; he chipped onto the green but failed to secure his putt for par. His heart sank as he suffered a bogey-five on the fourth hole.

Julie tried to comfort him, but he acted as if he was in another world. *"Relax dear; you'll go get the next one!"*

Number four was a critical cornerstone for Schuyler because he felt pressure for the first time and concluded Julie's alliance would be of great necessity throughout the rest of the way.

Number five was another par four, similar to number four. It measured 350 yards with a dogleg to the left.

The entire threesome hit playable drives on the fifth hole. As Schuyler walked down the sunny fairway, he appreciated the early tee-off time.

He recognized the significance of starting early. The morning sun finally kicked into high gear on this hole recognizing the advantage of an early tee-off time.

With positive thoughts throughout his mind, he hit his second shot onto the green allowing an easy two-putt for par. A refreshment stand awaited them as they strolled off the fifth green with all three of them securing a par-four on the hole. Schuyler ordered a Mountain Dew from the refreshment stand as both of the Central players bought bottled water. He asked them why they picked water instead of soda. Justin explained to him the effectiveness of drinking water during extensive golfing. He informed Schuyler of the dehydration factor caused by caffeine and influenced him to purchase an extra bottle of water to carry with him. With Justin's advice, he consumed a bottle of water immediately after enjoying his Mountain Dew. In fact, he was ready to resume play.

The sixth hole, 370 yards, was similar to the past two holes. It was also a par four, but contained a bit of water on the left side of the fairway.

Julie spoke with him before he hit. *"Justin is correct about the caffeine factor and you should force fluids during vigorous sporting events."*

Schuyler joined the others down the fairway with a sweet shot of a drive. Feeling good about the hole, his second shot hit the green in regulation again allowing a two-putt to gain par.

Once on the green, Justin told Shannon to putt first. "You are away, shows us how to putt!"

Both Shannon and Justin eventually made their putts for par, applying pressure on his putt for par. As he shaded his eyes from the late morning sun, he looked over his three-foot par putt and approached the ball.

With the utmost confidence, he delivered a sinking putt for par into the cup. He had matched the two Central golfers again with a par of his own.

After six holes of play, Justin was one stroke under par and Shannon was two strokes above par. Schuyler, on the other hand, was playing way above his head with a current score of only one stroke over par.

Schuyler was anxious to begin play on number seven. A 500-yard par five awaited him, instilling an excellent opportunity to explore birdie territory. Justin and Shannon were even more anxious to challenge birdie frontier as they both warmed-up their drivers.

Cautiously Schuyler drove his shot down the center of the fairway being careful to avoid fairway sand. His proceeding shot, a four-iron, traveled enough distance to allocate a short eight-iron shot onto the green. Even though he was well short of Justin and Shannon on his second shot, he was extremely confident he would still hit the green in regulation.

Julie was impressed with his two conservative shots. *"I like your chances on this hole. You seem to be playing smart."*

He looked upon the green, prior to hitting his third shot. His eight-iron addressed the ball a little fat and he pushed the ball short of the green. Luckily his shot was so short that it fell short of the trap also, leaving him with a difficult chip onto the green.

Julie calmly reassured him by informing him to be strong and don't lose his composure. She was worried he would lose control of his temper and miss his next shot. *"Sugar, don't worry about the past shot. Just think of hitting the next one sound and straight."*

Julie's reassurance worked like a charm, because his ensuing chip shot lofted over the sand trap, onto the green, and rolled easily within ten feet of the pin.

"Excellent shot," shouted Justin.

"Ditto," exclaimed Shannon.

He had stunned them both by his miracle shot. After watching Justin putt on the curvy green, he strategically aligned his putter behind his ball and went for the par. His putt for a par-five rolled around the cup once and dropped in.

"Used the entire cup there, Schuyler!" Justin joked, but later formerly congratulated him.

Julie responded to his putt by hugging him telepathically. *"Schuyler, you were great!"*

He was much satisfied with the par. Both Justin and Shannon scored pars themselves, but not nearly the same way. He, with Julie's assurance, had faced a great challenge and accomplished much achievement.

The seventh hole was a good sign for him, defining future strategies. His next challenge would be number eight, a 180-yard par three. After watching the other two golfers hit good tee shots, he selected a six-iron to hit. As he approached the tee, preparing to hit his six-iron, the wind changed directions. Instead of a tail wind, a crosswind that caused his tee shot to fall shy of the right of the green into a sand trap challenged him.

Julie was afraid to say anything to him concerning the shot.

As he looked at his lie in the trap, he informed her that he was going to have to play for a bogey. It was too risky to play for an up-and-down shot.

Julie accepted what he said. *"Okay, we will just have to accept a bogey on this hole and try to improve on the next one."*

Following his sand chip, he secured his bogey by two-putting the green. Both he and his telepathic spectator accepted his four in the scorecard.

Joining the other two golfers on the ninth tee, he ensured not to complain about his recent bogey. His character strengthened as he accepted losing the hole to both Justin and Shannon.

The ninth hole, 275-yard par four, beckoned his courage to perform above levels of expectation.

As he watched Justin and Shannon hit excellent drives, he prepared for his drive also. He followed suit by hitting his tee shot within fairway boundaries providing good shape for a straight second shot onto the green. A smooth iron shot into the heart of the green generated an easy two-putt par opportunity. The ninth hole was kind to the entire threesome as they secured par-fours finishing out the first nine holes in excellent fashion.

Schuyler was very much satisfied to finish the front side being only two strokes above par. His front nine score of 38 was his best nine-hole score ever, and he offered much credit to his telepathic companion. Justin fired a sizzling 35 and Shannon matched Schuyler with a 38. A mutual agreement among Justin's playing partners credited his leadership as a vital factor in their game improvement.

They were allocated a fifteen-minute break between sides. His order of Mountain Dew, water, and a hot dog would have to be enough nourishment to get him through the back side.

Justin was the first to report to the tenth tee. He was already prepared to hit before the others got there. His drive on the tenth hole, a 375-yard par four, was an excellent shot on one of the toughest holes of the back nine. His distance alone put him within 5-iron range of the green.

Shannon followed with a weak, short drive down the left of the fairway that caused him to become fluttered a bit. "Schuyler, don't hit as poorly as I did."

He hit his shot about as bad as Shannon's drive, but not quite as bad. As he walked with him to hit the second shot, he encouraged him on his proceeding shot. With a good distance from the hole and his lie not that good, he preferred to play safe again and just hit a four-iron at the green. After watching Shannon muff his second shot and Justin hit the green with his second shot, he challenged himself to land his ball as close to the green as possible. Looking down at the pin, he stroked his shot just a little shy of the green. He was satisfied with the shape since he could easily chip onto the green and sink the putt.

Strong support from Julie enlightened his hope of saving par. *"I know you'll do well because you have me on your mind."*

Since his game was at pinnacle status he was almost assured a routine up-and-down to secure par. Her comforting voice worked like magic for him. He seemed to do little wrong on the golf course; also Justin's mentorship provided great benefit. Between Julie's inspirational direction and Justin's sterling example as a golfer, his complete golf game had improved vastly.

As expected, Schuyler chipped close enough to the hole to one-putt for par. His continuous success progressed throughout tough battles, resulting with his strength and determination being a good combination.

His par on the tenth hole gave him motivation. The next two par-four holes were of short distance opening a strong window of opportunity for him to excel. With one par already under his belt on the back nine and an extra bottle of water in his golf bag, he marched upon the two holes like a true infantry soldier. His perseverance established fortitude for him to continue his success as he recorded back-to-back pars on number eleven and number twelve. After the first three holes of the back nine, he was shooting even par, an achievement in itself.

As the threesome walked away from the twelfth green in route to number thirteen, Julie excitably congratulated Schuyler, *"I have never seen you play so well! I'm honored just to get to watch you play."*

He thanked her dearly for the flattering comment, instilling even more confidence throughout his physical presence that elevated his self-esteem toward pinnacle degrees.

"Schuyler, you are playing awful well for being a sixth man for your usual team," said Justin.

"I'm impressed with your game. You remain calm at almost every critical play in the sport." Shannon told Schuyler as they both picked their irons for the upcoming par-three thirteenth hole.

"You seem to be well versed on the course also," said Justin. "You place your shots in good position regularly."

Schuyler nodded his head and told them that he had been blessed today with his success. He stated that the leadership of them both paved the way for him to excel.

Hole-number thirteen was only 160-yards, an easy chance for par. All three of them hit their drives on the green, eventually two-putting for scores of three each.

As Justin recorded their scores, Shannon washed his ball and Schuyler opened his reserve bottle of water. The next refreshment stand was not until the sixteenth hole, thus he needed something now to hold him over until then.

The par-five fourteenth hole covered almost 500 yards with two doglegs and multiple sand traps along the way. The threesome knew this would be the toughest challenged yet on the back nine.

Julie reminded him of the danger of the traps and the changing wind current. *"Play your heart out, my love. You've come so far the past few days."*

As Julie as his guiding inspiration, he drove off the tee with vigor and diligence high above the fairway. His initial shot had cleared a few traps and was in excellent shape for his proceeding shot.

"Play a sure shot," informed Julie.

Sweat was now flowing down his brow causing difficulty in his vision. He brushed the moisture from his eye, aligned his second shot, and stroked a four-iron straight down the fairway in adequate position to hit the green on the next shot. Indeed, he was much farther from the green than Justin and Shannon. His ensuing third shot was well over a hundred yards, but at least it appeared straight into the green, free of sand.

Justin and Schuyler both hit the green on their third shots. Justin was in good position to birdie while Schuyler was a long way from the cup.

Shannon had sand trouble that eventually led to a bogey six. The large putting surface presented a big problem for Schuyler. The long, downhill putt scared him into putting too weak resulting in a good stout putt to follow. He suffered a three-putt on the fourteenth green recording a six, matching Shannon's bogey. Justin held his lead with his two-putt par.

In admittance of a tough putting surface, he accepted his bogey and prepared for the ensuing fifteenth hole, a 333-yard par four. He was still on track to shoot his lowest score in his own short history, but he knew stiff competition awaited him.

The par-four fifteenth hole played very easily for the entire threesome with a score of four for all three of them.

"We all shot par!" reported Justin as his pencil marked the scorecard.

Schuyler informed Julie of his satisfied feeling from the ease of the past hole. He began to feel extra special about this eighteen-hole round.

"I understand your feelings. By reading your mind, I comprehend your expressions along with your thoughts," Julie affirmed her confidence.

As he ordered his Mountain Dew at the refreshment stand for the final three holes, he could only dream about his relationship with his telepathic goddess formulating sensations that would have to wait until he got home.

After fifteen holes of play, he was three strokes above par. Shannon was one shot behind him and Justin was setting a tough standard of one stroke under par.

The next three holes would be make-or-break for him if he were to have any chance to qualify for The Regional Tournament.

Number sixteen, 529 yards, was the longest hole on the entire course.

It was the course's monster hole and even Justin was a little scared of the size it possessed. In the past, this hole challenged many top-ranked golfers and Schuyler Ballantine had no immunity from its legacy.

He played number sixteen similar to any other par-five hole, but he did make one adjustment. After a nice, playable drive, he selected a four-wood for his second shot. Although he had not used any fairway woods during the round, he still decided to utilize his Ben Hogan model four-wood club. The club was a gift from Lyndon, his cousin from Tennessee, and it possessed a bit of accuracy too. The club gripped his hand as it was made for him and the ensuing shot he made with it would have made his cousin proud. The four-wood's magic left his ball within a hundred yards of the pin; and after a seven-iron chip onto the green, he eventually two-putt for par. His conquer of the sixteenth hole surpassed any expectation delivered. The outcome measured during this most recent par attained results in the delight of both him and his dream girl.

Number seventeen, a par-three, was uphill with water prior to the green provided much chance for failure. As Justin and Shannon hit over the water near the green, he contemplated his tee shot. Since they seemed to do well with their iron shots, he decided to use his trusty four-iron and loft it high over the water toward the green. The sun beamed down upon him as he aimed his tee shot beyond the glimmer of the pond's view. As he addressed his crucial four-iron shot, a strange exciting feeling flowed throughout his body that propelled strength and allowed him to hit a magnificent shot onto the green within twenty feet of the pin. His superb stroke had left him with an outstanding chance for a two-putt par.

A strong sigh of content beheld him when he tapped his putt for par into the cup. Again, he had matched par with both Justin and Shannon.

The eighteenth hole, the final hole, tested both his skill and compassion for the game. It being a 395-yard par four presented another obstacle for him to conquer.

Julie was worried about the long hole. *"Don't be afraid of the distance. You did alright on the prior hole; maybe this one will be just as easy."*

The monstrous number eighteen was not so easy for the threesome. Justin failed to hit the green in regulation resulting in his first bogey of the day. He finished with a spectacular score of 72. Shannon suffered greatly on his last hole by three-putting the green for a bogey also. His final score of 77 left him behind Schuyler by one stroke because Schuyler bogeyed in concert with the others resulting in a career-best score of 76. As they walked off the green, Shannon congratulated Schuyler. "I lost to a great golfer today."

"Maybe we'll both make the cut for the regional," he responded.

Justin shot even par; his date was already set for The Regional Tournament; but for his two playing partners, they would have to wait the numbers game.

After Shannon and Schuyler attested Justin's scorecard, they went into the clubhouse to eat a long, awaited meal. Justin, having the best score of threesome, offered to pay for the late lunch and Schuyler did not oppose, he was very hungry and appreciated the kind offer greatly.

The District Tournament results were not official until 1700 hours due to a late start by two of threesomes, but he knew his chances were excellent of making the final cut. The suspense grew more and more as he waited for his original team members to finish. Richard and Tony completed their rounds about an hour later than he did. Tony, who had been playing real well for the team lately, exceeded expectations by shooting a 75. Richard was not so fortunate, his game delivered a disappointing 81.

"Schuyler, how did you shoot?" Tony asked.

He informed him that he shot a career-best 76 and gave much credit to the playing experience of the Central golfers guiding him throughout most of the day.

"Don't ask what I shot," added Richard.

He eventually learned that his 81 was not an encouraging topic of conversation and the three of them anxiously waited for Mark and Kent to come in. Mark was in the last threesome, and Kent was in one of the next-to-last threesomes still out on the course. Thus, Kent would be completing the last hole soon.

Julie was extremely confident about his chances. *"I really like your chances since both Shannon and Richard finished behind you. Your 76 should hold up unless more golfers in the likes of Tony are still out there playing."*

As the scores were being posted, he noticed that Justin's 72 was tied for first place and Tony's 75 looked like a sure bet, but his own scored of 76 was going to be on the bubble until the last group completed.

Kent's group finished up the ninth hole, their final hole, with Kent's 77 being the threesomes' best score. Thus, he had survived past the entire threesome with only six golfers, 2 pairs of threesomes, left on the course.

"You'll be playing in the regional, I can feel it," said Julie.

With doubt in his expression, he informed her that he might still be forced to have a playoff for tie-breaking conditions.

"Don't worry, my sugar, you will earn your victory," assured Julie.

He paced back-and-forth as the remaining golfers finished. Out of the six remaining golfers, only three of them finished with scores of 76 or less. Mark, along with Tony secured a spot in The Regional Tournament with his score of 75.

Justin, who just received the final results, quietly approached Schuyler and informed him that he was successful. "Congratulations Schuyler, you have succeeded in earning a spot in the regional. Your 76-score was enough to qualify."

He shook Justin's hand and thanked him again for his mentorship and proceeding to go congratulate Mark for his performance.

The District Tournament was not just an important milestone in his golf career, but it was the beginning of a lasting unique relationship among two newly, found friends. This cohesive bond, beginning with the night prior to the tournament, spearheaded his character development that would become the basis for a young high school senior to embark upon the world. In partnership with a lover in which he has never met, he found the loving touch his spirit requested.

As Mark drove Doug and him back home, he learned Doug failed to qualify also with his score of 78.

"Schuyler, what is your secret weapon?' asked Doug.

He looked back at him and told him that he just lucky.

"Schuyler played with Justin today, "responded Mark.

"He tied with low score with two others. He sure is a great golfer," sounded Doug.

"He was my mentor most of the way. He is the master of the putting green." Schuyler nodded his head.

Mark and Doug just pretended to not recognize his telepathic romance as they conversed all the way home. But they knew in their mind Schuyler had gone through some eventful transformation.

Eventually Doug aired, *"Schuyler, you are the dream of a lifetime and we are plenty thankful just to be a part of it."*

As he continued to daydream to himself about his golf game, he asked Julie what she thought about him.

"You are the dream, sugar. Let me be the one to experience it with you?" inquired Julie.

His trip home was enjoyable; he couldn't wait to tell his parents the good news. When he arrived at his house, his anxiety levels increased as his father greeted him at the door.

The breaking news sent a mountain of happiness throughout the Ballantine household. His golfing success created much laudatory praise, elevating emotions in such a manner he fought to keep from crying. The feeling of achieving success that instilled espirit de corps among the family was almost too much of an experience for his subtle shyness. The happiness of his family was a very pleasant experience for him, but his sequential reward from Julie would come later.

Chapter 7

The social activities seemed to go well with Julie by his side. After the golf tournament on Saturday, the telepathic couple took a well deserving rest for the remainder of the weekend. Math assignments, golf practice, and other usual chores were postponed until Monday. This weekend was a time for them to get acquainted with each other and to explore newly, discovered lifestyle avenues. The couple practiced telepathic communication throughout the day enhancing his lifestyle. Wherever he ventured, she instilled her enthusiast dialogue. Her extensive knowledge paved the way for him to visualize life aspects from an entirely different point of view. Often, she expanded emotional abilities reducing anxiety through implementation of stress management techniques. She was his friend, advisor, therapist, and lover. His forever dream girl was only a thought away.

Monday morning came quick creating busy schedules for both of them. She had her own thing to do and he was plenty busy with his events also. Julie, upon his request, still would provide helpful communication during tight situations. Every evening after supper, her focused presence created a perfect atmosphere for homework environment. Dedication to mathematical enhancement spearheaded their relationship from the homework setting to bedroom activity. At the conclusion of schoolwork assignments, her character role transformed as mathematical subject-matter-expert into lustful lover.

Schuyler's calendar compressed activities such as daily golf practice, a Tuesday math examination, a Thursday medical appointment, and Saturday's regional golf tournament. The golf practice he could endure, the math test, with Julie's involvement, he could sustain, the golf tournament would be a challenge of pure enjoyment, but the medical appointment generated much doubt in his mind. His uncertainty of Dr. Walton haunted him throughout most of the week.

The night prior to his math exam, they studied together for over an hour. Utilizing their strategy-based study habits, they mastered the easiest material initially and proceeded to practice on more difficult algebraic equations. As the evening grew late, the most dreaded lessons were calculated. With Julie's help, he prepared himself for even the most difficult questions possible.

Julie offered reassurance by putting her arm around his neck. *"Schuyler, we have completed almost everything we can. Your improvement is superb! I don't think you will need my help during your test."*

Do you think I can pass my exam on my own?

"Yes, you have it down. If you run into trouble, just ask me for help."

I wish I had as much confidence in myself as you do!

She massaged his shoulders as he sat motionless at his desk. *"You must believe in yourself; I do!"*

Julie, you are the one and only girl for me. No other girl pays any attention to me, but you take the time out of your busy schedule to help me.

"Don't worry about it; put some comfortable clothes on and go to bed."

Yes, Miss Crystal.

Being very surprised, she quickly corrected his mistake. *"You must have misunderstood me before when I told you my name."* She grasped his hand and informed him of her complete name. *"My name is Julie Crystal Flowers. Sorry, I did introduce myself as Julie Crystal. I like to be called Julie Crystal; is that alright?"*

Yes, I love the name Julie Crystal. Also, I love the way you touch me at night.

In quietness of the night, in his bedroom, the couple began touching one another, as lovers would do. They were both inexperienced, and learning as they went along. Neither had a teacher, any advice, or any real knowledge of sexual relations. The couple's wholesomeness stimulated sexual behavior beyond imagination. Lack of carnal knowledge benefited the couple as they experienced one another's sexual fantasies, leveraging one's sexual feelings upon another. She seemed to be the one in charge most of the time; she knew how to manipulate his sexual appetite demonstrating her control.

He, on the other hand, followed her lead well. His response to her seductive kiss illustrated his learning desire to become deserving of her companionship. After an exhausting climax, he was ready for rest. Tomorrow would be another day, a telepathic one at that.

The next morning seemed to travel like the speed of light as a subsequent math examination awaited him after lunch. He took enough time to adjust fire in preparation for his test. When he marched into his math class, his mind was set to achieve good, sound results through usage of strategy-based techniques.

Schuyler's heart pounded as the examinations were disseminated; disappearing moisture in his mouth eventually caused his mouth to become so parched that the desiccation prevented him from speaking.

True, he was showing numerous symptoms of being nervous. As he initially examined the test, he noticed the very first problem was too difficult for him to solve. Panic bestowed upon him as another student laughed at him via air, but the champion in him prevailed as he overcame the distraction and proceeded with the next question. The subsequent nine questions strengthened his confidence. He easily could comprehend eight of them, thus he was certain of 80% success rate of the first ten questions.

Julie, as coy as she could be, assured him that she knew how to solve the first question. *"Hey Schuyler, do you want me to do the first problem for you? I overheard your friend laughing at you because you didn't know how to solve it."*

He thanked Julie, and told her of his need for the psychological edge to get him over the hump during the exam.

Her guidance was saved until the difficult problems were evaluated. As his set strategy had recommended, the complicated questions were delayed until closure. His examination balanced algebraic problems, pre-calculus equations, along with probability introduction. As he drove throughout the course of the test, his stamina adjusted for the final session of the exam. This final session incorporated the toughest challenge he faced throughout any previous test; his acceptance of this challenge was based upon the faith he had of Julie's expertise.

She scanned the remainder of the test; through his eyes she discovered that only four problems remained. *"I know how to solve two of the four final problems."*

With her assistance, he completed and relinquished his examination. As he dismissed himself from the classroom, Julie issued a strong hug congratulating him. She knew his results would be at least 80%, a superior improvement.

Schuyler thanked his telepathic companion greatly and asked her for her opinion concerning the test.

Julie provided her analysis of his performance. *"You did well and I'm so proud of your performance. You handled yourself well during tight situations. This is something we need to strategize, because you being The Dream might create more incidents in the future."*

Joyful bliss conceptualized his accomplishment. He achieved exceeding gratification, something he could only wish for, and this feeling of euphoria handling conquered his emotional state of being. Truly, it was another victorious day.

"Schuyler, your success has been blessed by your recent achievements with golf and math," responded Julie.

My recent accomplishments could not have been if it was not for your help, Julie Crystal.

The successful mathematical adventure, along with the golf tournament, stimulated his confidence, but in the back of his mind he knew that his psychology appointment on Thursday would be his real test.

An awkward feeling haunted him throughout the entire day at school. Even though his math results reported an 83% on his recent examination, his exodus from school that particular day precluded an antagonizing session with his shrink.

He arrived at Dr. Walton's office in plenty of time. He really needed to practice his sand wedge, but the scheduled appointment had precedence.

Dr. Walton greeted him with a handshake. "Glad you could make it here so quickly!"

"I left school a little bit earlier than usual."

The doctor walked him into his office offered him a chair and preceded to allow Schuyler to discuss his recent events. "Tell me Schuyler, what has occurred in your life these past two weeks?"

"My golf game has been successful; I earned a position in the upcoming regional golf tournament. Also, I've improved in my mathematical studies."

He pretended to examine his patient's diagnosis. "Can you remember your early childhood?"

"A little bit, I remember when my parents moved here when I was only two years of age."

"Did you ever have the feeling that you came from a place far away?" Dr. Walton inquired.

"No, why do you ask?"

Being startled, he spoke off the top of his head attempting to barter his reply. "No real reason. I just thought I would inquire."

Suspicious feelings overcame Schuyler's presence. He avoided almost every following question asked. He became leery of the doctor's intentions and began clock-watching.

Dr. Walton shifted position in his easy chair and stumbled with his words. "Schuyler, have you ever listened to voices in your head?"

Without hesitation, he replied to the doctor, "Doctor, I do not know what you mean."

Disgusted with his answer, Dr Walton quickly ended the conversation sending Schuyler home with an appointment to be scheduled at a latter date. He could not disguise his disappointment with his results from their appointment, thus his patient's early dismal was well warranted.

On the way home from his appointment, his discussion of his appointment's outcome was of hottest topic of the telepathic couple.

"Believe me Schuyler, your shrink is completely out of control. His insinuations concerning your past and voice telepathy were completely unfair." She harped aimlessly at him.

I did not know what to do about the question about being far away, but I did all right with the "voices in my head" question. Maybe he thinks I'm an alien?

Julie caressed his neck as he drove closer to home. *"I assure you sugar, you aren't an alien."*

In mutual agreement that the week was still a great success, even with a doctor who thinks he's from the twilight zone, the couple set their sights on The Regional Golf Tournament.

The Regional Golf Tournament was an event capturing glimmer and hopes of a huge handful of high school golfers. The event encompassed promising golfers from the entire Lexington/Richmond surrounding. Only the very best could participate in this strongly competitive tournament that showcased the area's golfing elite. College scouts viewed these types of tournaments as future resource evaluation. The competitiveness at this level advertised future prospects for college-level success, and among them was Schuyler Ballantine.

As a former sixth man of his team, he had to be one of the biggest underdogs in the tournament. The others were dominant figures representing their schools as selected few from their cream of crop. Quality players on the level of Central's Justin would be challenging him at all fronts, governing an atmosphere in which he could perform at levels well beyond his imagination. True, his talent was well below most of the others, but in his heart he knew everything was to gain and nothing to lose.

Arriving at the course with Mark and Tony, Schuyler noticed the coach waiting in the parking lot. The coach was very excited about the tournament. He had a good, strong feeling that all three of his players had an excellent chance of earning a state berth.

Walking toward the clubhouse, Mark instilled confidence in Schuyler's spirit. "Play with your lucky charm again today and you may defeat us all."

Schuyler glanced over his shoulder at Mark. "Maybe I will play with Justin from Central High School like I did last week."

"Just do it," encouraged Tony.

Schuyler began daydreaming to himself, wondering what exactly Mark and Tony meant. He focused upon them both. "I am prepared to play with as little pressure as possible," he responded.

"The sky is the limit in this tournament," added Mark.

"I feel everything is to gain and nothing to lose," responded Schuyler as he entered the clubhouse area.

Tony placed his hand on his shoulder. "I like your attitude. You impressed us last week and you will also do it again today."

Schuyler offered much gratitude toward both Mark and Tony as the coach approached them with their starting times. Mark and Tony were scheduled tee times at 0920 hours and 1140 hours respectively on the front nine. Schuyler's nerves roared as he was notified of his late tee time of 1120 hours. Yes, he would be playing the entire eighteen-hole round in the heat of the day.

With the late tee time, he enjoyed himself with food and drink. He mingled with the other golfers like he was a former champion. The competitiveness was tight among the golfers, but he overcame his fear when he discovered Justin was in his threesome. Yes, it was a mild miracle. Justin would be playing with him again for the second straight week.

Prior to mounting the first tee, he ensured to purchase several bottles of water in preparation of the play. Even if he didn't require the excess water, the possession of multiple water bottles might inhibit a good impression upon Justin. He idolized his talent, along with his character as a mentor of the game. Thus, he began to pattern his golf practices from his symbolism.

"Do it one more time, Schuyler," spoke Justin.

"Yes, we're back on the links again."

Justin informed him that the third member of the threesome was Leo, another golfer, from a high school on the other side of Lexington. He was only a junior and showed much potential.

Schuyler was so excited to hit with Justin, he didn't even care if he shot well because in his mind he knew that just watching him play was more of a lesson than playing himself. Justin was an artist.

"You want me to watch you play?" Julie inquired.

Of course, this is an once-in-a-lifetime opportunity. Julie, this will probably be the most outstanding golf tournament I will ever play.

She got excited and gave him a little rub on the bottom. *"I feel special just to get to follow you around on your dream."*

Schuyler played along with the other two golfers as comfortable as can be. The environmental setting was ideal for him to experience competitiveness from future college golfers. He savored the moment as he cherished the exposure to shine. Even though he bogeyed the first hole, his achieving admirations were not hampered.

Throughout the front side he visualized Justin's techniques in benefit of his own. Justin shot par throughout the entire front nine; his game was shaky at times, but he always managed to save par.

After the front nine, Justin inquired of Schuyler. "Remember last week when you consistently got up-and-down?"

"I only did it a few times, Justin."

"Your skill around the green saved numerous strokes," reminded Justin. "I often utilized your chipping method around the green; your chip and roll shots render outstanding results."

While Leo tallied the scores, Schuyler thanked Justin for his laudatory comments.

"You thought you would learn from him, but actually he was learning from you," reported Julie.

Flattered by her dialogue, his self-esteem illustrated an appearance granting maturity assurance among his tournament competition. This maturity would latter initiate milestones from his transformation from boy into man.

The break after the front nine was twenty minutes allowing plenty of time for the threesome to replenish their energy. Schuyler followed Justin's lead in purchasing bottled water for the back nine, but he still could not resist his Mountain Dew.

"Let's get back to the tenth tee, guys," said Justin.

Schuyler and Leo quickly gathered their equipment, with their junk food in their hands, and marched urgently behind their leader.

Prior to teeing-off on the tenth hole, Justin reviewed the scores. "During the front nine: I had a 36, Leo shot 39, and Schuyler's 40 showed good promise. So let's go out there on the back nine and tear it up!"

Schuyler respected his mentor, admiring every swing he took, but in his heart he knew an important impact was placed on Justin's game. His chip-and-roll style around the green might save Justin future strokes, strengthening his chances to advance to The State Tournament.

Schuyler's play on the early holes of the back nine presided ensuing disappointment; he suffered back-to-back bogies on number eleven and twelve causing shifting emotions that defined a need for external assistance.

Demonstrating her concern for him, she attempted to rally her troop. *"You are almost finished with your round. There is no pressure; you are aware of your chances for the state qualification. Just play your game and enjoy yourself; that's all I can ask. I love you, Schuyler."*

He pondered about his future; he accepted the fact that these next six holes would be his swan song. He realized his destiny; it was not to advance to the state, but to govern the lessons learned here at the regional. He was playing beyond his expected dreams anyway; he reorganized his strategy and pursued other available avenues of approach.

During play on number thirteen, he found the opportunity to speak with Justin concerning his golfing future. "Do you plan to play in college?"

Justin had shot par throughout the first three holes of the back side, remaining even par for the entire round. As he approached the green expected another 2-putt par, "Schuyler I plan to play college somewhere, but I'm not sure where yet."

The threesome putted-out for pars around the board, and proceeded to the fourteenth hole. In route to the next green, Schuyler persuaded Justin to elaborate on his college prospectus. "Justin, which colleges have you considered?"

"I'm mainly interested in Cincinnati, but if I have to play locally then I will," Justin informed him as they checked the scorecard for distances of the next two holes.

"I'm sure Cincinnati will be more than happy to offer you a spot on their team. Nobody can match your consistent play around the greens," responded Schuyler.

The scorecard reported back-to-back par fives. Number fourteen was a long dogleg to the right and number fifteen featured a straight fairway with its green on a steep hilltop. Even Justin was challenged by the layout.

After his drive on number fourteen, Schuyler used his trusty four-wood to hit his second shot. He aligned the club head in his desired direction and hit a magnificent, towering shot in the general direction of the green. His shot might have been a little to the right, but its distance spoke for itself.

"Excellent shot, I hope I can do the same," spoke Justin.

Schuyler put his club back into his bag. "Thanks, I hope I can survive this monstrous hole."

"Schuyler, what club did you use?" asked Justin.

"My Ben Hogan four-wood," he responded.

Leo was due to hit his second shot next. *"That's the club he got from his cousin from Tennessee,"* he aired. He felt it was all right to comment, via air, concerning Schuyler favorite fairway wood; he then proceeded to hit a fine shot of his own.

Once they got to the green, the entire threesome possessed excellent opportunity to secure par. In succession, they each two-putted for par. Securing their golf equipment they maneuvered toward the fifteenth tee to challenge the second leg of the double par-five combination. The proceeding hole might be another challenging obstacle for Schuyler, but it was just another milestone in Justin's quest to earn a birth in The State Golf Tournament.

Schuyler anxiously watched Justin hit his drive. Justin was the only golfer out of their group with any feasible chance to advance to state. Both Schuyler and Leo had damaged their chances with numerous bogies. As all eyes watched Justin, his masterly play carried him through 16 holes of play with a score of one stroke under par.

The remaining three holes consisted of a short par-three hole and two par-four holes, allowing focus upon good iron play to maintain prominence in the game. Justin appeared primed for state competition.

After each of them finished playing the sixteenth hole, earning a par a piece, Leo calculated the individual scores. He informed Schuyler he was four strokes over par and still was playing an excellent round.

Schuyler thanked Leo for the compliment, and prepared to finish the remaining two holes in grand fashion.

The heat of the afternoon sun facilitated fatigue and weakness throughout his physical presence, affecting both his golf game and mental telepathy. His ineffective golf game translated into two bogies on the remaining two holes that resulted in an eighteen-hole score of 83, far below qualification status. Also during the final two holes, his telepathic communication began to fade.

"I realize you are getting tired because you're not daydreaming near as much as usual," reported Julie.

He hesitated in his response. His brain seemed to slow down to almost a normal level. It normally could not seize to rest between issues, illustrating visions continuously concerning abstract observations and personal feelings. Intermittent pauses in his almost virtual perpetual thinking publicized decline in energy and alertness.

Julie instilled strength into his identity. *"You did well, I'm very proud of your accomplishments."*

At tournament closing, he walked proudly along with his mentor as the threesome marched quietly toward the center for tournament operations. Prior to reporting their final results, Leo congratulated Justin for his outstanding score of 71. Leo shot a score of 81, two strokes better than Schuyler.

Justin's 71 appeared to be a challenging score. "You might finish near the top," said Schuyler.

Leo finalized the scorecard, with attests from both Justin and Schuyler, and submitted it to the tournament director.

Schuyler had noticed Mark speaking rather loudly about his game. His loud, boasting voice traveled far enough for Schuyler to recognize. Before Schuyler accompanied him, he verified Justin's position in the tournament. His score of 71 was top score with only two other threesomes still out on the course.

"Justin, we are blessed to watch your play," spoke Schuyler.

Leo firmly shook his hand and aired, *"the whole world probably watched you play outstandingly today."* Gaining his composure, Leo confirmed Schuyler laudatory comment, "you are the best we have ever seen and we expect great accomplishments in the future!"

Schuyler, stunned from the excitement, gleamed at his playing partners in experience to the spectacular event. Deep in mind, his intellect knew that this milestone would be an important benchmark in transformation from boy to man.

Justin graciously thanked both Leo and Schuyler for their sportsmanship, and asked to be excused to put his equipment away. As he walked to his car, Justin could not resist airing, *"playing with that Schuyler is like playing in a dream; too bad that I can't play with him every time."*

"Schuyler, you may not have performed well today with the golf clubs, but your influenced upon Justin has impressed me greatly," reported Julie.

Schuyler finally met up with Mark and learned that he had shot a magnificent 74. With the scores already tallied, he was almost a sure bet for the state.

Mark enjoying the moment, "Schuyler, I might make The State Tournament!"

"Is Tony finished yet?" He studied the final scores posted on the board.

"He's still out there, he's in the final threesome!" said Mark as he put his arm around Schuyler and boasted about his game. Mark was the type when he did well; he made sure that everybody knew it.

Finally the entire scores were captured. Tony completed his round with a 77, not good enough to qualify for the state. Mark's 74 secured a state birth. Justin achieved the distinguished honor of shooting the lowest score. He was recognized greatly by The Regional Tournament Director as the best golfer within the entire regional area. Victoriously, Justin accepted the winning trophy. During his acceptance speech, the modest champion graciously thanked his playing partners and set his goal of a placing soundly at the top at the state.

After all the congratulations were rendered, Schuyler got to speak with the champion receiving an achievement of his own, Justin's electronic mail account address.

"Someday, you'll be a golf star in Cincinnati and I'll come to watch you play," Schuyler congratulated Justin one last time.

The road trip back home was an event in itself. He got to listen to Mark recite his tournament's play-by-play.

Chapter 8

The golf season ended with the completion of The Regional Golf Tournament, Schuyler's high school golfing career terminated with quantifiable success. The unknown sixth man from a local area school exceeded expectations throughout the entire season, especially at district and regional levels. Cinderella storybook fashion of his own, catalogued a series of unexpected performances proliferating talent and sportsmanship among his golfing peers. The District Tournament alone, stimulated professional growth and fostered attributes that influenced transformation from boy to man. His newfound maturity made it possible for him to venture out on his own, blessed by his telepathic lover.

His cluttered mind sorted schedule matrixes as he went upon his daily routine. His day was filled with much tension. His mathematical final was approaching, creating uncontrollable anxiety Julie often struggled to control. She prepared him as professionally as possible, resulting in noticeable improvement. Doctor Walton had schedule another psychological appointment intervening in two weeks causing him to experience intermittent migraine headaches generated from induced tension. His future was in question? What would he do after graduation? But with all of these dilemmas, Julie Crystal captured his heart and gifted him with her unique loving touch.

She transmitted unparalleled loyalty to her companion. *"Whatever you do in life, Schuyler, I will be with you. When you excel, I will be there to offer congratulations and if you fail, then I will be the one to restore confidence in your heart. I will come to your rescue, at any cost."*

Schuyler's good fortune kept building. Julie's transmissions influenced decision-making processes that allowed him to adapt to his surroundings. Gradually his shyness shrunk, programming him toward an outward direction. He conversed more frequently, distributing concealed convictions among his family and friends. With Julie Crystal at his side, his leadership abilities grew higher and higher. Yes, he was now ready to accept duties of increasing responsibilities.

The school year was concluding quickly and he knew only his math final would present any problems. Utilization of developed study strategies spearheaded his ultimate opportunity to excel at mathematical equations. Julie, almost every evening, organized a short study session dedicated to math alone. He anxiously looked forward to the study sessions, because ensuing telepathic romance followed.

At the Jupiter, Morrison and Boyd prepared their presentations concerning The Air. Morrison's admiration to follow the air throughout adulthood accelerated. "We have structured a fine development with The Air; he has matured enough to leave his nest and view the world."

Boyd struggled to organize his thoughts as he intensely studied his notes, with pizza on order for lunch. "I'm interested in the girl. Her life is hidden. We know what The Vision is doing at all times, but we don't know what she is doing."

"Only The Air has the phenomena," spoke Morrison ignoring any relative important of Julie. "She does exist in his mind, but her physical presence is not viewed." Hurrying outside to receive his lunch, Boyd dreamed of the day when their research focused upon Julie Crystal, not Schuyler. As he returned with an anxious stomach, Boyd got comfortable to listen to a long speech from Morrison.

Morrison poured himself a small pitcher of coffee and began lecturing Boyd. With pizza stuffed in his mouth, he pleasurably experienced Morrison's lecture. The senior partner explained the process to synthesize The Air from his current status into a leading member of the community. He ensured The Air would be granted some token government job due to his phenomena. "They have to keep him under complete surveillance some how. A gift of his nature cannot be exposed to the free market."

Boyd cut into his lecture. "You mean The Vision will be denied to live a natural life? To be labeled as limited access only?" He looked at Morrison, but quickly looked away and continued concentrating on his pizza.

Tasting his coffee for texture, he agreed with Boyd's comments. But he assured the government would be overprotective of "their Air", and attempt greatly to protect him from private investors. "The Air is a much unique phenomena and whoever has access to him controls destiny."

Both of the partners agreed that development of Schuyler's air phenomena would be top priority for some organization, but through what means? The Air fabricated new avenues toward fantasy experiences. Julie had proven her fantasies could be his, and vice versa. The Air would live a life with no privacy, with no inner secrets, and no avoidance from the ones that love him. He would be somewhere for everybody, and everybody would be somewhere with him.

The date with Doctor Walton would preclude any major upcoming event. Since his golf was finished, only graduating high school would present an intense emotional state. But his psychological appointment would be an obstacle he would have to hurdle prior to graduation.

Schuyler prepared for his psychology appointment with the aid of Julie. They practiced possible questions, and appropriate replies. Areas of concentrations were voices in his mind, alien lifestyles, and mental stimulation. They plotted to completely have him deny any trace of voices being transmitted through his mind. The doctor had attempted to extract this kind of information from him before, but he avoided the questioning well. If the doctor had any question what so ever concerning outer space, Julie directed him to pretend to be misinformed of the question. Thus, avoid rendering any knowledgeable response to any alien activity inquiry. Mental stimulation, on the other hand, would be a topic he could elaborate upon. In preparation for any mental stimulus questioning, she mapped outlines encompassing a large variety of inquiries. Her diagrams of possible cause-and-effect situations were devised in preparation of herself. She knew that the better she was prepared for his appointment, the better she would be to assist him with his answers. Thus, usage of air phenomena would enable Schuyler to cope with his psychological conversation.

Schuyler dreaded his meeting with Doctor Walton. Even with Julie's expertise, he could not shed his nervousness. The drive to Doctor Walton's office seemly lasted a strong eternity. While he was driving, he often dreamed of getting lost and never appearing for his get-together with his shrink. But he quickly understood he couldn't avoid him forever, and submitted to the idea of arriving with further delay.

The waiting area was quiet as he cautiously informed the receptionist of his presence.

"Good day Schuyler Ballantine, glad you could make," said the receptionist with a sham smile.

He responded back to her in confidence of enjoyment to be there, even though he wished he wasn't. The office's atmosphere sullied his hopes of achieving admiration of his sense of worth.

A fearing voice spoke, "Schuyler, are you ready?"

"Yes sir," he responded, but wished for Julie's assistance.

Doctor Walton had him sit down in his office and view magazines from various foreign countries. Periodicals from Japan, France, German, and Italy were available for his examination. "Schuyler, please admire these exotic magazines and give me some feedback of your feelings."

Schuyler looked at the periodicals for almost a full hour, dreaming of the particular lifestyles of each foreign country. He urged Julie to assist with him formulating a review of the articles read. Even without translation, Julie enjoyed the Italian articles. The photography of Venice exhibited notable historical uniqueness that influenced her significantly. But their combined conclusion delivered the Japanese literature as superior.

The doctor walked into the room, noticed the clock, and pursued feedback from his subject. "Are you interested in any foreign material that might illustrate sheltered inhibitions?"

After gaining feedback from Julie, Schuyler assembled the material and issued it back to Doctor Walton. "I liked the Italian articles, but overall the magazines expressing the Japanese art techniques interested me more."

The doctor became fascinated with his response and coaxed for more extensive information. "What Japanese cultural aspects invest your concern?"

Waiting for feedback from Julie, he slowly demonstrated confidence in his response. "I like their formulation of their written communication, instead of letters; they use characters that are distinctive compared to the western world."

"Would you like to live in Japan someday?" Doctor Walton inquired.

Waiting again for feedback from Julie, he finally submitted a response. "It would be an experience I would never forget." Nervously, he stared at the clock attempting to prevent further questioning.

Doctor Walton seized his questioning, but continued to pay attention to his subject. After a few minutes of silence, *"I know your thinking to the outside and I want to get in on it. I want to be the center of all thinking and channel all mental thinking through my presence,"* aired the doctor.

Stunned by the air transmission, he sat straight in his chair and continued to watch the doctor. In his mind he knew the doctor was acting crazy, but had no real feasible way to respond. Thus, he stayed frozen as long as the doctor remained silent.

"You may think I'm crazy, but I plan to be included on this thinking phenomenon," aired Doctor Walton.

Julie interrupted their telepathic communication, informed Schuyler to remain calm and quickly terminate the conversation. *"Sugar, don't let him think to you without speaking orally. I don't trust his intent. Please belong to me."*

"Can I please be dismissed?" asked Schuyler.

"I will speak to you in the future," responded Doctor Walton.

As he was leaving the office building, he bypassed the receptionist and maneuvered his way out the door and on his merry way home. He had little intention to book another appointment. As he drove away, he finally realized he was not going to be able to avoid Doctor Walton. The trap was set for him to become his personal experiment. Schuyler, in collaboration with Julie, challenged himself to strive to gain control of his own life, and not let others interfere with his priceless connection with his telepathic companion.

Schuyler had performed academically well during his senior year, verifying his motivation to succeed as a student athlete. Excluding his mathematics final exam, all other subject areas were covered with above satisfactory grades. Thus, his final math test would be the clincher before graduation. Even if he performed miserable on his math final he would still graduate, but he challenged himself to ensure accomplishment in this particular subject.

During finals week, Julie spent extensive time tutoring mathematics in preparation of the big test. Her three-tier study strategy progressed him from a marginal student to a strong college-entry prospect. With all other subject areas clicking on all cylinders, only mathematics required special attention and she was the subject-matter-expert to provide it.

Fortunately his math final would be the last exam he would take in his high school career, allocating maximum time to study for his monumental examination.

"Remember Schuyler, answer the easy questions prior to the difficult ones and leave the ones you can't solve for my assistance at the end," she reminded.

I will execute accordingly. I have my marching orders and will proceed into battle!

"Just relax and answer each question to your fullest ability," she responded.

As the test proctor disseminated the exams, he started breathing rapidly and perspiring profusely. His sweaty hands grasped a pencil and began figuring. He jumped out of the gates quickly solving several problems within the initial fifteen minutes; his eagerness to get to the more difficult problems allocated a few more moments in reservation. He was tracking right on through with this exam with little hindrance, strengthening his chances to not just meet standards, but to exceed them.

"Good job! I expect you to cruise through the rest of the test, but I do see a couple of problems you may have trouble with because we never really studied them,"

exclaimed Julie. She knew some of the problems were too hard for him, but her assistance should resolve any conflict. *"I'm here for you at exam closure."*

He struggled a little bit with the second tier of problems, calculating equations indoctrinated from algebra, pre-calculus, and probability. The final tier of his feared exam concerned mostly trigonometry, and he counted seven questions requiring assistance. Luckily, Julie knew how to solve five of the seven problems resulting in a comforting sign of relief at examination closure. Yes, he appeared to have been successful on his mathematics final examination.

Schuyler went home after the mentally strenuous day of finals. He assured his parents of success.

"You think you did well today?" asked his mother.

He explained in great detail his strategic maneuvers on his finals, especially during his mathematics final.

"What is for supper?" asked his father as he walked into the room. He paused and directed his attention to Schuyler. "How was school?"

Schuyler nodded his head in agreement. "I believe to have success on all of my exams, even my math one."

"Very good son, it appears you are ready for college after all," responded his father. "How are things working out with Doctor Walton and yourself?"

Schuyler began to get nervous and avoided answering the question. He finally spoke to his father. "He presents a lot of strange questions that make little sense, but I guess he is just attempting to expand my mental capacity."

His parents were very impressed with his confidence, his achievement, and his dedication to higher learning. They praised him greatly for his academic accomplishment.

After supper, later than evening, Julie praised him for his accomplishment also, but in a very different way.

"Get ready for bed," demanded Julie.

He prepared himself for romantic integration of each other. As he positioned his handy towel next to his body, she began to instill thoughts into his mind displaying removal of her clothing.

She transmitted a very descriptive vision of herself mounting into position to engage interaction. His vision of her was so authentic he could actually feel her pubic muscles stimulating his member.

As he began to moan silently informing her of his enjoyment, her talent expanded into other enjoyable positions that persuaded him to commence relief. The telepathic couple manipulated each other sexually, striving to induce orgasm. She successfully brought her partner to climax causing him to tactfully utilize his towel as her mental stimulation produced an excitement that came close to soiling his bed sheets.

Satisfaction was detected at the other end where Julie transmitted pleasurable sounds of her own. In the comfort of her Louisiana bedroom, her wet fingers delivered bliss that transmitted signals throughout his pulsating circulatory system proposing a lasting, compassionate relationship. This pretentious compassion fabricated a tight, collaborative bond that preserved wholesomeness, purity, and integrity among their clear channels of telepathic communication. The couple endured only telepathic sexual activity, remaining untainted at all costs.

Graduation grew near, and young Schuyler's ambition beckoned life after graduation. Struggling through mathematics class slowly seized in conjunction with Julie's proficiency. The dynasty of mathematical dilemmas abruptly ended as long as his mentor offered her guidance. Their study strategies, learning dedication, and obligation to each other incorporated a new era of erudition that instilled newly found maturity into the telepathic couple, especially Schuyler. His enthusiasm for her telepathic presence, alone, was enough to sustain progressive transformation into adulthood. Likewise, Julie's attachment of his charismatic character amplified congruently with his personal success. His captured achievements energized her inner health to pinnacle status. Hence her success derived from his success, and vice versa. Together they brought out the best in one another, distributing intermittent light throughout their own society.

Julie wondered why Schuyler never got his math final results. *"Are you going to inquire of your math teacher concerning your final exam score?"*

Why? You know I passed. You watched me take to test in your mind.

"Do not be silly! I do not know what you actually scored, but I did watch you take the test and I know you did well."

We'll stop by and talk to my teacher today. I'm starting to get a little uneasy about the whole entire event.

"Do not be afraid to talk to your teacher! Look, you've got to be more out-going."

Schuyler agreed with her. He told her of his attempt to be not so shy and to assume more responsibility for his own actions.

The visit with his math teacher was short and sweet. Schuyler never spoke much and had a bad habit of avoiding conversation. After laudatory comments from his teacher, he accepted his grade of 86% on his final exam.

His math teacher gave him a little pat on the shoulder. "Schuyler Ballantine, you have improved greatly in my classroom and your enhancing commitment will preside continuously."

He thanked his teacher and proceeded to exit the classroom for the final time. As he walked away he overheard his teacher air, *"thank you Miss Julie for your guidance, and don't ever let your catch swim away."*

Astonished by his teacher's transmission, he proceeded to travel home realizing his personal tutor was even more special than expected.

The Ballantine house was warming to his return. His parents prepared a small pre-graduation celebration for him. Informing them of his math score of 86%, he commenced to receive much welcomed attention inaugurating their small, subtle celebration. At the party he learned his brother, Duncan, was planning to attend his graduation at the end of the week. Duncan was doing well in the Army and was traveling across the state, on a three-day pass, to watch his little brother graduate high school.

"Schuyler, do you have plans after graduation?" asked his mother.

He paused for a moment before he spoke; his hesitation prefaced an awaited response from Julie. "I'm not really sure; I might try to play golf at the local junior college."

Schuyler's father cut in on the conversation. His unhesitant response influenced his son's ambition. "Son, you can attend almost any college you wish. I will support your decision with earnest."

Confused and reserved, Schuyler's procrastination of forecasting his college ambitions presented possible altercations. If he did not act soon, he would not even get accepted into a university. Maybe that was what he wished. Maybe in his self-conscience he desired to procrastinate enough, ensuring his only choice could be junior college. Down deep in his heart he felt his maturity was not enough to make that giant leap from high school to university.

The quasi-graduation celebration went well. His parents seemed to be very much satisfied with his progress. His father praised his golfing growth. "You have improved so much in the past month. Not so long ago you were struggling to shoot in the eighties, and now you threaten to break eighty on any given day."

Schuyler opened his Mountain Dew and organized his potato chips on his plate. "Yes father, I've been playing better lately. My focus has been improved from playing with Central's Justin."

As his mother finished cutting the cake, she also stimulated interest in his golf game. "How did you meet this Justin fellow?"

Anticipating chocolate cake, he responded back to his mother. "I was paired with him during both district and regional tournaments, and he's an excellent golfer who has taught me a lot."

"You are a very celebrated sixth man from the high school golfing tour, advancing all the way to The Regional Tournament," proclaimed his father as he gleamed proudly of his son's accomplishment.

"The cake is ready," claimed Mrs. Ballantine as she proceeded to take a rest and allow the men the opportunity to converse.

Both Schuyler and his father enjoyed the cake as they discussed the epics of one another's golf game. His father was not too much of an avid golfer, but he did take pleasure in playing with his two sons.

"Next Saturday I have a tee time for your brother and us to play," informed Mr. Ballantine.

Nervously Schuyler ate his cake; he visualized anticipation of his brother's arrival. He spoke highly of his brother to his father, but in the back of his mind he felt his brother's presence being something special. Mentally he could not identify the importance of his brother's arrival, but a strong sensation flowed throughout his circulatory system creating a stimulus of feedback into his inner mind.

"Your brother will become a huge factor in your future; listen to him because his advice will be monumental," advised Julie.

The ensuing week crawled by, in anticipation of Duncan's visit. Eventually Friday approached and the arrival of Duncan was an elaborate event. His ranger-style haircut pronounced his handsome appearance, consequentially framing him as a model service member.

Duncan's appearance was a strong impact on the Ballantine household. "Brother Schuyler, I can see you have discovered pristine wisdom from your endeavors the past few weeks."

Schuyler blushed and froze in his speech. It was as if he was embarrassed about his brother's comments referring to his lifestyle during the past few weeks. His conscience knew his brother was fully aware of his telepathic love affair, translating intermittent mental impulses, requiring it very difficult to speak. But he did eventually spit out some words to his brother. "I did well in The District Tournament, qualifying for the regional; also I passed all of my final examination with flying colors."

"Brother, you have progressed well and are an exceptional credit to your school, your family, and yourself," replied Duncan.

Friday evening's graduation ceremony went quite well. Schuyler got his diploma and Duncan got a lot of attention from the high school girls. After the graduation ceremony, Duncan took his little brother out to dinner in accompany with two newly discovered female acquaintances.

With Duncan's persuasion, Schuyler had a little dinner date with a hot graduating senior from his class. As they drove off to the dinner club, Schuyler's compelling nervousness gave way to his hormonal desires. He had never really dated much and he was matched up with a short, blonde-haired appealing girl named Dawn. When she looked at Schuyler he almost melted upon sight. He was scared to touch her because he was afraid his fingers would surely be ablaze because this girl was hot, and a put-on-the-spot Schuyler could not hide the encounter from his telepathic girlfriend Julie.

Duncan's date resembled a real actual blonde bombshell. Her figure had more precisely measured curves than a racehorse track. At dinner, she sat almost in his lap while he controlled the conversation. His Army talk could capture the undivided attention from any teenage girl, which was lucky for Schuyler since he was not much at dominating a conversation.

Julie interrupted his date with her interjection. *"What are you doing with that girl? Please don't be with her!"*

In silence at the table, Schuyler informed Julie through telepathic communication that it was she who advised him to seek his brother's advice and it was Duncan who got him the date and he had to react accordingly.

Julie interrupted again demanding his fullest attention. *"Listen here young man, I'm your girl and I'm not allowing this relationship to commence any farther!"*

With Duncan entertaining the two beautiful girls with his charismatic display of Army jargon, Schuyler was pleading to Julie for her forgiveness and to allow him to enjoy some female companionship.

Julie finally seceded from her overprotective display of affection for Schuyler while the dinner date ultimately came to closure. But due to the telepathic controversy, Schuyler knew that his Louisiana friend with the sexy accent was going to be in his mind for a long time. Within the most inner sites of his mind, placed a mark on the significance of this controversy because in due time this telepathic relationship would be a catalyst in a very prominent phenomena.

The ride home from the dinner club generated even more discrepancy. Duncan ensured to provide opportunity for his little brother to spend a little time with Dawn. He purposely left them alone in the car for a little bit allowing them to enjoy one another's company.

Duncan parked the car along a park walkway, leaving Schuyler and Dawn alone in the back seat of the car, while he and his date went for a short stroll along the side of the park. Given an excellent opportunity, Schuyler and Dawn enjoyed the company of each other for a short, but unforgettable, period of time. The couple was still cherry and remained that way throughout their loving encounter, but sexual advancements were discovered by both parties transmitting strong sexual desires to one another. Introduced to pleasurable sexual foreplay, Schuyler received a little bit of sexual instruction from a more experienced Dawn and this instruction would be very instrumental in shaping his personal character. Even more significant, his relationship with Julie would be under challenge from Dawn, his newfound love.

As Schuyler and Dawn cuddled in the back of the car on the way home, Duncan carefully drove the long route to Dawn's home to allow the cherry couple more time together. After Schuyler kissed his date good night, Brother Duncan quickly took Schuyler home prior to escorting his date back to her residence. With both Schuyler and Dawn eliminated, Duncan could experience romantic interaction with his date in private seclusion.

The morning began early for the Ballantine brothers as they quickly prepared to venture out to the country club with their father. After virtually inhaling breakfast, the brothers were ready to hit the links.

The Ballantine family arrived at the country club with little time to spare. As their father made the arrangements for teeing-off, Schuyler requested Julie's attention.

With much anger, Julie resented his request. *"Why are you asking me now for attentiveness? You did not want me last night, but you inquire of me now?"*

He asked her to accept his apology, but with little success.

"Why don't you ask Dawn to dream with you since she had her tongue in your mouth and her hand in your pants last night?" Julie returned fire.

Again, he strongly requested her compliance, but again with limited success.

Julie's voice trembled as she struggled to communicate telepathically. *"Schuyler, young man, I never will speak to you again!"*

Astonished by her remarks, Schuyler began his golf play with a suffering heart. He understood his guilt of not being pure to his dream girl and what she said sufficiently placed him into a serious state of depression. He could not focus on his golf game, or anything else. Feeling lifeless without his telepathic companion, he quickly discovered the significance of Julie. Her compassion as his personal escort enlightened his life, and without her presence his life was barren. His humility and suffering advertised the world his immense loving affection he beheld for her, conceptualizing the emotional consequence of camaraderie separation. The dissolving of their solidarity would not only harm his maturity advancement, but it would cripple the enhancement of the air phenomena.

Distracted immensely, Schuyler played very poorly during his long-awaited golf match with his big brother. His poor performance synthesized attributes developing novel characteristic traits that would provide assistance later in life. The disastrous golf round proved to be a strong lesson learned for Schuyler. Humbly he submitted to a score of 91, shooting the worst eighteen-hole score in months. Scared from all of the turmoil, he realized without being in concert with Julie meant he was only nothing but a bogey golfer. It was her presence that provided his dedication, motivation, and strength to excel in those crucial golf matches and she was the light to his bright future, but his bright future would surely go dark as long as he remained alone.

Conversely, both Duncan and the father performed quite well on the links. Duncan shot a 93 and his father shot a 94. Excellent rounds for the two of them, especially for Duncan since he hadn't played in quite some time.

Duncan ignoring the Julie incident, "Schuyler, playing with a golfer of your magnitude makes my play so much better. I never break a hundred when I play in the Army."

"Thanks brother, I regret my game was not better," responded Schuyler.

Duncan immediately attempted to restore confidence in his brother's attitude. "Even if you played this poorly in the Army you could still play for our Battalion-level team."

With an attentive stare, Schuyler's eyes opened wide publishing an idea of his own. "Maybe I should play golf in the Army because I probably won't be consistent enough to play at the college level."

"That is a decision I would strongly support!" exclaimed Duncan as they walked together to the car discussing one of biggest decisions Schuyler ever would contemplate in his life.

Chapter 9

Schuyler's perspective grew dismal in lieu of an enchanting telepathic romance. He suffered throughout the ensuing days, experiencing guilt, from Julie' departure. Undergoing a serious of cluster headaches, along with stomach cramping, he spent the next several days alone with his personal thoughts. The sadness increased, as her silence continued. He turned to his brother for guidance.

Already back at his Army post, Duncan received a telephone call from his little brother who was seeking advice concerning his future. Duncan understood his situation well and offered advice. "Schuyler, do you want to visit for a couple of days here with me?"

Admiring his brother's Army fortune, Schuyler agreed to the proposal and arranged a short trip across the state to visit his brother for the weekend. He needed to visit this ensuing weekend because the next week portrayed his appointment with Doctor Walton.

With the approval from his parents, Schuyler planned his trip. His parents were in much agreement concerning the visit since it allowed ample opportunity for their son to finally reach a concluding decision about his future.

He packed excessively for the visit, not knowing what to expect. He had never been on a real Army post before, experiencing much curiosity about the lifestyle of a soldier.

His parents saluted him off on his venture, providing him with a generous amount of spending money, instilling much confidence in their timid, but growing, son. As he drove outside the county limits, his virgin ears heard a familiar voice. The voice he heard possessed a very distinct Louisiana accent.

"I'm worried about you," aired Julie.

Who's that speaking? Is that you? Please be Julie Crystal speaking to my lonely self!

"Yes, it is Julie speaking to you. I don't feel right about your visit with your brother," responded Julie.

What are you afraid of?

"I'm afraid you might meet a girl there, ignoring our relationship totally," added Julie.

He continued to drive carefully, as he usually did, down the isolated highway with his mind set only on pleasing her. He fantasized about their telepathic romantic encounters, proliferating his sexual wishes that reinforced his compelling commitment for compromise.

"I can read your mind, I know you aspire to be with me," Julie pleaded.

Checking his gauges, ensuring safety, he telepathically informed her of an earnest apology that requested her forgiveness.

Before he could finish his complete apology, she anticipated its conclusion and was deeply accepting his apology with fullest extent. *"Yes! I finally can stop the bleeding; my lonely heart yearns for your companionship."*

As his heart fervently pounded, he experienced a bulging sensation in his crotch. Her seductive voice brought stimulation creating a severe distraction to his driving. Listening to her soothing accent, he carefully massaged his enlargement in the privacy of his automobile. In due time, a trickle of ooze escaped soiling his underwear. After a gasoline stop and a much-needed trip to the restroom, he was back on the road with vivid thoughts of his newly rediscovered lover. Julie's telepathic presence was so vividly real that it often caused Schuyler to lose contact with actual reality. It appeared he desired the telepathic relationship so much he would often avoid social actuality. A daily schedule of daydreaming about his fantasy girl standardized his personal character indulging him into secluded introversion.

It was late afternoon before Schuyler arrived at the Army post. Brother Duncan had made arrangements for him to stay at an inexpensive motel for both Friday and Saturday nights. Thus, Schuyler had a whole entire weekend, with his brother, to indulge the Army way of life.

Outside the post's main gate, flickering lights of excitement attracted his attention causing sensual thoughts to saturate his brain. He could not impede these sensual transmissions flowing throughout his mind, much less to hide them from Julie.

"Listen here my man, I know what you are thinking and you are not going to a strip club on me!" Julie demanded.

Schuyler tried to ignore her, but he failed. He conceded to understanding that strip club attendance was definitely out of the question. Julie was perfectly clear with her demands; his relationship strength depended greatly upon compliance of these demands, structuring a strong cohesion between the couple.

Duncan programmed a little itinerary for his kid brother. After viewing the Friday night scene, Saturday would be spent on the post itself. Duncan planned to stimulate Schuyler's military interest by parading him throughout the post's landmarks. The post presented a lot of history of its own, and this nostalgia guaranteed fascination in his direction.

The Ballantine brothers ventured upon the local community, outside of the post's boundaries, in conservative fashion. Duncan introduced his little brother to his favorite launching pad bar, The Magic Light, indoctrinating him into the area's nightlife. This particular local bar was a good launching pad, preceding admission to more distinguished social establishments, due to the fact that its happy hour served free chicken wings until 2000 hours.

Allowing his brother to drive the car, Schuyler requested information concerning the evening's activity. "Where are we going tonight?"

Duncan cruised down the busy highway, "Schuyler we will initially stop at The Magic Light for some complimentary chicken wings and later go to Dixie Stampede's, a country-western night club establishment."

"Sounds good to me," exclaimed an enthusiastic Schuyler. As he rode with his brother down the highway, he asked his telepathic lover for her acceptance of their ensuing itinerary.

"I'm leery of any social activity you may encounter, but as long as it not a strip club then I'll accept. But remember you are my lover and no other girl needs to partner with you," proclaimed Julie.

Entrance into The Magic Light was a little awkward since neither brother was of legal age to drink alcohol, minimizing the chances of them being served at the bar. But with Duncan's persuasion, the bartender allowed them to feast on chicken wings as long as they consumed non-alcoholic beverages. Usually Duncan entered the bar with fellow soldiers of legal drinking age, infiltrating as a frequent customer. But with his brother, he did not intend to attempt to convince anybody of both of them being of legal drinking age and settled for a pitcher of Pepsi in replacement for beer.

Schuyler felt very comfortable at the bar, even though the other patrons were drinking beer; he still continued to absorb the scenery's atmosphere. "Are you going to be able to get us into the next club also, even if I'm with you?"

Duncan poured them another mug of Pepsi. "I know the door bouncer, and he should still let us in the club. But be sure not to drink any alcohol there, because if an incident did occur then you could get into a lot of trouble."

As Schuyler got up to retrieve some more chicken wings, an attractive, mature woman inquiring of his proceeding plans approached Duncan. After a bit of small talk, Duncan promised her of his venture to Dixie Stampede's.

Schuyler, just returning to the table, inquired of the woman his brother was entertaining. "You sure have a charismatic way of charming the ladies, because you always seem to attract their attention."

Checking his watch, anticipating what the evening may behold, Duncan gave his brother some advice. "The best strategy with dating is to always leave you available for anything to happen. Like tonight, I told her of our plans to go to the club and talk to her there, if nothing materializes then we latch on to someone else."

After a few plates of chicken wings, the brothers journeyed to Dixie Stampede's. They ensured to arrive early increasing the chances of Duncan's friend working the front door. Customers usually didn't arrive at this club until at least after 2200 hours, but Duncan's plan to pass through the door prior to 2200 hours allowed a stronger opportunity to get inside and claim an isolated table. He wished to obtain a table providing concealment for two reasons; the seclusion of his under age brother and privacy for when he encountered with a date.

Entering the club, with the assistance of Duncan's friend, they ventured to a remote section of the club. While Schuyler went to the restroom, avoiding the waitress, Duncan ordered a round of Pepsi. The alibi of being "a designated driver" served as an excellent rationale for him to consume a non-alcoholic beverage. Luckily she did not inquire about the other Pepsi drink ordered, because he really didn't have a prepared excuse for his brother.

The club's activity inspired Schuyler's excitement conceptualizing ideologies of social interaction among Army service members and the local community. Unfamiliar with this environment, he appeared sheltered from the nightspot's commotion. But his brother seemed well rehearsed to this preferred pastime, communicating with one girl after another.

Julie interrupted his pleasurable surroundings, reminding him of her monitoring his air phenomenon. *"I want you to leave and go home!"*

Initially he ignored her, but he knew the consequences if he did not respond back to her. He informed her of his brother's control of the entire situation.

"I understand, but be careful," replied Julie.

He was satisfied with his disposition; having Julie mentoring his life influenced decision-making processes that established standards justifying his commitment to her. His emotional feelings were reserved for her, but ecstasy distractions interfered immensely with his unique relationship in which the couple shared.

The evening traveled swiftly, Duncan had maneuvered himself pretty well in-and-out of the crowd obtaining a few possible female associates. He was very selective in obtaining his associates, and often his selectivity thwarted dating opportunities. Fortunate for Schuyler, and Julie's concern, his brother was too selective that evening at Dixie Stampede's terminating the evening a bit shorter than expected.

As they drove back to Schuyler's motel, he inquired of Duncan. "Did you do any good at the club?"

"I got a couple of phone numbers for later, maybe we'll go there again tomorrow night," responded Duncan.

The trip back to his motel room was quiet, even with the night being young; Schuyler was very pleased to return to his room alone with only himself and Julie's presence.

Julie greeted him as he secured the door. *"I very proud of you tonight; go get undressed and I'll give you what you've been wanting."*

He positioned himself naked in his warm bed allowing Julie full view of "her boy." Her presence carefully massaged her boy, signally him to initiate preliminary fondling in route to sexual gratification. Telepathically, she imitated oral sexual activity until his stimulation expanded into extravagantly excitement climaxing emotional feelings experienced by both telepathic partners. She satisfied, through her presence, his sexual desires and he also delivered sexual pleasure to her via his air phenomena. Because the sexual fantasies he had experienced were mentally transmitted, Julie obtained sexual gratification from Schuyler's own indulgence.

Brother Duncan got Schuyler up early Saturday morning to begin administration of an extensive tour of the post. After breakfast at a local pancake house, Duncan registered his brother as a guest of the post. The Army strictly enforced the flow of traffic entering and exiting its installation, regulating and accounting for all non-military identification card holders, a category that included Schuyler.

Impressed by the attention received from the military police at the main gate, his initial impression of the Army was an excellent one. The military tradition symbolizing the hardships endured as freedom guardians, generated visions of established loyal obligations beheld by military service members. The stark commitment to excellence, nation honor, and sense of duty illustrated soldierly attributes admired by him, influencing highly regarded viewpoints concerning the military.

The post was very widespread, requiring the use of a privately owned vehicle. Frequently visited locations consisted of a museum, an airfield, the Post Exchange, a repelling tower, a hospital, and the NCO Club. Duncan was prepared to present as much of the post as he could offer. Yes, Schuyler was in for a very eventful day.

After showing his brother the helicopters, they walked through the museum. The nostalgia of old Army aircraft fascinated the younger brother introducing him to historical development of aeronautical appliance.

Completing the museum tour, Schuyler became hungry. "Where are we going to eat at?"

"We'll go the PX and eat at the snack bar," responded Duncan.

The PX is the Army's version of a large department store, encompassing not only retail merchandise, but possessed an attached section harboring a barber shop, hair salon, and a food court.

As they walked by the barbershop, "Schuyler, do you want your hair cut?" Duncan joked.

"No, not today," he responded nervously.

The food court offered a smorgasbord of choices. Schuyler persuaded his brother to eat Chinese, even though he knew oriental food was not one of his brother's favorites. As they sampled the cuisine, Duncan pretended to enjoy the meal in behalf of his younger brother. Since Schuyler was the guest, he got the lead in particular decision-making processes.

"Where do we go after lunch?" Schuyler asked as his rumbling stomach slowly, but surely, obtained satisfaction.

Selectively Duncan finished his meal, directed his attention to Schuyler and informed him of their agenda continuation. "After the oriental lunch, I'll drive you by the repelling towers, the hospital, and the NCO Club."

In route to the hospital, the brothers drove near the repelling towers. After parking the car to allocate a nearby view, an amazed Schuyler inquired about the tall structures with hanging ropes. "What are the repelling towers used for?"

An assertive Duncan quickly rendered a knowledgeable response. "The repelling towers are used to train soldiers for helicopter assault missions."

Fantasized about the concept, Schuyler turned and asked about his brother's repelling capability. "Have you ever done any repelling, or any helicopter assault training?"

"Of course, almost everybody on this post has been trained for helicopter assault training, even the medics!" Duncan boasted.

"Where do the medics work at?" Schuyler asked.

Duncan paused for a moment, gathered his thoughts, and issued a direct response. "The medical corps works all over post, but a large majority of them are stationed at the hospital."

"How far away is the hospital?" Schuyler inquired with much anticipation.

Duncan led him back to the car in preparation for a short drive to the spacious hospital complex. "Not to far away; my buddy who formerly was assigned to The Office of the Surgeon General works in the ER there."

His brother escorted Schuyler within a small segment of the facility, to his delight familiarizing him with emergency, operating room, and intensive care services, along with ancillary functions such as pharmacy, radiology, and pathology.

In vast astonishment, Schuyler viewed the impressive facility. "It looks like something you would see on television."

Acknowledging his brother's comments, he ushered him out of the building to an ensuing visit to the NCO Club.

But along the way, Schuyler's interest was attracted to a facility labeled as a recreation center. "What's at the recreation center?"

Reversing the direction of the car, Duncan accompanied him into the recreation center that consisted of similar activities of a sports bar. The center was well supplied with television monitors, pool tables, table tennis tables, video games, card tables, and pizza. He liked the place so much that he asked Duncan to allow him to stay. "Can we hang out here for awhile?"

Duncan surprisingly looked at his brother and smiled with great satisfaction. "Yes, we can stay here. Since we are practically the only people currently in the facility at the moment, you almost have the whole place to yourself!"

With the enthusiasm of a child, Schuyler played video games and shot pool with his brother the entire day. At close of business, the big brother purchased pizza prior to going back to the motel. During the way home, Duncan ensured to drive by the golf course inducing his brother's opinion of the Army. This long day of eventful moments would greatly affect Schuyler's future.

After eating pizza at the motel, Schuyler thanked his big brother for the tour. "I really enjoyed the outing today, and appreciate the time you spent with me at the recreation center."

Pausing for a moment to swallow a piece of pizza, "Schuyler, I really welcome your compliment. I was just taking care of my brother, just like we do in the Army because in the Army we take care of soldiers."

The brothers ate the pizza prior to driving out to Dixie Stampede's. Duncan was scheduled to meet one of a host of probable girl friends, and Schuyler could only just follow along.

Duncan's door bouncer friend got them into the club with no problem. Since they were there the night before, it was even easier this time to gain entrance into the club. Again ensuring to only order non-alcoholic beverages, preventing any accelerated altercations from being under the legal drinking age.

Claiming similar seats as the night prior, Duncan quickly went to work conversing with the girls.

As Duncan was circulating the bar, Schuyler received a little advice from Julie. *"I see a lot of prospects out there. Go ahead and mingle, but don't go too far."*

Not too long into the night, Duncan invited two girls back to their secluded table. They seemed to be excited about him, and even interested in Brother Schuyler. Wisely, Duncan got them quickly onto the dance floor before they noticed the non-alcoholic drinks located on the table. Fortunately Schuyler could dance a little two-step, because that was the primary dance of the club's clientele.

"I'm really impressed with your ability to dance," announced Julie as she carefully supervised every move he made.

With all of the dancing, the evening turned into early morning very rapidly. Time gradually passed by without the girls even noticing both of the brothers were pretending to be designated drivers.

In respectful courtesy of his brother, Duncan did not attempt to go home with his date relieving his brother from any possible commitment ensuing from his encounter with his dancing partner.

Together in the parking lot as they were leaving, Schuyler's date positioned her for a romantic farewell kiss. Her experienced showed as her tongue, playing tonsil hockey, practically extracted his tongue out from his mouth. Astonished, but pleased, from her deep, sensual kiss, he lustfully enjoyed the moment in the arms of a loving woman.

"It's late, lets go home," interrupted Duncan after accepting his date's telephone number.

Schuyler's date ceased her kissing lesson, releasing him over to his brother. She waved farewell to her apprentice as he departed, leaving a substantial impact in young Schuyler's life.

Needless to say, Schuyler surely knew he would eventually take a sound scorning from his telepathic companion.

Later that night, Julie told him of the plan to discuss the incident in the morning. Schuyler suffered throughout the night, having difficulty sleeping due to anxiety concerning her disposition on the matter.

Sunday morning opened by means of Duncan taking his brother to the pancake house prior to voyage back home. The pancake house had been a big favorite of his and few paralleled its service. They drove two cars in order to allow Schuyler the opportunity to begin driving home immediately after the completion of his morning meal.

After checking out of the motel and sitting comfortably waiting for breakfast drinking a cup of coffee, Duncan could tell that something was wrong with his brother. "Did you not have a good time last night at Dixie Stampede's?"

Schuyler added more cream to his coffee. "Yes, but I have second thoughts about what happen in the parking lot."

"She was hot!" Duncan responded as he punched him in the shoulder in congratulations for his success.

"A little bit too much for me to handle," added Schuyler.

They both agreed their dates were actually out-of-their league, but they couldn't complain and pursued to devour a couple of stacks of hot cakes.

Duncan saluted him as he exited the parking lot of the pancake house; with confidence he alleged Schuyler's short visit might become influential in his decision concerning his future. Duncan knew he had much potential, but just needed time to mature.

The return drive back to the eastern part of state was very stressful. Not because of the Sunday traffic, but the confrontational dialogue initiated by Julie caused him to become agonized.

"Before I complain about your actions in the parking lot, I'm going to allow you the opportunity to defend your side of the argument," proposed Julie.

Steadily driving down the highway, Duncan's brain filtered through probable alibis searching for reasonable explanations for his conduct at Dixie Stampede's parking lot.

"Schuyler, don't be afraid to talk to me. Remember I can read your mind, like everybody else, and I know what you're thinking," projected Julie.

I know but I can't face up to the fact of enjoying myself among your presence!

"You still have to defend yourself!"

How?

"Let me show you! You were with your brother, a handsome soldier, and he introduced you to an attractive girl who enjoyed your company. It is very common for a couple to kiss prior to departing for the night. You really did nothing wrong, but I'm

so jealous I get upset and give you're the cold shoulder. Please forgive my behavior, but I'm very interested in you and I want you for myself. I understand my life is in another world and we will never meet, but I still have very strong feelings for your affection."

Shocked from her testimonial speech, his thought process virtually froze in place. His brain, accustomed to near perpetual activity, seized motion and paused for almost a whole minute before informing her of being flattered from what she said causing him to be speechless, and could not develop words describing his feelings toward her.

"I comprehend what you're trying to say. In due time you will discover the worth of the vision you behold. Just remember I'm here to help you employ your visional phenomena."

Schuyler continued to drive home, but in much better spirits than he was at the beginning of his trip. His learned lessons this past weekend created whole new avenues for his future. The Army factor, the romantic farewell kiss, and Julie's integration were all strong variables in future lifestyle development. But most of all he was educated in family cohesion and that even the wishes of his telepathic lover could not offset the togetherness he and his brother shared.

As he became near to home, he asked Julie of her opinion of possible military service.

"I can tell you really are interested in the Army and you should inquire in more detail about it."

It will be a great challenge!

"Maybe you could enlist for three or four years and earn money for future college. I know you are worried about college and an enlistment in the Army might improve your maturity. Not just might, I know it would help but just remember that anywhere you go, I will follow you via mind."

I think I will talk to my parents about it when I get home!

"Good idea sugar!"

He soon completed his trip, arriving home in plenty of time for supper. He planned to spring the idea on his parents after supper. But at the moment, he rested with an understanding his telepathic companion was with him forever; or at least for now. The weekend excursion distributed a wide range of dividends. Schuyler's accomplishments consisted of quality time spent with his brother, an educational observation of an Army post, an enchanted experience at a nightclub, a gourmet pancake breakfast, and an intriguing telepathic conversation with the girl he wished very dearly to belong to.

His ensuing objective would be to discuss military service entrance with his parents. During supper, he quietly ate his meal orchestrating his proposal to be delivered immediately after supper's completion.

Pork chops, black-eye peas, and corn on the cob satisfied their appetites in anticipation of his proposal. Before the actual closure of their meal, his father initiated their own assertion. "Son, what did you experience from your Army visit?'

He reached for enough courage for a prompt reply. "I learned that the Army's tradition is rich with loyalty to its nation and people; the military instills values of trust and integrity in its leaders providing guidance for its junior enlisted soldiers to grow and learn."

Mrs. Ballantine poured her husband an additional cup of coffee, gently moved into the conversation, and with a caring facial expression. "Are you interested in joining the Army, my son?"

Noticing an alarmed look on his father's face, "I have been thinking about it," he cautiously replied.

"What about your ambition to play college golf?" his father asked.

"The Army plays golf," responded Schuyler.

As she began clearing the table, an excited mother awaited the conclusion of the conversation she instigated. Her persistent conversational interjection alleviated the pressure placed upon Schuyler to submit his proposal. Her timely interjecting question concerning Army enlistment made it so much easier for her son to inquire about entering the Armed Forces, providing a united front minimizing communicating barriers between Schuyler and his father.

After a long, lengthy discussion with his father about the military, the two of them eventually concluded to an agreement. Mr. Ballantine consented to an Army enlistment, but with college financial incentives. He wanted his son to endure military training, but wished very strongly that college be forecasted in his future. In concurrence, Mr. Ballantine supported Schuyler's decision to inquire about military service.

Julie introduced herself into the conversation at the father's concluding dialogue. *"Things went easier than expected, thanks to your mom!"*

Experiencing numerous sighs of relief, he informed her of his gratefulness of his mother's assurance.

"Your mom knew you needed assistance in your proposal, thus she interjected her own proposal," analyzed Julie.

Julie and Schuyler concluded his father-to-son discussion was a success, and together they would seek more information concerning military service enlistment. Of all of the service branches, The United States Army would be on the top of their priority list.

A visit to the Army recruiter would preclude a very extensive week. Even though it was summer break, his weekly schedule still projected his mental health appointment on Thursday and a golfing outing with Doug on Friday.

The next morning he awoke to Julie's telepathic touch, and after about twenty minutes of comfort he showered, dressed, and ate breakfast in preparation for an exhausting day at the recruitment center. With both of his parents at work, he could only take his telepathic companion along to speak with the recruiter. The Army recruiting station was designed to capture the interest of potential prospects, including the recruiting sergeants dressed in their green suits displaying shiny decorations and ribbons. The salesman technique caught the attention of not just Schuyler, but Julie as well.

"Schuyler, you sure would look handsome in an Army uniform like the one the recruiter is wearing," addressed Julie.

After greetings and introductions, Schuyler gave the recruiter a short, brief story about being interested in the Army, and presented a brief summarization about his recent trip to his brother's post. He emphasized his appeal with the medical field and the college fund, targeting objectives to be achieved.

The recruiter recorded all of his specific information, scanned the computer for medical related careers, and made a couple of telephone calls. Medical corps training was not as widely available as some of the combat arms training, but Schuyler was not going to accept anything but The Army Medical Corps.

"Ensure whatever you do in the service, you are striving for college enhancement," advised Julie.

Schuyler patiently watched the Sergeant in attempt to secure a medical position, to obtain results about his anticipated possible future in the Army. He positioned himself in the chair, getting closer to the Sergeant's desk, in order to speak with confidence. "What's my outlook in the Army, or should I ask the Air Force if they have any openings?"

With quick response, the Army recruiter allocated a slot as a pharmacy specialist with a window of enlistment in the middle of August.

"What does a pharmacy specialist do?" he asked.

The recruiter gave a book definition of the job, but in summarization a pharmacy specialist is a pharmacy technician, military occupation skill code of 91Q, which assists the pharmacist in pharmaceutical practices both in the hospital and field environments.

"Ask him how long the enlistment is?" interjected Julie.

Schuyler stalled a few seconds while he got Julie's advice. "How long is the enlistment?"

The recruiter advised of the benefiting factors of a six-year enlistment, but Schuyler eventually bargained for an offer of a three-year stint. The Sergeant directed him to bring his diploma, birth certificate, and other pertinent information to the station the following day initiating proper procedures for enlisting in The United States Army.

Schuyler acknowledged the assistance granted by the recruiter, and proceeded to go back home to deliver the news to his parents. The drive home was very enjoyable because not just he was excited about his future, so was Julie.

Later that evening he informed his parents of his outlook in the Army. They appeared to be quite interested in his progress. Schuyler's mother even talked his father to go with him to talk to the recruiter the following day. Her influence, once again, benefited his cause.

With the required documents in hand, Schuyler with his father journeyed to meet the Army recruiter.

With open arms, the recruiter invited them into his station greeting them, as they were valuable clients. He had already prepared most of the paperwork in expectation of Schuyler's return; his toughest challenge was to sell Mr. Ballantine on his son's enlistment into the service.

Mr. Ballantine requested quite a lot of information concerning his son's future. He inquired about entitlements, benefits, and assignments. The recruiter did quite well with him, answering most of his questions and avoiding the ones he didn't want to answer. But Schuyler and his father got basically the required information they desired including basic training location, advanced individual training location, college fund amount, medical/dental benefits, insurance cost, and delayed-entry until the middle of August.

The recruiter inputted all of Schuyler's data into the computer, and informed him of his arrival at his house early Monday morning to pick him up and take him to have his physical done and get sworn in. The entrance exam scores, Schuyler had taken previously, were sufficient for his proposed training. Thus, he did not need to retake the examination again. He did warn Schuyler of required success on both a background security check and a medical physical prior to getting sworn in. But with encouragement, he welcomed Schuyler into the Army.

Schuyler and his father traveled home with some concern. Schuyler going off into the Army was a big event, strengthening his endeavor to make that giant step in his transformation from boy to man. His father was hasty at first about allowing his son to venture too far away from home, but he eventually understood the value in the long-term objective. The military service, even with only three years served, would build character, values, ethics, and personal courage required to succeed in life. He recognized the importance of mental, physical, and emotional attributes developed from military service. He had to accept the fact his son was about to mature into adulthood.

Schuyler spent most of the week performing odd chores for his mother, waiting for his mental health appointment. He anxiously awaited the appointment because he knew that it should be his last. The Army was an excellent alibi for shrink session termination, alleviating him of a totally miserable experience.

Julie kept in close contact throughout the entire week. Her presence shadowed almost every move, providing continuous advice and guidance into his life. Also, their nightly interaction kept the telepathic couple deeply entertained.

After a couple of days of near boredom, Schuyler had his much awaited appointment with Dr. Walton. Upon entrance into the mental health facility, he could feel a cold chill carrying throughout the air. Checking in at the receptionist's office, taking a seat, and pretending to read a magazine were all standard procedures prior to his interview.

"What are you going to tell your doctor?" asked Julie.

Schuyler had no set plan, but he knew his interjection about something concerning his plans to join the Army was on his agenda.

Sitting in the waiting room for over twenty minutes, he anxiously greeted his doctor when he finally arrived. "Good afternoon, Dr. Walton."

Cautiously Dr. Walton approached, appearing a bit distressed, he shook Schuyler's hand. "Glad you could make it, it has been quite some time since we last met."

After being escorted into his office, directed to take a seat, he began to speak nervously. "I-I graduated high s-school and did very well on my finals. Also, I advanced all the way to The Regional High School Golf Tournament."

Doctor Walton pretended to evaluate his patient. "What do you have planned for this summer?"

He slumped in chair, stumbling on his words, he informed him of his plans to enlist in the United States Army, with basic training beginning in August.

Acting surprised, but not doing a very job of it, the doctor glared into Schuyler's eyes. "How did you get into the Army?" Dr. Walton's voice inflection changed, as he seemed to become angry. "Does the Army know you are going under psychological treatment?" He continued to defy his enlistment.

"Why shouldn't I be in the Army?" spoke a puzzled Schuyler.

"Because I need you here! I mean you need psychological treatment." Dr. Walton frantically attempted to convince his patient.

Schuyler paused for a few seconds; "you mean the Army cannot help me stimulate my mental capacity like you were doing?"

"The Army cannot study your mental ability like I can," demanded an angry Dr. Walton.

"Am I being studied here? I thought I was being tested for mental strengthening?" he questioned the doctor.

"You are my patient and I need you available for my thinking phenomena studies," exclaimed Dr. Walton as he pretended to attempt to make an important phone call.

"You cannot leave, because if you do then I can't get in on the thinking phenomena frenzy."

"Schuyler, please leave ASAP because this shrink is nothing but trouble. It is obvious that all he wants to do is to profit from your gift," Julie warned.

Schuyler suddenly went silent, allowing the doctor to speak until he was blue in the face. After a constant span of silence, Schuyler finally was dismissed from his appointment at the dismay of his psychologist.

Once out the door, marching through the parking lot, mounting his vehicle, he drove away with the pleasant feeling on seeing his ex-shrink's office in his rear view mirror.

"Schuyler, the doctor seemed a little upset you joined the Army. I guess he's not going to get to use you as his private experiment." Julie enlighten, caressing his neck as he drove home.

I can't believe he acted that way! He must think that I'm some fool that would allow manipulation in that manner.

"Obviously your phenomena of being in vision of everyone must be worth something to him, she mentioned.

With your vision of myself, I understand I fortunately get to communicate with you, and I feel that it is very valuable, because with your assistance, I can adjust to almost any situation, achieving sustained success in my endeavors.

At the Ballantine household, Schuyler did not elaborate on his conversation with Doctor Walton. He did confirm, with his father, the termination of any future medical appointments with Dr. Walton due to his military obligation expectations.

The next morning at the golf course, Schuyler had the pleasure to inform Doug of his military plans. The other members of the school golf team had acquired summer jobs and didn't visit the country club too much, resulting in only them as a twosome for golfing that particular day.

Doug was very supported of Schuyler's military decision. "I hope you pass your medical exam! Should be a piece of cake."

As they approached the first tee, Schuyler explained the details of probable military commitment.

After they hit their drives, Doug walked along him inquiring several questions of the Army. It seemed he was getting more interested in the military as he received additional information concerning the topic. "How hard is the entrance exam?"

After watching Doug hit his shot onto the green, he explained, in great detail, about the extensiveness of the test. He took a pause in his conversation to hit his chip shot onto the green, and continued to explain the importance of having a good math and science background prior to going into the service.

"How much math and science do I need?" Doug inquired as he two-putted for a par.

Failing to get up-and-down for his par and settling for a bogey, he explained the levels of math comprehension, chemistry/physics knowledge, and clerical learning required of most of the Army's medical occupational skills.

As they played together on the front nine, Schuyler spent most of his time communicating with Doug about the Army. This was the first time in along while that the conversation on the links possessed more significance than the actual score.

At the conclusion of nine holes, the twosome ventured into the clubhouse to enjoy lunch. As expected, Mr. Jenkins noticed him entering the café. *"Going into the Army is a good decision son; we'll be following every marching step you make."*

Inside the café Ms. Hurt received their lunch requests, in allowance of ample time for Doug and him to relax before playing the second nine. As she issued lunch to Schuyler, she reminded him of his fortune with Julie. *"Don't let go of Miss Julie Crystal, because her affection cannot be rediscovered!"*

Comprehending the information, as well as he could, from Mr. Jenkins and Ms. Hurt, he finished his hamburger, fries, and pop and began play on the back nine with Doug.

"I got a good compliment from Ms. Hurt, didn't I?" Julie interjected.

He confirmed what she said, and continued to play along with Doug. Doug had shot a 39 on the front nine, in comparison to his 41. The back nine was a little more competitive, with less conversation and more play; but major emphasis was still placed upon the Army and not golf.

At conclusion of the golfing outing, they compared their scores of Doug's 79 and Schuyler's 81. Both of them experienced much fortune on the golf course today, structuring their strong cohesive bond in which they shared. Even in more significance, Doug found self-reassurance from obtaining useful knowledge about the importance of military service, instilling confidence in Schuyler's choice to pursue the military as an avenue for growth, education, and patriotism.

In congratulations of excellent play, Schuyler bid farewell to his playing partner initiating movement to his car.

Doug waved goodbye. *"You have not yet begun to achieve the fame you deserve."*

"Schuyler, I can tell when you leave for the Army you are going to miss your friend Doug," responded Julie.

As he packed his clubs in the car and commenced to drive home, he reminded her of his Army commitment would be for only three years and he would return home.

The golf round with Doug did him well; it gave him the opportunity to express himself. Doug seemed to respond to him the best of all of the other golfers, strengthening confidence in Schuyler's character for future undertakings.

The eventful week ended on a positive note, but his appointment with the Army recruiter could easily begin a whole new outlook on life.

Chapter 10

At the Jupiter, Morrison and Boyd were livid about the recent events concerning Schuyler's decision to enlist in the Army.

Morrison arrived to work early, preparing a pot of coffee even before Boyd came to work, cataloguing recent activities affecting his research of The Air. His enthusiasm had accelerated to a whole new dimension. In recent dialogue with his partner, he predicted The Air's future employment would be limited to governmental agencies in order to manipulate and protect the air phenomena. But he had no idea that military service would be a possibility. He felt that it was too risky for the government to allow The Air to be exposed to such a wide range of domestic and foreign interests. He felt the government would seclude his gift, not proliferate it.

About 0730 hours in the morning, Boyd arrived at the office submitting his projection of The Vision's future. "I think if he gets in the Army, it will be a giant leap for our research!"

Morrison, already on his second cup of coffee, assembled his slides and prepared to administer his short brief. "I feel that security is too risky for The Air to attend military training. His advertisement of today's Army would be a certain breach against national security."

"On the other side of the coin, his military involvement might deter opposition forces from challenging freedom," responded Boyd.

Nursing the coffee pot, pacing back-and-forth, he eventually coincided with Boyd's idea. "Either way, he will initiate and instigate more situational analysis than we will be able to track."

Boyd nodded his head in agreement with him. "It will be a supreme challenge, but the knowledge we gain from his Army service will benefit others to follow."

Morrison sat back down in his chair, shaking his head in bewilderment, processing analysis in correlation with The Air's past history and future possible military service. "In all of my research, I cannot locate any time in his past that he left home for any period of time except when he went to basketball camp for five days."

"It will be a huge lifestyle change, but the girl's assistance will provide comfort and guidance throughout the military's hardships," added Boyd.

"I am worried, what if something happens to him." He vented stressful inhibitions to Boyd. "If he goes, so does our project."

Eventually Boyd settled him down and synthesized convincing dictation establishing positive objectives of military service. "An Army career might do the Vision well. He'll be in safe hands, serving his country like normal people do. After his discharge, he'll reward us with even better data to study since he'll be an honorable discharged veteran upholding civil obligations in the defense of our nation."

His partner's lecture calmed him down. Morrison agreed that if The Air did get into the Army, then his acquired skills, character development, and military bearing would fortify his career opportunities in the civilian workforce. He was so enriched with satisfaction he offered to purchase Big K pizza for lunch, in honor of Boyd's influential feedback.

During a working lunch, the Jupiter partners constructed analysis concerning Dr. Walton's negative influence on their research subject.

Enjoying a ham and pineapple pizza slice, a favorite of his, John Boyd explained the importance of The Vision's avoidance of his psychologist. "I can't say anything good about the shrink; his attempt to manipulate The Vision's phenomenal gift was totally illicit."

Don Morrison, also taking pleasure in the pizza, soundly denounced Dr. Walton's intent. "He can't select himself as the center of all thinking phenomena; he's only confusing the boy's mind, in pursuit to his own fame."

Boyd got up from his desk to offer his partner some ice cream he had stored in the office's freezer. "Do you want some ice cream?"

"What flavor?' he asked.

"I only have plain vanilla," responded Boyd.

"That's fine." Being a connoisseur of ice cream, he understood the importance of developing a fine taste for the universal flavor of ice cream.

The two of them agreed Dr. Walton was a low individual in a high place, and their research project did not need to associate with an individual with such unacceptable, improper tactics as a psychologist. In concurrence, the Army might be a good idea even if avoidance of Dr. Walton was the only profit.

The jury was still out on Schuyler's entrance into the Army, until he completely finalized his entrance obstacles and got officially sworn into the Army, he was still a civilian.

Monday morning came quickly as the Army recruiter arrived at the Ballantine house very early in the morning to retrieve Schuyler in route to the Army's processing station.

The recruiter was delighted to have the opportunity to enlist a bright, new prospect into the Army. "Here we go Schuyler, soon we will be at the station; I have all the required paperwork and all you have to do is receive satisfactory results on your physical."

"Should be easy enough, I should be in good health," he responded.

"Just don't tell the physicians you have a drug problem or psychologically incapable of adapting to the Army," directed the recruiter.

He paused for a second and asked Julie for advice concerning the psychological question.

"Act like you never had been to see Doctor Walton. If they pursue the issue just tell them you were just expanding your mental ability," warned Julie.

At the processing station, everything went quite well except for when poor Schuyler had to get his bottom probed.

Julie watched him get his blood pressure checked, perform a urinalysis, get checked for a hernia, and get blood drawn, but the most memorable event was when he got poked about in the rear. *"Oh Schuyler! I could feel every painful twitch in your rectum when they prodded around in there; I'm so proud of your because you took it like a man."*

He thanked her for the condolences, but he felt the embarrassment was even more painful than the poking. He passed all of the required exams, including the cough-test procedure in which he could detect Julie's laughter all the way from Louisiana. Since his medical past lacked any major illness or surgery, he was proclaimed fit for military service.

"It *was easier than expected, but of course I know that you are one healthy boy!"* Julie declared.

After all of the interviewing by the medical staff and signing various documents, Schuyler was marched into a secluded room with about eleven other recruits. In this room he raised his right hand and swore to defend The United

States Constitution. At its conclusion, Schuyler was officially sworn into The United States Army.

A proud Julie awaited him as he walked out of the room. She presented him with a warm, intimate hug congratulating his achieved accomplishment. Even though she knew her destiny was attending college to play basketball, her attentive devotion was directed immediately at his military obligation. She seemed to be more excited about the Army than he was, because she could simultaneously attend college and monitor his military activity. Her interest in Schuyler's air phenomena bloomed due to his Army enlistment; it was like she could live her own life and still contribute to his.

Schuyler was flattered by her attention; he couldn't realize the basis for her involvement in his life. He was a shy, lonely golfer and she was an intelligent, admired future college basketball player having vast potential to succeed as both student and athlete. Without a doubt, her companionship was something to cherish.

Proudly, the Army recruiter drove him home with laudatory comments concerning both the Army and him. Schuyler was definitely sold on the Army and he was convinced to give the Army a good solid three years.

It was a long day about the time he got back home. His mother had already prepared supper, anticipating his arrival. The breaking news of his successful enlistment thundered throughout the household, enlightening faith among his parents. It was another huge celebration at their home bringing much happiness, including a telephone call to Duncan, to the entire family. The Army fixation stimulated growth among the family, bonding them with increasing strength and cohesiveness.

In the isolation of his room that night, he welcomed Julie's enchanted entertainment inspiring him to take pleasure in her preferred treatment as her presence provided him comfort until he fell into a very restful sleep.

During her telepathic visit, *"Schuyler, go play some romantic music so we can practice dancing together. Use your headphones so you can play the music a little more loudly than normal!"*

He hurriedly secured a favorite cassette tape, secured his headphones, and proceeded to test out his music. He asked for her opinion.

"I like it; hold me like we're slow dancing."

He positioned his arms around her body, tilting his head to his left side. She followed with grasping his body in such a fashion she could have been accused of groping him instead of dancing with him. If she got any friskier, she would require a search warrant.

"Practice moving with the music, following the rhythm with your body." Julie instructed as she caressed his scalp. *"I like your hair, it is so soft."*

The couple pretended to dance with each other to the music's tempo, allowing him to relax and focus on both the music and his dance partner simultaneously. He could tell she was a much more proficient dancer than he was, and her sexual caressing generated a stimulus craving ensuing supplementary activity.

"Prepare yourself sugar, I want to watch you enjoy enlarging yourself," she requested.

Is it big enough?

"It's plenty big," she assured.

With confidence, he continued to manipulate his enlargement in concert with telepathic stimulus. He could feel her presence pressing up against his rigid torso, transmitting sensual signals throughout each other's mind until pinnacle climax satisfied one another's sexual appetite.

After climax, she hugged him heartily consenting gratitude. *"I love to watch you receive so much pleasure from our relationship. Trust me; I am also receiving a great deal of pleasure myself at this end."*

A mutual point of view derived concluding results that the telepathic couple significantly conveyed affection toward one another, bonding togetherness in fashion alleviating unnecessary challenging pressures affecting their lives.

The Jupiter was buzzing after the news of Schuyler's successful enlistment, generating even more recognition than before. The Army presented a deep fairway of opportunity for The Air, publicizing his phenomena in fashion allowing Morrison and Boyd to continue research studies.

Morrison was still worried about exposing The Air to the public's view. "Being captive in a goldfish bowl as a soldier could cause a lot of altercations in the near future."

"Don't worry Dr. Morrison; he will be taken good care of. Remember the Army sergeants take care of their soldiers," responded Boyd.

Yearning for a cup of coffee, he accepted Boyd's suggestion. "I guess we must trust the Army to not penalize him for being The Air. I know it will be difficult for his superiors to not wish to watch him via air in order to scrutinize him."

"He will be an easy target since his seniors will be able to watch and anticipate every move he makes. Yes, he will be at a disadvantage since his mistakes will be advertised to the world, but I assure you that his achievements will overcome his deficiencies." Boyd tried to put his mind to ease.

Taking pleasure in his coffee, he carefully listened to Boyd. "Correct, the boy is very talented and is extremely capable of following orders. He'll probably be a model soldier, instilling leadership values, ethics, and integrity throughout his class of peers."

The partners came to closure on the issue, identifying strengths, weaknesses, opportunities, and threats of Army service for The Air in route to development of a strategy-based plan of action for The Air's evaluation.

Strengths of military service would include team building, group interaction, and leader development. Weaknesses of being in the Army presented possible altercations of The Air's failure or embarrassment. His call to military duty might turn sour causing a disgrace to his personal character. The Army could easily indoctrinate vast opportunities for the young troop expanding his individual persona through travel, achievement, and responsibility. The Army challenge poses threats due to the nature of its profession. The Air's military assignment could breach national security, enable opposition forces to gain useful knowledge, or produce critical personal injury.

Objectives, from each of the four perspectives, will be evaluated measuring success or failure throughout milestones of The Air's Army career. This strategy-based data should provide ample information for progression of The Jupiter's research project of tracking and projecting the life history of the air phenomena.

The rest of the summer went by quickly with Schuyler occupying his time by playing golf, performing household chores, and telepathically communicating with his distant lover. The couple reengineered the concept of sustaining a relationship. Schuyler could not show affection for any other woman than Julie without her knowledge. Julie, on the other hand, had to maintain his confidence of her fidelity. Thus, it was her responsibility to ensure faithfulness in this long-distance romantic relationship.

Chapter 11

August crept upon Schuyler before he knew it. The summer prior to enlistment was reaching closure, conceptualizing the reality of basic training being only a couple of weeks away. In preparation for departure, he corresponded with significant family members, including extended-family members. He telephoned Duncan for advice concerning the hardships of basic training and how to endure its strenuous training. A physical training program, implemented by his brother, primed him for basic training. He actively exercised almost daily by running two or three miles, along with his regular calisthenics. Counseling, disseminated from his father, strengthened his public awareness pertaining to societal behavioral patterns affecting his actions. A farewell event, planned by his golfing teammates, was scheduled for the upcoming weekend. Without doubt, his communicative interaction with Julie was the most vital correspondence since it structured a strong, mutual cohesive bond of lasting energy that would propel his transformation into Army's environment of adventure.

"I admire your courage. You could have made life easy on yourself and just attended junior college and possibly played on the golf team, but you decided to accept the challenge of being an Army soldier." Julie instilled spirit in his confidence.

Julie, do you think I'll be any good as a soldier?

"You are the man! You'll perform at levels exceeding expected standards."

Schuyler's confidence increased dramatically in motivation of his near departure to The Home of Armor, because he would embark on his military career, attending basic training at this prestigious post.

Mark, from the golf team, organized a farewell party for Schuyler on Friday evening at his parents' house. The house would be vacant, due to his parents' weekend vacation, presenting an excellent opportunity to throw a party. Of course his parents had advanced knowledge of the party, delegating responsibility to Mark for suitable conduct of his guests. Anyway, a social gathering with the boys was on schedule for Friday evening and Schuyler was the guest of honor.

"I know you are going out with the guys and I expect you to be on your best behavior," declared Julie, as she was busy preparing herself for college.

As Friday evening arrived, Schuyler had informed his parents of his farewell event over at Mark's house. With his parents' consent, his father drove him to the event in prevention of any vehicular misfortune. Upon his arrival, Mark introduced the guests including Doug, Tony, Kent, and Justin. A surprised Schuyler welcomed Justin to their neighborhood; in return he learned Justin had finished in third place in the State High School Golf Tournament and had accepted a scholarship to play college golf in Cincinnati.

"We are very proud of Justin's accomplishments and are very glad to see him here in Schuyler's honor," spoke Mark who had competed in the state tournament also, finishing among the top twenty golfers.

"I owe a lot to Schuyler; playing with him in the district and regional tournaments improved my short game immensely," responded Justin.

Doug, who was the youngest at the party, asked about the evening's agenda. "What is planned for tonight?"

Mark showed the basement to the partakers, containing a pool table and an open area suitable for dancing. "I plan to order pizza for food and Tony has made additional arrangements."

Tony stepped into the conversation. "I took the liberty of notifying my friend Connie of the occasion and she and a few of her friends should be coming."

"Schuyler, what are the girls doing at your party," exclaimed a frustrated Julie.

The room went silent for a moment as an astonished Schuyler tried to manufacture a response back to Julie. He eventually came to a conclusion that since he was the guest of honor he was expected to be there and he didn't invite the girls anyway, Tony did.

A disgruntled Julie Crystal had to accept his response. *"I guess you are correct, you had no advanced knowledge of Tony's additional arrangement."*

While Kent racked the pool balls for an ensuing break by Doug, Mark and Tony made telephone calls for pizza and female entertainment. Of course, Tony's phone call to Connie took precedence.

With Kent and Doug shooting pool and Mark and Tony busy with telephone duty, Schuyler enjoyed a Cubs' baseball game on television. "Justin, look the Cubs are already winning and it's only the second inning."

"Are you a Cubs' fan Schuyler?" asked Justin.

"Since I was seven years of age," as he offered him a Pepsi.

It wasn't long before Schuyler had Justin interested in Cubs' baseball, as they both worriedly awaited Mark and Tony. Because Justin knew in the back of his mind, Schuyler's telepathic girlfriend would not tolerate any female companionship within range of his friend Schuyler.

A couple of 8-ball games were played until the pizza arrived with Connie and her friends in route. Schuyler began to get nervous and suffered a little difficulty in speaking. He got nervous around girls and with Julie's protectiveness produced only a synergy effect causing his mouth to become parched inhibiting his speaking performance.

The pool match seized for a while in lieu of pizza consumption. With the Cubs still winning, Schuyler seemed to be in high spirits but deep down inside he felt guilty in consequent arrival of Connie and her friends.

Tony greeted the girls, four of them, and introduced them to the fellows. They were polite and friendly to the guys, especially Schuyler. As they teased Schuyler of both his bravery of joining the Army and his shyness around girls, he quickly became the center of attention.

Noticing the attention provided by the girls, Julie became jealous and tried to distract him away from them. *"Don't ya wanna watch the baseball game on TV? Check to see if the Cubs are still ahead."*

Justin alertly reminded him that the Cubs were still ahead and they were playing in the middle innings.

Schuyler introduced his friend Justin as one of the best golfers in the entire state to bait female attention. With some success, Justin impressed one particular girl by integrating his potential college golfing career into their conversation attaining her interest.

With wit on his side, Schuyler convinced his female companion to watch the Cubs' game allowing Justin to spend some quality time with his newfound date. Mark and Tony seemed to suddenly disappear, as Kent and Doug continued to play pool, leaving Schuyler alone with Connie's younger sister. Even her being a couple years younger than Connie, she still was very developed for her age. As she pretended to be interested in baseball, she slowly maneuvered herself closer to him until her body made contact with his.

"She is too close, leave now," argued Julie.

Before he could render a response, she lured him into her arms and began kissing him deeply. Her kissing sensation produced much gratification and her kissing technique seemed to almost extract his tongue out of his mouth, initiating addition sensual simulation to follow.

Luckily for Julie, Doug and Kent was still playing pool preventing ensuing excessive romantic advancements performed by Connie's sister. With much satisfaction, her kissing talent had conquered Schuyler, confirming her youth did not prohibit her ability to take control of a man's sexual desire. Yes, even at her age, she was too much girl for Schuyler to handle.

At festivity's closure, Schuyler received a ride back to his house with Justin who had cut his date short in order to comply with Schuyler's schedule of getting home on time. Justin had attained another girlfriend, providing him with even more selection as he ventured away to college. Schuyler, on the other hand, had gained affection from a younger girl, talented with much potential, generating sexual viewpoints in objection from Julie Crystal.

Driving home, Justin and Schuyler confirmed of an attempt to stay in touch as one went Army and the other went school. Justin progressively gained interest in Schuyler; his unique composure attracted the respect and consideration from his peers due to his honesty, integrity, and trustworthiness. Justin was one of the first individuals to invest on Schuyler's air phenomena. As he dropped Schuyler off at his house, Justin aired *"you are an investment of a lifetime."*

As he waved goodbye to one of the most talented golfers in the entire area, he wondered what he meant by him being someone's investment; but preparing to attend college in Louisiana, Julie Crystal Flowers realized even more the importance of her telepathic relationship.

As before, Schuyler was in the doghouse with Julie. She refused to communicate with him, isolating him as he went about dreaming along without her assistance. He knew of her eventually returning to his side, as he kept his focus on basic training. He continued to run almost every day in preparation for his future culture shock of being in the Army. Of course he still worried if Julie was ever going to come back to him, but the sense of urgency with Army preparation training relieved his mind of dreadful thoughts of suddenly becoming alone.

The day prior to traveling to basic training, via bus, he packed his suitcase in the loneliness of his empty bedroom. He could not repel the sorrow bestowed upon him without his telepathic companion, transmitting his sadness amongst air phenomena.

A concern transmittance interrupted his sorrow, *"Schuyler, I know you need me for alliance if you expect to be at peak performance during basic training."*

An excited Schuyler suddenly stopped in his tracks, paused for a moment to plan a response, and asked very kindly of her assistance during his military endeavor.

Julie welcomed his response with open arms. *"I support your decision to pursue the military, providing you with encouragement, praise, and confidence during tenure as a soldier."*

As he finished packing his suitcase, he greatly rendered appreciation in respect for her attentiveness.

The night before departure, the couple discussed their plans to maintain a relationship throughout his confinement at basic training. This discussion precluded a lasting memory of the telepathic couple's final night together before he ventured to The Home of Armor. Within the friendly confines of his bedroom, they experienced sexual relations, via air phenomenal transmission, allowing him to receive sensual pleasure prior to his voyage unto the unknown, basic training.

The next morning Schuyler's Army recruiter received him from his house, with his parents bidding farewell, he was off to the bus station in route across the state. A proud Army recruiter, earning his month's quota with his prospective recruit, escorted Schuyler to his bus.

"Good luck Schuyler, you'll be an outstanding soldier." The Army recruiter saluted Schuyler as he stepped onto the bus.

With confidence he relaxed during his bus ride because he knew with Julie at his side and his brother Duncan also in the service, he would do well.

"I can't wait until you are finished with basic training. Where will you go next?" Julie inquired.

He explained to her that after basic training he would attend pharmacy specialist school at Fort Sam Houston in San Antonio, Texas. As he got comfortable in his seat, he felt her massaging touch on his forehead relaxing his mind until sleep overcame.

It was only a couple of hours until the bus arrived at the Army post. As he gathered his baggage, he noticed the enchanting grove of trees surrounding the post. It appeared much different than Duncan's Army post with condensed, wooded areas throughout the installation compared to Duncan's openly spaced infantry post. Even with the initial trust of discipline from voices from drill sergeants, he felt right at home.

Basic training was a whole unique experience for Private Ballantine, indoctrinating numerous sets of rules and regulations in which he was to follow. He was expected to be a leader and a follower at the same time, demonstrating potential to progress as a leader soldier. They issued him various types of uniforms, requiring proper wear and appearance, in expectation he would expand his learning by teaching other privates the importance of good, correct uniform maintenance. In fact, the Army was grooming him for future benefit because he was carefully instructed to learn, grow, and lead others to do the same, instead of just learning the information required for graduation. The Army was about teamwork, cohesion, and most of all to never let your fellow soldier down. Indeed, Schuyler was greatly impacted by his drill sergeant beginning his transformation from high school graduate into freedom's guardian.

The perils of basic training involved training for twelve hours a day for 7 days a week, very little actual rest, repetitious meals, polishing combat boots, preparing a tight bunk, arranging an orderly wall locker, performing daily physical training, road marching, firing a M16A2 rifle and military instruction.

Military instruction consisted of map reading, Nuclear/Biological/Chemical agent protection, drill and ceremony, weapons maintenance, military courtesy, leadership, and other various practical lessons related to combat readiness.

Schuyler followed the drill sergeants' instructions well and eventually advanced to become a squad leader, responsible for the accountability of seven other privates. Even though he was only a private, wearing no insignia, he was handpicked to help the drill sergeants' oversee the rest of the recruits in his platoon.

"Help me with your military terminology. What is the difference between a platoon and a squad?" Julie inquired.

While he was in a mist of running a three-mile run, he informed that a platoon was a larger element than a squad and it took four squads to make a platoon. Each squad had eight or nine soldiers compiling a platoon of about thirty-three soldiers.

"When are you'll going to do the obstacle course?"

Huffing and puffing from the strenuous run, he managed to tell her of their plans to challenge the obstacle course this afternoon.

Julie was very interested in his Army training. The NBC training utilized much self-control due to being confined in a protective gas mask for hours. She anticipated his indoctrination of the gas chamber, scheduled in a couple of days.

Later in the day, an exhausted PVT Ballantine marched with his comrades to the obstacle course. It was only late afternoon and poor Schuyler was already fatigued. The obstacle course, or confidence course as it is often called, presented a tough, physical challenge. The drill sergeant aligned the soldiers and dispersed them in the direction of the first obstacle.

Amazed at how efficient the drill sergeant could dissolve his troops in accurate paths, he watched the others scale a high, wooden wall and carefully land on the opposite side in preparation of his turn to conquer the wall himself. Watch, learn, and execute was his motto to achievement. He watched the others climb the wall, learning the technique, and executing the drill to standard. With this process in mind, he had little problem overcoming the obstacle course's challenge.

The ladder climb, successive layers of wooden beams erected into the air, proposed a bit of a contest for most of soldiers, especially for Michael. Michael, a bit smaller and weaker than the rest of the platoon, had climbed to the top layer wooden beam and suddenly froze in place.

An alert Julie noticed Michael's predicament, via Schuyler's air phenomena. *"Schuyler you've got to do something, he's going to fall!"*

Schuyler seemed to be in suspended animation as he glazed at poor Michael stuck on the top beam and afraid to come down.

"Go get him down, you're his squad leader and you must ensure his safety!" Julie demanded.

At a moment's notice, Schuyler climbed up the wooden ladder, one beam at a time. Every layer got tougher, with the beams getting more far apart as the height increased. He slowly stretched out his arm to secure the second to the highest beam, clutching the beam and rolling over it to secure himself. Michael, being short, had much difficulty securing his feet onto the beam directly below him. Schuyler, assuring his own safety on the beam, carefully secured himself on the beam and reached for Michael's legs, guiding him down onto the same beam as he.

"Ensure Michael keeps grasping the top beam until you securely have him." Julie advised as she watched the turmoil from the comfort of her own home. *"And keep him calm by reassuring him."*

Schuyler did what Julie advised, carefully instructing Michael downward the ladder. He was successful in calming the frighten Michael, guiding him to safety.

Due to Michael's inability to climb down the ladder, the drill sergeant proceeded to scrutinize his bravery in a very harsh voice. In other words, poor Michael was getting yelled at because he froze on the ladder.

A disgruntled Julie expressed, *"don't scream at that poor boy for being scared, you're only ruining his confidence!"*

A silence filled the air; the drill sergeant looked at Schuyler and ceased yelling at Michael. He dismissed Michael back to his squad leader for further directives. Schuyler, pleased with Julie's intervention, thanked her for the assistance, but warned of possible ensuing repercussions.

At closure of a very eventful day, Schuyler showered and prepared for rest. Since he shared a room with three other soldiers, he and Julie's bedtime telepathic relationship had to be downsized immensely. In fact, he was so exhausted at close of business Julie needed very little sweet-talk to put him into a deep, sound sleep.

The next anticipated scheduled event was the gas chamber. Julie had warned Schuyler of the perils of inhaling the dreaded tear gas agent. The gas chamber involved the soldiers entering an enclosed facility containing tear gas, a riot control agent.

The morning of gas chamber visitation, the recruits ate a light breakfast guarding against probable upset stomach activity from tear gas agent inhalation.

Marching down the asphalt road in the direction of two massive hills, misery and agony, the platoon of recruits eventually arrived at the gas chamber site.

As before, the drill sergeants formulated the recruits and dispersed them in an orderly fashion into four equal ranks. Since the gas chamber facilitated four soldiers at a time, each rank would provide one individual at a time for training. Gas chamber training familiarized each individual with their gas mask, ensuring confidence in masking procedures, identifying strengths and weaknesses throughout the entire training.

Schuyler was slated to go into the chamber in the second foursome. As a leader, he could show signs of fear that might panic other recruits, such as Michael.

"Have Michael go in the chamber with you, he might panic and you'll be able to help him," warned Julie.

Schuyler requested the two of them would enter the chamber in the same group. The drill sergeant was hesitate at first, but agreed to allow both of them to experience the tear gas agent together.

"Be careful dear, and watch out for Michael!" Julie advised as she anxiously anticipated the ensuing event.

Prior to going into the chamber, the drill sergeant presented a brief. "You will enter the chamber, position yourself on the appropriate markings on the floor, upon the command UNMASK you will remove your mask for ten seconds, and then proceed out the exit door. Are there any questions?"

Schuyler understood pretty much what was going on, but Michael seemed a bit confused and too afraid to ask questions. Thus, Schuyler knew to keep a close eye on him.

The fearsome foursome slowly maneuvered into the chamber carefully studying the markings on the floor and gingerly positioning themselves in the appropriate locations. As they stood inside the chamber, completely masked, for about thirty seconds to ensure a proper seal of the mask, Schuyler noticed an uneasy feeling about Michael.

The chamber proctor, who was completely masked, ordered the four recruits to unmask and hold their breath for ten seconds and then exit. They followed the orders and everything seemed to be going well until Michael accidentally swallowed a big gulp of tear gas agent. With Schuyler's eyes burning from the agent, he quickly moved Michael to the front of the line to exit the door. A frantic Michael was gasping for air already and coughing profusely. After the longest ten seconds of their lives, the foursome gladly exited the door. As Michael lead the way out the door, he continued to cough and gag immensely until he vomited freely along the tree line. The light breakfast was indeed a good idea since several recruits, not just Michael, lost their stomach's contents.

Schuyler didn't throw up, but tears poured from his eyes due to the agent's irritation. As he continuous spit saliva from his mouth, he began recovering his squad members in assurance of their safety. The remaining recruits eventually came stumbling out of the chamber, ailing from the agent's effect, expressing much sigh of relief, instilling desired confidence in masking procedures from their intensive ordeal.

In amazement, Julie admired their courage enduring the suffering caused by the agent. "*Schuyler, you did well inside the chamber. You prevented Michael from inhaling more agent than he actually did.*"

With eyes still watery, he let her know of his appreciation of her assisting support and he would have not taken prompt action without her alarming interjection.

The gas chamber experience illustrated the authenticity of chemical agent warfare, identifying preventive measures for protective posture in a chemical environment.

At close of business, another day was in the books for PVT Ballantine and the other recruits. After a couple of weeks of this eight-week vigorous training cycle, Schuyler was feeling the pressure. The Army Physical Fitness Test would be their next challenge.

The ensuing week featured a physical fitness test evaluating muscle strength, muscle endurance, and cardio-respiratory endurance. The recruits were tested on push-ups, sit-ups, and a two-mile run.

Schuyler felt confident with his physical fitness; his brother's incorporated fitness plan had sufficiently prepared him for basic training physical training. Thus, his calisthenics and running prior to basic training paid a lot of dividends. He was prepared to challenge the physical training test.

By this point of his basic training, Julie Crystal Flowers was about to start college in Louisiana. She planned to juggle a full schedule of classes and basketball practice, along with attentiveness of Schuyler at boot camp. Her priorities were fuzzy, but she knew her schoolwork, basketball, and Schuyler had to receive top priority along with her family. She was destined to be a very busy girl.

The drill sergeants governed the physical training test, explaining in much detail the expected standards of each event. The entire platoon of recruits were first tested on push-ups, given a ten-minute break, and then tested on sit-ups. After another ten-minute break, they began a timed two-mile run.

At conclusion of the record Army Physical Fitness Test, PVT Ballantine had passed with flying colors. He was very proud of himself, scoring a 263 out of 300 possible points, but most of all he expressed much congratulations to Michael, who had also completed the rigorous testing procedure with a passing score.

The physical training test was another milestone for the basic trainees, strengthening their physical conditioning in preparation for upcoming events such as road marches, rifle marksmanship, and bivouac.

The days slowly proceeded by, with very structured lessons demonstrated on a daily basis that provided required guidance for success as a combat soldier. Road marches, from ten to fifteen miles, were conducted at least twice a week that strengthened physical stamina needed for combat readiness. A memorable road march occurred on a hot, muggy day in late August, challenging the platoon to perform a tactical road march for approximately fifteen miles. With supervision from the drill sergeants, and other supporting personnel, the recruits began a journey through the back section of post to included range road. Range road was a hardtop surface with three major hills, and all three of them were extremely steep, exhausting most of the recruits as they marched to its top. Dressed in full battle rattle consisting of pistol belt, suspenders, helmet, mask, and rucksack, they soldierly marched down range road at five-meter intervals.

"Schuyler, why do you walk five meters apart?" Julie was involved in classroom study, but was still interested in their tactical road march.

As he maintained his proper distance, he informed her of the importance to stay in line with the others and not to form a cluster, because an incoming round could inflict a much larger amount of injuries if the troops were bunched together.

Schuyler kept pace well, drinking water when needed. In remembrance of Justin's advice on the golf links, he made certain of plentiful water consumption not just for him but for squad members also.

The road march encompassed most of the morning, building a huge appetite, as tired, exhausted recruits returned back to garrison. They had conquered three of the toughest hills on the compound, expanding their heartiness resilience in groundwork for further grueling training. Army training prepared their soldiers in increments, allowing progression at one step at a time, compounding the development of soldiers' abilities from one stage to the next.

Basic training's mid-point incorporated numerous training increments including drill and ceremony, map reading, physical fitness testing, obstacle course, gas chamber, road marches, and other combat-related training. The final four weeks featured rifle marksmanship, bivouac, a final examination on several military subjects, and graduation.

Emphasis was placed on shooting the rifle, a critical subject area and principal milestone in the progression of a soldier during basic training.

"I can't wait to watch your shoot your gun!" Julie told him, pretending to be dumb.

He reminded her that the Army strictly prohibited calling the M16A2 rifle a gun. It is referred to as a weapon. A gun was something else.

She laughed at him. *"I know; I can't wait to watch you shoot your gun!"*

He eventually understood her true meaning and informed her of maybe after basic training she can watch him shoot his gun.

At the break of dawn, the drill sergeants marched the platoon of recruits down range road to a rifle range. PVT Ballantine, chosen by his drill sergeant, was selected to call cadence while they marched down the hardtop. As the other recruits kept in step, Schuyler sang a little Army song to stimulated espirit de corps among the troops. Even though, he wasn't really any good at calling cadence, he was highly commended by his drill sergeant for his effort.

His drill sergeant had taken much interest in his leadership development, maybe Julie's influence was a factor, but Schuyler's confidence as an individual seemed to mature everyday.

Rifle marksmanship consists of two main phases. The first phase was weapon zeroing in which the weapon was placed at mechanical zero, positioning both rear and front sights exactly in mid-range. After mechanical zero, the individual firer repositions the sights in adjustment of personal shooting vision. The second phase was the actual weapon's qualification consisting of forty targets of various distances.

The raw recruits were to practice zeroing their individual weapon for a couple of days until near perfect alignment. An adequate battlesight-zero alignment was three of three bullet shots inside a small circle, or very near, on a target of a distance of twenty-five meters. Thus for advancement to actual qualification, a firer would have to shoot three straight bullets very close to a small circle which was twenty-five meters away.

Schuyler explained to Julie the techniques of shooting the weapon. Breathing, aiming, trigger squeeze, and steady grip, illustrating the procedural skill involved in marksmanship.

Julie was busy with school, still keeping up with Schuyler's progress during basic training. *"It looks difficult. A lot of the guys are shooting numerous times in attempt to zero."*

He agreed! As he loaded his own rifle he informed her of their shooting for a couple of days to ensure proper alignment for actual qualification. He proceeded to shoot his three rounds into the target with little luck. He had one shot inside the circle, but the other two were scattered.

"PVT Ballantine, you need to work on your breathing," informed the drill sergeant. "Wait to shoot until the beginning of your exhaling part of your breathing cycle."

Schuyler's ensuing three-round shot group improved considerably, resulting in two of the three shots landing in the circle. After a couple of more three-shot rounds, he steadily improved.

"Let me give you assistance on this next shot group. I'll remind you to breath properly, aim straight through both sights, steady grip, and relax," offered Julie who was about to begin basketball practice in the late afternoon.

Schuyler, with Julie's as his coach, locked and loaded one three-round magazine. After placing the selector level from the safe position onto the semi position, he carefully shot his three rounds downrange. After the command of seize fire, a positive PVT Ballantine, his telepathic shooting coach, and his drill sergeant carefully walked downrange to inspect the zero target. With a gleam in his eyes, the drill sergeant informed him of his success zeroing his weapon. Even though two rounds were on the circle's line, he had possessed a tight-enough shot group for advancement to qualification later in the week.

"PVT Ballantine, you're finished with the zero-lane. Clean your weapon and be sure not to adjust your sights." Directed a stern drill sergeant impressed with Schuyler's ability to follow directions.

"Most affirmed, drill sergeant!" PVT Ballantine responded in a robust, hearty manner. After being dismissed off the range, a proud Schuyler gladly marched back to garrison. With much sighs of relief, he had completed the toughest part of rifle marksmanship, the battlesight zero range.

The platoon followed the same pattern the very next day, marching to the zero range in anticipation of achieving success for the rest of the recruits. Since Schuyler had already zeroed his weapon, he was assigned as a coach, directed by his drill sergeant, to ensure Michael zeroed his weapon by the end of the day. Thus, the remaining non-zeroed firers would be assisted by coaching peers and have the entire day to successfully zero their weapon.

"Watch Michael carefully, guarantee his advancement to the qualification phase," requested Julie.

As he paired off with Michael about to range walk to his firing point, he asked Julie about her basketball practice?

"Doing well; Coach Jackson likes me a lot." An enthused Julie Crystal reported to her telepathic companion.

Michael was a little afraid of his weapon, a common problem with several recruits. He had trouble concentrating and staying focused while he was on his range point. He seemed to be distracted frequently, forgetting to follow simple instructions from the tower. Schuyler's number one task was to get Michael in the proper frame of mind to successfully overcome the zero range's challenge.

As Schuyler instructed Michael, "relax at your firing point, stay calm, listen to the drill sergeant and myself, and focus on the little black circle on the target."

Michael, nervously positioned himself in the foxhole at his point, obtained a comfortable firing position and commenced to fire his three rounds downrange. After failing to obtain a tight-shot group, he felt depressed and began to worry if he would actually get to the qualification phase.

The drill sergeant adjusted his sights again and pursued to assist another problem firer. Schuyler offered additional supportive advice. The day got longer with every attempt at zeroing the weapon, but eventually in the late afternoon Michael fired three consecutive rounds in a close enough tight group to advance to the qualification phase of marksmanship. Actually, everyone eventually graduated the zero range prior to darkness. Thus, the drill sergeants were not going to prohibit any recruit from advancing to shoot at the actual qualification targets.

Julie commended Schuyler for his dedicated commitment in assistance toward his shy squad member. *"You did well out there at your range point. Maybe tomorrow both little Michael and you will qualify."*

The following day began the rifle marksmanship phase featuring a variation of targets, ranging from 50 meters to 300 meters. A warm morning would surely lead to a miserable hot afternoon, presenting an advantage of firing as earliest as possible. Schuyler tried to get into the first firing order, but had to settle for the second of four firing orders. Similar to golf, an earlier tee-off time had advantages in order to avoid the hot sun of the afternoon. Second firing order was still good, ensuring he would get to shoot prior to lunch. It was stressful; the other recruits were struggling to fire well enough to earn their marksmanship badges as Schuyler watched from behind. The badges consisted of three levels expert, sharpshooter, and marksman. The expert badge required 36 of 40 targets, the pinnacle of marksmanship sought by every soldier in the Army.

Julie was active in school, but following the dramatics of rifle marksmanship. *"When will Michael shoot?"*

In response to Julie's request, he searched for Michael eventually learning that his turn was in the fourth firing order. Thus, he was going to shoot last. The drill sergeants arrange the firing orders by precedence, attempting to qualify as many firers as possible the first day by ensuring the better firers shoot early.

As the pounding noise of bullets being shot through the barrel of M16A2 rifles, he watched how the pop-up targets were positioned throughout the range providing intelligence in preparation of qualification.

Fortunately for Schuyler, he positioned himself in the foxhole awaiting to lock and load a magazine in preparation to fire before the day got very hot. It was still mid-morning, similar period of time as front nine holes of golf during an eighteen-hole match, an invitation to shoot down some pop-up targets prior to lunch.

"I'm still watching you, sugar," strong support from Julie. *"Remember to do your breathing techniques and steady grip on the rifle."*

After receiving the commands from the tower, he carefully watched his lane for targets to appear. The targets seemed to spring-up from the ground, begging to be shot down. They resembled little soldiers holding a rifle of their own across their chest. With confidence he shot his initial ten rounds expecting good result, after removing his spent magazine and replacing it with a fresh one containing ten rounds, he continued to shoot down little plastic men down range with greater than expected success.

After twenty spent rounds, half the rounds of qualification, the tower requested the firers to shoot any remaining alibi bullets. He had a little pause until firing the remaining twenty rounds, changing from the foxhole position to the prone, unsupported position.

Julie anticipated good results. *"Looks like you are shooting about par for the course."*

The next twenty rounds of fire went by quickly; he positioned for the targets ensuring strong success of the targets of 50, 100,150, and 200 meters. The 250 and 300 meter targets were a little far for him, resulting in frequent misses at these particular targets.

At conclusion of his second twenty rounds, after all of the alibi shots were fired, he was instructed to leave his firing point, with weapon pointed down range, and travel to the tower.

With a cleared weapon, he was allowed to go back to the containment area and await his results. The drill sergeant would not return any actual results until all firers had the opportunity to shoot, but in his heart he expected good results.

Julie awarded her congratulations. *"Good shooting, I know you shot at least sharpshooter!"*

A nervous Schuyler had to wait until the very late afternoon to receive the bad news of his lack of qualification. His heart sank in denial of his failure, his expectations dissipated into thin air as his lengthy day came to such an abrupt ending.

Without Schuyler's knowledge, his drill sergeant failed to qualify him for a specific reason. Schuyler was only one shot away from sharpshooter and even though he scored high enough to qualify with marksman, his drill sergeant insisted to have Schuyler shoot again the next day in expectations of a higher score. Also his drill sergeant had planned to pair Schuyler with Michael at the same firing point, projecting his leadership in hope of elevating Michael's shooting ability. As expected, Michael was very far from qualification and needed Schuyler's assistance greatly.

Schuyler's character grew from his thought of failure, but being provided another chance at shooting sharpshooter was a benefit only provided to him. Because his drill sergeant knew PVT Ballantine possessed an uncanny leadership quality, Schuyler was selected to provide much needed assistance to a fellow soldier. PVT Ballantine was only doing his duty as a leader, to take care of soldiers.

The recycled firers rode out to the firing range the next morning with expectations of success. As they arrived, Schuyler was selected to be in the initial firing order. He was, of course, paired with Michael on the sixth firing point.

The tower voiced instructions, familiarizing the firers with quick-firing fundamental instructions, reinforcing range procedures as they prepared to shoot.

On the command of commence firing, Schuyler began to light up the range with consecutive direct-hits on various pop-up targets. The morning dew pronounced the target's locations, enhancing landscape detection of decisive targets, ensuring achieved success on the rifle qualification range. He breezed through the foxhole, supported position and the prone, unsupported position in route to shooting a better than expected score than yesterday. Unlike yesterday, his drill sergeant made it a vital priority to stop by the sixth firing point and inform PVT

Ballantine of his sharpshooter qualification. With Schuyler's sharpshooter badge earned, the first half of the drill sergeant's plan was deemed successful. It was now Michael's turn to shoot, and as expected it would be a long day for Schuyler as his coach.

With a congratulating hug, Julie expressed her satisfaction toward Schuyler for his accomplished achievement. *"Good shooting; I bet you are even better with your gun, than your rifle."*

Michael still had trouble focusing on his quick-firing fundamentals. His breathing was bad, he rushed his shots, and he really didn't aim well either. His worst shortcoming was his lack of attention to detail, because once when the tower asked for alibi shots to be fired he almost shot his own foot. Wondering if he had any alibi rounds remaining in the magazine to be fired, he failed to aim the rifle downrange to shoot; instead he pointed his rifle at the ground in front of him and pulled the trigger and fired his alibi round in front of his feet. Luckily, no other sole on that entire range responded to the mishap. It was completely ignored, like it had never happen, avoiding possible immense disciplinary action.

Later in the afternoon with Michael still trying to qualify, their drill sergeant added about five extra rounds in each of the four banana-clip magazine enhancing Michael chances of qualification.

"Private, you better qualify now because you've got twenty extra rounds to fire with," directed the drill sergeant.

"Michael, concentrate on shooting the short targets; shoot three bullets at them if you have to." Schuyler encouraged his strategy.

After firing a total of sixty rounds at targets ranging from 50 meters to 200 meters, a proud Michael finally qualified marksman. The strategy had worked like a charm; by avoiding the 250 meter and 300 meter targets and shooting two or three bullets at the other targets, Michael acquired marksman status.

After a long, stressful day at the range, Schuyler returned back to garrison in the comfort of Julie's telepathic touch.

Julie touched her telepathic companion in all of the right places on the ride back to garrison. She continued relaxing his aching body by massaging his tender muscles, stimulating a restful sleep. The next major obstacle of basic training was a three-day bivouac, but at least the rifle marksmanship phase was completed.

In garrison, the recruits prepared for a long road march to the bivouac site. A hike of over fifteen miles awaited them, transporting to a location designed for a few days of camp. The bivouac detailed setting up two-man pup tents, constructing hasty fighting positions, guard duty, land navigation, first aid training, and

NBC confidence training. The highlight of the camping trip exhibited night maneuvers, incorporating NBC protective posture and patrolling techniques.

After Schuyler prepared his squad members for the midnight patrol, he rallied with the platoon sergeant in preparation for the maneuver. The platoon dispersed by squads, one at a time, with Schuyler's squad proceeding in the second order. As the platoon of recruits carefully paced along the tree line, Schuyler ensured his squad remained in position for an attack at all times.

"When will you'll get attacked?" inquired Julie.

Awaiting further instructions from the platoon sergeant, he informed her that an ambush awaited them very soon.

The platoon's patrol came to a sudden halt and the squad leaders assembled with the platoon sergeant. After receiving his warning order, Schuyler immediately rallied his squad and directed them to be prepared to don their protective mask and commence low crawling.

In the quietness of the night, the troops slowly patrolled ahead in great expectation of immediate danger. The tree line was deadly silent, until without notice, the sound of machine gun fire initiated the expelling of tear gas agent. In hast, the recruits donned their protective masks and began low crawling along the tree line.

The machine gun bullets sounded appeared to be traveling immediately over their heads, strongly persuading them to crawl quickly and very near the ground. The tear gas agent fear, along with the machine gun fire, was too frightening for several of the recruits. But strong leadership from the squad leaders, and other supporting individuals, strengthened the confidence of the frighten recruits, tactically transporting them to safety. The entire platoon survived the assault, with minimal injuries, due to leadership expertise.

At conclusion of the midnight maneuver, the drill sergeants expressed vast laudatory comments toward the platoon as a whole. They have performed bravely in the face of danger and were extensively commended for their achieved accomplishments.

"Schuyler, I was so scared during the ambush that I was afraid to think to you in fear that I might be a distraction. I can't believe how good of a job you did leading all those scared soldiers to safety!" Julie administered her own congratulatory comments to her hero.

The bivouac as a whole was a success. The trainees received experience in the field environment, including reacting to hostile fire in combination of chemical agent protection. They also qualified with hand grenades during the bivouac operation, broadening their ability to succeed in combat.

The only remaining increment remaining of basic training was the final practical test. PVT Ballantine was charged to provide necessary individual training to ensure his squad successfully passed the test. This was a test designed to ensure 100% achievement throughout the entire platoon.

It was a practical examination consisting of all increments of basic training such as guard duty, map reading, drill and ceremony, reporting procedures, Army history, customs and courtesies, weapons maintenance, risk assessment, and a few other additional Army tasks.

The platoon sergeant, squad leaders, and a few other selected trainees were allowed to test in the first order. In expectations of outstanding results, these individuals would complete the test initially, and then provide assistance to marginal recruits as strategy to ensure everyone passed the final increment.

PVT Ballantine, along with a few others, completed the final increment of testing with a perfect score. Excited about his results, he could not do much celebrating because his toughest challenge of mentoring trainees still remained ahead.

Julie was very impressed with his results. She was very busy with school and basketball, but soon became very knowledgeable of the Army. *"The final increment was a breeze; now do your job as a leader and ensure your troops are taken care of!"*

Schuyler wasn't sure to take orders from his drill sergeant or Julie; they both seemed to coincide with each other providing guidance in behalf of his leader development.

After a few recycled stations, his squad members finally achieved the final increment's standards, granting advancement toward graduation.

In surprise, Michael had completed the final increment's test with only two recycled stations. His elevated confidence, due to Schuyler's extensive guidance, expanded his military knowledge in path to successful completion of basic training, accomplishing all required objectives.

Basic training came to conclusion at graduation. The trainees dressed in their Class A uniform, with spit-shined low quarters formulated into a rectangular company formation. Even though Schuyler did not earn any individual award, his drill sergeant commended his leadership attributes, values, and knowledge in the presence of his parents. "Mr. and Mrs. Ballantine, your son had been a valuable asset to our mission and he exceeded expected standards as a soldier, squad leader, and a leader. He is a fine credit to himself, the platoon, and the United States Army."

After Schuyler's parents thanked the drill sergeant for his dedicated mentorship, they proceeded to walk to the reception tent. The reception tent, containing punch and cake, presented much opportunity for the parents to mingle with the command personnel.

"Where is Duncan?" Schuyler asked his mother.

"He should be in route, and arriving shortly."

After brief conversations with other graduates and their parents, SGT Duncan Ballantine joined Schuyler at the reception dressed in his starched battle dressed uniform with spit-shined jump boots.

Duncan, as usual, seemed to suddenly be the center of attraction, synthesizing conservation with numerous individuals. Schuyler was very proud of his brother, but not near as proud as Duncan was of him. "Brother, you made a good choice in joining the Army and you have done well, but remember it has just begun."

CHAPTER 12

Basic training demonstrated Schuyler's ability to adapt to changing environments. Being placed in a leadership position posed specific challenges enabling Schuyler to grow as a leader, indoctrinating flexible competencies to achieve set goals. As a squad leader, he withstood battlefield-setting challenges ensuring his squad members were provided worthy guidance throughout all phases of vigorous training. Through caring, courage, and commitment PVT Ballantine's complete squad graduated a grueling basic training.

Only a few of the trainees from Schuyler's basic training traveled to Fort Sam for advanced individual training. Most of the other recruits were to attend tank mechanic school, but Schuyler and Michael were off to hot San Antonio to complete their training. Schuyler, of course, was scheduled to begin pharmacy technician school in adjacent to Michael's dietary technician's training.

At the Jupiter, Morrison breathed huge sighs of relief as The Air successfully exceeded standards in practically all phases of basic training. In deep worrisome self, he gladly accepted the fact The Air possessed much more self-discipline than expected. Without a doubt, The Air revealed his true ability to extract provided leadership principles and guidelines, establishing applications in directing his troops to accomplish desired goals.

Boyd was even more flabbergasted, he raved about Julie Crystal's interventions providing informative suggestions throughout the entire training cycle. Her alertness supported key incremental activities such as the obstacle course, the rifle range, bivouac, and especially the gas chamber. Indeed, her telepathic assistance defined a new concept of today's Army.

With a coffee cup clutched in hand, Morrison gazed out the window at the streets of Lexington. "Do you think he will have any problems in the big city?"

"He has proven to overcome the experience of basic training, demonstrating abilities not recorded in our research." A positive Boyd attempted to reassure Morrison of the achievements accomplished by The Vision.

Morrison, making himself comfortable, sat back down in his chair and analyzed a bit of The Air's past. "To my knowledge, The Air has never peaked in maturity as much as he has in the past six months."

"Because of Julie's involvement, his transformation has reached pinnacle levels," responded Boyd.

Morrison nodded to Boyd, in restoration of confidence in his research project, coming to agreement with Boyd's hypothesis. "The girl is an affirmative aspect, providing aid in his cause. No other single individual can compare with her influence, in such this matter, to benefit our undertaking."

Together the Morrison and Boyd tandem patiently awaited his venture to San Antonio, generating research data to enhance their mission of tracking his air phenomena.

The Home of the Combat Medic appeared kind to Schuyler, alleviating a lot of stress stored from the Home of Armor outing. Fort Sam appeared completely different, almost a 180-degree twist from basic training. They too had drill sergeants, but this training cycle deemed much more relaxing than the past one.

Advanced individual training, incorporated classroom study within a training environment. The student-trainees marched to class at the Academy, under drill sergeant direction, attending classroom instruction throughout the entire day. The evenings and weekends were liberally freelanced, integrating extracurricular activities with Army technical training.

Schuyler, quiet and posed, performed well during the early increments of A.I.T. maintaining a very much respectable class average. His prior knowledge of Math, Biology, and Chemistry propelled him through several of the initial basic modules. Julie was thrilled almost daily at his progress, utilizing her subject-matter-expertise minimally.

While Schuyler was occupied at pharmacy technician school, Julie had finished her first semester establishing a grade point average of 3.5 and performing well on the basketball court. As she balanced a full load of college courses, she firmly established herself on the basketball team. The Louisiana native gave South Eastern State a breath of fresh air, coming off the bench in a substitute role. Coach Jackson's recruitment included two freshmen guards, two freshmen forwards, and Julie. Already, the team was set for the future. These were the rebuilding years, nourishing the five young freshmen for seasons to come.

A final math examination awaited him, requiring her assistance, during a latter week of the academic phase. It would involve a lot of IV additive solution problems, featuring ratio and proportion principles, metric system conversions, calculations involving sodium chloride equivalents and hyperalimentation solutions, dilution of dry powders, and intravenous flow rates. Sounded real complex, but most of the actual problems were similar, involving cross-multiplication techniques.

Julie had done an excellent job preparing him for his mathematical testing. She adapted well to pharmacy's style of solving formulas and equations, implementing her own format in solving pharmaceutical calculations. In addition to his mathematics exam, he also would undertake a chemistry and biology final the same week. These three major examinations were a huge piece of the academic phase requiring focus at his fullest extent.

In preparation of the three significant examinations, Julie convinced him to stay alone overnight at a local motel in fashion to spend some quality time with her. She knew what he needed to excel in mathematical studies and she was dedicating herself in his behalf. Thus the ensuing week would make, or break, Schuyler's academic performance during fundamental modules establishing himself as a competitive student.

Early Saturday morning, Schuyler prepared himself for a short hike off post to a nearby motel. With a backpack filled with study material and a change of clothes, he proceeded to individually road march a few miles outside the back portion of the post. Being his first time walking this main street, located in the older section of San Antonio, he carefully walked along this melancholy street in search of an acceptable room to spend the night. The streets were filled with restaurants, shops, and motels. A lot of the motels were quite aged, appearing to be frequently utilized by hoochie girls.

Julie had a big basketball game that particular Saturday; she balanced concentrating on her dribbling skills as she monitored which motel her telepathic boyfriend shopped for. *"Don't even think about staying in one of those tramp motels; try down a little bit farther down the road."*

Eventually, he located a clean, affordable motel room. He wasn't too distant from the post, but well hidden from the rest of the soldiers. After he assembled his belongings, he walked next door to order a box of chicken to satisfy his high noon hunger. But before he actually began to study, Julie directed him to strip down and stand naked in front of a mirror allowing her to peek at his frontal exposure. Due to his air phenomena, when he looked at himself in the mirror, she thus viewed whatever he did, transmitting his vision to her mind.

"I see you are glad to finally be alone with me, unfortunately everybody else can vision you also," informed Julie.

It has been a long time!

"Sugar, pleasure me by pleasuring yourself!"

Warming-up before a basketball game, Julie Crystal Flowers viewed her telepathic lover perform a sensual dance in plain view of the bathroom mirror stimulating her sexual desire. As she shot pre-game free throws, her sexual excitement grew distracting her touch on the free-throw line.

"Are you alright Julie? You seem to have lost your focus." Teammate Brittney inquired. "Don't let Coach Jackson catch you not being 100% focused during pre-game as well as during the game."

A little prior to the game, Schuyler began massaging himself in delight of Julie. Luckily for her, she usually sat the bench until at least the second half. During a large percentage of the entire first half, Julie sat on the bench deeply involved with the encouragement of Schuyler's pleasuring ejaculation.

As her team played, she fantasized with Schuyler until he soiled the bed sheets with multiple detonations.

As Julie continued to ride the pine, he cleaned himself and prepared to study biology. Julie requested he study the math later during the evening. *"Schuyler, I'm busy with a basketball game now. Begin with biology, follow with chemistry, and save the math for later."*

The basketball game went well with Julie's team winning easily, but the Coach neglected to play Julie until very late in the game. Brittney played a lot at forward, representing the freshman class, as Julie observed from the bench.

At the motel, Schuyler eliminated a lot of stress from his sexual fantasy with Julie. He was now primed to begin studying for his module examinations. As he leisurely studied, he wondered about his telepathic companion. He dreamed about her existence as a college basketball player, requesting interpretation of its lifestyle excitement.

Julie explained the livelihood of playing college basketball. The commitment to schoolwork, intense practices, travel scheduling, and game preparations highlighted the lifestyle of the college student athlete. Indeed, playing basketball maybe wasn't as grueling as basic training, but sounded like a lot of work also.

After he completed his biology and chemistry preparation, he initiated mathematical problem solving processes. As the night grew long, Julie and he had mastered almost all of the testable practical exercises in his module. At closure, they figured to have a strong majority of the math conquered in preparation of the eventful math module final examination.

Julie's confidence synthesized his ambition to achieve results higher than expectations, enhancing his status as a prominent soldier student in the United States Army Medical Corps.

The lengthy day of schoolwork indeed offered a good reason for a restful sleep, but early next morning he awaken with a very compelling desire to engage in fantasy sexual relations with Julie. With clear-cut compliance from Julie, his fantasy lasted for over an hour obtaining sexual satisfaction for him and providing mental stimulation toward her. It was an unforgettable stay at the motel.

With the aid of her expertise, he breezed through all three final examinations exceeding standards established within the academic module. He had accepted the challenge of self-study, accomplishing desired objectives as he obtained anticipated results.

At the halfway point of advanced individual training, Schuyler had attained much success with the academic subjects. The second half of the training would feature pharmaceutical practicing procedures such as prescription dispensing, sterile products, manufacturing, and computer-entry techniques. These ensuing modules were practical applications, requiring Schuyler to act independently as he learned to perform proficiently in the field of pharmacy.

Even though Julie could not intervene to a great extent during these practical modules, her warming companionship lifted his spirits in flourishing directions. Her inspirational motivation was the accurate medicated dosage to treat any ailment of fear he might face.

Julie was excelling in her schoolwork, achieving more progress in the classroom than on the hardwood. Her choice of study was drama, attempting to achieve a life-long dream to be an actress. Of course, she did well in all of her classes, but her primary area of concentration was drama in pursuit of stardom.

In the middle of the month of February, PVT Ballantine gained advancement to PV2 earning his private mosquito wings. A PVT wore no insignia compared to the single stripe of a PV2; this single stripe is often referred as a mosquito wing.

A resilient PV2 Ballantine, from his recent advancement, spent quite a lot of hours preparing for his practical examinations. He, after duty hours, would receive additional instruction from SSG Lynch, his counselor, ensuring progression in the course. SSG Lynch spent numerous hours in direct contact with PV2 Ballantine making certain that proper applicative techniques were presented to the fullest extent in the majority of the practical modules. Even Julie admired the sergeant's dedication, melding Schuyler into the sharpest pharmacy technician possible.

Both Schuyler and Julie achieved exceptional results in their academic endeavors during the remainder of the spring. The warmth of the spring air dispersed energy across the southlands, including Texas and Louisiana. Her basketball season derived superb results with the team finishing in second place within the conference, improving from the past season. The coach matured the five freshmen, granting them plenty of playing time in progression for seasons to come. Nicknamed "The Fresh Five", all reserve players, were often placed into tight games to rejuvenate the squad. Indeed, the future looked bright for Julie Crystal Flowers and the remainder of The Fresh Five.

PV2 Ballantine performed above standards in most of his practical performance modules. He excelled in computer-entry applications and sterile products. He developed exceptional skills in IV additive medication therapy, marketing his pharmaceutical calculations capability. With Julie's calculations expertise, he was a natural in the laminar flow hood preparing IV additive mixtures.

The increased heat of San Antonio administered progression in Schuyler's pharmacy technician training. It wasn't long before it was graduation time. After a little three-day field training exercise, nothing compared to basic training, and a comprehensive examination, the advanced individual training pharmacy technician students were primed for graduation. Compared to basic training's graduation, it was minor league. The ceremony was conducted in a theatre, with no reception, and very few guests compared to basic training's ceremony. Schuyler, following suit with most of the other students, did not bring any guests what so ever to the ceremony. The graduation ceremony at Fort Sam deemed much less traditional than his prior one, conceptualizing the fact that Army basic training was the real heart and soul of a recruit's indoctrination of the military.

With both phases of training completed, basic training and advanced individual training, Schuyler was ready to advance to permanent party status. After a three-week leave, he would venture to his initial duty station assigned as a pharmacy technician. To quite surprise, his initial duty assignment would be Korea.

Both training cycles, basic training and advanced individual training, were an astounding success spearheading his transformation from recruit to soldier. His initial-entry training was completed, transporting him into regular Army.

Flying back home on leave status, his parents at the Lexington airport with open arms welcomed him. The gratification of pleasing his parents inspired devotional outcomes from his military service. Even within just a short period of service, his devotion to exceed standards rendered good, solid results.

"You look so handsome with your hair style," spoke his mother.

Schuyler ran his fingers through his hair. "Its kind of like Duncan's hair cut, isn't it?"

"Your brother will be here tomorrow, unless he has duty." His mother embraced her baby boy in knowledge of his much venturous excursions throughout his training.

His father was worrisome of his ensuing assignment. He feared the unknown, and having his son travel halfway across the globe was fearsome enough. "How do you feel about Korea?"

As Schuyler noticed a little bit of doubt in his father's tone of voice, he tried to convince him that it was a secure assignment. "I'll be in good hands there; only the best soldiers go to Korea for duty and I'll receive the very best leadership that the Army can offer."

His father, in the back of his mind, knew his youngest son really didn't know that much about Korea and was only trying to settle his nerves. "Schuyler, maybe your brother Duncan can provide valuable information concerning the subject."

"Let's talk to him when he arrives?" Schuyler agreed with his father also hoping Duncan could shed some light on the Korean subject.

Later that evening, alone in his old room, Schuyler discussed his Korean assignment with Julie. She was very supportive of his effort as a soldier. *"Schuyler, I will follow you wherever you go. My thoughts will track you down even as far away as Korea. It's getting late, so get my boy out and get busy because I have been waiting for it!"*

Schuyler pleased her to a great extent, as he obtained his own pleasure as she injected visional fantasies into his mind. Their fantasy sexual relationship was in a class of its own, illustrating how a geographical-separated couple fashioned sensual engagement.

As Schuyler awaited his brother's arrival the next day, he performed routine tasks such as his father's yard work to avoid stress from the anticipation. By cutting the grass and edging the sidewalks, he shunned fearful anxiety of his brother's visit. Because he knew his brother would know extensive information about Korea, and he might discover facts he didn't wish to know concerning the peninsula.

Later that evening, Duncan arrived home with news of his own. He had been selected to take part in a deployment comprising of a six-month tour in the Balkans. The exact location was unknown, due to security reasons, but he would be at that general vicinity for 180 days. This type of deployment meant greater responsibility as a soldier, earning even more respect from his younger brother.

At conclusion of Duncan's informative briefing, the father inquired profusely about Schuyler's Korean deployment. "Tell me son, what is the current situation over in Korea?"

Duncan immediately attracted attention. "To the best of my knowledge, the Korean peninsula is still an ongoing ceasefire. It is occupied by a joint command with Korean Army augments establishing a freedom guardian with adjacent support from forces stationed in Japan and Hawaii."

"Yes, but is it safe for Schuyler?" asked the father.

Duncan smiled, "he'll be in good hands." He directed even more attention to his father. "Dad, the Army takes care of its own. He'll be just as safe there as he would be if he was living in a college dorm."

The father accepted Duncan's word because he was a seasoned soldier with vast knowledge of the Army. In a way Duncan had put his worrisome father in his place, because he knew his brother had to choose his life and he had chosen a life of being a soldier. Duncan knew, from past experiences, his brother was ready for deployment due to the fact he viewed him all through his initial-entry training.

As Duncan addressed both his father and brother, "Schuyler's a quality leader, incorporating numerous traits melding together, that attests his ability to direct and manage subordinates at decentralized levels."

Schuyler was flattered by Duncan's laudatory remarks. "I expected to be working in a pharmacy when I get there; I don't expect much of a management position."

"Don't sell yourself short, I know your potential," responded Duncan as he began forging for food in his mother's refrigerator.

Schuyler joined his search for food, cutting short the conversation, progressing into a more social environment in allowance of relaxing family intervention.

Acknowledging the Army language placed stress upon the father, the two sons quickly got involved in the baseball game on television. In fact, the game engaged the Cubs battling a rival early in the season.

His vacation time, prior to flying to Korea, was spent graciously among several activities such as golf, leisure time with his father, and lending a hand to his mother around the house. He stayed relatively busy, but he ensured to stay in faithful touch with Julie. Even though she was completing her spring semester of school, she entertained him virtually throughout the day. Becoming a nightly ritual, she sexually fantasized with him guaranteeing satisfaction.

At the Jupiter, Morrison and Boyd both hailed their soldier subject. They were much impressed with his Army pharmacy tech school success, projecting greater returns in the future.

Morrison praised the Army! "The service has done him well, providing him the tools to succeed on his own."

"His progress is well above expected," agreed Boyd.

Morrison opened a fresh carton of vanilla ice cream in lieu of brewing another pot of coffee. Currently, he was on the ice cream habit and primed to indulge. "I'm still worried about Korea. I know his brother was pretty convincing, but having The Air on foreign ground worries me."

"It will be quite a battlefield challenge!" Boyd remarked as he put a little bit of Morrison's ice cream on his slice of hot pizza. "That's the chance we have to take!"

Morrison began remembering his Korean trip. "You know, being in Korea is more dangerous than you think!"

"What do you mean?" asked Boyd.

As he smiled, "there is more in Korea than just the military."

A worried Boyd agreed, "I wonder how the girl will behave when temptation strikes The Vision?"

As Morrison consumed the rest of his ice cream, "I guess we will just have to strategize it as a threat."

The Morrison and Boyd tandem proclaimed the Korean assignment presented much more threats than stateside counterparts. Even at low risk, an overseas assignment manufactured threats not apparent stateside. The language barrier alone, not to mention enemy menace, elevates any threat level. On the other side of the coin, his overseas assignment presented mammoth opportunities expanding horizons for The Air. His growth and maturity could extend extensively from the host country's cultural aspects. They concluded the opportunities outweighed the threats, furthering adulthood transformation while advancing as a soldier. Identifiable strengths and weaknesses remained relatively constant during military transitions, but opportunities and threats reaped quantities of potential outcomes.

As Morrison and Boyd pondered thoughts of achieving success in their research, actuality was about to come about because very soon PV2 Schuyler Ballantine was about to board a large airplane and fly to a foreign land called Korea.

His parents provided him with a bit of farewell prior to reporting for overseas duty. Brother Duncan was unavailable due to a field training exercise, but his father did take him to the racetrack, wagering their luck on the horses.

In their state, it was almost a national pastime to frequently experience horseracing attractions and the racetrack deemed appropriate since it facilitated entertainment not available in Korea.

Schuyler had an enjoyable day, wagering with his father, in anticipation of a winning long shot. They faired well that day, breaking about even, challenging their horse betting knowledge amongst the rest of the crowd.

At conclusion of his eventful vacation, his parents drove him to the airport to embark upon a very extensive airplane ride that would last almost an entire day. Even with the long flight, the most difficult task involved his luggage dilemma due to his military clothing requirement.

Once aboard the plane, after a long wait at the check-in station, he soon got very relaxed. Since it was an international flight, he was afforded the opportunity to drink alcoholic beverages. After indulging in a couple of beers, he was coaxed asleep by a soothing sound of a sexy Louisiana accent. The frequent dozing shortened the trip, alleviating a lot of tension of the enduring flight.

Landing at the international airport in Seoul, he was rounded up by the military liaison and channeled through customs along with other military travelers. Again, his most troublesome venture was the awkward transportation of his luggage.

Before he could even attempt to call home to the states, he was on the bus heading for the Army hotel with an ensuing date with the Army replacement center the very next morning.

At the replacement center, he was indoctrinated into Korea's sector of the United States Army by the liaisons assigned to the replacement center. By the end of the day, suffering from weary jet lag, he learned of his assignment at Seoul's Community Hospital, located on the same camp as the replacement center. What luck! He would be afforded the opportunity to live and work on the largest camp in all of Korea, the home of the Commanding Officer of United States Forces Korea. Obviously, this was a prestigious assignment and Schuyler was going to make the best of it.

"The city is beautiful; the high-rise buildings reach for the sky. You will stay busy here, I assure you." Julie reinforced any doubt in his weary mind. She seemed to be more excited about Korea than he was. Having her telepathic companion in the Army stationed in Seoul, conceptualized herself being there also.

He informed her of his intimidation of being unfamiliar with the language, along with the huge population contained in such a massive city.

"When will you start working at the hospital?" she asked, as she was currently finishing up the last month of second semester.

As he was being integrated into the camp, he suggested a time span of two or three weeks until he actually started working full time in the pharmacy. After he was fully indoctrinated into the unit, he was assigned to work in the inpatient pharmacy, a section designated to provide direct patient care to hospital wards. With this assignment, his sergeant had placed much individual responsibility upon the shoulders of his newly assigned private. Schuyler would be given every opportunity to grow and develop as a pharmacy technician.

During his unit integration, Schuyler had been introduced to the unit's NBC NCO, SGT Canini. The sergeant persuaded Schuyler to work with him on the NBC team, assisting in the preparation, teaching, and evaluation of unit-level NBC readiness training. It sounded like a good opportunity, acquiring additional skills that enhanced combat readiness. The NBC team usually met one or two Saturdays a month, maintaining proficiency in skills and abilities in preparation for instruction during scheduled NBC training.

To a surprise, he had located an old acquaintance while he was enjoying breakfast in the dining facility. Michael, from basic training, was also assigned at the hospital but as a dietary food service specialist. They had never crossed paths during advanced individual training, but through seemingly a stroke of luck were assigned as permanent party at the same unit.

Julie was anxious to learn about his living quarters. *"Schuyler, where are you going to permanently live?"*

Sitting at the breakfast table, he suggested he needed to return back to the billeting NCO and inquire about his permanent room. At the moment, he had been living in a transient room with two other soldiers.

"Try to get a single room so we can still be together!"

He affirmed her inquiry.

Her anxiety level began to grow because she wanted very much to be afforded privacy with Schuyler alone in his room.

By close of business, Schuyler had reported to the billeting sergeant to inquire about his future living conditions. "Sergeant, I'm Private Ballantine requesting my room assignment."

The billeting sergeant was in his office with SGT Canini, the NBC NCO. The billeting sergeant asked, "soldier, how long have you been in the transient room?"

"Sergeant, I have stayed four nights in the transient room," replied Schuyler.

The billeting sergeant carefully examined his room listing. "All I have opened are one-man rooms." He looked back and forth at SGT Canini and PV2 Ballantine. "I normally provide my more senior soldiers the opportunity of the single rooms."

Julie cut in on the conversation, *"SGT Canini do what you can to hook him up with a single room please!"*

Immediately, SGT Canini responded, "Private Ballantine is with my NBC team." He paused for a moment, "good potential for advancement and highly recommend providing him with a one-man room."

The billeting sergeant paused, stared into space for a while, and assigned Schuyler a one-man room. "Private Ballantine, you'll get your single room immediately but only from the recommendation of SGT Canini, one of the highest-speed NCOs we have in the entire command.

Julie aired screams of joy heard around the world as she graciously thanked SGT Canini.

Growing so excited, her excitement pulsated the heart of Schuyler causing him to nervously blink his eyes rapidly as he sat in the billeting sergeant's office awaiting issuance of keys to his new room, a room to be worshiped by the telepathic couple for months to come.

After Schuyler secured his keys to his private, single room, Julie offered her opinion of his living conditions. *"Sugar, I can't wait to get you alone tonight. I want to see it!"*

He promised her of his intentions to do even more tonight than just let her see it; then pursued to move his belongings into his room, a room he could claim his very own, or at least for now.

Schuyler was pretty much fixed in one place for a while. He had landed a job in the pharmacy working as an inpatient pharmacy technician, introduced into the unit's NBC team, and secured a one-man room in the barracks. Yes, he firmly situated himself as a permanent party soldier on the most prominent camp of the entire peninsula.

Chapter 13

Schuyler was settled a little bit in the Korean environmental setting. SGT Canini, a fine looking man at age 25, quickly became his mentor. He possessed a charisma that seemed to overpower his adversaries, managing to be influential both on-duty and off-duty. His ability to charm the ladies was quickly noticed by Julie, generating a bit of worrisome jealously she couldn't repel.

After completing her second semester of school with outstanding grades, Julie was granted during the summer break a fully paid trip to New York to attend a private drama school. The school entailed individual instruction enhancing students' acting knowledge and techniques. Her drama curriculum consisted of a six-week term, worth six semester hours of college credit, offered for three successive summers enhancing her core curriculum as a drama major at South Eastern State.

Julie had matured also over the past year, developing into a very attractive woman. Her soft, blonde hair complimented her healthy, vigorous frame proliferating her appearance as an eye-catching female athlete. Besides being nearly a straight A student, she was "easy on the eyes" in such she was very desirable to look upon. Often, she would attempt to visualize herself to Schuyler in such a manner she would telepathically display her image into his mind, familiarizing him with her actual physical representation.

Excited about her news of her drama scholarship, she immediately notified Schuyler. *"Guess what dear? I have been granted a full scholarship to attend drama school in New York for six weeks of the summer."*

That's great! How did you manage that?

"My coordinator in the drama department got me in!"

You got the hook-up?

"Kind of, I guess playing basketball helped."

Will it affect your basketball?

"No, the coach said that it would not affect it at all and to take advantage of any extra funding that would progress my acting career."

Your coach sounds like a good woman.

"Actually she's a real bitch, but extremely fair and impartial. She has high optimism of winning the league tournament and advancing to the National Tournament in the near future."

As Schuyler grasped all this newly discovered information, he congratulated her on the scholarship and wished her the best of luck in both her drama endeavors and basketball future.

Thus as Schuyler spent his summer dodging either hot, muggy climate or rain cultivated from the monsoon season, Julie would be full of activity at drama school as a promising actress. Julie's most distinctive concern entailed not her drama pursuit, but to keep her telepathic lover dedicated to her. An apprehensive undertaking that agonized her continuously as she followed her enchanted boyfriend throughout the uncertainty of the lifestyle of an Army soldier stationed in Seoul, within artillery-range of communist neighbors just north of the DMZ.

At the Jupiter, Morrison and Boyd analyzed The Air's current situation. They updated their strategy scorecard instilling imperative concerns for probable threats throughout the Korean peninsula.

"I have been to Seoul. I assure you that his safety will be in jeopardy his entire time in country," discussed Morrison.

Boyd was bothered also with the unknown. Seoul was a big city, encompassing a wide spectrum of multi-national inhabitants located within The Vision's vicinity. "I see The Vision being exposed to their culture a great deal. This publicity may be positive enriching his characteristic traits, or may be negative permitting display to unfriendly opportunists."

As Morrison charted The Air's progress, he allocated some excess room on his scorecard for future evaluation. "I feel his social integration should escalate, publicizing his air phenomena throughout abundant communicative sources."

Boyd added input to his strategy scorecard. "The more people he makes contact with, the more additional airing we recognize. Already when he walks along the streets, strangers are anxious to air responses to him."

"Good observation, a prominent measuring tool to track air phenomena would be to actually determine the amount of individuals that air responses to The Air compared to those who completely ignore his phenomena and continue with their normal lives." Morrison projected a possible case analysis to Boyd for future study.

"Yes, I have noticed a gradual increase in air activity. Some how I need to measure the amount of air activity increase and its affect upon The Vision himself." Boyd sighed a big relief, in acknowledgement of a huge task ahead.

Morrison agreed with his partner. "The proliferation of air phenomena is your objective to be annotated on our strategy scorecard."

"Will it be a threat or opportunity?" asked Boyd

"Hopefully it will be an opportunity for society to grow and understand The Air's phenomena is truly an asset in today's world, shining light throughout American interest at home and abroad." Morrison summarized his analysis by vowing to accept The Air as his own self, instead of just a subject of his research work.

Morrison and Boyd were proud of their work, publishing data concerning The Air's revolution. Even with the dangers of foreign intervention, especially in Korea, the military served as an excellent medium for advancement of Schuyler's unique characteristic trait labeled air phenomena.

With Julie off at drama school, Schuyler was familiarizing himself to routine Army life. The two training phases, prior to coming to Korea, were completing different situations. Unlike tedious training environments of the past, he was a part of set regimes such as pharmacy duties, physical fitness training, guard duties, and bus transportation schedules. His life was pretty much set for him by his leaders. They told him where to be, what to wear, and what to do. He learned very quickly soldiers are no better than the leaders who direct them. Fortunately for him, he was provided some of the best leadership available; efforts committed by the Commanding General vastly strengthened quality of life issues not just in the Seoul Community, but also throughout the entire peninsula.

Schuyler was well versed in spectrums such as pharmacy skills and physical fitness. He had little problem manufacturing sterile products or passing an Army Physical Fitness Test. Even performing guard duties, provided little mental challenge. His sergeant approached him with a concept of challenging the soldier of the month board. This board consisted of an oral presentation, with structure of military questions, self-improvement, military bearing, and appearance. The sergeant provided him with a little booklet, called a promotion board study guide. The same as soldier of month boards, a soldier was required to appear before an oral board in order to be promoted to the rank of sergeant. Thus, good preparation for the promotion board was to make an appearance before soldier of the month boards.

Schuyler's immediate supervisor was Staff Sergeant Bishop, a sergeant in charge of the inpatient pharmacy, who noticed potential in PV2 Ballantine. SSG Bishop, an assertive leader who tried to obtain as much progressive out of his soldiers as he could, selected Schuyler as a candidate for soldier of the month.

SSG Bishop directed PV2 Ballantine to report to his office. "PV2 Ballantine, I have two objectives for you. First, you will be my next candidate for soldier of the month and second, you will be competing next month as a Private First Class."

Standing at parade rest, "Sergeant does that mean I'm getting promoted to Private First Class next month?" Schuyler asked the sergeant in an astonished voice.

SSG Bishop put him at ease, and sat him down in a chair immediately in front of his desk. "Yes, you will be pinning on PFC (E-3) rank on the first of the ensuing month."

"Thank you sergeant, I will do well on the soldier of the month board," promised Schuyler who didn't really know what a soldier of the month board was. "Uh sergeant, what do I use to study for this board?"

Schuyler's sergeant then went into great detail about the board process and issued him an official unit promotion study guide. Schuyler was ready to obtain board knowledge, a requirement for advancement in the Army.

The soldier of the month board puzzled him, generating numerous questions requiring answers, directing him to SGT Canini for advice.

SGT Canini was about to secure his shop, after a long, lengthy week, in route to his hooch. "Private Ballantine, you need help with your board?"

"Yes SGT C, my board will be next month. I'm getting promoted to Private First Class and will be appearing before the board."

"Meet me at the lodge in about an hour and we'll eat at the Italian restaurant." As SGT C logged himself out on the security form of his door. "My treat!"

"I'll be ready." Schuyler hurried onto the bus back to the billets in preparation of his meeting with SGT C.

The lodge was an enormous hotel featuring several restaurants, a bar, a gym, and a swimming pool. SGT C loved to eat at the Italian restaurant there, a popular place on Friday evenings.

Schuyler, nervously, walked into the lodge in pursuit of the Italian restaurant. Maneuvering through the crowd, he eventually located SGT C in front of the restaurant.

"Are you ready to eat?" SGT C directed his guest in through the door.

Schuyler told his mentor he was grateful for the invitation and any assistance he could provide concerning board preparation.

As they ate their fettuccini and clam sauce, SGT C diagnosed board procedures to an attentive Schuyler. Stressing reporting procedures, clarity of voice, along with addressing the board members properly highlighted his overview of board proceedings. Of course, he explained the subject areas for study expanding on the need to study an hour per day progressively learning board material to obtain maximized effect.

After dinner, SGT C planned to take him off post to the Korean club scene. Julie felt threatened due to Schuyler being invited to go off post with the sergeant. *"Schuyler, don't you go out with him! You'll meet Korean girls and me something might happen."*

Schuyler did not know what to say to her. He hesitated for a moment, he tried to convince her of SGT C's good influence and he helped him get his single room and also knew a lot about board proceedings.

"Don't even try it, I can read your mind and anticipate every more you make, I don't trust you downtown with him." Julie tried her best to prevent him to associate with the sergeant, persuading him to not go to the Korean clubs.

Schuyler's heart rate increased, his mouth became dry, and he tried again to convince her of the need to affirm his invitation from the sergeant. He begged for her to allow him to go downtown.

She finally allowed him to go, *"OK, you can go but be careful and remember that even if I'm here in the states, I still watching you!"*

He gratefully thanked her for beholding trust in him, but then he thought again at the situation, he really did not know what to expect. What would he do; what would he say if approached by a Korean, or American, girl?

Later, SGT C and Schuyler ventured downtown to SGT C's favorite dancing spot. He was an avid dancer, attracting much attention throughout the female persuasion at the club. He had the knack of getting the girls out on the dance floor, influencing them to initiate activity. Often he would have two or three girls dancing with him at a time, publishing opportunities for his cohorts.

After a short while as SGT C was busy entertaining a past acquaintance, a Korean girl named Suk persuaded Schuyler to dance with her. She was a tall, mature woman with long black hair who seemed to have interest in Schuyler.

Speechless, he tried to avoid dancing but she relentlessly overcame his avoidance, and soon they were on the dance floor together.

"Schuyler, why are you dancing with her? You leave now!" An angry Julie demanded. She became very jealous, asserting her stipulations upon him.

He tried to ignore her, but ultimately pleaded with her to let him be. His plea struck her silence, calming all air transmission between them. He continued to dance with Suk, but could only focus on the fact his fantasy girl had separated. His air phenomenon was preventing him from having female companionship, becoming a hindrance instead of assistance. His dancing partner continued to show interest, but his heart was stymied as he felt the disappointment of losing transmission with Julie Crystal.

Noticing Schuyler's problem with his telepathic girlfriend, SGT C prevented any further damage to the situation.

He ensured Schuyler made it home safely, without any ensuing tribulations from Suk also, as he carefully communicated with their female companions for a later encounter at the club.

With Julie continuing to be silent, Schuyler began studying for his soldier of the month board. As SGT C directed, he ensured to study one complete hour each day too slowly, but surely, encompass all testable material. He felt uneasy; he was neither sad nor happy. His anxiety level remained unchanged; he exhibited little motivation and presented a bleak, bland appearance. Although he still performed at work, his social activity participation declined a great deal identifying specific desired social needs. Schuyler did go to the Korean club with SGT C a few times within the following month, prior to his board, but in respect for his former, but not forgotten girlfriend Julie, he never initiated any sexual activity with his Korean girlfriend.

Back in the states at The Jupiter, Don Morrison summarized his Korean descriptive analysis. "I feel good about his progress. The sergeant has provided The Air the necessary exposure and protection required to supplement my research."

"Wait a couple of minutes Don, I have to go outside for a minute," noted Boyd. Returning back from tipping the Big K pizza deliveryman, John Boyd immediately scanned his data as he anxiously prepared a pizza slice for both him and his partner. "The sergeant has provided good, solid leadership for The Vision, but without the girl he will never reach his full potential."

Accepting his pizza slice and stirring a hot cup of coffee, Morrison ignored the comment about the girl by changing the subject. "How is your process analysis coming along with air transmission frequency?"

Boyd quickly finished chewing his slice, swallowing it almost whole. He uploaded his data and briefed his partner. "Air transmission has actually decreased in the past month probably due to the girl ignoring The Vision."

Morrison's face appeared worried as he checked Boyd's data himself. He shook his head in disbelief, questioning the consequence of the girl's affect on total overall air transmission. "What if the girl doesn't come back to him? Then what?"

"We have to keep the faith that her emotional love is absolute and will generate a continuing relationship with The Vision." Boyd looked at his partner for accepting agreement.

Morrison placed his coffee mug down on his desk, walked over to the window, and peered out toward the sky. "I guess we are to accept the girl as a significant piece to our puzzle in proliferating air transmission throughout American interest in the world."

The days progressed swiftly, with still no response from Julie, advancing closer and closer to Schuyler's big date with the soldier of the month board. It was late summer, nearing Labor Day, and he knew his lost love was due to be back at college. He longed to hear her Louisiana accent serenading him at night, along with her presence caressing his body with her sensual touch, as he suffered immensely from her abrupt dismissal from his life.

Even with board preparation assistance from SGT Canini, PFC Ballantine suffered an astounding defeat. Out of five candidates, he finished a disappointing fourth place.

He did well with his reporting procedures and addressing the board members properly, but lacked bold voice inflection when responding to the board members' questions. Also he missed several questions, forgetting much of the material due to nervousness. He vowed to appear again before the board, seeking improvement, attempting to be recognized as a quality soldier not only within his department, but also throughout his command.

After a dismal board appearance, Schuyler sought advice from both SSG Bishop and SGT Canini. But his most cherished advice came from an old acquaintance; a secret personal confidant rendered her own counsel.

"Schuyler, I've been watching you the past month and I want to go back to being your friend." Julie offered to get back together with Schuyler. Beginning her second year of college, she quickly felt a desire to rekindle the fire.

Schuyler was blissful to hear from his past girlfriend. His heart froze for a moment and then began to pound fiercely, he tried to respond back to Julie but so many thoughts rushed into his mind he could not formulate an appropriate response.

"That's OK; I understand your feelings toward me. Just your heartbeat alone transmits your mind-set." Julie acknowledged his confused way of thinking, telegraphing signals of good intent.

His mind finally settled from the enormous intensity derived from her air transmission. Luckily, it was after duty hours and he was alone in his room. He inquired of her if she was ready to commence fantasizing with him.

She encouraged him to appear naked in front of a mirror in allowance of her to observe what she had been missing for quite some time.

Her self-established punishment specified he would engage into self-indulgence, as she would be forced to only observe, with no telepathic interaction.

She anxiously gazed at her lover as his stimulation aroused her sexuality. She hastily joined him, being a spectator was not sufficient. *"Sugar, I'm initiating fantasy sexual activity because I can't take it any longer!"* She knew how to get inside his mind and to provide her lover with sexual fantasies that no man could resist. Her imaginary connotations of sexual nature amplified his sensual desire from her presence as his lover.

As she telepathically performed for him, he cried joyfully in dispositions of ecstasy as her mental telepathy conquered any sexual desire imaginable. As she could stimulate his inner mind, he could provide his own sexual arousal with his telepathic stimulus. His air phenomena, uncannily, induced a magnifying affect on his telepathic sexual performance activating sensory impulses in his partner's mind never manipulated before. Their togetherness was indifferent than any other romance, integrating mystical interactions of unknown prior occurrence.

Julie was full of activity at college. She, in her sophomore year, balanced her schoolwork with her basketball career. Coach Jackson had high expectations of the upcoming season, utilizing her amongst the other four of The Fresh Five indoctrinating a paradigm shift in the school's basketball program. Excelling in the classroom, she maintained almost straight A's in rapid pursuit of her degree in drama and her New York performing arts school had already provided a good foundation in that direction.

Interested in her summer school, he inquired of her trials and tribulations in the big city.

"Being from a small southern town, I was shell-shocked from the traffic alone. Taxi cabs everywhere, people parading down walkways, and all the high-rise buildings."

Sounds a lot like Seoul!

"Yes, it is very similar except New Yorkers speak English!"

How was your drama school?

"I met a lot of talented people there, strengthening my theatrical forte from specialized instruction." She explained to him of her willingness to give up her summer vacations in return for a chance of acquiring a promising calling.

Satisfied with her progress as a student athlete, Schuyler wondered how he could improve himself as well. He admired her in such a way he knew in reality he didn't measure up to her potential, but still felt he could contribute something in her behalf.

For the next few weeks, he sought guidance in self-development. Between his pharmacy sergeant and the NBC team's sergeant, he gathered some feedback to develop a strategic plan.

During a meeting for the NBC team, SGT Canini instructed PFC Ballantine to communicate with him after close of business. "PFC Ballantine, I have my bowling league tonight. Meet me at the bowling alley in a few hours and we'll outline your self-development plan."

"Yes SGT C, will comply," replied Schuyler.

Schuyler owed a lot to SGT C, his mentor, but most of all he could always count on him to solve any occurring problem. He was a valuable asset to any element, guaranteeing clear-cut guidance that instilled disciple, integrity, and justice characteristics in all subordinates he influenced. It was indeed a privilege to be granted his leadership. Every soldier should be afforded eminent supervision; also all soldiers require a compassionate leader who understands his job, his soldiers, and human nature. Indeed, SGT Canini fit that specific mold as a leader.

At the bowling alley, SGT C was a superb bowler carrying a 170 average. He loved to talk about his bowling art, especially to the ladies. Undeniably, he was a show of his own. Between his bowling acrobatics and his female persuasion, he was very a difficult person to get a chance to speak with. Schuyler at times seemed to be waiting in line, holding a number, in anticipation of his attention.

Between games SGT C approached him, informing him of change of plans. "Hey, we're going to the club after bowling."

Schuyler, worried about what Julie might think, acknowledged going to the club after bowling ended. He really didn't know what to expect, but he did fear SGT C's mentorship and Julie telepathic relationship would surely collide creating an ethical dilemma affecting two of his most strongly held values.

"You are not going to the club!" demanded an angry Julie.

Schuyler didn't know what to say in return, excessive anxiety prohibited the formulation of an appropriate response, signaling confusion between the telepathic couple.

"Are you going with them, or staying with me?" Questioned a distressed Julie Crystal.

Schuyler promised her that even if he went with SGT C to whatever club he was going to; he would be on his best behavior requesting an opportunity to prove his loyalty to her.

Relentlessly, she eventually gave into his offer. She couldn't interfere with his appointment with SGT Canini; she accepted that social integration was a common occurrence and her boyfriend really needed social activity.

Schuyler, along with SGT C and his cronies, walked over to the NCO Club for the rest of the evening. Dancing only sparingly, Schuyler stayed occupied consolidating ideas for his strategic plan. SGT C offered excellent advice, and his girlfriends were very informative also, as Schuyler composed a listing of objectives to enhance self-development. At the head of his list, five main objectives tallying college, soldier of the month, physical fitness, NBC competency, and pharmacy technician progression endorsed areas of concentration, escalating self-improvement.

At the club's close of business, as they exited the building; Stacey, a female acquaintance, provided Schuyler with a very sexy goodbye kiss. She was a private first class who worked in the unit's mailroom; her blonde hair and blue eyes captivated his attention as she embraced his warm body transmitting a tingling sensation down his spine. He enjoyed her company a lot, but was extremely satisfied when she opted to return to her own quarters, instead of his.

As expected Julie was silent until the next day, she eventually responded to him, but very gingerly. *"Schuyler, that Stacey girl might be right for you. Treat her with respect, but don't pursue too far."*

A little shocked, Schuyler acknowledged her transmission and replied to her of their relationship being only as friends.

Uniquely, Julie dreamed a vision of herself making an expression on her face informing him of his last comment being not even close to being believable. She had developed a way to dream her image into Schuyler's mind, allowing him to visualize her physical appearance.

As time passed, they settled their differences. But a verifiable fact arose from the incident; Schuyler could never hide any romantic tendencies from his Louisiana comrade, even half way around the world. Private First Class Ballantine survived his initial six months in Korea. Progressively he achieved at work well above expectations, his pharmacy sergeant encouraged him to extend his overseas tour for another year. Staying in Korea was a big decision for Schuyler; he consulted advice from SGT Canini, Brother Duncan, and his parents.

SGT C suggested an extension would benefit both Schuyler and his organization. He would be allowed to continue college at the same school, challenge the soldier of the month board, and work with him on the NBC team.

Duncan supported staying in Korea for his entire enlistment. According to Duncan, if Schuyler was doing well at this duty station then he should stay there as long as he could. Especially if he has a lot of career-enhancing possibilities, then he should capitalize on them as great as possible.

Schuyler's parents were a little leery about having their youngest son live in Seoul for a little over two years, but an extension would render an incentive of additional thirty days of earned leave. Thus, Schuyler could come home for whole month without using his regular leave.

Even with encouraging support from SGT C, Duncan, and parents, his ultimate counsel came from Julie Crystal Flowers. *"Schuyler, if you stay there in Korea then you can stay in your own room. Get it?"*

Well, it didn't take much more than her suggestive influence to convince him to apply for extension. True, Korea offered everything he could want, but what he really wanted was to extend his relationship with Julie. And if a tour extension could assist in sustaining a romantic relationship with his dream girl, then he would put up a strong fight to stay in Korea and keep his private room.

As the months rolled along, Schuyler was getting pretty close to his next promotion. As a PFC, he was still junior to almost every enlisted soldier in the hospital. Michael and he were both at the bottom of their respective totem poles, but with promising potential. To surprise, both of them were due to take the Army Physical Fitness Test the preceding week of their advancements to the rank of Specialist.

As springtime was about to cross over to summer, Julie had completed her second basketball season in grand fashion. Her playing time had doubled since her freshman year, surpassing not just her expectations, but the coach's also. She quickly became a vital asset off the bench, contributing to newfound maturity of The Fresh Five. Julie and her partners off the bench energized the team to several victories during the season. Contributions from The Fresh Five, providing necessary vigor during critical situations, propelled South Eastern State to the Conference's Championship Game for the second year in a row, experiencing defeat in similar fashion. Again, Coach Jackson had to accept second place, no trip to the National Tournament, and prepare for next season. But the savory, dynamic motivator as she was, the team knew that their championship was near.

As Julie was progressing at college, both Schuyler and Michael were moving along in the service also. With two years of service almost under their belts, their military careers would be coming to conclusion sooner than expected.

The morning of the Army Physical Fitness Test, fallen dew and darkness staged the physical training test. Both Michael and Schuyler had been running together enhancing their cardio-respiratory endurance. Training in push-ups, developing muscle strength, and sit-ups, developing muscular endurance, prepared them for the physical training test as well as running.

Testing always began with the push-up event, followed by sit-ups, and closing with a two-mile run. Schuyler endured both the push-up event and sit-ups with ease; Michael struggled a little bit, but successfully passed both of the events.

Waiting to run the two-miler, Schuyler dressed in his Army physical fitness uniform met with Michael. "How do you think you'll do?"

Michael was a little winded from the other two events. "I'll do well enough to pass, don't worry about me."

The participating soldiers assembled along the starting line and started running on the command of "go". Schuyler's pace was well within range, but as he was running he noticed a concern voice.

Julie, being well versed with the event's competitiveness, inquired of Michael's status. *"Schuyler, I know you are doing well, but what about Michael?"*

Schuyler suddenly turned his head, searching for Michael, ultimately spotting him in the back of a large pack of runners displaying visual image of his status to Julie.

"He looks like he's hurting!"

Julie, how can you tell?

Julie informed him of her feeling that he might have trouble during the run and was worried about him.

Finishing the run with a comfortable time, Schuyler assertively hunted for Michael's location on the track. After a few seconds, he spotted Michael's position on the track.

"He looks like he needs help; go run with him!" With fright, she beckoned Schuyler's response.

In a short second, he dashed to his aid providing moral support. As he ran aside Michael, he offered encouragement to energize Michael's performance. As Julie cheered them along via air transmission, Schuyler called cadence in Michael's behalf throughout the remainder of the run. Exhausted from the grueling event, Michael gleamed with joy as he received his qualifying time. With the aid of Schuyler and his telepathic companion, Michael had successfully passed the two-mile run. Thus, both of them would be getting promoted together the proceeding week.

Promotion day was just around the corner, and Schuyler was preparing himself for the ceremonial event. A starched uniform, spit-shined boots and a good haircut were ordered for his promotion ceremony. A memorable experience, as expected, highlighted the day as both Schuyler and Michael were pinned the rank of Specialist.

During the reading of the promotion orders, Julie had a question concerning his new rank. *"So Schuyler, what is the difference between Specialist and Corporal?"*

Getting ready to be pinned by his commanding officer, Schuyler explained to her that a Specialist shares the same pay grade as a Corporal, but lacks NCO duties and responsibilities. Thus a Corporal belongs to the NCO Corps, earning a greater degree of precedence in the NCO Support Channel.

A reception followed a triumphant ceremony, congratulations from individuals ranging from Private to Colonel, including SGT Canini, SSG Bishop, First Sergeant, Company Commander, and the Hospital Commander concluded an event to be archived in lasting memories of both Schuyler and Michael. Because if neither re-enlisted in the Army, it would surely be their last promotion.

Schuyler's first objective as a newly promoted specialist was to challenge the Soldier of the Month Board, demonstrating his worthiness in his new pay grade. In preparation for the board, Julie and he diagnosed achievable objectives focusing on subject-area board material.

Julie was way ahead of the game. She had a certain plan of action for this next board. *"Schuyler, I want you to read all of the probable questions to me so I can write them down with their corresponding answers."*

Why?

"I know that it will take a long tine, but if I have a majority of the answers in my possession than you can always rely on my assistance during board procedures. Get it?"

Schuyler thought about it for a short while. He finally figured it out that if Julie could give him the answers on the board then he could answer almost every available question. In realization of the golden opportunity, they hurriedly began outlining testable subject areas.

Ensuring clarity, she logged all data into her computer as he provided it. Her organizational skills were put to use because her assembly of notes now would pay great dividends in the future. Time being a critical factor during board procedures; Julie needed to be organized to transmit necessary information in a timely manner. Together, calculated tactics were assembled suddenly via air phenomena.

The table was being set for Schuyler to surmount board material reaction, exemplifying measures designed to maximize all available resources in pursuit of the best board performance possible. Indeed, it would take very shrewd coordination to launch SPC Ballantine as reigning soldier of the month.

Growth as a soldier of month candidate developed, as he participated in coinciding battle-focus training. As the NBC team structured lane training, enhancing soldier readiness, SGT C decentralized evaluation of individualized tasks upon two-man teams. As a valuable member of the NBC team, Schuyler responded accordingly to SGT C's command decisions equipping his evaluating partner with subject-matter expertise. He too was very knowledgeable on specific NBC aspects, complimenting his partner suitably as lane training reached top speed.

NBC proficiency, an essential element in combat survival, polished soldiers' capability to attain victory on the battlefield and SGT C was a master at integrating multiple tasks into lane training. He devised a way to amalgamate NBC training with land navigation. Lane training would require soldiers to navigate unfamiliar terrain, utilizing dead reckoning and terrain association, in route to locate plotted points on a topographical map. Thus, the soldiers would have to first use map reading and land navigation skills in order to find NBC stations for further evaluation.

Schuyler was a little rusty on his navigational skills. "SGT C, how can I locate my position if I get lost?"

"By use of resection, a position can be discovered by virtue of shooting two or more azimuths upon known targets and then computing back azimuths from respective targets." SGT Canini attempted to explain the concept of resection to SPC Ballantine.

"SGT C, how do you compute back azimuths?" Schuyler looked at SGT C with a puzzled look on his face.

The sergeant removed a compass from his pocket, referring to it as a training aid, and showed Schuyler how a complete compass rotation consisted of 360 degrees. "A back azimuth is a 180 degree opposite direction of the actual azimuth. Thus, if an azimuth was 180 degrees, then its back azimuth would be zero."

Schuyler received the compass from SGT C, pointed it at Seoul Tower, and noted the correct azimuth. After noting the azimuth from the tallest point in the city of Seoul, he figured 180 degrees in the opposite direction attaining a correct back azimuth. "SGT C, is this correct?"

The sergeant checked his calculations, nodded his head in agreement, and responded to his prize student. "Affirmative, you are a go at this station. The ability of performing resection may save your life some day!"

An impressed SPC Ballantine, but astonished from all of the dramatics, acknowledged his mentor. "Most affirmed, maybe I will get one of those Army watches with the compass built into it?"

The sergeant saluted his suggestion. "Sounds like a soldier prepared to go to combat and return home victorious."

When the sergeant talked like that, it made Schuyler want to go grab a weapon and start shooting the enemy! Even though Schuyler worked as a garrison pharmacy technician, he still was responsible for some type of combat readiness. With SGT C as his mentor, he would have no problem being a motivated, highly dedicated, Army soldier fit to fight the enemy at any front.

After the lane training finally ended, Schuyler's knowledge of NBC and land navigation enhanced greatly his board material wisdom illustrating the importance of mentor expertise in The United States Army.

Attending college in Korea was actually quite simple. By the means of working a lot of weekends, Schuyler had the opportunity to attend University of Maryland during weeknights in attempt to obtain as much college credit as possible prior to departing the service. A stellar student, attaining honor roll status throughout the entire period, he achieved substantial recognition from his superb efforts.

His college student endeavor, not only produced almost a full year of college credit, but also was an asset toward his military livelihood.

A strong portion of soldier of the month boards consisted of self-improvement, insinuating that off-duty college attendance was very impressive. Schuyler, in fact, did utilize his free time while in Korea to his advantage. Besides being a sterling example of a soldier, he prepared for later civilian life by accumulating a good deal of college credit during his tenure in the service.

Off-duty lifestyle was fine, making suitable use of his private single room. Besides his frequent telepathic romantic voyages, he spent a lot of quiet time with either homework or board material. Actually, his progression in the military seemed to accelerate almost daily as he continued his valiant term.

The days dashed by with every evening spent practicing for his ultimate chance at stardom, a board appearance. Julie and he were synchronizing themselves in preparation of a very eventful period of his military career. Every preliminary process, pre-combat checks as the military called it, needed to be in place prior to his board appearance.

As board day commenced, Schuyler learned of his expectation to report to the board after lunch. This was perfect timing, because the time difference between Louisiana and Seoul made it much simpler for collaboration. Thus with Schuyler competing during afternoon hours, Julie in the seclusion of her room would be stationed at her computer ready for quick responses. The plan was set, all the telepathic couple needed to do was to execute.

Dressing for the board was a chore; from carefully shaving to apply edge dressing to his low quarters, it was a very meticulous course of action. But the accurate and proper placement of appurtenances, his badges and ribbons, on his Class A uniform gave him such a problem he needed to ask SGT C for assistance.

With no haste, SGT C responded to Schuyler's request and within an hour had his Class A uniform squared-up to the max and all set for the board.

SGT C was a great asset to Schuyler's enhancement as a soldier. Besides ensuring his uniform was squared away for the board, he mentored board procedural techniques that could easily provide the necessary edge to propel Schuyler over the top, earning him definitive recognition as Hospital Soldier of the Month.

Standing nervously in the hallway, urgently waiting for his turn to report to the board's president, he mentally primed himself for his ensuing board appearance. Of course, Julie was stationed at her computer terminal with itchy fingers in great anticipation of the upcoming event.

Sweat began to formulate in his palms, the first sign of board pressure, as he was informed he would be next. As the preceding candidate exited the boardroom, Schuyler's heartbeat suddenly increased in strong anticipation. Two deliberate knocks on the door, a pronounced entrance into the room, and a straight and stalwart approach to the board's president initiated board appearance.

"First Sergeant, Specialist Ballantine reports to the president of the board as directed." Schuyler saluted the president and waited for directives. After preliminary movements, he was seated.

"Doing good so far champ, your reporting procedures were superb." Julie rendered confidence, even though she was just as, if even more, nervous than Schuyler was.

After board member introduction, he delivered a brief biography of himself stressing his college success and NBC team performance.

"I'm ready when you are ready," she anxiously awaited.

The initial sergeant asking questions introduced herself and informed Schuyler she would be asking questions pertaining current events, military programs, drill and ceremonies, and counseling.

As the sergeant asked about current events, Julie went straight to the Internet in preparation of any probable question. Schuyler ensured to hesitate a little bit before responding to allow for maximum feedback from Julie.

Luckily, the sergeant asked him to provide her with as much current media news as possible within a one-minute time span. Thus with Julie transmitting the news' headlines to him via air phenomena, Schuyler was soundly answering the sergeant's proposed question to fullest extent. Julie's information was on key as Schuyler greatly surprised the board members with his limitless current event knowledge.

"Good start; just give me about five seconds to locate an answer."

Like clockwork, when the sergeant asked a question from the unit's study guide, he proceeded to recite the book answer, in amazement to the board members. It was like he was programmed to hear the question, pause for a few seconds, and then present a book answer.

Prior to the next sergeant's questions, *"so far so good,"* as Julie kept pace with board proceedings.

The next sergeant was to ask questions on military justice, NBC, weapons, and first aid. Schuyler being an avid member of the NBC team did not need any assistance with the NBC portion. But, Julie's telepathic reference provided him enough correct answers to get him through the remainder of this sergeant's phase.

As before, her timing was critical in order to allow Schuyler ample opportunity to delivery correct responses to a huge majority of the questions.

The final sergeant to quiz SPC Ballantine was one of the toughest sergeants in the entire unit. His presence itself caused Schuyler to tremble in his chair. Even with Julie's telepathic assistance, Schuyler stumbled through the final increment of the board. With soaked palms perspiring onto the knees of his pants, a parched tongue struggled to answer questions concerning flags, military courtesy, leadership, and chain of command. It was obvious the sergeant had intimated him; even with knowledgeable responses he didn't really impress the judging council.

"Wow! That last sergeant was really scary. He even made me squirm in my chair and I'm not even there!" Julie breathed a big sigh of relief, acknowledging conclusion in a very short bit.

The board's president commended his performance, presented closing remarks, and dismissed SPC Ballantine from the board. Later, he would soon learn of his unanimously selection as soldier of the month and would compete the ensuing month for soldier of the quarter.

The board president congratulated him, "SPC Ballantine, you seem to have all the answers to our study guide memorized?"

He hesitated, and then responded to the First Sergeant. "Affirmative Top, I tried to study as much as possible."

"Keep it up soldier and you'll go far." The First Sergeant offered a reassuring pat on the back confirming Schuyler's board performance was highly regarded.

"Schuyler, why did you refer to him as Top?"

He explained to her that it was customary to call the senior enlisted person "Top" and this title is usually reserved for first sergeants. Thus, it was a compliment to be referred to as Top.

Julie happily comforted her champion, offering a lot more gratuities that what the unit offered. She had already made arrangements for the evening promising that it would be a very eventful telepathic session.

As reigning soldier of the month, he received numerous laudatory comments from the pharmacy department, the company commander, and especially SGT Canini.

A proud SGT C greeted him, patting him on the back, already strategizing for the quarter board. "SPC Ballantine, I heard you are almost unbeatable at the board and a strong favorite at the quarter board."

Indeed, SPC Schuyler Ballantine had made his mark on the command via aid from a telepathic companion named Julie Crystal Flowers; this partnership appeared to be a vital key in career progression.

CHAPTER 14

The days rolled along, his life remained the same, and Schuyler was courted almost every day to re-enlist in the Army. He was a prime candidate. In fact, he was one of the most eligible soldiers for re-enlistment in the entire command. Being soldier of the month, responsible at work, good in physical training, and a valuable member of the NBC team attracted a great deal of attention. Confused on what to actually tell the re-enlistment NCO, he attempted to avoid any contact what so ever.

Julie, his biggest confidant, was worried about the perception he was making upon his superiors from his lack of re-enlistment commitment. *"Schuyler, I love you dearly but do not leave the Army on my account. You know I want you back home, in safety, attending college."*

Yearning for home himself, he believed her message was a persuasive sign in plea of a change of lifestyle. The Army had graciously accepted him, developed his character, and transformed him from a boy to a man. In his opinion, the military had done its job; Schuyler Ballantine had been melded into not just a soldier, but also a man capable of being accountable for his actions and seeking avenues to improve not just his life, but also the lives of his subordinates. Flexible leadership, open-minded judgment, and value-based initiatives structured this newly transformed leader, publicizing the effectiveness of military service.

The basketball season had already escalated; South Eastern State was becoming a conference powerhouse. The Fresh Five was now the starting five, all but Julie. Her valuable asset was her uncanny ability to come off the bench and resuscitate the team. Her role was not as a starter, but as the team's sixth man, giving the breath of life to the team in tight situations.

It was Julie's junior year in college. With two additional performing arts internship summer sessions, she was well on her way toward graduation. Her vigor on the basketball court, measured only second to her theatrical inclination. But with basketball at full tilt, her main focus was winning a championship for Coach Jackson.

As she was away at college, she urged Schuyler to pursue his education. *"If you go back home to college, you might can come watch me play basketball."*

Enjoying the thought of actually watching her perform on the court, he pondered the notion of being a college student. But in reality, his Army days were still numerous and quickly returned focus to near-term objectives.

With the Soldier of the Quarter Board around the corner, Schuyler traded thoughts between the board and re-enlistment. Either way, SGT C's confidant status governed guidance. Dedicated to Schuyler's progression, he worked with Schuyler every day for at least one hour on board material.

During study sessions, Schuyler would pick SGT C's brain for supplementary information. "SGT C, you are an experienced NCO. What do you think about re-enlisting in the Army?" Schuyler eagerly looked upon his mentor for wisdom.

SGT Canini set the study material aside, looked at his prize soldier. "SPC Ballantine, do you want my honest opinion as a straight-shooter?"

"Yes SGT C, your judgment is of high importance." In deep anticipation, he promptly directed fullest attention to his mentor.

SGT C was a seasoned sergeant, with extensive knowledge of military operations, "I really think you should not re-enlist, and out-process the Army."

A surprised Schuyler asked, "Why?"

With mental knowledge of his telepathic ability, SGT C offered a promising alternative. "A soldier of your caliber needs not to tread water as an enlisted soldier, instead you deserve much better. I highly recommend a ROTC scholarship in pursue of a commission."

Influenced by his mentor, Schuyler immediately discovered a viable avenue of approach toward re-enlistment. Alleviated from career-decision stress, his plan to exit the Army was settled. Even if he didn't get a ROTC scholarship, he would be exiting the military on good terms providing a comfort zone in preparation for his upcoming board.

Due to his relationship with SPC Ballantine, SGT Canini had to analyze his entire perspective. Balancing performance and personal aspects, he ultimately chose to guide him in a direction for personal benefit. It was a tough decision for him; SPC Ballantine was a tremendous asset to the Army, but his personal life beckoned a return to civilian life. The definitive issue was the telepathic relationship that could possibly be tarnished with military service continuation, identifying an intangible prerequisite in sustaining this unique relationship, a relationship like no other on record.

A date with the quarter board awaited Schuyler, carefully prepared operations with Julie increased his chances of winning. They nearly had the study guide memorized between them; actually she probably could have won the board herself.

As board day came, the telepathic couple had a little altercation. With Julie's basketball game conflicting with his board occasion, he would not be afforded the luxury of her prompt assistance. Schuyler's board schedule was in the morning, coinciding with Julie's basketball game. Thus, there was no way for Julie to feed Schuyler the answers as she did before.

Schuyler waited nervously in the hallway on the morning of his board. He wished his telepathic companion much luck in her upcoming game.

Warming up prior to the game, Julie tried her best to predict when exactly Schuyler would be performing. *"Schuyler, I have a plan! Since I'm not in the starting line-up, I can help you answer a few questions by memory."*

A great idea! His confidence level soared, but he eventually realized he would be mostly on his own. In prompt timing, SGT Canini surprisingly appeared to give him reassurance.

"SGT C, how do you think I will do?"

"Relax breath in and out, carefully evaluate the question, properly address the board member, and deliver a confident answer." SGT Canini had just turned a tight situation into a promising condition.

As Schuyler wondered to himself how conveniently SGT C appeared suddenly in his behalf, he was now ready to challenge the board even if he had to do it solo. An enthusiastic soldier reported to the board that morning with derived confidence from his mentor's sudden appearance.

As suspected, this sudden appearance by SGT Canini consequently prevented much despair and anguish. Applauding Schuyler's courage, he detected a faint pat on the back; in response he turned his head in recognition, but was completely alone. Tingling sensations flowed down his spine, with emerging tears he gazed into space realizing the genuine air phenomena that was introduced into his life. Bewildered for a moment, he heard a distant Louisianan voice, *"thank you for watching over my prize possession."*

During board proceedings, Julie had started her game, as usual, on the bench. Early in the first half, with no warning, Flowers was sent into the game, replacing Wanda at the second guard position. With Schuyler in the middle of his quarter board and Julie on the hardwood, an ethical dilemma faced South Eastern State's Flowers during competitive intensity.

At the board, SPC Ballantine's performance began strong but was fading fast. Even with aggressive study preparation with SGT Canini, he often hesitated in anticipation of Julie's response.

In a heated rivalry match, Flowers' passion for the game and thrusting energy kept her team in the game. Thus she had no time to spend on Schuyler's behalf; but during a free throw attempt by teammate Brittney, she took a golden opportunity to reinforce his board performance.

During the momentary break of Brittney's two foul shots, she provided Schuyler with three straight correct answers in the current events' category. With luck, Brittney took her sweet time shooting her two free throws, allowing Julie plenty of time to assist Schuyler with his current events.

After board dismal, he gratefully thanked her for her input. Her current event knowledge, increasing his board performance, projected him victoriously at conclusion of the quarter board. In fact, final tabulations announced SPC Ballantine as Hospital Soldier of the Quarter.

Shaking his hand, "you showed strong perseverance in there and we are proud of you!" SGT Canini paraded through the congratulating line.

Schuyler, in gleam, wondered what he meant in reference of "we are proud of you" since SGT C was alone when he shook his hand. Nevertheless, SPC Schuyler Ballantine was the champion at the quarter board and he did it almost all by himself.

On the hardwood, halftime finally presented Julie a break. *"Sorry I couldn't help much but I was pretty busy out there! Glad you won!"* She simultaneously, telepathically, gave him a very sexy kiss and a squeeze in the crotch for his performing achievement.

Schuyler's board performances were stellar, even with Julie's assistance or not. He presented himself well and was recognized to great extent for his accomplishment. As for further board appearances, this quarter board appeared to be his last military board. But character development would last forever.

With Schuyler on the downhill slide of his military career, succeeding in both civilian education and military learning, Julie, on the other hand, was at full trust in her collegiate endeavor. She was a junior, performing on the hardwood like an up-and-coming champion, budding as a dependable asset off the bench. It was mixed emotions; the other four members of the Fresh Five were all starters, but still as sixth man she was the catalyst of the team.

Being a student-athlete created compromising situations. Tough decisions transpired conflicting basketball with school, not to mention her social life. Under Coach Jackson's watchful eye, the value of winning was top priority in front of anything else. The coach expected her team to wear their game faces from season's start to finish; she was hungry for a championship and would act in accordance in achieving one.

Basketball hiatus became a rarity of its own, but Julie's stellar student status kept sustaining pace in the classroom. With only minimal time away from basketball, time-management applications drove her study scheduling. Including a final summer session at her New York performing arts school, proposed plans predicted completion of requirements for her Bachelor's Degree in Drama by conclusion of next year's fall semester. True, she was well ahead of pace for college graduation.

Even though extremely popular as a student-athlete, her unbroken commitment toward her telepathic lover remained untainted. Collecting a few prospects along the way, but she never sullied the purity of what Schuyler and she had between them.

In Korea, Schuyler could vaguely follow the success of her basketball team. News was pretty much the same as the states, but not quite as targeted on women's college sports as other aspects of sporting news. But through media channels, he still could obtain basketball scores, including South Eastern State.

As her basketball season developed, a junior college transfer from Tennessee solidified defensive strength. Coach Jackson had the uncanny ability of locating talented players from the most remote sites. Her prize catch was this junior college center, Monique, who was playing basketball somewhere in the hills of Tennessee. Monique's appearance would scare anybody from even thinking about driving down the lane in attempt to score. She was the final piece to the puzzle, augmenting The Fresh Five in search for a conference championship and a national tournament berth. Indeed, Monique's defensive stronghold just might be what the doctor ordered for Coach Jackson's championship season.

After every game, Julie would provide Schuyler with an executive summary of the decisive events determining victory, or not. Also, she gave a little box score summarization identifying the team's strengths and weaknesses. He was very much interested, yearning for next season in attempt to follow her progress even closer.

As Schuyler performed his status quo pharmacy duties, she strived to please Coach Jackson, nickname Fickle Fisherwoman, or FF for short, providing this one iron clad bitch of a coach all the energy she could offer for team success.

Schuyler had asked her once why the coach had such a particular nickname. Julie being unsure could not answer his question. Nobody on the team could verify the originality of the nickname, except Jennifer who was a senior guard who spent a lot of time on the bench listening to team gossip. To Jennifer's account, Coach Jackson was 99% pure bitch allowing no man to persuade her lifestyle. An old boyfriend labeled her Fickle Fisherwoman due to her technique of catching any man, like a fish, that she desired and throwing him back in the water at her leisure. She caught and discarded boyfriend after boyfriend in dominance of any man that got in her way. The term FF was never spoken in her presence due to possible terrifying wrath in retribution. But among the players, the coach was often called FF in remembrance of the overbearing woman she was both on and off the court. True she was very intimating, not allowing any male referee, or opposing coach, to get the best of her. Being FF meant her superiority over men would be the bridge her players would eventually have to walk across in order to reach destiny at the national tournament.

Coach Jackson, or FF, was not just an overwhelming dedicated recruiter, but an extremely talented teacher of the game. Her recruits often came from various isolated backgrounds, but they were always molded into the finest players imaginable. Yes, FF was the supreme captain of her ship and she would not hesitate to make anybody walk the plank if the good of the team was at stake, including herself. Her selfless service earned her players' respect, providing cohesive bonding necessary to achieve desired ambitions of winning the championship, a current aspiration within reach.

The season went well for Flowers and her teammates, achieving the highest win total in the history of the school. The Monique addition proved to be a bright move, stimulating oomph in the lineup, but to no travail since FF and her team faltered in the championship game for the third straight year. Even with progress from the previous years, three consecutive runner-ups yielded no satisfaction for The Fresh Five, FF, and the remainder of the team. A vow for a championship season rallied the team in preparation for next season. Why not a championship? The Fresh Five, including Monique, would all be seniors establishing a good, solid foundation for FF to build upon in the subsequent year.

In Korea, Schuyler was routinely performing his duties in a military manner.

With the news from Julie of the final basketball results, he offered his condolence. He promised Julie that next season would be different since he would be back in the states residing in a new environment, providing her supplementary comfort during her final year at college. Also, he told her to go off to New York for the summer, enjoy herself, and return back to Louisiana and focus on winning a championship for FF.

"Next year will be different, I hope. As long as we are together, I expect to do fine. A confident Julie addressed her companion as she continued with her collegiate studies.

Schuyler, fascinated with her life as a student-athlete, inquired of her accomplishments on a regular basis. He was becoming quite a basketball fan, interjecting her life into his. Compelling feelings that desired her livelihood to correspond with his life coincided with her constant observation of his distinctive lifestyle, upon display to the world via air phenomena.

As the winds of the spring launched the dog days of summer, a hot, muggy summer captured Schuyler's awareness. Before the monsoon season arrived, softball climbed to notability through intramural leagues and tournament play. Never before did Schuyler earn a position on the hospital's team, but this season triggered change.

Michael, an avid softball pitcher, used his influence to get Schuyler on the hospital softball team. Since the team often played shorthanded, Schuyler had little difficulty earning a spot of the team as a substitute. Michael, on the other hand, was actually a talented pitcher. His knuckleball pitch baffled batters from all walks of life, sending the best of hitters back to dugout in bewilderment.

The team appeared pretty strong to Schuyler who spent most of the time warming the bench. With consistent hitting, balanced with dependable fielding, the team was one of the favorites during intramural championship play. Along with signal and personnel, the hospital offered the greatest threat.

At this particular time in Schuyler's Army career, his days were short. He had less than a month left in the Army with intramural championship on his mind. They had played together for the past few months, providing challenging opportunities for him on the diamond. Even as a substitute, frequently he saw action.

Opportune post tournament scheduling was not the case, as SPC Ballantine was tasked for force protection the evening of the very first game. Due to the tasking conflict, Schuyler would miss the initial round of the camp's softball tournament. Of course he responded well to the disappointment, understanding fully that force protection was essential to the camp's security.

The force protection duty was a very critical task, providing additional security to service members, family members, and civilian employees. It not just provided vehicle checks, but roaming guards keep under observation the camp's exterior walls.

As tournament play commenced, Schuyler received his force protection directives dictating guard duty at the entrance gate nearest the hospital. His duty imposed surveillance, assessment, and inspection of incoming vehicles through the gate, a very tiring duty involving extensive vehicle investigative requirements.

Throughout the evening, Schuyler wondered how his team was doing on the diamond. It was a bit of a distracter, but he felt his performance was still at peak intensity.

Julie, in New York, was concerned about Schuyler's force protection duty. *"Are you sure what you are supposed to be doing?"*

As he positioned a mirror around the undercarriage of a car, *"I'm supposed to check underneath the cars for possible bombs!"*

"Schuyler, you never have really done this before. Have you?"

After he completed his mirror check, he informed the military police that his check was completed. *"See Julie, this is all I have to do. Also, we check the trunk and underneath the hood!"*

"I'm leery about you doing this, but the MPs are there also to render assistance." She attempted to reassure herself, but carefully anticipated every action he committed.

Darkness overtook them, as the guard force grew weary. Schuyler, still worried about the ball game, became relaxed in his duty.

"Schuyler don't you start to slack off! This job is important and don't lose your focus." She warned him.

But as a few hours dissipated into the night, the duty became routinely boring, affecting his persistence. Vehicles passed through seemingly at will, without any inspection what so ever.

Julie noticed Schuyler letting his guard down. *"It appears that a whole lot of cars are getting to enter the gate without getting stopped?"*

"Don't worry Julie. If the MPs are not worried, than I'm not worried." He stopped the next vehicle. It was a dirty cargo van expelling enough exhaust to kill every mosquito along the countryside. *"Just to please you, I'll use my mirror."*

The MP walked up to him and pretended to be interested in the inspection of the van. "Got a lot of exhaust there SPC Ballantine; just let him go through!"

As the MP was about to wave the smoking van through the checkpoint, Julie interrupted, *"wait, I saw something in Schuyler's mirror that I haven't seen yet!"*

Responding to her voice, the MP delayed his decision of allowing the van to proceed. The MP directed SPC Ballantine to continue his mirror inspection of the van's undercarriage. Noticing unconnected wiring beneath the van caused the MP to become suspicious. The MP was fully aware of potential car bombs that possessed excessive wiring, concluding that this unconnected wiring could be an unused segment of a car bomb.

"Please dismount your vehicle," ordered the MP.

The driver, pretending to not understand English, responded to the MP's demand by throwing white powder out the window of the van's passenger's side in attempt to distract the MP.

In panic, the MP transmitted a message back to the Military Police Station requesting the hazardous material team. During the confusion, the van's driver tried to drive through the checkpoint in avoidance of a barricaded entrance, but was securely blocked by a military police tactical vehicle.

After Schuyler donned his protection mask, he assisted the MP in arresting the mysterious driver of the van. Julie, watching the entire incident via Schuyler, and gave much credit to military police. *"I'm so impressed how you, the MPs, and the guard force captured the driver and secured the area in anticipation of the hazardous material team's arrival."*

As the MPs detained the van's driver, the HAZMAT team tested the peculiar white powder concluding the substance to be non-toxic. Obviously, it was only used as a distraction to get the van through the checkpoint.

After the all-clear sign with the biological threat, inspection of the van proved not to contain a bomb either. Further inspection revealed that the mystifying van contained illegal drugs as barter for high-technical military equipment. Among all of this chaos with white powder, a possible car bombing, and barricade intrusion, the force protection team thwarted one of the biggest black-marketing conspiracies throughout the entire peninsula. His timely inspection of a dirty van led to uncovering a criminal network gaining profit from the military system. Of course, an innocent bystander who happens to be located in New York played even more of a significant part since she had convinced, via air phenomena, the MP to adjust his fire and have SPC Ballantine re-inspect a polluted, old van.

What a day! Schuyler had missed his softball game, but was instrumental in eliminating fraud within the military procurement system.

"Way to go champ! You helped arrest a whole lot of government criminals." Julie praised her little Army hero.

But the entire planet knew the rest of the story, a New York drama student, interested in the life of an Army soldier, alertly thwarted a widespread underground operation in behalf of the largest military installation on the Korean peninsula.

The next day, Schuyler was an instant hero. Being on gate guard duty, when the drug smuggler got caught, achieved grand recognition. Suddenly, he was one of the most publicized individuals in the community.

From his pharmacy sergeant to the Hospital Commander, he received congratulatory accommodations in reaction to his heroic measures taken during the checkpoint encroachment.

Following even closer, than before, to Schuyler's adventures, *"You've become quite a celebrity. Get any more publicity, and you'll be on TV!"*

It was a day to remember, besides the softball team winning the night prior; Schuyler spent a great deal of the day getting interviewed by the media. As he spoke to the press, he could only think of what Julie had told him early about being on television.

The force protection achievement carried into his softball activity also; by virtue of being suddenly a celebrity enabled him to gain a position in the line-up of today's game.

The softball coach informed Schuyler of his duty as catcher, a position responsible of guarding home plate. Since Michael was pitching, it seemed fit for Schuyler to catch him.

Their team's opposition would be a transportation team, comprised of at least one player who had played for the installation's team. Transportation provided some stiff competition with an outstanding outfielder named Alamo. He could hit, field, and run creating much difficulty for the Hospital.

As the game began, Transportation scored two runs in the top of the first inning as Alamo hit a two-run home run off of Michael's knuckleball to put their team on top 2-0. But as the game went along, Michael settled down a little bit limiting Transportation to only 4 runs through the first five innings.

Trailing 4-0 in the bottom of the fifth, the Hospital got consecutive hits from Antonio, Mike, and Scotty to load the bases for Primo.

"Primo, step into the pitch!" The coach yelled encouraging his power hitter to stride through the pitch as he swung.

With a 2-0 count, Primo hit a tremendous home run over the left field fence to tie the score 4-4.

After a scoreless sixth inning, Transportation scored two runs in the top of the seventh when Alamo drove in two runs with a double to put their team in front 6-4.

After a pep talk from Ivy, the Hospital's team captain, the hitting vowed to increase intensity. Schuyler, leading off the inning, drew a base on balls allowing the tying run to come to the plate.

"Rico you're up next, be careful with the pitches!" The coach had a strong desire for another base on balls.

But instead of waiting for bad pitches, Rico pulled a pitch down the left field line allowing Schuyler to go to third base while he trotted to second base. With no outs, runners were on second and third with LB coming up to the plate.

"Wait for your pitch!" The coach hoped for another hit.

LB stepped out of the box, ensuring the ladies took notice, and got prepared to bat. He didn't get a hit, but he flew deeply to left field in allowance of Schuyler to score and Rico, a very slow runner, to advance to third. Good play, putting Rico in good position to score with only one out. Westbrook stepped into the batter's box ready to hit. Obviously a long fly ball would tie the score 6-6, but Westbrook being the hitter he was ensured that not only he would hit a long fly ball, but he hit a long, towering 2-run home run deep over the left field fence tallying the score 7-6 in victory for the Hospital's team.

As the team ran onto the field, in celebration of the victory, Schuyler's emotions peaked from all of the recent excitement. Between gate guarding and home plate guarding, the past two days presented a little too much excitement for him to handle.

"Can't wait until you get back to your room, champ." Julie's voice inflection altered a bit, *"I wanna watch some other ball playing tonight!"*

We play again tomorrow, Julie!

"Who do you play?" Julie watched Schuyler get a ride back to his room, along with Michael, from Rico.

Riding in Rico's car, he asked, "Rico, who do we play tomorrow?"

"Personnel," responded Rico. "They only have one good player!"

"Who is he?" asked Michael interjecting into the conversation.

Rico slowed his car down a bit, turning his head toward his passengers, "Mario!" he spoke. "The fastest player on this entire installation!"

As Schuyler entered his room, securing a Mountain Dew, and getting comfortable, he asked Julie if she was interested in the game tomorrow.

"Oh yes, I think it will be very entertaining. I can't wait to watch LB play in his tight shorts." Julie pretended to be joking, but actually was pretty much sincere relating to LB's playing attire.

It didn't take long for Julie to coerce Schuyler into performing for her in the way she desired. She was fascinated with him satisfying himself upon her command. She encouraged it, just as long as she got to participate. As he satisfied himself, she transmitted sensual acts throughout his brain causing both partners to telepathically experience sexual intercourse induced by air phenomena. Sexual acts transmitted, back and forth, consequentially produced climaxing stimulus, finalizing an intensified day as she soothed him to rest.

The week was not over yet, plenty of softball to take place. As Schuyler's days in the Army were counting down, his softball commitment had just begun. The Personnel game was a late evening game, allowing maximum time for preparation. The Hospital team took batting practice prior to the game, commanded by Ivy, the team captain.

With the entire team at the game, the coach decided to keep Schuyler out of the starting line-up. Schuyler, showing good sportsmanship, sat on the bench and supported the starting line-up. Often more difficult than playing, good sportsmanship on the bench was an art a lot of players did not possess.

With the winner advancing to the championship game, the Hospital took an early lead and continued success as they defeated Personnel 9-3. Michael pitched a very good game, Primo and Ivy hit home runs, and Johnny V played a tough shortstop. With the victory, the Hospital advanced to play Signal in the finals.

It was late July, Schuyler was about to begin out-processing the Army and one last award ceremony awaited him. But before he got out of the Army he desired a championship, and this softball tournament would be his final chance.

All day long, he dreamed to Julie about winning the championship. She informed him that if their basketball team desired to win as much as he did than they might just win the national championship next season.

Schuyler learned prior to the game he would be catching Michael during the Signal game. "Michael, does Signal have any good hitters?" Schuyler inquired, as they got loose prior to the game.

Michael practiced his knuckleball in deep concentration. "Schuyler, to my knowledge they have Seda, Parker, and some kid named Abe," he replied.

Catching a short-hop, "who's the most dangerous hitter?" he asked.

Michael manipulated the ball to throw his knuckleball. "Abe no doubt, he's the most awesome hitter in the league."

The coach called out the starting line-up, with the sound of clapping hands, Mike, Johnny V, Westbrook, Ivy, Primo, Rico, Scotty, LB, Michael, and Schuyler.

"Sounds like a few runs!" shouted Ivy. "We're cutting first!"

Since a pumped-up Signal was home team, the Hospital batted first. In the top half of the first inning, the first seven hitters hit safety in route to a seven run first inning. The highlight of the inning was Scotty's bases clearing three-run triple.

With the big lead, the game was pretty much in Michael's hands. Even with a seven-run lead, he still had to pitch carefully to their big guns, especially Abe.

Throughout the first three innings, a familiar chant from the coach. "Get it up, get it up, they can't hit you if you get the ball up."

In the bottom of the third, with a 9-1 lead, Michael continued to put sufficient arch on his pitch to satisfy his coach.

The innings flew by, with little excitement, until the sixth inning. With the Hospital ahead by nine runs, 10-1, Seda hit a home run with Parker aboard cutting the score to 10-3. Following Seda's homer, Abe crushed a knuckleball at least 350 feet into dead away center field. Abe's homerun trot worried Michael's coach enough he came out to the mound in reassurance.

Michael got out of the sixth inning with a 10-4 lead. The Hospital failed to score in their top half of the seventh inning, placing the game's conclusion on Michael's shoulders.

With a 10-4 lead, Michael continued to pitch his own game. He began to pitch wild and walked a batter after recording the initial out.

Schuyler suddenly called time. "Blue, time!"

"Schuyler, you go talk to Michael and let him know he is going to get the other two outs and win the game." Julie began coaching via air phenomena.

Schuyler walked to the mound to converse with Michael, but not about pitching strategy. "Michael, where are we going for dinner after the game because I'm buying?"

Michael smiled, "Townhouse, of course."

Michael, relaxed from Schuyler's invitation, proceeded to dance his knuckleball even better than before as he forced the following two batters to hit weak ground balls in the direction of Johnny V's glove.

After the final out, the team congratulated Signal's team for sportsmanship and proceeded to celebrate their championship. Indeed it was a tough battle, but the best team came out on top.

At closure, Ivy spoke to the team. "Guys, it was a good season. We played together; we showed our capability to take a team out like we did by putting up that seven spot in the first, but most of all we had fun and that it what it is all about."

The coach cut in, "thanks team, you are the best!" And later gave both Michael and Schuyler an autographed photo of a famous professional basketball player. The professional basketball player was a personal friend of their coach, and the two of them were extremely proud to be a part of his championship team.

With championship trophies, Schuyler and Michael went to the Townhouse to celebrate victory. A memorable championship it was, concluding a wonderful military career for both of them.

The only significant activities remaining for both of them were an award ceremony and the freedom flight home to the states. A couple of exemplary Army careers were about to bring to a close.

CHAPTER 15

The rain fell heavy; disturbing Schuyler's out-processing of the Army. Leaving the Army was a very difficult decision, a choice dedicated to him. The remaining stop on this journey through the military incurred at his award ceremony, finalizing his career. Along with Michael, he will be awarded an Army Commendation Medal for his dedicated duty while serving in Korea. His three-year military commitment, seemingly flew by, delivering character that would be greatly used in the future.

Fortunately the sun broke through the rain clouds, bringing heat to the day much earlier than expected. With both soldiers taking break from out-processing, the award ceremony requested their presence. With their supervising sergeants, SSG Hatchet and SSG Bishop, they were seated in anticipation of ensuing commands from the master of ceremony. Nervously they both sat, awaiting their cue to approach the stage. Following tradition, each awarded soldier's supervisor pinned the appropriated award onto the uniform.

As each awarded soldier received congratulations from a receiving line, Schuyler received a congratulatory handshake from his mentor SGT Canini. "Good tour here in Korea," mentioned SGT C. "You'll make good officer material some day."

Peering into his eyes, he acknowledged his mentor; "thanks SGT C for doing everything you did!"

As the ceremony was becoming quite a success as the outgoing soldiers received appropriate recognition, Julie showed concern of his military exodus. *"Schuyler, I'm sure glad you're coming home soon because I've been following news of Korea, and frankly I was getting a little worried about your well-being."*

Heavily involved in her New York performing arts studies, she anxiously watched Schuyler out-process his final station and board his freedom flight home in conclusion of an outstanding Army career. *"You have made me so happy demonstrating your bravery in the Army. Indeed, both Michael and you are a credit to the United States Army and yourselves."*

Uncannily, Julie returned from her final New York session almost the same day Schuyler returned from Seoul. Two of the largest cities in the world had groomed this telepathic couple, both of them originally from small towns, through their transformation process. Eventually, Julie went back to college as Schuyler took up residence back home with his parents. After an excellent military career, it was time for him to be integrated into the collegiate scene.

Back home, Schuyler experienced much down time. Lacking a rigorously military schedule directing him, he felt out of place as is he was suddenly in another dimension. Life was so different as a civilian, no PT, no uniform, and no paycheck. Even though his college registration was last minute, he did get to enroll into a few classes at the local junior college. With his military experience and credits from University of Maryland, the local junior college was more than happy to accommodate him.

At the junior college, his advisor fixed him up with twelve hours of classes allowing Schuyler to attain full-time student status. Gary, his academic advisor, presented him his schedule of classes. "Schuyler, I've done the best I could to get you into a pre-pharmacy curriculum. Biology, chemistry, and calculus are all four-hour classes.

Schuyler paused in thought, accepting the challenging schedule, "Gary, I think I can handle those three classes."

"Biology and chemistry are Monday, Wednesday, and Friday classes with biology lab on Tuesday afternoon and chemistry lab scheduled for Wednesday afternoons. Also, calculus would be Monday, Tuesday, Wednesday, and Friday." Gary handed the schedule to Schuyler welcoming him to their school.

As Schuyler read his class schedule, Julie was already planning his activities for him. *"Schuyler, Gary did a very good job getting those classes at specific times. Chemistry from 0800-0850, biology from 0900-0950, and calculus from 1100-1150 gives plenty of time for your afternoon labs, not to mention free time for addition study."*

He told her he planned to get a weekend job at the hospital pharmacy to earn some spending money.

"Oh, I know with your Army education money and a part-time pharmacy job, you will do quite well!"

With his school schedule set, he visited the local hospital to inquire about work. Due to his past military experience as an IV pharmacy technician, he had little trouble obtaining a weekend job. He was offered a position as a weekend technician with third shift duty. Usually an undesirable shift, but it did fit into his schedule well. Thus, he had a part-time job at the local hospital working the graveyard shift on both Friday and Saturday nights as a pharmacy tech without interference with his college curriculum.

"Good job Schuyler, you'll doing well. You've got school and work already integrated into your new life!"

With your help Julie, I'm sure to do fine!

At the Jupiter, Morrison and Boyd were delighted with the military career of The Air. Morrison, who had aged quite a bit during the past three years, presented his executive summary. "As expected, The Air did not disappoint us as a soldier. As he progressed from basic training, advanced individual training, and his Korean tour, The Air characterized a model soldier. His actions symbolized the slogan of being all one can be. Truly, his call to military duty proved to be a wonderful research specimen."

Boyd, who had developed a matrix scorecard from air phenomena measures, elaborated on his findings. "During the past two years, air phenomena feedback increased regardless of environmental setting."

"Do you have an environmental relationship?" Morrison interrupted, "I'm interested in any outcome measures?"

"Metrics show that almost every situation The Vision encountered, air phenomena feedback measured a strong response." Boyd opened his desktop computer. "Everywhere The Vision visited, strangers consistently aired responses back to him."

Morrison, overlooking Boyd's shoulder, noticed a sharp decrease in his metrics. "Where did this extremely low level of air phenomena feedback occur?"

"The Vision received very little response as he traveled on Korean public transportation, such as the subway." Boyd further explained is greater detail. "Communication, overall, is less frequent on their public transportation system, explaining reason for little air response in those certain situations."

Morrison carefully studied Boyd's scorecard, concluding both Americans and Koreans alike were contributing heavily to air phenomena feedback. "Even though the public had very little to say, they almost always recognized his air phenomena trait by uttering some form of air transmission back to him."

"Often, the young girls would air the name of Julie to him in recognition of their relationship." Boyd made an important verification of Flowers' impact on air phenomena proliferation.

Morrison smiled, "Boyd, you're theory of the girl being the key to air phenomena proliferation might prove to be correct." He handed Boyd back his scorecard. "Your metrics does prove that as The Air goes, so does his phenomena."

"Yes, air response will ultimately follow The Vision." Boyd filed his scorecard and looked toward his partner for additional instructions.

Morrison printed his evaluations from his analysis of The Air's strengths, weaknesses, opportunities, and threats from his military service. His four slides referenced the four major areas of evaluation. "Strengths revealed The Air's military service as great benefit. The vigorously training, commitment to discipline, and leadership transformed him into adulthood much more effectively than expected."

"Yes, his maturity accelerated very quickly," added Boyd.

Morrison's second slide reflected weaknesses sustained during his tenure in the Army. "Family separation interrupted The Air's cohesion with his family."

The opportunities slide expanded into much detail from cultural influences to leadership enhancement. "The Air's exposure to the military instilled confidence, leader development, and vast integration among Americans and Koreans introducing him to their unique customs and traditions." Morrison presented the slide to Boyd for his evaluation.

Boyd viewed the slides, but used his own point of view. "I feel a strong opportunity perspective was the effect governed from The Vision's actions in the Army. By viewing his conduct, both his hardships and rewards derived from the Army, were transmitted throughout society."

Morrison nodded his head in agreement. "The Air's military experiences advertised the Army in good faith, identifying the Army as a viable segment of our Gross National Product."

With The Air safe at home, the threat portion of his brief was scaled down. Previous candidate measures for threat perspective consisted of possible physical harm directed at The Air. Morrison explained, "our only real threat incurred was that our enemies could watch him exist in the Army."

"Good point, Don, but The Vision verified our military's strength in deterrence of any opponent."

The research analysis went well, measuring and evaluating The Air's growth and the affect upon his environmental setting. The Jupiter strongly rewarded

Don Morrison and John Boyd for their analytical research. Boyd's scorecard showed a strong relationship among The Vision's social diversity and air phenomena feedback.

Metrics verified an increase in individual responses as he expanded his exposure to society. Morrison's contributions from his evaluations of strengths, weaknesses, opportunities, and threats from his military service presented the Jupiter with excellent perspective on The Air's transformation from high school graduate to honorably discharged from the military. With The Air's military adventure behind him, Morrison and Boyd would have to look deeply into further applicative objectives for study. They did not wish to accept their best years of evaluation were behind them.

Schuyler settled into civilian life, leaving the military in the past, providing Julie the comfort needed in pursuit of her dream.

"Schuyler, you know I will have enough credit to qualify for graduation by the end of fall semester."

Will you graduate then, or wait until end of spring semester?

"I'll probably wait until spring. I can always take drama or music electives in constructing a course load to get me through basketball season and spring semester."

Is FF still being a bitch?

"More than ever, she is pushing us hard this season in hunt for a title!"

As the fall semester crept along, Schuyler continued to work part-time at the hospital pharmacy. His talent in the laminar flow hood strengthened his position as a qualified pharmacy tech. Even though he worked third shift, his involvement in workflow processes continued to enlarge.

Julie, on the other hand, had already started her basketball season. As a senior, she would have to set aside her life in pursuit of a championship for FF. A student maintaining practically straight A's, she was a standing member of the Dean's List during her extensive career.

As the fall semester ceased, both Julie and Schuyler successfully achieved fine grades. Julie's report card consisted of three A's and one B, while Schuyler received a string of B's. His calculus class gave him the most trouble, but with Julie's help he attained a composite B grade.

Due to his recent collegiate success, Schuyler registered for the second semester of each of his classes for the spring. Working with a similar schedule as the fall, his pharmacy job was not affected.

At the holiday break, South Eastern State traveled to play in a Christmas basketball tournament in the mystical city of New Orleans. As Julie entered the arena, she looked around at the massive enclosure. *"I'm in New Orleans to play basketball!"*

Schuyler was at home spending Christmas with his parents. He asked her if she planned to visit the French Quarter.

"No, but I feel honored to be here playing against some of the larger schools in the region." She laced her shoes in preparation of the game.

Interested in her team, Schuyler asked her to describe some of her teammates?

Pre-game drills were a routine ritual, providing optimal time to introduce a few of her teammates to her telepathic companion. *"You already know about FF, our coach, and a little about Monique. Our starting guards are Yogi and Wanda."*

Schuyler asked her for more details?

"Yogi, a member of The Fresh Five, was of Korean descent. Out of high school, she had very few scholarship offers. An unknown prospect, this dynamic ball-handler could dribble through a minefield. Her crossover dribbling technique was awesome, making her very hard to guard in the backcourt. Yogi didn't shoot much during the game, but she could beat you from the foul line."

He asked if Yogi was a senior.

"Yes, we are all seniors!" Julie continued to get ready for game time. *"Wanda plays the other guard position and she's an excellent ball handler also causing double trouble in the backcourt if any team attempts to full-court press. Wanda was recruited by FF from a small, rural town in East Tennessee. As the lone African-American player of The Fresh Five, her addition to the team energized the play of the others. Her defensive quickness and sharp passing skills earned her the nickname Wicked Wanda, identifying her dominance in the open court."*

Julie watched Yogi and Wanda warm-up together. *"Even though they are both lacking in height, they both match-up tough against anyone!"*

Coach Jackson directed the team to begin shooting foul shots in anticipation of a tightly officiated game.

"Schuyler, we have co-captains at the two forward positions." She checked-out the pre-game crowd, *"the co-captains are called the trailer park twins."* Julie continued to prepare for the game. *"Heather and Brittney were both raised in trailer parks. Even I feel high society compared to them, and I come from a very small Louisianan town."*

Schuyler interrupted her, asking if the twins looked much alike.

"Kind of alike, they both are tall with long blonde hair." She paused to shoot five straight foul shots making all five of them. *"Both Heather and Brittney were prominent figures of The Fresh Five and FF encouraged them both to shoot the ball as*

much as possible. Between them both, the twins often scored over half of the team's points.

Schuyler asked if the twins socialized together off the court.

"Socialized together? I heard they were dating the same guy!"

Who could manage both of them, asked Schuyler?

"Some pitcher from the baseball team!"

He asked if she ever was in the starting line-up.

"No, I always relieve from the bench early in the game. I'm the only member of The Fresh Five not starting, but I still play as much as Yogi and Wicked Wanda."

Is Monique still a fearsome center? Schuyler remembered her defensive dominating factor.

"Yes, Monique patrols the lane, not allowing anybody much penetration!" Julie concluded her introduction of the starting five. She sat patiently on the bench acknowledging her role as the team's sixth man.

Back at the Ballantine household, Schuyler anticipated the arrival of his brother for Christmas break. Duncan, newly promoted to the rank of Sergeant, was still stationed down at the southern end of the state. Although he had a six-month deployment, his original duty assignment never changed.

Schuyler's parents, proud of his military accomplishments, prepared the house for the eldest son's arrival. Since his discharge, Schuyler had only seen his brother twice. He was close to his brother, and not being overseas in Korea made it more convenient to spend quality time with his immediate family members.

In little notice, Duncan walked in through the door. It was a chilly winter day, with only a faint hope of snow in sight. Wearing his airborne sweatshirt, Duncan entered the household with Christmas gifts in hand. "Merry Christmas, how's school Schuyler?"

Schuyler offered his brother a living room seat. "Earned all B's in my last semester."

"Son, how many credit hours did you earn while in Korea?" His mother approached the two brothers with a tempting offering of her famed monster cookies.

As he reached for a monster cookie, a combination oatmeal and peanut butter cookie with a mixture of nuts contained within, "I have twenty-one semester hours from University of Maryland.

Eyeing the monster cookies with huge appetite; "you know college credit is available from military experience!" Duncan stood up from his comfortable seat to secure a couple of cookies. "Don't worry; you can apply for the credits later; just pass your calculus class!"

Schuyler gave his brother a strange look. "How did you know I was taking calculus?"

Duncan paused in his tracks, looked around the room, and informed Schuyler he wasn't sure how he knew that information.

The holiday seasonal break produced an excellent opportunity for the brothers to visit. Duncan needed a break from stressful military commitments; Schuyler required encouragement in pursuit of college success. The brothers were different as they were alike. One brother lived to dream, as the other existed to protect.

Duncan, the big brother, was always dominant in command, but his mind knew his little brother's unlimited destiny would carry him far. Schuyler displayed admirable respect for his brother's courage as a soldier, because his own Army experience provided much reinforcement of his perspective pertaining to his brother. Being recently discharged from the Army, Schuyler's future outlook articulated warrior spirit in preparation for life's hardships. The two brothers would be together for a few more days, but the bond created between them gave structure to both of their lives.

In New Orleans, Julie spent her holiday in a bit different note. In a heated tournament, she and her cohorts were constantly under the thumb of their coach. FF established clear lines of authority, attempting to steer her talented team to earn first place in this holiday tourney. She accepted nothing less than victory. Throughout play, Julie transmitted game highlights to Schuyler periodically. With two victories under their belts, they had earned a birth in the finals.

Prior to the championship game, FF expressed her concern of their opponent, the Tigers. "Tonight we will place our undefeated record on the line against a team from a much larger conference. Even though they are nationally ranked, we will not be intimidated."

On her command, the players exited the locker room and marched onto the court. They were overshadowed by the awesome size of the Tigers, casting doubt upon The Fresh Five. It was a classic match between "the haves and the have-nots." Tiny South Eastern State was apparently little contest for their ensuing competition.

From tip-off to the final tick of the clock, the Tigers were dominant eliminating any doubt they were truly in a league above their opponents. As Heather picked-and-rolled with Brittney, Wicked Wanda captained the ship, but a piece of the puzzle was missing as they could not challenge Tiger strength.

From the courtside, a furious FF worked the referees in attempt of persuasion. Bargaining the officiating was an art of FF, her classic gesture of pointing at her crotch alerted the referees' attention. As she pointed, she would yell "right here" to the referees symbolizing her dominating figure headship as a female coach. FF definitely earned officiating respect; her male ascendancy character offered much intimidation. As a coach, she walked a fine line of getting a technical or not, disputing male officiating throughout the south. Nothing pulled the team together as when FF sounded off with a timely "right her!" Her gestures left many of referees in stark embarrassment, providing faith in her team; her unwelcome indications, even in disgrace, never warranted a technical foul. With FF at the helm, the team's fate was sealed.

Even with a crushing loss to the Tiger five, FF and her team pledged to rise to the occasion and let the region know their season ahead would not be taken lightly.

Suffering their first loss of the season to the teeth of the Tigers, FF praised her players in the mist of defeat. "We were outclassed today, but tomorrow will be another mission!"

The players all stood on their feet, in acknowledgement of FF, and took turns exhibiting their thoughts in the quietness of their locker room's dim light.

Heather spoke first, "this loss may have been humiliating, but it will definitely be our last!"

Brittney followed suit, "we vow to keep faith in our team and believe in ourselves in pursuit of our quest to win it all!"

Julie shouted, "faith will be our battle cry rallying our troops in quest of victory; faith will doctrine our mission, accomplishing milestones to achieve designed objectives."

As the team oddly stared at Julie, FF interrupted her speech. "Julie, you sound like a company commander in the Army."

"Do you have a friend in the Army, or something? Wicked Wanda smiled as she joked, "maybe you should have enrolled into ROTC instead of performing arts during the summers."

"No, not really!" A startled Julie replied in haste. "I really can't explain why I sounded that way."

In dismissal, Julie walked with Yogi to their dorm. Since the beginning of their freshman year, they had lived in same dormitory suite. Sharing a bathroom, they each had individual rooms that connected to each other. Often together with little verbal conversation between them, they both followed The Dream. As Julie communicated with Schuyler, Yogi listened along.

"You know Julie, often you do act like you're in the Army." Yogi marched in stride with her suitemate.

She smiled at Yogi, "you know me too well."

The Christmas tournament was the beginning of the grooming of an enchanted college team. Faith would guide them down the path of success, keeping in mind the leader would have to lead to keep faith alive.

Schuyler saluted his brother as he drove off to return to the land of helicopters. Schuyler's admiration for his brother grew, acknowledging that his military service would not have been if it weren't for Duncan's influence. As soon as Duncan's vehicle disappeared down the road, he asked Julie about her basketball endeavors?

Julie, relaxing comfortably in her dorm, presented a synopsis of the entire tournament. With emphasis of the impact of the two initial victories, she captioned the emotion of the championship game. *"Schuyler, we played our hearts out, but came up short on the scoreboard."*

How bad did you'll lose?

"We lost by about twenty points."

Schuyler's mind began to experience multiple thoughts, collaborating various personal questions he wished to ask her.

"Settle down dear, I can tell you are nervous about me. Don't worry; I'm still your girl!"

Julie, I was worried since I wasn't in the Army anymore you might not be still interested in me.

"This is not so, just remember I'm only a thought away and I will always be by your side."

Her telepathic rhetoric put his mind to ease. Fear of losing his telepathic companion raced through his mind frequently, he experienced much difficulty in acceptance of her involved interest in his life. In fact, she was far superior to him as a prominent collegiate student athlete compared to his simple life as a junior college student.

She, expressing her concern, prepared him for nightly rest as her soothing voice eased him to sleep. Awakening the next morning, his heart experienced a big sigh of relief as he detected her distinct voice giving encouragement to begin another day of his life.

The spring semester introduced another challenge in Schuyler's behalf. Besides a three-class schedule, an inquiry of the school golf team presented a proposition of being a competitive golfer again. Since his class schedule was relatively light, involvement with the golf team was a strong possibility. An enthusiastic Schuyler had a major obstacle; the golf team had already been selected and had started play during early in the fall semester. But since it was a split season of fall and spring, the coach allowed Schuyler to join the team as an alternate member.

An excited Julie, *"Schuyler, you got on the team; all you have to do is prove yourself worthy of the honor."*

He explained, I really hadn't been playing much and might not be any good.

"Ridiculous! If you can conquer challenges presented by the Army, then you can surely adapt to playing golf again."

You are right, Julie. If you think I can compete, then I will do so. You always seem to have the correct answer.

With college-life pretty much on automatic, he turned to his pharmacy job for challenging entertainment. Even though he worked only two eight-hour shifts per week, he seemed to pretty much know a great deal of the operation. As the IV tech, his priority assignment was to mix IV-additive solutions to be distributed to the requesting ward. His co-worker, Victor, distributed the unit dose mediations and ordered supplies. Rounding out the trio was Robert, the supervising pharmacist, ensuring all pharmaceutical procedures were followed correctly.

Schuyler performed in the laminar flow hood very efficiently; he was told he was much quicker than the IV tech he replaced. Due to his efficiency, he often completed his batch of IV's ahead of schedule providing ample opportunity to survey the pharmacy's area of operation.

Victor was a little older than Schuyler, but with less pharmacy experience. He was of similar height and build, but his excessive hair length set him aside to much extent. Even though they worked together, they appeared worlds apart.

Robert, Victor's cohort, was at least the age of forty and spoke with a very loud voice. At times he seemed a little odd, giving explanation for his nickname "Crazy Bob."

The three of them seemed to work pretty well together; Crazy Bob and Victor worked a regular 40-hour week providing continuity to the work place.

At South Eastern State, Julie was enrolled in a bare minimum of courses. After all she had already completed the requirement for her Bachelor's Degree at her school, thus she only took the required twelve semester hours for athletic eligibility. Her academic record was strong, setting an excellent example for her junior classmates to follow. In basketball, her tolerant compliance on the bench promoted good espirit de corps throughout the team. The team continued to win, the coach was happy, and Julie was an important ingredient toward team achievement.

Schuyler's college schedule had a little bit of pressure. Chemistry and biology required moderate out-of-class study, and calculus always kept an upbeat tone.

Of course Julie prepared him for his calculus assignments, ensuring he studied every night. It was almost a ritual, calculus homework followed by telepathic sexual activity. Indeed Schuyler looked forward to completing his calculus homework in a timely manner, allotting maximum time to spend with his telepathic lover before he went to sleep.

Late in January, Schuyler's routine pharmacy job added a bit if a twist. As he had just finished up with a batch of IV's, a short, bearded man, suddenly appeared at the pharmacy requesting Victor's signature for a small shipment of medication.

Victor walked to the door and let the supply guy into the pharmacy. "Scratchy, what do you have for me?"

"Sign here!" The bearded man issued a small sample of medications to Victor.

Victor inspected the invoice, hunting for a specific item. "Good, you have the growth hormone." Satisfied with the shipment he escorted him to the door. "Thanks Scratchy, for the delivery."

Standing in the IV room, Schuyler was a little suspicious of the transaction. Since he had never seem this bearded man before, he became apprehensive of the relationship between Victor and Scratchy.

"Schuyler, who was that strange man with the beard and why is Crazy Bob pretending not to be involved?" Julie alerted him to her own ill feeling about the incident.

Crazy Bob finished his paperwork and instructed Schuyler to take a break and visit the snack shack down in the basement. Ahead of his own schedule, he ventured down the stairs to purchase a Mountain Dew.

"Schuyler, how often does Crazy Bob tell you to take a break?"

As he located his Pepsi machine, he bought his soda and wondered about what she had just said. In return, he pondered the thought and still could not give her a viable response.

"It is strange? Scratchy coming to the pharmacy and then Crazy Bob inviting you away from the shop?"

As Schuyler returned to the pharmacy, in surprise he found Victor in the hood mixing an IV solution.

Crazy Bob interjected, "Schuyler, I had Vic go ahead and mix up the growth hormone IV."

Schuyler sat down with his soda and experienced some down time. He rarely had seen Victor in the hood before and grew even more suspicious.

"Something about the growth hormone must be special because Victor has ensured to personally take care of it." Julie interjected a bit of her own as she kept Schuyler's eyes on Victor.

Victor stopped suddenly after he injected the growth hormone. "Bob, I put too much into the bag!"

Crazy Bob walked up to the hood. "Discard it and make another one." He watched Victor remanufacture the IV solution with another vial of growth hormone for a little while, and then went back to his paperwork.

Julie interrupted Schuyler's thought process. *"The pharmacist didn't seem too upset Victor wasted a whole entire vial of growth hormone."*

He agreed with her. Something looked fishy about the whole ordeal, and it appeared Crazy Bob was in on it with Victor and possibly Scratchy.

Julie was worried about Schuyler's job. She did not know for sure, but something didn't add up. The incident with the growth hormone, a steroid used on the streets to build body muscle, was a little too scary for her taste. Along with her, Schuyler felt uncomfortable about the incident also. Wondering about what actually happened to the discarded IV bag containing the growth hormone, he continued his work as if nothing distinctive had happen.

With the spring semester well into swing for the telepathic couple, they seemly were headed in different directions. Julie, a college senior, had the conference basketball tournament in her windshield and Schuyler, a junior college student, was subject to work in a pharmacy in which ethical practices were questionable. Nevertheless, this couple was still together. Even living in two different worlds, they continued to save themselves for one another.

CHAPTER 16

The Louisianan winter began to dissipate as the basketball season progressed. Tournament time was drawing near, an enthusiastic FF synthesized motivation in the clubhouse, and a charismatic Julie Crystal Flowers kept pace in the classroom, on the hardwood, and with Schuyler's affairs. It was an enchanted moment for the basketball team, a squad of eleven playing for a coach demanding nothing less than near perfection. With still only one loss attached to their record, South Eastern State was on a roll and hoped to continue rolling all the way through their conference tournament.

A week preceded entrance into the month of March, an innovative Coach Jackson had every coach in the conference stalking her strategic implementations designed to put a championship trophy in the school's trophy case. She was the talk of the region, her winning streak was one of the longest in the entire nation, and opposition coaches feared her competitive instinct to fullest extent. Simply, she was the leader of the pack overshadowing the rest of the conference by leaps and bounds.

Every practice until the conference tournament was a stressful situation for Julie. Awareness of its importance, she prepared to place her life in the coach's hands in pursuit of a dream to qualify for the national tournament.

During the final practice prior to the tournament, FF counseled her eleven players. "As the out-right league champion of our conference, no team should even come close to competing us in the upcoming tournament. As we know, even as league champions we must still win the tournament to qualify for the national tournament."

Heather raised her hand and gained permission to speak. "How high of a seed do we expect to get?"

"Not certain!" FF interrupted and glimpsed at her notebook. "Even with an at-large bid, I expect at least an eight seed." She paused in her rhetoric, "I don't even want to think about an at-large bid because that would have meant we lost our tournament."

Brittney gained permission to speak. "High importance of winning the conference tournament; we can't let our guard down!"

"Most affirmative! We must shoot, move, and communicate while on the court as well as determine sectors of fire." reported an outspoken Julie as the rest of the team strangely glanced at her.

"Julie is correct; you'll need to diagram shooting projectiles at preferred spots on the court." Wondering how she knew Army jargon, FF reinforced Julie's intent of predetermining shooting lanes on the hardwood.

As FF concluded the meeting, she emphasized their upcoming weekend trip to Biloxi, host site of the conference tournament, and programmed noble expectations into the hearts of her eleven players. The entire team was ready to play, but an exceptional goal of The Fresh Five was to earn a national championship birth after four long years of hard work. This was their year and they vowed to do what ever it took in order to accomplishment mission number one, to win it all!

Biloxi greeted Team FF with warming sunshine spreading high expectations throughout the hearts of the teammates. Sandy beaches, temperate waterfront, and beautiful casino hotels framed the city's landscape in host of a conference tournament, beholding South Eastern State as the overwhelming favorite.

Coach Jackson, exerting her power, established clear lines of authority by implementation of harsh curfew principles, even more severe than before, protecting her team's interest as they proceeded to enter tournament play.

Schuyler, always interested in his telepathic companion's activity, questioned Julie about her upcoming tournament. He had been following the team's success in the sports page, acquiring much knowledge about the squad's destiny.

"Schuyler, I'm in Biloxi to play basketball for the weekend. Win or lose, we should still get a bid to the national tournament. But, of course, I want to win this championship so bad I'll do anything for accomplishment."

How is Biloxi?

"Even though FF has us on strict lockdown, it is actually quite a lovely environment."

The sports' columnist already has your team picked as a possible Cinderella team for the upcoming national tournament, reported Schuyler.

"FF has high hopes for the team; she expects a pretty good seed in the tournament, anticipating a first-class presentation."

He wished her much luck as he continued his college routine, eager to obtain updated tournament results, via air; he went about his business as usual.

In Biloxi, Team FF was gearing up to play its first game. Thursday night's game pitted the Eagles and the Cardinals against one another with the winner advancing to play South Eastern State on Friday night. In the grandstands, Julie and her teammates carefully watched the Eagles defeat their opponents in advancement to the quarterfinals.

As the team's sixth man, Julie prepared both mentally and physically for a crucial quarterfinal game against the Eagles. With confidence, she had a strong feeling the Eagles would be little match against their mobile 1-3-1 zone defense. When Julie entered the game for either Yogi or Wicked Wanda, FF always applied a flexible 1-3-1 zone defense utilizing Julie at the baseline defensive position.

Preparing for nightly rest was a big chore for Julie; she was overly hyped for the ensuing game the next day. In need of soothing comfort, she turned to Schuyler for assistance. *"Schuyler I know you're currently busy with your family, but could you talk to me for awhile because I'm very stressed about tomorrow's game?"*

A delighted Schuyler responded to her beckoned request. With sense of important duty on hand, he cherished the moment of providing comfort to the woman he admired and loved. For the first time, it was Schuyler preparing Julie for competitive battle instead of the vice versa. It was a time for him to shine, because discovering his specific impact upon her led him to experience self-gratification as increasing self esteem rose to near pinnacle level.

Friday's game exhibited grand opportunity for FF to showcase her squad. During pre-game interviews, this calm, cool, and collective coach advertised her team's talent as little as possible. It was like she was the leader in the clubhouse at the U.S. Open Golf Tournament, interviewing with pleasure being in total control of the situation.

Sweat rolled down Julie's forehead, as tip-off time grew near. Evaluating the circumstances, her game face appeared. She understood that everything she had worked for would be put to test; it was her chance to excel during this opportune time.

As she sat on the bench during early minutes in the game, her focus set on the opposition in preparation for consequent play. Her duty as sixth man would be put to test; she must learn the opposing team's system prior to participation.

With Yogi and Wicked Wanda at guard, Brittney and Heather at Forward, a power center Monique quickly tested Eagle strength in the middle.

In early minutes of the first half, Team FF had opened a ten-point lead. Monique appeared too dominant for the opposition, as a man-to-man defense stymied any opposing offensive threat. FF liked to open the game with a tight man-to-man defense allowing both Yogi and Wicked Wanda to pressure the ball. It was very effective, synthesizing several fast break opportunities generating a lot of breakaway points for both Brittney and Heather.

On the bench almost the entire first half, Julie patiently waited for her playing time to materialize. With the half-time score in favor of Team FF by over twenty points, Coach Jackson proportionally rested her starting team during the entire second half. A rested Julie took no time in taking command of the court. She opened up the second half with six straight points and did not let up until FF cleared the bench with a little over four minutes to play in the game. A twenty-two-point halftime lead swiftly ballooned into a forty-point lead due to the sharp shooting of Flowers; her twenty-four points in the second half commanded South Eastern State to an 83–51 victory over the Eagles.

Immediately after the contest, Julie notified her telepathic companion of the good news. *"Schuyler, we won our game easily and we will play tomorrow!"*

He acknowledged her signal and informed her to elaborate later in the day about the game, giving him more details.

A joyful Coach Jackson, in the locker room, praised the play of the entire team. "You'll were clicking on all cylinders!" She patted Julie on the back. "Julie was sure crystal clear with her shooting." She pointed at Monique, "your fifteen rebounds impressed me a lot also."

After a little post-game celebration, the team enjoyed refreshments at the arena awaiting ensuing results of the current game. Drinking pink lemonade, Julie sat with Yogi and watched the Bobcats defeat their opponents in another quarterfinal game. The Bobcat victory granted a date with Team FF the subsequent day. Saturday's semifinal game would match South Eastern State against a scrappy Bobcat team. As the team departed to their hotel, Julie and Yogi assured each other the team would perform admirably as long as they played together.

"If we play our game, our talent will shine over any Bobcat chance of hope," said Yogi.

"Fit to fight!" Responded Julie as she reported back to her living quarters with teammate Yogi.

In the comfort of their room, Yogi listened to Julie analyze the Eagle game to Schuyler. *"Our victory over the Eagles will pit the Bobcats against us tomorrow.*

Monique dominated the boards, Heather and Brittney scored about twenty points a piece, and Yogi who is with me now dished out over ten assists."

Schuyler was happy to hear more details of the victory. Being very pleased, he asked her if she scored many points.

With Yogi watching her air, Julie described the game to Schuyler. *"I scored twenty-four points, all of them in the second half!"* She could read his mind thoroughly as joyful thoughts raced through his head. From his notions, Julie translated his feeling into joy of her own. Julie's detection of his mental happiness stimulated encouragement in her heart. True, it was only his thoughts, but his air phenomena expressions influenced her life to a great degree.

Lying in bed, she asked him again for his relaxing aid. *"Sugar, can you please give me comfort like you did last night?"*

A blissful Schuyler complied with her wishes, because it made him feel like he was an actual participant of Team FF. Communicating with her, via air phenomena, caused him to imagine he was actually at the tournament with her, being of assistance in common cause of winning a championship.

Daylight broke early Saturday morning, Julie had her game face ready, and her teammates began focusing on nothing but the semifinal game. Arrival at the arena encompassed a multitude of emotions, publicizing a multi-talented team in quest of another victory. Coach Jackson, settling her nerves, ordered a cup of coffee as the team gathered in clubhouse. Her intensity peaked as she entered her team's locker room; shunning nervous tension she delivered encouragement to her eleven players. "Yesterday was an excellent day, today will be even better, stay aggressive, but play smart!" FF asked for any comments from the players.

Receiving permission to speak, co-captain Heather addressed her team, "seriously, we are much better than our competition and we have shown it all year long. Lets utilized our strengths, and attack their weaknesses."

Co-captain Brittney added, "Heather is correct! We control the game, not vice versa. If one of us gets hot during the contest, then feed them the ball."

Julie looked at Yogi, encouraging her to speak. "Yogi, you are going to get us the ball?"

Yogi, who seldom speaks, uttered, "I'll find you'll when you are open, and a lot points will be scored."

A proud FF rallied her team one last time prior to court entrance; the trailer park twins led the charge in preparation for the Bobcat team. Prior to the game, Julie's inspiration climbed as pre-game drills vitalized her potency. As the maneuvered along the hardwood, *"Schuyler, we're about to start the game against the Bobcats; wish me luck!"*

He acknowledged her transmitted request, in motivating thought he conveyed high expectations of her consequent game. Delivering encouragement from hundreds of miles away, Schuyler by virtue of his assistance rejoiced in satisfying fashion. A paradigm shift formulated as it was him supporting her into competition instead of the vice versa.

Game time approached, as the starting line-up positioned on the floor. Julie, sitting next to FF, began her analogy of the opposition. It was an art how she could scout the opposing players during the early minutes of the game.

As the sixth man, she utilized this opportune time to visualize herself in action against her opposition forces. Like a reconnaissance mission, she analyzed her enemy before she attacked. Therefore when she entered the game, her mental preparation was already established.

Similar to the Eagle game, the Bobcats began the first initial minutes inferior in the paint. Again, Monique relinquished little traffic down the lane illustrating a dominating force factoring heavily on the side of Team FF. With Yogi and Wicked Wanda in the backcourt shuffling out assists right and left, the trailer park twins generated a quick fifteen-point lead late in the first half. As with the Eagle game, Julie stayed on the bench for most of the first half waiting for her chance to reveal her talent at the conference tournament.

The Bobcat five suffered greatly in attempt to adjust from a high-pressure man-to-man defense to a flexible 1-3-1 zone defense. With Julie guarding the baseline, and the trailer park twins at the wings, the opposing forces were stifled during the last five minutes of the half. Coach Jackson's rotation among Yogi, Julie, and Wicked Wanda kept the Bobcats off balance, providing establishment of strong coaching strategy precedence.

In the locker room at halftime, FF was very pleased with the performance of her players. She paced back-and-forth in front of her team of eleven praising the first-rate play of Monique and The Fresh Five. "Girls, you look even better tonight than yesterday! In the second half, we will continue with Julie on the floor but rotate Heather and Brittney out to begin with." She directed her attention to Julie, "you will go to forward as our defense will match-up with a 2-3 zone defense."

Julie, a versatile player, changed positions in accordance with which player was being rested. If she wasn't playing, they played man-to-man; if she replaced Yogi or Wicked Wanda, they went to a 1-3-1 zone defense; if she replaced Heather or Brittney, they switched to a 2-3 zone defense; if she replaced Monique, the team went to a full-court or half-court press. Hence, Julie Crystal Flowers was interchangeable with any player of the starting five. After the top six players, FF didn't play anyone much else. She strictly lived and died with the six players, producing well as long as two of them didn't get into foul trouble at the same time. If needed, Jamie Lee could substitute at the guard position and Patti could spare Monique for a breather at center.

The second half opened quickly for Julie and Wicked Wanda as they combined for fifteen points in the initial six minutes of play. The zone defense appeared vulnerable for a few short minutes; but tighten promptly. At the forward position, Julie played strong by scoring from the baseline on frequent occasions and contributed to rebounding strength in aid to Monique. Even with a trailer park twin on the bench, South Eastern State firmly stood their ground eliminating any chance of their opposing forces to cut into the lead.

Midway in the second half, Wicked Wanda was called for charging. Being a questionable call, FF challenged the official's viewpoint. Not happy with the call or the viewpoint, FF gave the tourney officials a taste of her savvy. With her classic gesture, she shouted, "right here ref, right here!"

An alarmed referee pretended to ignore her actions, but her players did not. In response, FF removed Monique for a spell, revising her line-up with an indoctrination of The Fresh Five.

She had the original five recruits out on the court running a man-to-man, full-court press at the Bobcats. After a couple of good fast breaks, they switched to a half-court press maintaining the tight man-to-man hustle defense. In a manner of moments, if seemed Julie practically took the game over with her agile maneuvering up-and-down the hardwood. She virtually broke the game open with four consecutive baskets, as the Bobcat defense could not contain her.

With a little over five minutes left to play in the game, FF called time out. She huddled her team, "our twenty-five point lead looks good now, but don't underestimate your opponents!" She sent her players back onto the court, leaving Yogi and Wicked Wanda on the bench. Jamie Lee received the nod at guard, complimenting Flowers.

Julie hadn't played much with Jamie Lee, but she liked her potential. Julie detected Schuyler's mind worrying about the game's outcome. *"Schuyler, don't worry because we are up by twenty-five points with little time left."* She received his acknowledgement and went back to business.

Responding to Julie's air, Yogi started daydreaming on the bench. *"Too bad Schuyler's not here at the game, he's really interested in Julie."*

FF, in astonishment from Yogi's air, contemplated the effects of having The Dream at her game. She asked herself, what possible effect could it have to play in front of the one possessing air phenomena?

In conclusion of the game, FF replaced Monique with Patti for a few minutes giving both Jamie Lee and Patti some playing time. Team FF finished off the Bobcats by a score of 77–54.

A sounding victory is was as the trailer park twins combined for a total of forty-four points, Julie contributed seventeen points, Wicked Wanda had ten points, and Yogi collected a six-point total. Both Jamie Lee and Patti failed to score, but played quite well in relief.

With the victory under her belt, FF looked ahead at the championship game. Within a few hours, it was quite evident South Eastern State would face the Raiderettes in the finals. The Raiderettes had FF in fear all along throughout the tournament due to their size under the boards.

At conclusion of the evening's events, Yogi and Julie went back to their room. In route, Julie diagnosed the Bobcat game. *"Schuyler, we played like champs tonight. They were little contest for our transition game."*

Schuyler was on his way to work; excited about the triumph he wondered how she did in the game.

With Yogi following along, *"I scored seventeen points, a few buckets behind Heather and Brittney,"* responded Julie.

"Tell him about me, please?" Yogi asked her as they entered the hotel, avoiding the casino room.

"Also, my roommate scored six points and tallied eight assists. Her name is Yogi and she plays guard." Julie gazed over at the casino room. *"We have a casino in our hotel, too bad it's off limits."*

Schuyler thought about the numerous slot machines in Korea. He remembered how a lot of soldiers lost their money playing the one-arm bandits.

"Yes, I know it! But it does look exciting." Julie rode the elevator to the fifth floor and located her room. She was happy to be back in the room; because it was obvious she needed as much rest as possible. Because tomorrow afternoon would be the championship game and she could not let her guard down. The Raiderettes could not be taken softly, she understood her "A" game would be needed for a convincing championship win.

Sunday's championship contest featured two powerful opponents, publicizing the game's importance in great detail. One of the nation's longest winning streaks was on the line for South Eastern State. No defeat had crossed their paths since the disappointing defeat at the hands of the Tigers back in late December. Team FF had demonstrated courage compiling a string of victories, the most in school history, in search of national recognition.

With success on her mind, Julie met with her teammates in route to the arena. The team arrived a little early, attempting to resolve any deficiencies before play began. A noon shoot-around gave The Fresh Five a bit of opportunity to sharpen their shooting eyes. Sighting in on the basket, Yogi practiced extensively on her fifteen-foot shot in the lane. Being an excellent shot from the free throw line, she adapted very well to her fifteen-foot jumper along the foul line. Normally not a frequent shooter, she was asked by FF to practice this particular shot. As a good soldier, she received her warning order and proceeded with the mission. Along with Yogi, the others practiced their favorite shots. Wicked Wanda aimed at three-pointers from the top of the key, as Julie's three-pointers projected from the wing positions.

The trailer park twins, having little preference, fired projectiles from a wide range spectrum. In a crucial championship game, air supremacy was important and The Fresh Five had the ability to utilize both short-range and long-range bombing in very effective manner.

The shoot-around set the stage for a productive day, defining objectives to be achieved by The Fresh Five. Virtually, it was their day; four years of hard work compressed into one day determined their lives. The day would be the cutting edge for FF; presiding as one of the region's foremost leaders, her coaching legacy pended on this single day.

An interested Schuyler, informed by additional news media coverage, consistently kept in contact with Julie throughout the day. He wished to be there greatly, but of course was out of the question. Julie, via air, kept him informed of the current activities but the setting was not the same as when Schuyler's performance was on the line. Since he possessed the air phenomena, Julie's activities were not via air in the same sense as Schuyler's presence. Thus, he could not watch Julie perform as sixth man in the same procedure as she could watch Schuyler exist his entire life.

Pre-game talk left FF almost speechless; an experienced, boisterous speaker was without words. She only a few, short comments to administer, "you'll know what needs to be done in order to accomplish the mission." She asked for any other comments from the team?

"Coach, we are ready and willing to earn this championship today. We will not let you down!" Heather offered her encouragement.

On that final note, the team exited the locker room and marched onto the court once again to illustrate dictating talent above the level of their competitors. The game was soon to begin!

In pre-game, Julie practiced her battlesight zeroing of her targets from wing positions. *"Schuyler, we are about to start; right now I'm warming my shooting arm."* Reading his mind, she responded to his ensuing question concerning her pre-game shooting accuracy. *"My aim is on target. I will not disappoint you tonight!"*

Sitting next to FF, Julie could feel her heart pounding, as it was her own; awaiting the ceremonial tossing of the initial jump ball. The two of them sat together, palms sweating, as the game began. Anticipating an early lead, Coach Jackson kept her sixth man informed of resulting prescribed duties. Besides scouting the opposition for later action, Julie's additional duty involved assisting the coach in staying focused on the transition game. FF preached good ball movement up-and-down the floor, enhancing scoring opportunities for the trailer park twins. The scoring they provided was the lifeblood of the team, distinguishing the necessity of good transition. Also upon game entrance, Julie's vast court mobility contributed to numerous points off the fast break.

Early in the game didn't go their way, Monique suffered a couple of fouls and Yogi coughed up a few turnovers. Down by six points, Flowers entered the game in relief of Monique. With the original Fresh Five on the court together, Team FF went directly into a mix of both full-court and half-court press depending on the situation.

Pointing at Yogi, Wicked Wanda, and Julie, "trap the ball!" Shouted FF as she sat next to Monique on the bench.

"Cut the dribble off!" Julie approached a Raiderette in appliance of a double-team trap. She waited for Yogi to stop the Raiderette's dribble, and then dislodged the ball free.

"I got it!" Yogi secured the loose ball penetrated into the lane, shot a fifteen-foot jumper, scoring two points that cut the Raiderette lead to four points.

Another scoring chance was made available when Wicked Wanda forced an errant pass, intercepted by Brittney in route to an easy lay-up. The score was eventually tied when Yogi stole the ball from a dribbling Raiderette, delivering an assist to an open Julie. A stimulated Team FF, from aggressive pressure, stifled the opposing forces alleviating some pressure off their offense.

With Monique still on the bench, FF called time out and addressed her players. "Only three minutes left in the half and were still tied." She pointed at Yogi and Wicked Wanda, "get the ball to Brittney and Heather at the post while Julie spots up on the outside."

The subsequent two times down the floor registered back-to-back three pointers from the hands of Julie. With the defense insistently guarding the twins, an open Julie made two three-point shots in a row from the right corner. Attracting immediate defensive attention, Julie's ensuing decoy allowed the twins to score two baskets a piece before halftime.

The implemented strategy paid quick dividends, propelling South Eastern State to a ten-point lead at halftime.

At intermission, FF demanded utmost attention as she designed a couple of offensive rotations, allowing the twins more freedom near the goal.

With Monique reporting back into the game at the beginning of the half, FF could orchestrate her 1-3-1 zone defense with either Yogi or Wicked Wanda at the top and Julie on the bottom. The twins would bookend Monique along the middle. Morale was high, spirit even higher as FF deployed her troops back into battle. It appeared the Raiderettes would fight to the finish; an allocated lead of ten points was no cushion to rest upon.

Julie could do nothing but imagine a victory for her team, a chance to shine where few have done before. She alarmed her telepathic companion of her quest only moments prior to tip-off. *"Schuyler, our ten-point lead at intermission will survive; I plan to give everything I got in the second half."*

As play began in the second half, Team FF attempted to seal off the middle of the lane on defense controlling the tempo of the game. Even if the opposition scored, Julie immediately in-bounded the ball to Wicked Wanda as quick as possible to generate hasty transition offense. After receiving Julie's in-bound pass, Wicked Wanda would alertly locate Heather or Brittney for instant offense. Quick passing, vigilant ball maneuvering, and first-class shot selection totaled numerous baskets for the twins. Before Julie even got down the court, points were being tallied. Not being left out, Julie and Wicked Wanda zeroed-in a few three-pointers themselves as South Eastern State quickly took control of the game and along with it, their destiny. Monique, staying in her lane, concentrated on defense in balance of a swift offensive that initiated a scoring disparity well into the second half.

With a cushion of twenty points, FF inducted Jamie Lee and Patti into the contest along with Yogi. The trio joined the twins on the hardwood in stiff competition with the Raiderettes, establishing a little bench strength of their own.

Ridiculed for lack of bench depth, Coach Jackson rationed a little playing time for both Jamie Lee and Patti. The latest formation granted both Heather and Brittney supplementary scoring opportunities, employing Yogi's ball handling as the floor sergeant distributing the ball to the twins at opportune scoring localities. FF, with the taste of victory already on her breath, carefully watched Yogi slow the pace down and milk a little clock.

Yogi, an excellent ball handler by trademark, could control the clock with the best of them. She alternated a few passes between Jamie Lee, but as the shot clock ticked down she would continuously spot one of the twins with the ball for an ample shot attempt.

As the lead remained above twenty points, FF replaced the twins for a few, short minutes with Julie and Wicked Wanda. The current rotation now featured four good, steady ball handlers of Yogi, Wicked Wanda, Jamie Lee, and Julie. Even though they suffered in size, this new rotation managed to kill a lot of clock. As the premier shooter on the court, Julie delivered a few baskets maintaining the comfortable lead. Also, Wicked Wanda found a scoring niche of her own as she scored consecutive times down the court in an ensuing victory over the Raiderettes by a score of 89 to 71. A convincing win it was as South Eastern State claimed their first conference championship in more than two decades.

After the victory, a proud FF and her team awaited following award recognition. With a celebration of their own, cheerfully hugging each other, Team FF enjoyed the moment.

Breaking away for another celebration, Julie telepathically hugged Schuyler, *"we won the championship dear!"*

He asked who was MVP?

"We don't know yet, but either Heather or Brittney because they both played outstandingly!"

Coach Jackson, fighting off tears of pure enjoyment, interviewed with the media in elaboration of her team's success. In praise of her seniors, she offered recognition to a very much deserving cast who sacrificed their lives for the past four years in honor of this basketball program.

The award ceremony brought the team close together, the All-Tournament Team announcement left Julie stunned as she was named to the seven-player tourney field. Excitement was felt throughout the air, as both Heather and Brittney were named Most Valuable Player. The twins were co-MVPs of the conference tournament leading the way on the all-tournament selection.

Astonished, pleased, and exhausted described Flowers as she accepted an all-tournament selection trophy. As she was congratulated by a host of dignitaries, she relayed her achievement, via air, to Schuyler. *"Schuyler, during the award ceremony I was selected on the All-Tournament Team along with Heather and Brittney! The two trailer park twins earned co-MVPs."*

Julie, smiling with happiness to the crowd, could read Schuyler's emotional mind state. His transmittance was in strong favor of her accomplishment. Her heartbeat began to race to keep pace with the heartbeat of her distant lover; his emotional feelings translated pure contentment.

True, it was a colossal event for Julie Crystal Flowers. The championship, the all-tournament selection, and Schuyler's feelings toward her were almost too much for this woman to absorb. Her transformation process, similar to Schuyler's, from teenager to adult was apparently in full force. Julie, due to her success of the championship event, took a giant step toward adulthood. A giant step it was, but the true test would transpire during the ensuing national tournament; a tournament in destiny for not just for her, but for the entire team.

Celebration was sweet for Team FF. The fanfare was enormous as Julie and the rest of the team returned back to Louisiana as crowned conference champions. It was evident the national tournament selection board would definitely consider South Eastern State as a potent team for any bracket. The team had a winning record of 26–1, with a consecutive winning streak of twenty-two games. Talk throughout some media suggested weak conference competition profited South Eastern State's consecutive winning streak.

Coach Jackson informed the media, "my team maybe unknown to the rest of the country, but in our region we are a corps to me reckoned with." Notifying the disbelievers, she stood tooth and nail to any interviewer in doubt of her team, a squad capable of playing with anyone in any arena.

As selection time grew near, the team gathered on selection Sunday at the athletic department in anticipation of a favorable position in the bracket. But as the selection process unfolded, news of a ninth seed momentarily wilted the spirits of the team.

"Number nine seed in the Mideast Regional against the number eight seeded Hilltoppers," announced FF. "I'm a little insulted with only a number nine seed, but I do like our regional!"

"Yes, we go to Lexington for the first two rounds and then off to Cincinnati to maybe face the Tigers again." Heather added to the coach's announcement.

Standing up, Brittney enthusiastically spoke in favor of playing the Tigers once again. "Look team, we need to win through our bracket and match-up again with the Tigers because their overconfidence will be in our favor!"

FF settled down the commotion, dismissed her players to their dorms in preparation of an ensuing trip to Lexington in a few days.

Julie notified Schuyler, via air, of their selection to play the Hilltoppers in his nearby town of Lexington. He acknowledged her transmission, responding of a strong eagerness to watch the game in person.

FF, listening to the telepathic couple's air transmission, signaled an idea in her mind. Aware of Schuyler's telepathic condition, she planned strategy of her own. Schuyler's physical appearance at the game might be distracting, but the promising potential of achievement might be what the team required. Without another thought, FF initiated strategic action.

CHAPTER 17

The March mornings came quickly as Schuyler prepared himself for school as he forged his way through his classes. He adapted well to college environment, familiarizing himself to cafeteria food in replacement of military dining facility cuisine. As his college studies and pharmacy job began to become routine, he focused on women's college basketball. He tracked his favorite team, South Eastern State, publicizing their profits, via air transmission, to the public. His interest in Julie had transpired from college student and New York performing arts apprentice into the March madness of the basketball world. It was an exciting period, defining the true pride of collegiate espirit de corps.

On the afternoon of Wednesday, the madness of March became real when a special delivery letter landed in the hands of Schuyler Ballantine. Nervously he signed for the letter, thanked the delivery source, and opened the mysterious letter. Contents of the letter revealed two tickets to both rounds of the regional tournament to be played in Lexington. Alarmed, but elated, he did not question where the tickets came from, but only accepted them in honor of the event itself. Schuyler, in his own hands, possessed first and second round tickets to the national tournament of women's basketball. The seed for destiny was planted.

The past few weeks for Schuyler had been a bit hectic, balancing school with pharmacy commitments. Feeling anxiety, due to Julie's basketball challenges, he still had the mental strength to confront his part-time pharmacy job. A scandalous environment was brewing at the hospital pharmacy, manipulating Schuyler's integrity as a trusted employee.

Every weekend, he seemed to detect unethical activities in practice. Besides the growth hormone incident, he noticed excessive requisitioning of antibiotics and antiviral pharmaceuticals. Cutting drugs of the top was a common occurrence among pharmacy practice, proliferating profit for a selected few. Schuyler's suspect, due to the covert operations as present, translated alert to the actions of Victor, Crazy Bob, and Scratchy. Eventually, he matched a connection with the trio since they often worked the same shift on Friday night. Prescribing a strong relationship of Victor's excessive requisitioning of expensive medications in coordination with Scratchy influenced his perspective of the pharmacy's working environment.

Team FF arrived in Lexington on the day prior to their Friday afternoon game. A brief practice session ensued on Thursday evening in preparation for the regional opening game featuring South Eastern State and the Hilltoppers.

Coach Jackson, attempting to dodge the media as much as possible, ensured time management allowing ample opportunity for her to spend quality time with her team. She was almost inseparable with her players, her participating leadership style integrated player involvement in the decision making process. Her unique coaching approach earned respect among her players, peers, and opposing forces alike. Coach Cheryl Jackson, standing tall in the spot light, illuminated her team to the world of women's college basketball, a team led by a reverent coach in quest of more than just respect.

After a vigilant practice cataloguing offensive rotations, zone and man-to-man defenses, and ball maneuvering transitioning, FF held her team meeting. Expressing her concerns of the consequent first-round game, she asked her players for feedback that might enhance their victory over the Hilltoppers.

Brittney and Heather each offered their advice promoting team achievement and success. Also, Wicked Wanda encouraged the transition play of both Yogi and Julie stressing quick, precise passing in transition.

"You'll need to communicate to each other on the court; if possible I would like everyone to know where everyone else is at all time," requested FF.

Julie reminded herself of the possibility of Schuyler being present at the game, understanding the potential opportunity of benefiting from his telepathic ability. With Schuyler's potential presence at the game, she began to visualize the effect in her mind. Developing an advantage, Julie planned her game strategy.

Lexington's arena was extremely large with seats stretching from all points inside. The team was allowed to have a little practice session, familiarizing them to the huge stadium. Except for the arena in New Orleans, this stadium exceeded all others visited by leaps and bounds. Indeed it would take a whole lot of fans to fill this arena, but the size of the ship was not as important as the talent of the sailors aboard it.

Expecting the arrival of her telepathic boyfriend at the game transmitted nervous tension throughout Julie's physical state. In suspense, she did not know what to expect of the encounter. Unsure of the situation, she asked Schuyler his intentions. *"Are you coming to the game, Schuyler?"*

Of course Julie, I have tickets and plan to attend the game. I don't know exactly where I will be sitting, but I'm looking forward to watch your performance.

"I feel a little awkward, because I've never played before air. It will be unique watching me play via air phenomena."

Reminding her, he thought confident images across transmitting links between himself and her. Through mental telepathy, Schuyler was preparing Julie for battlefield challenge.

As game time crept near, eagerness to get on the hardwood grew. It was a stressful time, but FF handled her team with much promise. Leadership doctrine emphasized application of routine tasks to fight battle stress, influenced by this doctrine FF ensured her players stayed busy throughout the day with enjoyable activities. She believed if the players kept their minds off the game, then they would be less tense as they entered the arena.

Bewildered, an anxiety-stricken Schuyler worried about his attire for the big game. It was his first opportunity to be in same location as his dream girl. It was awkward, she being a star basketball player compared to his minimalist status. An opportunity was knocking at the door beholding a possibility of Julie gaining benefit from Schuyler's presence. In the past Julie's mentorship guided Schuyler to the High School Regional Golf Tournament, but this window of opportunity could be the ticket for him to return the favor. He could only imagine the consequences of his air phenomena presence at the Mideast Regional Tournament.

Friday afternoon came upon Team FF in quick manner; the Fickle Fisherwoman coordinated her team in fashion to upstart this tournament with grand temperament. Vow from The Fresh Five, and their teammates, granted promise throughout the entire state of Louisiana. The game would be a match-up between a perennial national tournament team against a small Louisiana school patiently waiting its destiny.

Excitement filled the Lexington arena, as a non-televised tournament game would commence in the presence of a telepathic spectator named Schuyler Ballantine. The Hilltoppers, dressed in white trimmed in maroon, faced their opponents clad in black with gold. As game time grew, Julie awaited the arrival of an invited guest.

Prior to tip-off, FF signaled her troops for huddle. "We are a team of one with one thought on our mind—to be victorious!"

After a brief prayer by Wicked Wanda, the starting team broke for the center of the court. Just as Monique prepared for the initial jump ball, a sparse crowd focused upon a young man wandering alone throughout the facility in search of his seat. He was an individual unlike any other at the event, as onlookers gazed at him the contest began before he reached his seat. This individual was beckoned to this tournament by a coach searching for anything possible to advantage her team. His presence alone set forth a precedence publicizing a possible paradigm shift in the way a coach utilizes strategy.

Schuyler, dressed conservatively in a white polo shirt bearing a U.S. Army logo, eventually located his seat. By design, his seat was conveniently positioned opposite the bench of South Eastern State in plain view of the entire court. With love in his eyes, he could only watch his dream girl sit patiently on the bench next to Coach Jackson.

"Hi Schuyler, glad you could make it. But please watch the game, informing our players of the opposition's location as much as possible. Kind of like a SALUTE report you used to do in the Army!" Julie presented the operation order to Schuyler.

Schuyler reported back, Lima Charlie! In strong attempt to keep from staring at his lost love, he promptly initiated action to analyze opposing force capabilities both offensively and defensively.

With his perspective from a pre-positioned seat, FF immediately designed transitional movement in attack of her opposition. Having another viewpoint gave FF an opportune advantage, since by reading Schuyler's telepathic mind she could adjust fire throughout the course of the game. Indeed, FF initiated a twist in the game of basketball by planting an observation post in the crowd. With high expectations, FF could only dream of further success.

Sitting on the bench, Julie studied the Hilltoppers through her eyes and the eyes of Schuyler. With the score tied at twelve, she entered the game substituting for Yogi.

Almost immediately, momentum adjusted in favor of Team FF. Julie began to take charge of the offense relying on Schuyler's input; maneuvering the ball down the floor like the captain of a ship, she continuously found an open Heather or Brittney in plain view of a high-percentage shot. Uncanny as it was, she sparkled almost every time she touched the ball. Through Schuyler's vision, she detected and attacked her opponent's weaknesses in deliverance of timely passes and shots. Within five minutes of her induction into the game, South Eastern State's lead spread to ten points.

On defense, Julie guarded the base line as their 1-3-1 zone defense stifled the Hilltoppers. Again, Schuyler's telepathic vision informed her of opponent's strength under the basket. With knowledge of opposing force position, she managed to block passing lanes in the paint initiating fast break opportunities.

By halftime, the Hilltoppers found themselves in a deficient of fourteen points. Flowers' play had spurred her team on both ends of the court. A triple-threat, she brought seven assists, four steals, and eight points into the locker room at intermission.

Schuyler, a pleased spectator in the crowd at halftime, could only mention one main thought to her, *"Julie, I'm so proud of you!"*

"I'm so happy you came to watch me play," Julie aired back to him as she sat patiently in the locker room waiting for ensuing orders from FF. *"Your presence makes all the difference in the world!"*

At the intermission, FF was so excited she couldn't speak. Her voiced crackled every time in attempt to speak. She managed, "keep it up!"

Brittney stepped forward, "stay focused out there, we have them on the run!"

"You bet, let me get you the ball inside." Wicked Wanda encouraged, "I feel good about this game."

Coach Jackson could only listen to her players chat about future success, dreaming about the possibilities of Schuyler's air phenomena in her arsenal.

As the team marched back onto the court, Schuyler sat alone in his seat in continuous thought. Surrounded by spectators, he could only think about Hilltopper basketball and avenues of approach to contain their potent scoring machine. Harnessing his mental telepathy revised Coach Jackson's entire method of scouting a team.

FF began the second half with the starting team on the court. With Julie by her side, she commenced to reevaluate the opposing force for any adjustments in the second half.

Yogi opened the second half with a couple of good passes to the twins in perfect position to score. Attempting to restart where Julie stopped, she asked for assistance from their guest spectator. *"Help me stay focused out there, allow me also to vision the game in my mind as I play a part in this contest."*

Even with a two-digit lead, their man-to-man defense sacrificed several easy baskets along the baseline. With the lead being cut to ten points, FF wasted no time by inserting Flowers back into the game replacing Wicked Wanda.

Upon entrance, Julie eyed Yogi and then gazed upon her telepathic companion in the crowd. Energizing her team she directed her voice at Yogi. "Let's do it!"

The sparse Louisiana contingency applauded Julie as she initiated explosive transition derived from her alert, precise passing. Frequently after a Hilltopper score, Julie would throw an inbound pass halfway up the court to a fleeing Yogi who would relay the pass to one of the twins for fast break score. Amazing, but practical, Julie initiated a passing attack on the hardwood. By knowing Yogi's location of the court, she fired mid-length court passes to her, as she was a pass receiver. If Yogi was guarded, then she would look for another receiver in the likes of Heather or Brittney. Through Schuyler's eyes, she possessed almost full vision of the court even if her head was turned; advantage was in her favor as long as Schuyler kept her informed.

Defense promoted improvement as re-implementation of the 1-3-1 zone defense kept Flowers down low along the baseline. Her hustle alone thwarted several Hilltopper scoring opportunities, recording quite a few steals in the process. The only short-coming of this air phenomena assistance was that is caused Julie a considerable increase in fatigue due to all her hustling. FF identified her fatigue, rewarding her with a break on the bench, immediately inserted Wicked Wanda back into the game to protect a sixteen point lead with less than eight minutes to play in the game.

Yogi, utilizing their eye in the sky, slowed the pace up a bit with some handy ball control along with Wicked Wanda. Even confronted by Hilltopper trapping defense, they kept the ball between themselves awaiting golden opportunities for the twins to score. But uniquely among the trapping defense and the ball control, Monique was often left unguarded in the paint. As soon as Schuyler noticed Monique open for an easy shot, an alert pass landed in her arms in excellent shooting position. Like clockwork, an open Monique received the ball and proceeded with a golden scoring opportunity. With the clock ticking down, Monique was adding points to the scoreboard.

In the final few minutes, FF traded Julie for Monique on the court in preparation for subsequent free throw shooting. Julie was one of the better free throw shooters on the team, along with Yogi and Brittney, establishing a strong front against possible excessive fouling by the opposition.

South Eastern State possessed a 74–60 lead as Julie entered the game. Upon entrance she huddled with the rest of The Fresh Five allowing Heather to provide encouragement.

"We have come too far to let our guard down now," said Heather.

"Remember, stay in your lane!" Brittney reminded as she broke the huddle directing the others back to their positions.

As Schuyler admired the scoreboard, the Louisiana faithful cheered their team's effort. Due to Julie's superb performance, excitedly he sat patiently awaiting further accomplishments.

Feeling pressure from the tension, Julie managed to keep her game in full swing. After a couple of slick steals, causing fast break opportunities, she connected with Yogi for back-to-back easy baskets.

Eventually the Hilltoppers, pressing for points, fouled one of the members of The Fresh Five. First Heather was fouled, then Brittney was fouled, and then Julie went twice to the foul line to shoot. After Heather made one or two free throws and Brittney made both of hers, Julie secured four of four free throws to enlarge the lead to 88–70. With only seconds remaining, FF inserted Patti and Jamie Lee into the game for good measure allowing them both some official tournament playing time.

As the game ended, with the score 88-74, South Eastern State celebrated victory in the center of the floor with Schuyler looking upon. After congratulating the Hilltoppers for good sportsmanship, Team FF endured the sweetness of triumph. The game set precedence, since it was the first national tournament game ever played before air phenomena, and it was indeed a milestone.

Coach Jackson assembled her troops in the locker room in preparation for an after action review. Even though it was hard to settle down the players, she used assertiveness to obtain their attentions. "Settle down; let me give the statistical report." She opened her book and began to announce, "Yogi had ten points and ten assists; Wicked Wanda had eleven points and seven assists; Monique contributed ten points and eleven rebounds; Heather scored twenty points with eleven rebounds; Brittney added another twenty points with ten rebounds; Julie produced seventeen points, ten rebounds, eleven assists, and ten steals."

"Way to go Julie!" Announced an excited Jamie Lee and was the first to shake her hand. "You had a quadruple double with your points, rebounds, assists, and steals totals."

As the others followed suit congratulating her also, Coach Jackson offered a finishing statement. "True it was a great win, but on Sunday we will face a tougher opponent."

Heather looked at the coach, "I expect to play the Senators, the top-seeded team in the regional,"

"I expect so also, they are a huge favorite in their first round game!" Agreeing with Heather, she dismissed the team for personal hygiene.

Julie, dazed and confused, was bubbling with emotion. *"Schuyler, I received the news of my quadruple double!"*

Schuyler, walking to the parking lot, congratulated her performance. His mind was so active; no single though was transmitted without interference from another inspiration. It was like a dream coming through, as he cherished the thought of Julie being a famous basketball player.

"I read you loud and clear Schuyler, are you coming to the game on Sunday?"

With emotion pouring from his eyes, he promised a commitment from him at Sunday's game.

Julie reading his mind, *"I know you will come, nothing will prevent your presence at my game!"*

The game, as expected, was a complete success. Schuyler's air phenomenon was just what the doctor ordered. But how long could the magic last?

CHAPTER 18

The Hilltopper victory initiated confidence in Coach Jackson's team. With a convincing triumph, Team FF advanced to play the Senators. Besides being the regional number one seed, their conference play was at a much higher level compared to South Eastern State. An evenly balanced team, the Senators presided as strong favorites over their opponents, an unheard team from Louisiana. Alone in her war room, the underdog FF began to analyze her opposing forces by the virtue of a distinct spectator. She recognized and strongly understood the team's potential through the eyes of Schuyler's air phenomena.

Flowers' success buzzed excitement throughout Jupiter's think tank. The Morrison and Boyd collation strengthened in coincidence to Schuyler's successful interjections. Receiving laudatory comments from their studies, they evaluated Flowers' relationship with The Air and projected its outcome.

Morrison, occupied with coffee, examined the local newspaper revealing editorial comments concerning the upset-minded South Eastern State. "Even though the girl's success will be short-lived, her quadruple double will make its mark on history."

Boyd interrupted, "why it that? The team will not repeat its superb performance with the aid of The Vision."

Sitting with his legs crossed at his desk, Morrison explained, "according to the sports page, the Senators will win easily." He looked at his partner and read the article verbatim. "This is no Cinderella Team! A one-game wonder will fall to the hands of our Senators on Sunday."

Boyd, with pizza and chicken wings on his mind for lunch, ignored the article's suggestive influence. "I understand we both graduated from their school, but the Senators have never played before the presence of The Vision. An uncharted contingency never introduced in this fashion into the game of women's collegiate basketball."

Without response, Morrison's concern of The Air's effect upon the game grew stronger creating a dilemma among his loyalty to his school and his personal study of air phenomena. "If The Air makes it to the game then the event's outcome could be altered." He paused, and then added, "I question if we should attempt to divert his prompt arrival to the contest?"

"I realize a loss for the Senators would be dreadful, but interfering with his air phenomena would only weaken our research." Boyd's proposal landed on a good note, persuading his partner to leave it alone.

The Ballantine household was pleased with Schuyler's success in the classroom, but uncomfortable working conditions worried both Schuyler and his parents. Mismanagement of the pharmacy was one thing, but the diversion of pricey drugs was another. He had spoken with his parents concerning the issue, resolving little question. In fact, Friday night's duty offered even more controversy as he observed Victor making another mistake with the growth hormone injection. It was like clockwork, a growth hormone mistake occurred about once a month telegraphing signals of corruption in the pharmacy. Not to mention the excess requisitioning of specific mediations such as expensive antibiotic and antiviral medicine.

Confused about his working relations with the hospital pharmacy, Schuyler asked advice from his telepathic cohort. He inquired of what actions should be taken? Should he quit his job? Should he report the scandal? Or should he ignore it and go about his business. With these alternatives, he consulted Julie.

Focusing upon directives from FF, she had little time to fully examine possible courses of action. *"Schuyler, I love you and I don't want you to get into trouble."* She analyzed the situation, *"maybe you should get another job?"*

He alleged her advice as golden and proceeded to make arrangements to find another job, but he still would have to visit the hospital on Monday to give his two-week notice. His choice to end his current job eased her mind; allowing her to concentrate on winning basketball games, her current short-term goal.

As Julie attended practice for an ensuing game the next day, a furious FF spoke with a few of the players criticizing the press. "I don't think they realize our threat to their number one seed here in Lexington. Cinderella, or not, we can play at not just their level, but at anybody's level."

"What should we say about it?" Heather asked before taking the court to warm-up with Julie.

"At this moment, we remain silent." She watched Julie shoot a three-pointer, "the Senators could easily enter tomorrow's game with a little too much chip on their shoulder."

As Heather ran onto the court to join Julie, "lets knock it off!"

Practice was status quo, the same as usual, but FF kept in the back of her mind that the true test would appear once a specific spectator arrived.

She wondered over near Julie, pretending to watch her shoot, and asked via air, *"Julie, can you ensure your friend will be at the game?"*

Julie shot another three-pointer, *"Schuyler, are you coming to the game tomorrow?"* Confirming his affirmative response, she nodded to her coach in positive confirmation.

Once again, Schuyler felt proud of being a part of this event. His uniqueness offered benefit to the team. Even the coach beckoned his service, marketing his assistance to the girl he dreamed about since high school. Excitedly he planned his venture to Sunday's regional game in high expectations of an upset. His emotions ran high as he anticipated a Cinderella story of his own, a story influenced by his admiration of a distant relationship.

In route to work, late Saturday evening, he could only dream of the ensuing basketball game the next day. Arriving promptly at the hospital, he noticed a group of blind people assembling together outside of a hotel. Never previously contemplating the idea, he wondered the affect air phenomena placed upon the blind.

"Schuyler if I can see the blind people through your mind, then they must be able to see themselves also." Convincing him, Julie persuaded his air phenomena provided a form of sight for the blind. *"Even though they can't see themselves, your vision provides sight from the eyes you behold."*

In persuasion, he peered at the blind people in attempt to receive some form of feedback from the group. But no one responded via air transmittance, thus verification of a communicative connection was still unknown.

"Unique isn't it? How no single individual from the blind group responded to your calling?" An astonished Julie described the ability of the blind to ignore Schuyler's presence even in appearance of his air phenomena.

Walking past the group of blind people, being as silent as possible, he entered the hospital in route to the pharmacy. A little unsure of himself, he proceeded into the pharmacy for his usual graveyard shift. It was a distinctive feeling, reporting to work in knowledge that quitting as soon as possible was the only real priority. The job facilitated self-esteem, but the risks outweighed the benefits.

Julie warned, *"stay away from the others if you can; don't allow them to corrupt you."*

With her thoughts in mind, he tried his best to stay busy in the laminar flow hood manufacturing IV additive products. The shift would be hard to endure, but anticipation of the basketball game kept him focused throughout the night.

Sunday's landmark match between South Eastern State and the number one-seeded Senators drew little attention. Every basketball analyst from coast to coast denied FF advancement to the next round. One analyst described, "a big fish in a little pond." Another wrote, "a pretty good team, but not ready for major league play." A non-televised game, due to its mismatch, formulated little urgency throughout the Senator faithful.

Pre-game anxiety plagued Team FF, the expectation of a huge crowd compounded interest to the anxiety virus. Julie tried her best to hide her nervousness, but couldn't shun the sensation. The team was tight, and the coach knew it. During pre-game rituals, she kept it simple.

Similar to a commander introducing fresh troops into battle, emphasizing routine tasks to lower battlefield stress slowly implemented familiarity among the soldiers about to head into battle. Her warm-up routine featured a few passing lay-up drills and an extensive set of free throws for The Fresh Five, Monique, and if time permitted, Jamie Lee. It was show time and FF ensured her team was ready to show.

A little weary from his graveyard shift, Schuyler hurried to the arena ensuring prompt arrival at Julie's game. Wearing his lucky Cubs' shirt, he brought an appetite to the arena. Once inside, he prepared his stomach for the contest by engulfing his hands with a hot dog and Pepsi. Unlike last game, the seats contained numerous fans bearing Senator blue. Similar to the way he walked past the blind, he crept down the aisle to his usual seat. Detecting a bit of tension, he began studying the opposition's mannerisms in preparation for the actual game. Comparable to pre-game conditioning drills; he initiated strategy-based planning defining probable objectives for analysis.

On the free throw line, Julie eyed at him, *"our team is scared, give us some enchanted hope of achievement."*

Coach Jackson ended the pre-game routine, rallied her troops near the bench, and presented a little pep talk. "We didn't come this far to lose to them or anybody else, remember to follow our game plan, and never forget our legacy."

Heather gave the final word, "lets go out there and just have fun!" On her command the starting five broke camp and assembled at center court.

As the rest of the team positioned along the bench, Schuyler transmitted encouragement to them. *"Don't be afraid of the unknown, life's biggest rewards come from challenging fear derived from the unknown, and remember to play your heart out as it was your last game of your life."* His speech, broadcasted throughout the entire air circuit, urged his favorite team to accept the battlefield challenge and overcome any obstacle in route to conquest.

Beginning play, Monique surrendered the tip to her opponent. Within seconds, the Senators scored an easy basket. Even with Schuyler in the stands, the team felt the pressure as Wicked Wanda dribbled the ball off her foot, turning the ball over to the other team. Playing a tight man-to-man defense, South Eastern State kept pressure on the ball avoiding any further easy baskets, but the twins on offense had trouble finding a sweet spot themselves.

With the game starting to look ugly, FF leaned toward Julie. "Get ready to go in for Wicked Wanda." She looked at the scoreboard. "I'm not waiting any longer, this game is too important."

Julie removed her warm-up jacket, reported to the scorer's table, and waited for an opportunity to report into the game. Meanwhile the Senators had extended their lead to 10–4, questioning the play of Team FF in a tough match. Eventually Monique fouled her opponent, stopping the clock, and allowing Julie's entrance into the game.

Transferring to a 1-3-1 zone defense with Julie positioning on the baseline, South Eastern State momentarily stunned their opposing forces into a couple of turnovers. With Yogi bringing the ball down the court and Julie following her lead, the twins began to pick-and-roll with each other in attempt to position for a sweet shot.

Julie, after receiving the ball on the wing position, continued to locate one of the twins for a high-percentage shot. After a couple of baskets by the twins, and a steal by Yogi, the Senator lead was cut to two points.

An offensive foul placed Monique on the bench, the team went to a full court press as Wicked Wanda entered back into the game. Again, the Senators observed problems adjusting to a different defensive style. As Julie sighted the court through the eyes of Schuyler's air phenomena, she uncannily attacked her opponent's weakness in almost every aspect of the game.

Sitting among the crowd, Schuyler informed Julie of golden opportunities at both ends of the court. He could detect flaws in the Senator formations, illustrating avenues of approach for scoring prospects. Installing a trick play, Julie would fake a shot and with his air vision could detect prime occasions to draw a shooting foul. Also if an opposing player attempted to steal the ball from Julie, then she would divert her dribble and maneuver down the court in transition. Not to mention the countless passes she cut off due to knowledge of opposing positioning. Again, she was at a big advantage with her telepathic companion present at the game.

The first half featured a series of scoring stretches, misfortunes, and blown opportunities at both ends of the court. The Senators had a ten-point unanswered scoring spell, followed by eight straight points tallied by SE State. Personal foul tribulations plagued SE State as feisty play by Monique, Brittney, Julie, and Wicked Wanda warranted them all two fouls a piece at intermission.

Monique had played very little in the first half due to two early fouls, allocating more engagement by The Fresh Five. Missed opportunities significantly affected the Senators; even with excessive trips to the free throw line, they could only manage six of fourteen baskets from the charity stripe.

Critical half court pressure by Yogi, Julie, and Wicked Wanda, prevented the Senators' superb inside game to get on track, but eventually Senator-size distributed a heavy burden upon the trailer park twins precluding scoring likelihood throughout the first half.

As the final seconds of the first half ticked off the clock and both teams headed for their locker room, the scoreboard disclosed the true evidence of this second-round regional contest between the top-seeded Senators and their suspect opponents. The scoreboard revealed the Senators 37 and South Eastern State 32.

In the seclusion of the locker room, FF pledged a commitment from her players to fight to the finish. "Lets get physical with them, don't let their size bully you'll around, and don't play apprehensively." She looked at both of the twins, "we expect more offense from you two since Monique will be back in the game for protection."

Heather asked for permission to speak, and her request was granted. "I know we looked a little off balance out there, but the second half will be our stepping stone into the final four."

"You bet, we will show the world the determining factor for winning in a big game," added Brittney.

On Brittney's note, Coach Jackson deployed her troops back onto the floor to clash against their enemy.

Even down by five points at intermission, her mind knew that mission number one was to utilize Schuyler's telepathic ability to instruct her team via air transmission.

With Julie at her side, FF sat at courtside anticipating the second half tip-off. She requested Julie, "keep me informed of their weaknesses before you check back into the game in a few minutes."

"Roger that," reported Julie.

Unlike the beginning of the first half, the Senators did not take the upper hand. Concentration on the twins, allocated openings for Monique to produce offensively, Yogi and Wicked Wanda manipulated their way through Senator-pressure locating the ball to her. Within in the first initial minutes of play, Monique had scored four points setting the pace for the second half. As the game progressed, alert passes directed to the twins tallied supplementary scoring in challenge of the Senators but never cutting the lead with any significance.

A third personal foul called against Yogi, introduced Julie back onto the floor in replacement. As the Louisiana faithful cheered, "Julie, Julie, Julie!" Schuyler made eye contact with her, *"we start mobilization now!"*

Huddling with her teammates, Julie listened to Heather's encouragement. Wearing black with gold, she began her conquest. Fearing only the clock, she knew of little reason why the Senators could not be defeated. True, their size was a huge advantage executing havoc in the paint.

As she positioned on defense, she followed Schuyler's sight in knowledge of opposing forces even if located to her rear.

Back-to-back times down court she intercepted a Senator pass, establishing a dominating figure within the paint. Along with Flowers' two steals, Monique blocked a shot and retrieved a couple of rebounds. This aggressive defensive play delighted FF, enhancing expectations in the second half. Even with resilient defense, the Senators refused to relinquish their five-point lead.

Forcing a few turnovers, the aggressive defensive play by Team FF penetrated Senator offensive maneuvers enabling shooting capability from the two wing positions. With Wicked Wanda being charged with her fourth foul, the Senators gained another ensuing opportunity to score from the charity line. Fortunate for SE State, the struggling Senator free throw shooters were a measly nine for twenty at the foul line. Realizing their deficiency, FF didn't mind giving up a few extra fouls as long as her players did not foul out of the game.

A hustling Julie Crystal kept her team in the game with frequent steals, a few rebounds, and numerous assists. Closing in on another triple double, she continuously passed the ball to open teammates in allowance of easy scoring likelihood. Effectively using the in-bound pass play, Yogi would receive the pass from Julie near midcourt and relay an assist to one of the twins. The play worked like a charm, tallying a lot of points for the trailer park combination. After each Senator score, Schuyler would locate Yogi on the court and after she received the ball from Julie, then he would shift to locate an open twin in superior position to score.

In utilization of Julie's ability to draw fouls against her opponent, she ventured to the free thrown line numerous times. With only three minutes left to play in the game, she had made all ten of her free throws throughout the entire course of the game.

Her valiant play, indeed, kept her team within reach during the remaining three minutes of the game.

A timeout by FF rallied her troops in quest of one last chance to dethrone the Senators. With encouragement, "we got to make up those five points that we've been trailing by since halftime!" She discussed the foul situation, "if you have any fouls to give start giving them up when we go under two minutes." She pointed at Julie, "make it happen, get us back in the game."

As the team broke huddle, Yogi looked at Julie, "I'll get you the ball when you are open!"

The Senators, utilizing their height advantage, added an additional two points to their lead when they scored another easy basket in the paint. Good alert passing by Yogi and Julie permitted back-to-back three point shots by the twins, cutting the Senator lead to one point.

A fourth foul by Yogi gave way to Wicked Wanda's entrance back into the game. Unfortunately a charging call against her rendered a fifth foul, eliminating her from the contest and reinstatement of Yogi back onto the court. With only ninety seconds remaining, SE State foul troubles escalated with both Yogi and Monique playing on the hardwood with four fouls respectively.

A Senator three-pointer opened the lead 70–66. In response, Yogi fed the ball back to Julie from the in-bound pass in attempt to initiate transition. Reading the defense through Schuyler's eyes, her crossover dribbling instigated contact from her defender in consequence of another trip to the foul line.

The chant of "sink it Julie, sink it" from the Louisiana faithful inspired immense concentration on ensuing free throws.

"Do it again, Julie. Make both of these free throws! Watching her prepare to shoot, Schuyler offered encouragement.

The Senator crowd looked upon Flowers in disgust as her skillful shooting touch added another two points on the scoreboard.

After the second free throw tallied a point, Schuyler informed her of her streak. *"Julie, you have not missed a single foul shot this entire game! To top that, you haven't missed a single foul shot during this entire tournament!"*

Down by two points and with only a minute to play in the game, Julie received her fourth foul as a steal attempt went sour. A mistimed steal effort triggered the referee's whistle, bringing FF off the bench to challenge the call against Julie.

Pointing at her crotch, "right here ref," she voiced her opinion of the call. Quickly sitting back down in her chair, avoiding a technical foul, she patiently sat in hope of another free throw miss by the Senators.

As the Senator fans cheered encouragement to the Senator foul shooter, an excited Schuyler transmitted the results of only one of the two foul shot attempts being made. A minor battle achievement for FF as she only surrendered one point from Julie's defensive foul.

Seconds began to tick off the clock with little notice. Senator ball-control prevented any turnover prospect. An obviously foul by Brittney, her fourth, put another Senator on the charity stripe.

"Maybe she'll miss them both?" Schuyler dreamed wishful thoughts as the Senator shooter zeroed her sights on the hoop.

Louisiana emotion roared when two consecutive free throws rattled off the rim, providing still a bit of hope among the South Eastern State fans.

Dribbling the ball down the court, trailing by three points, Julie once more found a gap in the Senator defense. Cutting back against the grain, her crossover dribble drew another foul from the opposition and a consequent trip to the charity line.

Chanting "sink it Julie, sink it," Schuyler and the rest of the Louisiana loyal viewed two more successful free throws, stretching her streak to sixteen straight triumphant free throw attempts. The Senator lead was now only one point with twenty seconds remaining on the clock.

Calling her final timeout, FF counseled her subordinates. "We have to foul again, but try not to let it be a fifth foul." She paused, "don't worry about a fifth-foul; we must get the ball to Julie." On her command, Team FF reported back to work.

"Keep me informed dear!" Julie eyed her telepathic companion in the grandstand.

In attempt to foul out Flowers, the Senators gave the ball to Julie's opponent. With critical time ticking off the clock, Yogi sacrificed herself by fouling Julie's opponent suffering her fifth foul and disqualification from the contest. With honor, Yogi received an outstanding ovation as she marched to the bench.

Yogi's fifth foul proved to be huge as the Senator shooter missed the first free throw, but sank the second one. The lead was now two points with only eleven seconds left in the game.

With both Yogi and Wicked Wanda on the bench fouled out, Brittney threw the inbound pass to Julie. As seconds quickly ticked off the clock, Julie maneuvered the ball down the court. In attempt to position for a tying shot, she passed the ball to Heather at the high-post position about fifteen feet from the basket.

"Go to the wing position and wait for the ball," aired Heather. Diverting attention in protection of Julie, she faked a shot and then delivered a behind-the-back pass back to an open Julie for a three-point attempt. *"Win the game for us, Julie!"*

A crowd on its feet noticed Flowers wide open on the right wing position with the ball about to deliver the final shot. Focusing upon her shooting style, a stunned Senator partisan crowd watched in disbelief as their season ended when Flowers sank a three point shot at the buzzer.

"You did it; you won the game with the three-pointer!" An excited Schuyler rendered congratulations to his heroic idol.

On her knees in joyful bliss, she was praised by her teammates in a celebration transmitted throughout the world via air phenomena. With the scoreboard's final results showing 73–72 in favor of South Eastern State, the entire team could savor the victorious feeling of upsetting the number one seed in the regional.

As Coach Jackson watched Schuyler walk to the exit, she asked Julie. *"Can you get him to come to Cincinnati for the next two rounds?"*

Inhibiting much self-satisfaction, Julie requested from Schuyler. *"Please come back to watch me play again?"* Reading his mind, she expected he would make every effort to make the trip to Cincinnati.

In the seclusion of the locker room, Coach Jackson delivered a speech to her players. "I don't know what to say, this is a cherish moment in my life." She started to shed emotion, "you'll proved to be worthy of your recent accomplishments and will continue to verify warrant to much more than just defeating the regional top seed."

Granted permission to speak, Heather focused on the next round. "We can't savor our victory for too long because the games in Cincinnati will be tough."

"Lets do a quick after action review," mentioned Coach Jackson. "What was positive?"

"Free throw shooting!" Yogi sounded off. She looked at Julie, "Julie made every free throw she shot!"

"Transition game!" Jamie Lee submitted input, "Brittney and Heather scored a lot of points off the break."

Monique responded, "our defense kept the Senators in check most of the game." Referring to Julie, "she had a few crucial steals initiating fast break points."

FF addressed, "can you add something, Julie?

Julie, attempting her best to not shed too much emotion, carefully positioned herself in front of her teammates. "A positive factor in our success derives from the will and the strength that our heart provides. Due to the stress demanded of the team, we withstood the battlefield challenge and won the contest." She took a deep breath, "we showed real class out there on the court and lets show the court who has class."

"Very good, the remarks were outstanding!" A proud FF complimented her players. "Now, lets have some negative feedback."

Brittney, pretending to be shy, spoke quietly, "we rushed too many shots early in the game because maybe we were intimidated by the enemy."

Wicked Wanda added, "I was scared at first, but after learning of their vulnerabilities, I overcame my fears."

"We fouled a lot," interjected Heather. "But it worked to our advantage."

"True, our faults led to their failure," agreed FF. "Does anybody else have anything to say?" She waited for responses, "then I have the individual data."

As the team became silent, Yogi asked, "did Julie have another quadruple double?"

Coach Jackson read from the data sheet. "Monique scored four points and had eleven rebounds; Wicked Wanda tallied six points with six assists; Yogi contributed four points and nine assists; Brittney totaled eighteen points and seven rebounds; Heather marked another eighteen points, seven rebounds, and six assists; Julie attained twenty-three points, ten steals, and ten assists to earn a triple double; Jamie Lee and Patti played but did not score."

After the players all congratulated each other, especially Julie's performance, they went about their business and headed back to the hotel. With Coach Jackson involved with a post-game press conference, the players sighed much relief as they concluded business at the Lexington Arena.

Julie, full of joy and glee, requested a favor from her telepathic lover. *"Schuyler, can you do that for me tonight?"*

You mean?

"Yes, I want to watch you pleasure yourself while we dream about sexual relations with each other."

Checking his Army watch, he agreed to a telepathic sexual rendezvous around 2300 hours that night.

Later that evening as Julie and Yogi sat alone in their hotel, they conversed about the effect of the big upset upon their lives. Watching their heroics on the late night sports' news, Julie and Yogi felt similar sensations concerning their impact on the tournament.

"Now they are claiming us as Cinderella's at the big dance. Before the game hardly a media source even recognized our existence." Julie directed her comment to Yogi.

As Yogi turned the sound to the television up a little bit, "our game wasn't even televised, now we are national news."

"I just hope FF is happy, she has been very pressed for the past four years." Julie prepared for her shower.

"After my shower Julie, I might walk down to the lobby for about twenty minutes." Yogi added, "I'll leave to go downstairs about eleven o'clock."

Thinking to herself, Julie appreciated Yogi's allowance of her to be alone when Schuyler performs his magic.

Yogi ventured away, leaving Julie alone with her thoughts. Schuyler, as promised, gave his telepathic lover a little treat. Alone in his bedroom, he manipulated himself in fashion making certain she endured mental sensation.

It was much welcome interaction as each other's presence inspired desired passion in allowance of pleasurable sexual telepathy. Together the couple expressed romantic feelings held within, never shared with any other partner.

Deeply aroused, a breathless Julie, *"your touch compares with no other, my love."* Gratified, she prepared for a restful sleep.

On the end of the telepathic link, Schuyler completed enjoying his own comfort in route to sleep. As proud as can be, he relayed an affirmative mental answer in response to her question.

CHAPTER 19

All roads led to Cincinnati, as South Eastern State's upset of the top seed in the Mideast Regional opened a huge window of opportunity for Team FF. Freshly labeled by the media as a "Cinderella Team," the Fickle Fisherwoman and her eleven players zeroed their battle sights for their consequent opposition, the Warriors. As the number four seed of the regional, the Warriors were still heavy favorites in match against a minuscule basketball team from Louisiana. In avoidance of every barracuda from the press, a confident FF planned strategy to enhance the blossoming of her flower.

Again, Flowers' success affected Morrison and Boyd. The defeat of their Senators tarnished the affect. True, the monumental victory made headlines and enhanced research studies, but a crushing trounce of their home team indoctrinated dejection within them. Mixed emotions surrounded the think tank due to strong basketball contingencies inhabiting spirits throughout the Jupiter.

Morrison, enjoying his early morning coffee as usual; he toughest opponent has been conquered, The Final Four is reachable!"

"Sports reporters are all claiming credit for the upset!" An angry Boyd showed him a national newspaper. "Upset not unexpected, only unpredictable!" He added, "what do they mean by that?"

Morrison tried to analyze, "maybe they're afraid of reality." He followed, "jumping on the bandwagon might be a trend?"

"I don't care for it at all! The girl's team earned the victory with no help from the press," added Boyd.

Morrison calmed his partner to ease by reminding him of air phenomena proliferation. "Remember, the frequency of air transmission has grown a lot in the past week."

He looked at Morrison. "Affirmative, but The Vision still has to live his own life!"

Morrison nodded his head. "Obstacles at his job might prove trouble for The Air."

With air phenomena at a peak, the Morrison and Boyd collaboration still followed the personal life of The Air with proximity of carefulness.

Monday afternoon after school, Schuyler visited the hospital to speak with human resources. His pharmacy job was convenient, with the back-to-back graveyard shifts, but work discomfort encouraged his decision to pursue alternative avenues of employment.

Arriving at the hospital, he listened to Julie's advice. She insisted, *"terminate your job, and find something else until the summer."* She understood his fear at work, guiding his personal safety, in attempt to sway him away from a dishonest working environment.

As he waited to meet with Mrs. Garman, brain thoughts rushed through his head. Uncontrollable thinking bothered him severely, advertising to the world his nervousness disposition.

Finally, Mrs. Garman invited him into her office. She was a short, attractive woman with heavy eyebrows illuminating supplementary facial features. She quickly put Schuyler to ease. "Please state your business," she said in a quiet, petite voice.

Nervously he answered Mrs. Garman as short and concise as possible. "Ma'am, I wish to terminate my pharmacy position."

She smiled at his timid expression, "our pharmacy offers you little challenge." She peered at his personnel file, "your qualifications exceed our standards." Fishing for an appropriated response, "do you have another job offer somewhere else?"

Attempting to keep from holding his breath while his heart pounded profusely; "no ma'am, I don't p-plan to w-work only go to school."

Waiting for him to finished stuttering, she paused in mid-thought and asked a following question. "Is there something wrong at your pharmacy job here?"

He shook his head, "no, n-not really."

Looking deep into his eyes, "Schuyler, are your sure there isn't a problem at your pharmacy job?"

"It's ok, I just want to t-terminate my assignment please." Schuyler could no longer try to convince Mrs. Garman of his innocence.

"Thank you for your work here with us, Mr. Ballantine." She directed him to the finance office. "You are officially terminated; your final check will be mailed to you in about four working days."

With tears in his eyes, he gratefully thanked Mrs. Garman and exited the hospital for the last time. What an ordeal! Schuyler's meeting was too much for him to handle and Mrs. Garman noticed.

Before close of business, Mrs. Garman initiated paperwork to delete Schuyler Ballantine from the personnel listing and activated background investigations involving selected pharmacy personnel.

Schuyler, unaware of future implications, returned back to his parents' house unemployed by his own choice.

"Good job Schuyler, now you don't have to work with those crooks at the hospital pharmacy." Julie satisfied with his termination. *"You did appear a little nervous when you were talking with Mrs. Garman."*

I don't know why I couldn't talk; I guess she was too intimidating.

"You did well Schuyler, you are lucky to be who you are." Julie welcomed his courage in discussing unnerving issues with Mrs. Garman.

Alone in his studies, he quickly prepared for the week's studies. An eventful period it was with conflicting values of school, work, and basketball colliding together throughout the course of one week. Of course, the basketball factor presented priority as Schuyler prepared to attend the contest. As before, two regional tickets appeared mysteriously in the mail for Schuyler Ballantine. But this time, the games were to be played in Cincinnati. With an extra ticket in hand, he sent e-mail to his former golfing cohort, Justin.

Justin, in his senior year of college, was still playing competitive golf at a Cincinnati area college. With much gratitude, he welcomed Schuyler's offer of attendance at the regional match. Thus for Friday's game of South Eastern State versus the Warriors, both Justin and Schuyler would be attending.

Schuyler, not having to appear at the event alone, felt assured by having Justin there with him at the game while he transmitted signals to Team FF via air phenomena. Another challenge was placed upon his unique style of transmitting communication in benefit of others.

The week was short, as Schuyler cut out of class as quick as he could in route to Cincinnati to rally with Justin. In a few brief hours, they would have the opportunity to watch a "Sweet Sixteen" regional basket ball game amongst a crowd of enthusiastic fans from the state of Louisiana.

Prior to the contest between Team FF and the Warriors, Coach Jackson had to fight off the press almost at every turn of a corner. But in compliance, she did voice her opinion describing her squad being prepared to play against any team at any level. Interviewers consistently inquired about the school's strength of schedule affecting the winning streak. Also, the term "Cinderella" was used in almost every connotation as possible in portrayal of South Eastern State's enormous victory over the Senators.

In her pre-game press release, "our hard-working athletes derive from a culture that places emphasis on selfless service, sense of duty, and organizational loyalty." She glazed over the media crowd, "their background, possessing enthusiastic spirit, accepts nothing less than the best than they can be; undivided unity is our watchword guiding the principles that foundation our economy of force." Coach Jackson finalized her speech by complimenting her senior leadership, "my top six players, all seniors, have sacrificed their lives during their entire tenure with myself." She ran her fingers through her hair and continued, "I would play any game, at any time, with my players, and today we will play again." In exit, she thanked the press for allowing her to express her viewpoint.

One hour prior to tip-off, a rendezvous between Schuyler and Justin set the stage for a reunion of old golfing adversaries. With Schuyler freshly discharged from the Army and Justin about to graduated from school, the twosome had much exchange of communication if affect of glory days.

During pre-game warm-up, Team FF was tight once more. Trailer park twin shooting drew frequent iron, Monique had butterflies in her stomach, Wicked Wanda and Yogi became worrisome of the twins' shooting inabilities, and Julie could only anticipate the arrival of Schuyler in order to restore confidence and hope in the hearts of her team mates. His appearance wagered noble influence upon the mental readiness of the entire team. She completely understood success would be derived if Schuyler appeared at their game.

A huge sigh of relief overwhelmed Team FF and their faithful fans as Schuyler entered the arena. With Justin as his tour guide, he had little difficulty locating the facility. They had choice seats, as near to center court as possible, offering an excellent viewpoint for air phenomena transmittance.

Astonished by the choice seats, "how did you get such good seats?" Justin addressed his question to Schuyler.

With quick thinking, Schuyler responded with a safe answer. "My Uncle Fred has connections and got me the tickets." He paused, looked back at Justin, "I guess I just got lucky!"

Justin, playing along with the conversation, "is he from Louisiana?"

"Uh yes, he's a big fan of South Eastern State." Schuyler swayed in his seat, "thus I follow their success also."

The twosome sat comfortably in their seats awaiting tip-off. Justin ordered the popcorn, as Schuyler secured the Pepsi. Indeed, they were ready for a basketball classic to remember.

The favorite Warriors, dressed in white with purple trim, greeted their opponents at midcourt for the tip-off. South Eastern State, bearing black with gold lettering, started the game with the usual five. As the game opened, Julie sat patiently on the bench as sixth man. As before, she studied the opposing offensive and defensive patterns. But with Schuyler's presence, her perspective diagnosed both ends of the court simultaneous. If he was watching one side of the court, then in collaboration she watched the other side. Within the first initial minutes of play, she was already mentally prepared to enter the game.

Warrior quickness spearheaded an early lead. Two swift baskets off the fast break set Team FF back 4-0. Yogi maintained control of the tempo and worked the ball inside to Heather for a basket and fed Brittney for a three-pointer to suddenly take the lead 5-4. But a turnover by Wicked Wanda led to another easy Warrior score and an offensive charging foul against Yogi gave the Warriors back the ball, eventually acquiring a three-pointer of their own.

It was a back-and-forth game, scoreboard points changed frequently, and Team FF was making a statement of their ability to play along the fierce Warriors. With the score tied 12-12; Julie entered the game in replacement of Yogi.

A chant from the Louisiana cheering section, "Julie, Julie, Julie!" Standing and cheering with the crowd was Justin and Schuyler.

"Who is this Julie?" Pretending to be coy, Justin inquired.

Schuyler, still cheering her entrance into the game, responded, "she's the best sixth man in college basketball." He took a swallow of Pepsi. "She makes it happen all over the court."

With the Louisiana faithful still on their feet, Flowers immediately scored a three-pointer, converted a steal for a fast-break score, and added another assist by locating Wicked Wanda open on the wing for a three-pointer. Her introduction into the game had already paid great dividends; with the score in favor of Team FF 19-18 a television timeout was called to order.

Warrior power proved stalwart as their front line crashed the offensive boards, capitalizing on the extra shooting attempts and tallying crucial points. But Team FF didn't let up, they kept pace with the opposition as the twins continued to score from the three-point stripe.

Justin admiring the shooting fest, "I notice the two forwards are always open from three-point range." He clutched another handful of popcorn. "And when they get open, Julie always gets them the ball in plenty of time to shoot."

"Amazing isn't?" Schuyler responded, but kept studying the game with passion. "The two forwards are Brittney and Heather, they usually score most of the points."

With the Warriors in a hot streak, Wicked Wanda slowed down the pace giving Julie a chance to catch her breath from all of her maneuvering in transition. The strategy was useful as once Julie received the pass from Wicked Wanda; she immediately connected with one of the twins for a three-point shot. With Schuyler's visual aid, Julie was indeed in charge of the game's tempo. She knew every move the twins made and when to furnish them the ball.

Another timeout break put Yogi back into the game in charge of the offense. Monique remained in the middle with the twins spread out on the wing positions.

Julie's task was to penetrate Warrior defense as much as possible and either feed the ball to the twins or take it to the hoop. FF requested more help on the defensive boards, as Monique could not keep pace with opposing front line support.

As the game progressed in the first half, SE State couldn't overtake the Warriors even with several three-pointers from Heather and Brittney. Warrior power in the middle flanked the trailer park twins, leaving only Monique available for rebounding position. FF realized the sharp perimeter shooting would not be enough to overtake the Warrior lead on the scoreboard.

Justin, addressing Schuyler, "what defense does South Eastern State play?"

"If Julie is in the game for either Yogi or Wicked Wanda, then they play a 1-3-1 zone defense with Julie on the baseline." He waved the Pepsi vendor down for a refill of his beverage. "The starting five start the game with a man-to-man defense and if Julie, Yogi, and Wicked Wanda are all three in the game together, then they usually employ a full-court or half-court press."

"Good defensive mix, it should keep the opposition off guard." Justin responded. "I really think they can handle the Warriors, but they need to involve Julie more in the offense." Admiring Schuyler's watch, "where did you get that watch at?"

"It's my Army watch, it contains a compass." Enjoying his Pepsi, he went back to scouting the opposing forces.

Newly entered into the game, Yogi manipulated the Warrior backcourt with her dribbling talent; attempting to commit both Warrior guards in defense of her, she spotted Julie the ball along the perimeter allowing her the opportunity to either shoot, penetrate, or feed off to one of the twins. It was an awesome prototype display of offensive power, affording Julie the opportunity to monitor twin-killing point production during half-court offensive maneuvers.

Charged with their seventh team foul, the Warriors plunked SE State's Flowers on the free throw line shooting a one-and-one penalty free throw. The crowd, on its feet, shouted "sink it Julie, sink it!" With a streak of twenty-seven successful free throws, she converted both foul shots extending her consecutive streak to twenty-nine foul shots made in a row.

Within the final minutes, Julie kept trying to penetrate Warrior defense in attempt to receive consequent trips to the charity stripe. By dribbling amongst congestion in the lane, she accomplished her ambition. Back-to-back trips down the court, Julie got fouled and went to the free throw line and made both ends of the one-and-one. With the additional four points from the charity stripe, she extended her streak to thirty-three.

As the end of the first half, with the Louisiana stronghold cheering, Team FF trailed the Warriors by only one point. The scoreboard, in favor of the Warriors, displayed a score of 46–45.

In the locker room, FF commended her team in their courageous effort. Scoring by Heather, fifteen points, and Brittney, fourteen points, paved the way for SE State.

Julie, of course, was in route to another triple double with her six steals, eight assists, and eight points. Morale was high, espirit de corps elevated spirits, and optimism ascended to pinnacle levels as the Fickle Fisherwoman and her Cinderella cast prepared for an encore performance in the second half.

Justin and Schuyler sat patiently in the midst of the Louisiana partisan, diagnosing analysis in accomplishment of their favorite team's objectives. They both approved of Coach Jackson's offensive strategy of spreading out the twins at the wing position allowing for open attempts at three-pointers, but Julie's talent at the free thrown line will be the most significant note of the song's stanza. Heather and Brittney could not defeat their opponents alone; Julie would have to step up to the plate.

As the second half began, FF decided to open up with Julie on the bench concealing her intended strategy for the ensuing half. With Julie not on the court yet, the Warriors could not really predict the second half's fate.

"Julie, look how they are trying to check both Heather and Brittney out deep on the perimeter." FF observed the Warrior defensive adjustment. "In counterattack, we will move Monique to the high post and roll Heather behind her with

Brittney following suit from the other side." She squeezed the rolled-up program in her hand. "We must get the two of them to get open inside for some easy baskets."

"Coach, maybe as Heather screens by Monique, then I can get the ball to her and she can feed Brittney on the backdoor play."

"I like that idea!" Coach Jackson immediately called a quick timeout to issue the operation order to the rest of the team.

Team FF broke huddle with Yogi on the bench, coordinating with each other on implementation of the plan. Within minutes of play, both Heather and Brittney had scored easily from aid of a Monique screen. Julie, in fact, had orchestrated the offensive movement in benefit of the easy buckets, representing superior leadership on the floor.

Schuyler followed the action, *"Julie, once you pass off to Heather or Brittney they quit guarding you and fall back to aid in defense of others."*

Following along, FF added, *"yes Julie, look for the give-and-go with either Brittney or Heather."* With multiple thoughts, *"watch for Monique as they double-team the others."*

Unfortunately instead of keeping on track with the scoring spree, Julie got a whistle on a steal attempt. Suffering her third foul, she went back to the bench for a short break. But Yogi picked up her slack by coming off the bench with two finesse assists of her own, minimizing the Warrior lead back to only one point. Wicked Wanda added a three-pointer to take a momentarily two-point lead and Monique snatched a couple of key rebounds preventing the Warriors from converting on second-chance scoring. Even with Julie on the bench, Team FF kept the locomotion running and sustained a one-point lead midway through the second half.

With the stretch run determining their fate, FF replaced Yogi again for Julie. Although the twins had scored most of the team's points, Julie had specific instructions from her coach to take the ball to the hoop in attempt to draw some fouls. She knew Julie's free throw shooting would decide the outcome.

With the Warriors at edge 75-74, Julie went to work penetrating the ball inside to the twins. As Brittney picked for Heather coming off a Monique screen, Julie spotted Heather for another three-pointer. The ensuing trip down court, Wicked Wanda found Brittney alone under the basket for an easy two points. Within minutes they found themselves in front 79-75, but the Warriors bounced back with six unanswered points of their own forcing FF to call a time out.

In the huddle, "we have only a little over four minutes to play and we are on the penalty bonus, let Julie take in down the lane and either draw the foul or dish off to somebody." FF gave the marching orders.

Off the dribble, Julie got fouled as she darted between two defenders. Trailing by two points, her free throws would be much beneficial. Standing on the charity line, alone on her stage, she carefully fulfilled her task by sinking both foul shots to tie the score at 81.

Warrior sharpshooters responded with a three-point goal, instilling an answer from Team FF. Driving in the lane once again, Julie drew defensive company, but passed off to an open Brittney down low in the paint for an easy two points to tie the score at 83.

A foul by Monique put her opposing center on the line for two shots. Luckily, a conversion of only one of two free throws gave Team FF an excellent opportunity to take the lead. The lead did change hands again as Julie found Brittney again for another effortless two points to take a one-point lead.

Inside the final minute, disaster struck SE State as Julie committed her fourth foul in allowance of another two Warrior free throw attempts.

Not as lucky as before, the Warrior free throw shooter converted on both attempts and pushed the Warrior advantage 85-84. Also, a turnover by Wicked Wanda allowed an uncontested Warrior two points adding to their lead at 87-84.

A final time out by Coach Jackson provided opportunity to overcome emotional distress inhibiting the team's concentration. In her huddle, she calmed the team down and stressed the requirement of a three-point play.

Walking back onto the court, *"Schuyler, let me know my situation."* Julie prepared her counterpart for the final verse in her song.

As the final seconds ticked off the clock and SE State behind by three points, Julie brought the ball down the court eyeing the twins for a perimeter shot. At closure of the game, Julie passed the ball to Brittney at the high post in route to Heather for the game tying three-point shot at the top of key. With all eyes focused upon the blonde-haired Heather, an open Julie stood at the right wing, her favorite spot, waiting for Heather's pass.

"Julie's open on the right wing!" Schuyler informed her teammate.

Without hesitation, Heather passed the ball to an open Julie Crystal Flowers with little, if any, time left on the clock. After retrieving the pass, Julie faked a three-point shot drawing her defender off her feet.

"Now, Julie!" Exclaimed Schuyler. *"She is off her feet!"*

In observance of his command, she leaned her body toward her defender in attempt to draw the foul as she attempted a desperation three-point shot. Drawing defender contact, her desperation three-pointer was not altered.

In the eyes of Schuyler, a view transmitted throughout all known world locations watched as her three-pointer sank securely in the hoop to tie the score at 87. Celebration through the state of Louisiana erupted when the referee counted her three-point shot and gave Flowers a free trip to the foul line in opportunity to win the game.

Justin, along with Schuyler, was amazed at the feat. "I can't believe she made that shot, and got fouled in the process!"

"Justin, she's going to win the game right here!"

After a Warrior timeout in attempt to hinder Flowers' winning free throw attempt, she walked alone back onto the court with no time remaining on the clock. With the score locked at 87, a drama student from a tiny Louisianan town held the ball at the free throw line.

"The stage is yours," Schuyler encouraged.

"I will not let you down." Julie eyed the goal.

On that final thought, in the midst of silence, she flicked the ball into the hoop securing victory 88-87. As she fell to her knees in tearful bliss, her teammates swarmed the floor in celebration of this historical event.

As Louisiana faithful shouted, "Julie, Julie, Julie," Schuyler and Justin cherished the moment. The scene of ecstasy endured much excitement as South Eastern State advanced to the quarterfinals.

Looking into Schuyler eyes from across the court, Coach Jackson offered her thanks to her secret weapon. *"Schuyler Ballantine, I have much appreciation for what you have down for this organization."* Joyful emotion flowed from her eyes, *"your value cannot be calculated."*

Eventually, the happiness dispersed from the floor to make way for the ensuing regional game featuring the number two-seeded Tigers. The favorite Tigers were the only team to defeat South Eastern State during the year. With a good chance of a rematch, Team FF awaited the opportunity.

Following post-game interviews, FF finally made it back to the clubhouse. In entrance, "hey! I'm back from the media's torture and ready to get down to business." She retrieved her notes, "here's the individual results." Catching her breath, "Yogi had two points and ten assists, Wicked Wanda added nine points and six assists, Monique pulled six points and eleven rebounds, Brittney tallied twenty-eight points with eight rebounds, Heather contributed another twenty-eight points and seven rebounds, and Julie supplied fifteen points, eight steals, seven rebounds, and fourteen assists."

"Another double-double, almost another quadruple-double!" Exclaimed Jamie Lee.

"What about Brittney and Heather scoring twenty-eight points a piece!" Patti shared a high-five with Jamie Lee.

The group began to mingle with each other on behalf of the outstanding results achieved by the individual players. Letting them be, FF exited the clubhouse in route to another lackluster interview. During her media conversations, she ensured to commend solid team play and outstanding fan support in inspiration as her team advanced to the quarterfinals. When asked about her team's performance, her favorite response was "everyone stayed in her lane."

The Warrior triumph awarded Coach Jackson even more recognition as her "Cinderella Team" advanced into the quarterfinals upsetting three quality basketball teams in a row. Also her success established South Eastern State as a team to be reckoned with on a national level, and players in the likes of Heather, Brittney, and Julie were gaining acknowledgment after every game. The time was now, and the hard work invested during the past four years was paying off big dividends for The Fresh Five.

Upon departure from Cincinnati, Schuyler made plans with Justin to return on Sunday for the quarterfinal game. A converted SE State fan, Justin looked forward to Sunday's game. Schuyler's drive back home was an enjoyable one, making available much time to ponder his thoughts with Julie.

Julie, near close of business with her post-game personal hygiene, initiated communication with Schuyler. *"Drive carefully dear, and don't drive back up here on Sunday with those bald tires."*

"Affirmative, I'll get them changed tomorrow." He quickly checked his vehicle's speedometer and fuel gage. *"Even though Saturday morning will be busy, I'm sure I can get Don to mount some fresh rubber on my Olds."*

"I really want to thank you for coming all the way up here to watch us play." She applied the finishing touch to her attire. *"Your presence makes all the difference; you ease tension among the team, and provide us with an added edge through your vision of the game."* She motioned at Yogi, getting her attention, and together they ventured to the grandstand to watch the Tigers play.

"Maybe I should have stayed to watch the second game?" He continued to drive southward down the interstate. *"I'm only a little over two hours away."*

Sitting in the stands, drinking pink lemonade with Yogi, Julie kept her eyes on the Tiger game, but her mind remained focused upon Schuyler's activity. Even during the pinnacle of her basketball career, she still persistently kept track of his personal lifestyle in persuasion for continuation of his purity and unsullied essence.

No other relationship existed as theirs did. A telepathic romance would normally seem ludicrous, but they have proven through perilous periods of time that telepathic stimulation could satisfy the sexual appetite of a pure, unsullied couple in desire of nothing less but to inspire immeasurable achievement upon one another.

CHAPTER 20

Luminary success was slowly capturing Julie's imagination. Her basketball heroics were transcribed in almost every sports page from coast to coast. Accomplishing feats bringing new spirit in her life, the three straight tournament victories were the ends that justified the means. It was a time in her life beyond compare; it would be a tough act to follow.

Schuyler, a humble, timid college student, continued as the misunderstood individual he portrayed. Beyond his grueling Army days, he sought contentment from mental telepathy engagement through Julie Crystal Flowers. Blessed with time on his side, due to being unemployed, his passion for the game of women's basketball elevated his force of life.

The Saturday preceding the big game drew opposite roles. As Julie prepared for Sunday's game by attending team meetings and participating in light practice workouts, Schuyler studied for a critical chemistry exam.

"Hi Schuyler!" Julie, via air phenomena, pretended to walk pass him and punch him in the shoulder. *"Too bad I don't know much about chemistry, or I would help you out next Tuesday on your test."*

In the quietness of his home, he acknowledged her transmittance and suggested she follow along with his chemistry studies anyway.

Interpretation of his mental thoughts; *"I might be of some help to you; at least I want to stay involved with your lessons."*

She continued to read his mind and anticipate his actions in pursuit of providing him with desired comfort from her afforded attention. Coach Jackson, energized from the glamour, had her team in full overdrive. A new atmosphere had overhauled her team of eleven players. The Fresh Five, in accomplishment of set objectives, initiated performance drivers guiding FF past three intimidating opponents in heartbreaker fashion. In coordination of her rehearsals that day, FF didn't know to feel content with the three tournament victories or to be preoccupied with the ensuing rematch with the Tigers. Again, as before, the Tigers were still a clear-cut favorite over her team, but this time, not as before, she would have at her leisure, an eye in the crowd among the Louisiana stronghold.

At the Jupiter, Morrison praised the work of The Air. "He is practically making college basketball history with his air phenomena interjection."

"Most affirmative, not only Flowers is following his lead but the others in complement appear to be involved with the aerial attack also." Boyd mention.

Sitting at his desk and looking through the sports page, Morrison reported. "Ah, here it is! Cajun Cinderella Team reaches Elite Eight." He took a sip of coffee. "Look here John at this article." He offered the paper to his partner.

Boyd examined the news release, "Flowers does it again! Sinks final shot at buzzer to lift Jackson Five over Warriors in major upset." He sat the paper down on his tabletop. "Too bad we had to play them in the second round!"

Morrison walked over to the window, "John, the word out on the streets is Flowers may not be legitimate."

"How can that be, her record is unblemished!"

"John I've only heard rumors, but an independent source is trying their best to discredit her."

In deep sadness, John Boyd could not accept the possibility of The Vision's dream girl being sullied at any degree. Becoming fond of her charismatic influence, any thought of dishonor acutely assailed his spirit. Nausea overcame him as he shunned any faint consideration of discredit.

Game day approached elevating espirit de corps throughout the southland. A pending quarter final match with South Eastern State and the Tigers would decide one of the pieces of the final four puzzle. The Tigers, number two seeded, featured a versatile offense incorporating star-shooting guard play complementing strong low-post strength. Team captain Alesha, an All-American forward, contributed heavy scoring from driving along the baseline. Her agile operations, dissecting defenses throughout the bracket, delivered potent offense establishing herself as the lead-candidate for Regional Most Valuable Player. In supplement to Alesha, the Tigers highlighted Jennifer and Jessica at the guard positions. These two guards, often referred to as the "blonde bombers", offered zone-busting, long-range shooting techniques that opened avenues for Alesha along baseline pathways. Indeed the rival Tigers appeared much stronger on paper than Team

FF, but once rival opponents step onto the court, momentum can easily influence outcomes rather than paper statistics.

On game day, as before, Schuyler drove to Lexington in rendezvous with Justin. A pleasant drive it was as he communicated with Julie along the way. She appeared to be quite composed, considering uneasy reactions triggered from a televised game, exhibiting tranquility and coolness during pre-game preparation.

Coach Jackson had her team in fast-forward mode in rehearsal for the huge event. All systems were status quo, except for additional maintenance with Yogi's scoring potential. A traditional weak shooter, Yogi had worked much overtime in her shooting ability. In utilization of strong ability to shoot free throws, she developed a sweet touch from the foul line area. In harmony with FF, Yogi composed an offensive maneuver by implementing penetration toward the free throw stripe, stopping about fifteen feet from the basket, and firing an uncontested shot.

"Yogi, if your opponent does not attempt to prevent you from shooting your fifteen-footer along the charity stripe, then fire away." An urging FF instilled confidence in Yogi's shooting talent.

"Lima, Charley! I read you loud and clear coach, I have been working on my shot in the middle for a long time." Yogi continued to consistently convert on her fifteen-footer inside the key.

In the clubhouse, prior to tip-off, Team FF sat quietly in pure focus of only upsetting the highly favorite Tigers. Coach Jackson went over game strategies, requesting feedback, and providing encouragement. Even with quality preparation, the game's outcome rested upon the shoulders of the players. Julie recognized the need for a near perfect game from The Fresh Five, a group with a tight relationship that would be tested maybe for the last time together.

Arrival by Schuyler was prompt, within plenty of time to join Justin, at the arena. With the same seats as before, they wondered into the huge facility in quest of viewing a gigantic upset.

"I like the seats your Uncle got us," Justin complimented.

"We have a complete view of the court here, I'm really satisfied!" Schuyler got up from his seat. "I'll go get a couple of Pepsis before they get started!"

As Schuyler returned from the vending stand, South Eastern State had taken the court. Admiring his telepathic sweetheart, he could only fantasize about her because even though she was within sight, they were still worlds apart. Often she would gaze into the stands to see what he looked like, as she maintained near constant mental contact with him throughout the contest. Acknowledging the fact that this might be their final meeting, Schuyler pressed hard to satisfy her telepathic demands.

In pre-game conditioning drills, Julie was approached by FF as she practiced her game winning shot from the right wing position. FF watched her shoot a couple of three-pointers. "Same as before, do it again Julie!"

Coach Jackson, walking among her players, appeared proud and confident in front of the large crowd. In her mind, she knew her team would perform well due to an added ingredient in her possession. As the players nervously shot practice free throws, she asked Schuyler to provide assurance.

Sitting in the middle of SE State fans, he delivered advice to the free throw shooters. *"Focus, breath, and shoot."* He followed on the next shooter, *"same as before, stay focused and breath out right before you shoot."* Similar to shooting a rifle, good breathing techniques improved results.

As game time came near, FF gathered her squad together for one last huddle. "We have proven to be the best in this regional, our only loss is to this team, and we will not relinquish our winning streak to them."

Breaking them from the huddle, FF sat down on the bench next to Julie as the starting five headed toward midcourt to encounter with the Tiger five.

"Julie, get ready to come in!"

"Coach, the game hasn't started yet."

Together they watched the opening tip-off lead to an easy Tiger basket. A turnover by Wicked Wanda and a Monique foul allowed the Tigers to extend their lead to 6–0. Yogi responded to the unchallenged six points by driving down the middle of the key and feeding Brittney on the wing, sinking a three-pointer to cut the lead in half.

"Notice when Yogi threw to Brittney her defender left her alone and tried to double Brittany." FF alerted Julie.

Julie acknowledged the strategic objective and continued to study opposing force engagement patterns. She watched Alesha drive the base line for another two points, as the blonde bombers kept the defense spread out. Fear of their perimeter shooting talent, prevented backside defensive assistance on Alesha.

Finally after the Tigers had tallied ten points, Heather scored two points from the low post to cut the lead to five points, 10–5. Within moments, FF sent Julie to the scorer's table.

Taking off her warm-up jacket, she felt the crowd's energy as they anticipated her entrance into the game. A standing ovation greeted her as she entered the game. With the chant of "Julie, Julie, Julie" she replaced Wicked Wanda on the floor and immediately informed Yogi of the strategic objective.

It was a difficult first half as the blonde bombers consistently converted three-pointers, preventing SE State to get back into the game. Even when the trailer park twins countered with a couple of baskets themselves, Alesha added points from her offensive rebounding domination. With the lead growing larger and larger, Yogi and Julie initiated play action of their own. After Julie received the pass from Yogi, she would hesitate a bit to allow Yogi to get open along the foul line, and in response would throw the ball back to Yogi. With little defense placed upon her, Yogi found herself very open for a sure fifteen-foot shot. The same fifteen-foot shot she had been practicing for at least two weeks. Finally, a bit of hope shined upon Team FF as Yogi made consecutive baskets to slice the Tiger lead to eight points, 26–18.

In turmoil, FF called for a timeout. She immediately requested team unity, deliberate passing, and patience during this panic stage of the game. "Don't try to get all the deficit back at once, just keep cutting into the lead little by little, and don't be intimidated." As the team broke huddle, Coach Cheryl Jackson pulled Julie Crystal Flowers to the side for a woman-to-woman talk. "Julie, nobody is better than you on the floor." She looked into Julie's eyes, "this game means a lot and only you can make it happen!"

FF looked into the stands, searching for Schuyler Ballantine. *"Schuyler, wherever you are at, we need you as our air traffic control."*

In route from the latrine, *"coach, that's an affirmative!"*

Even with the timeout, SE State could not crack the Tiger lead. Alesha collected a couple of baskets on garbage opportunities.

She had the knack of being in the right place at the right time in order to capitalize on loose balls bounding off the rim indirectly. Alesha, indeed, hustled her way into a lot of scoring prospects. Along with Alesha's hustle points, Jennifer and Jessica contributed with a basket a piece off the fast break. Suddenly the Tiger lead ballooned to fourteen points, 34–20.

In deeper mayhem, FF searched for a way to stop the bleeding. A charging foul against Yogi, her third foul, lifted FF out of her seat delivering a message to the referee who made the call. "Right here ref, got it right here!" She pointed to her crotch trying her best to intimidate the referee. With everyone expecting a technical foul to be charged to Coach Jackson, the referee turned his head the other way and pursed other matters. Obviously her actions did not warrant a technical, but her point got through to her players. Inspired from coaching tactics, Team FF got busy. Julie, on the transition, listened for directions from Schuyler. As he informed her of the open player, and their location on the court, she without haste delivered them the ball. She began quarterbacking the offense.

"Brittney in the left corner!" Schuyler aired as Julie dribbled up the court. Alertly, she feed Brittney for an easy bucket.

The next time down court, *"Heather down low, behind Monique!"* Schuyler aired again to Julie as she waited for Monique to set a screen prior to a snap throw to Heather for another two points.

With Yogi on the bench with three fouls, Wicked Wanda and Julie captained the ship in the backcourt.

As the blonde bombers covered Julie, Wicked Wanda broke open along the left wing. Julie, with aid of Schuyler's directives, shoveled a bounce pass to Wicked Wanda for an ensuing two points. Like magic, Team FF closed the gap to 36–26.

On defense, Julie stepped up and sealed off the baseline preventing Alesha from maneuvering along it in route to uncontested scoring. Also on the defensive end of the floor, Schuyler kept Julie notified of Alesha's whereabouts at all times. Preventing Alesha from dominating the offensive boards was almost an impossible task, but Schuyler's continuously directives significantly disallowed Alesha from getting rebound position as Julie hustled to box her out permitting Monique and the twins to gather defensive rebounds.

In closure of the first half, Julie eventually got to the free throw line for a couple of foul shots as she collided knees with Jana, the Tiger's small forward. Being her first trip to the line, the crowd suffered a long drought of not being able to cheer "sink it Julie, sink it!"

In full concentration, Julie drained both free throw attempts extending her streak to thirty-eight in a row. In the midst of cheering fans, a prescribed Tiger timeout slowed momentum setting the stage for one final drive before halftime.

Within the remaining two minutes, the Tigers collected a couple of three-pointers from Alesha from deep in the corner. Good team passing, a screen of Julie, and alertness freed Alesha for back-to-back three-point shots giving them a 42–28 lead.

Counter-offensive by Julie discovered Monique alone in the paint, since the Tigers were reluctant to guard her by virtue of heavy concentration on both Brittney and Heather.

Also, a Flowers steal led to a Wicked Wanda driving bank shot cutting the lead to ten points, 42–32. But even with precision floor orchestration from Team FF, the Tigers still held a commanding edge.

The first half ended with Jana, of the Tigers, scoring a three-point play via a two-point bank shot in the paint with a subsequent free throw from being fouled by Brittney. At the end of play, South Eastern State trailed their opposition 45–32.

"They look a little shook up," spoke Justin.

"Wait until the second half, Yogi will be back in the game." Schuyler reported as he applied mustard to his hot dog. "A thirteen-point deficit does appear bleak, but I expect the second half will be a completely different story."

In the clubhouse, FF remained calm. Intimidating her players through coercive measures was not her style. Instead, she rallied her troops via means of constructive criticism offering feedback to derive positive outcomes.

"Maybe we should open up with a full-court press?" Heather interjected.

"How about a box-and-one?" Brittney suggested. "Put someone on Alesha at all times."

Julie approached the coach and asked permission to speak. "After they score I'm going to start throwing the ball down court as soon as I can." She looked at Yogi, "so be ready."

With analysis of the feedback, FF decided to try the box-in-one with Yogi and Julie up top, Heather and Monique down low, and Brittney shadowing Alesha. Implementing the new objective, FF commanded her troops back into battle. She pulled Julie and Yogi to the side, "Julie throw that ball deep to Yogi on the side, and Yogi anticipate Heather or Brittney open for three-pointers."

After the second half tip-off, Team FF opened with a three-point shot by Julie. After a Tiger turnover, Julie found Yogi alone in the key for another fifteen-foot jumper slicing the lead to 45–37. After Jennifer and Heather traded baskets, Jessica made two free throws from being fouled by Monique, and Jana got open for a driving bank shot, Team FF was still struggling to maintain composure with the Tigers.

The box-and-one defense had proven no significant advantage with other Tigers, besides Alesha, picking up the slack. Responding after two Monique points, Jessica and Jennifer began pounding SE State with baseline shots elevating the lead to 57–41.

Gleaming at the scoreboard, FF called a timeout to alter strategy. In the huddle, "scratch the box-and-one and go to a full-court press." Replacing Monique with Wicked Wanda, she sent The Fresh Five onto the court in desperation.

Within minutes, a turnaround of six points occurred. Jana committed a costly turnover allowing Julie to score on an easy lay-up, Yogi scored again on a wide-open shot in the lane, and Wicked Wanda was left unguarded once more scoring a routine bank shot. The full-court press appeared successful, penetrating the Tiger lead, but a hacking-foul charged against Yogi placed her on the bench with her fourth foul.

Again, FF shuffled her line-up replacing Yogi with Monique. The full-court press remained in order, but with a little twist with Monique on the floor. South Eastern State performed well under the pressure; Julie utilized Wicked Wanda as her receiver on her long in-bound passes initiating multiple scoring opportunities by the twins, Monique found herself available for an open shot in the low post, and Julie contributed to the cause with a couple of two-point baskets herself.

The Tigers, in counter attack, found refuge as Alesha continued her scoring spree and the blonde bombers adjusted the sights with some long-range artillery. The offsetting scoring kept the Tigers in command with a ten-point advantage, 67–57.

Slowly but surely, SE State crept back into the game. The Tigers had secured a comfort zone consistently maintaining a double-digit lead over their opponents. FF had introduced defenses including man-to-man, 1-3-1 zone, box-in-one, and a full-court pressure in order to thwart Tiger offensives. Currently, employment of the full-court press presented a bit of a problem for the Tigers, but still Alesha's versatility granted her team the means to stay in front.

Midway through the second half, Julie's aerial attack guided Team FF with quick scoring opportunities as Wicked Wanda, Heather, and Brittney gained benefit from Julie's passing arm by tallying decisive points keeping pace with Tiger scoring generated mostly from Alesha and the blonde bombers. Another Julie three-pointer decreased the Tiger lead to 73–66.

A timeout was generated with five minutes to play; FF contemplated admitting Yogi back in the game, but later changed her mind. Due to the aggressive full-court pressure, FF didn't want to risk Yogi's fifth foul.

Instead, she kept the same five in the contest and asked them to turn up the heat on the Tigers.

A Tiger turnover gave the ball back in Julie's hands and she maneuvered through two defenders into the lane and was fouled attempting to shoot (another golden opportunity to cut into the lead and extend her free throw shooting streak). In immense pressure, Julie eyed the rim and delivered two more consecutive free throws slicing the lead margin to five points. Also, the two converted foul shots generated a perfect forty-out-of-forty free throws made during the entire tournament.

With SE State on verge of a comeback, a setback was in store as Julie collided again with Jana injuring her knee, surrendering to the bench. Yogi, as her replacement, reported into the game already bearing four fouls. The crowd felt Flowers' pain as she sat hopeless on the bench.

"Is this end of the Julie era?" Justin turned to Schuyler in fear.

"I don't know," responded Schuyler. *"Julie, can you play?"*

"Not right now! I have no strength in my knee, only pain!" She sat next to FF in embarrassment. For once she was rendered helpless against her opposition, a feeling she had never experienced before.

A little over two minutes remained in the game as Brittney stripped Jana of the ball and passed to Wicked Wanda who feed Yogi for another quick two points. After Jessica responded with a three-pointer, Heather matched her with a three-point score of her own. As the score being 76–73, the Tigers slowed the ball down in attempt to waste clock.

An alert Brittney fouled the Tigers' Betsy, currently in the game for Jana, sending her to charity stripe for a one-and-one.

A timeout by FF, prior to the Betsy's free throw, gave her enough opportunity to diagram an in-bound pass play. Since Julie was not in the game, Brittney would have to throw the in-bound pass in endeavor of a scoring transition.

After the timeout, Betsy converted the first free throw but missed the second one allowing SE State another chance to decrease the advantage margin. Monique rebounded the missed free throw, threw to Yogi who located Brittney along the right wing in position for a three-point shot, but a traveling violation called against Yogi turned the ball back to the Tigers.

A furious FF ejected from her seat, "how can you call traveling at this stage of the game if you haven't called it throughout the rest of the game?" She initiated the action of pointing at her crotch even though the referee was watching her every move.

Julie, sitting next to her on the bench, "no coach, don't do it because you might get a technical foul called on you!"

Schuyler added, *"not the time to draw a technical!"*

Refraining from delivering her classic "right here" gesture, FF pulled her finger away from her crotch and sat back down on the bench next to Julie. "Thanks Julie, the ref was eyeing me for a technical." She looked at Julie's knee, "can you play?"

"Coach, I don't think so."

The incident calmed down, but the Tigers still had the ball with a three-point advantage with under a minute to play and precious time ticking away.

With Jennifer holding the ball, the same referee who called the traveling on Yogi called a three-second-lane infraction on Alesha.

In a great deal of alarm, the Tiger coach yelled at the referee coming near to a technical foul himself. In challenge of the lane infraction, he attempted to work the ref a little bit too. But the damage had been done; the ball was in the hands of SE State with only twenty-five seconds left on the clock.

Down by four points with the score 77–73, Wicked Wanda received the in-bound pass from Brittney and dribbled up the court to set-up the offense.

Schuyler alerted Team FF, *"look at Monique; she is open at the high post."*

At his command, Wicked Wanda feed Monique at the high post. Awaiting instructions from Schuyler, Monique held the ball for a couple of seconds.

"Monique, check Wicked Wanda at the top of the key!"

On his command, Monique passed to Wicked Wanda for a three-point goal to cut into the lead at 77–76. Faithful fans applauded the score, but the Tigers still had the ball with a one-point advantage.

Only fifteen seconds remained as the Tigers threw the in-bound pass. Team FF knew that a foul would have to come within a few seconds. With eleven seconds on the clock, Yogi committed her fifth foul dismissing her from the contest. She had fouled Jana, not one of the sharp-shooting blonde bombers, and placed a 66% free throw shooter on the line.

With Yogi ineligible to play, FF looked toward Julie for assistance. "You have to go in the game for Yogi, she has fouled out!"

In tears, "coach I can hardly walk, much less run." She searched for Schuyler in the crowd.

A standing Schuyler, *"please Julie, ignore the pain, report back into the game and do it again!"*

FF put her arm around Julie. "You are our only hope."

Julie sprung from her seat, "coach I'm ready to win the game, give me the basketball."

Limping on the court, Julie was greeted by a deafening applause. "Julie, Julie, Julie." Acknowledging her teammates, she hobbled down to the other end of the court in the opposite direction of Jana's free throws.

Jana, on the foul line with a one-point lead with only eleven seconds on the clock, was prepared to shoot a one-and-one. With all eyes, including Schuyler's telepathic vision, upon Jana, she ripped the net clean scoring on the front end of the one-and-one. As the scoreboard presented a score of 78–76, Jana eyed the mark and delivered her foul shot at the goal. The crowd, holding their breath, watched Jana's shot bounced around the rim and fall off into the hands of Heather.

Disregarding a possible timeout, Heather immediately passed the ball to Brittney who dribbled the ball down the court as time slowly ticked away. Julie, standing in pain at her favorite spot on the right wing, watched Brittney attract Tiger attention.

Less than five seconds remained as Schuyler rendered his final commanding order, *"Brittney, Julie is open on the right wing!"* He sighed, *"The right flank is clear for Julie to shoot the winning shot!"*

Upon his command, Brittney prepared to shoot a three-point shot from the top of the key. Instead of shooting, she faked the shot and attracted both of the blonde bombers toward her, causing Julie to be unattended on the right wing in position to shoot a three-pointer in attempt to win the game. Anticipating a three-pointer by Brittney, the crowd viewed Julie receiving Brittney's pass in perfect position to shoot. Shooting just prior to the buzzer, Julie hit a three-point shot that was transmitted around the world. Yes, her three-pointer lifted South Eastern State to a 79–78 victory over the rival Tigers.

In complete celebration, *"Julie, you came through in the clutch again!"* Schuyler continued to transmit signals of happiness via air phenomena.

Justin, along side of Schuyler in celebration; "She's a true champion; she has my vote for Most Valuable Player."

"Well deserved, but advancing to the Final Four is the major objective accomplished." Schuyler responded as he continued his standing ovation.

As her teammates emotionally congratulated her, Julie feel to the floor in tears. Not knowing the tears was from pain or joy; the trailer park twins carried her off the floor in triumph.

After congratulating the opposition in good sportsmanship and avoiding the media, Coach Jackson directed her team without delay to their victorious bench to savor the moment and wait for award presentations.

A thrilling event it was as the Regional Championship Trophy was presented to Coach Cheryl Jackson. The entire team, in unison posed for the photographer, portraying the huge, magnificent trophy.

Prior to the All-Tournament Team announcement, Julie nervously tried to ignore any idea of her not being selected to the team. She tried to focus on Schuyler, her drama schooling, or even childhood activities in attempt to block out the notion of her non-selection.

Feeling her distress, FF approached Julie whispering something in her ear. "Don't be upset when your name isn't on the All Tournament Team because you are The MVP."

"Thank you very much," Julie began to cry. *"Schuyler, wait for the MVP announcement!"*

"You got my vote!" Schuyler patiently waited for the MVP results to be announced.

As the Mideast Regional All Tournament Team was announced with the Tigers being represented with Jennifer, Jessica, and Alesha. Also, Heather and Brittney both claimed a spot on the prestigious list along side of the Tiger trio.

Standing next to FF, Julie anticipated the Most Valuable Player announcement. *"I'm ready Schuyler!"*

With all eyes, including Schuyler's air phenomena, on Julie, the master of ceremonies spoke, "and for Most Valuable Player for the Mideast Regional Tournament." The MC paused, "from South Eastern State, Julie Crystal Flowers!"

A tremendous ovation congratulated her as she limped to the MC to accept the MVP trophy. An emotional wreck, she tried her best to hold back tears of joy but ultimately lost the battle.

Finally after all the hard work, it was her moment on the stage. This event in her life was like no other before; an occasion of enormous gratification hailing her as the chosen champion.

Justin and Schuyler hung around for a bit of the celebration and eventually dispersed from the arena. In an emotional state, Schuyler wished Justin good luck with his golfing career and promised to stay in touch via e-mail. As Schuyler walked away to his vehicle, his heart suffered depression recognizing that this game might be the end to the Julie era. With her leaving the area, heading to San Antonio for the semi-finals, and later back to Louisiana, he might not ever see her again. There was a good chance that their relationship might falter due to separation. He was sadden, the two games in Lexington and the two games in Cincinnati elevated mystical sensations captured within his essence. Mental passion grew as he followed his dream girl throughout the final days of her college basketball career; all he could was to imagine about his fantasy girl becoming a star.

The stunning upset, the award presentations, and the excitement of traveling to San Antonio to play in semi-finals was due cause for a little celebration. In the locker room, a pleased FF delivered a final message. "I'm so proud of you'll! Even with a fourteen-point deficit, a comeback victory was not in question." Her congratulations to the entire team set precedence for the ensuing trip to Texas. The semi-finals would be an event for all to remember, a dramatic episode in the lives of everyone in collaboration of this fine organization. She opened her scorebook, passing it along to Marsha to read the results.

Marsha, a reserve forward, was the statistical expert. "Monique had four points and eight rebounds; Wicked Wanda added ten points with five assists; Yogi collected another ten points with eight assists; Brittney tallied nineteen points and seven rebounds; Heather contributed another nineteen points with six rebounds; and Julie attained seventeen points, fourteen assists, six steals, and five rebounds." Marsha raised her hand in order to make another announcement. "Throughout the entire tournament, Julie did not miss a single free throw in conversion of forty out of forty."

At last Julie, with roommate Yogi, gathered up their things in route to the airport. The team had booked the late flight with arrival into Baton Rouge around eleven o'clock that evening. It was going to be a long trip home, just getting to Baton Rouge would take a few hours not to mention getting back to campus.

As the two of them strolled out of the arena on their way to the bus, a group of Louisiana faithful was waiting patiently to view Julie. Recognizing the blonde superstar hobbling along side of her Asian counterpart, a flurry of fans rushed in request of autographs.

"I feel like a celebrity," spoke Julie as she signed her signature for the cheering fans.

"Me too! I'm not even the star." A flattered Yogi responded to fans also asking for her autograph.

Within minutes a rush of screaming fans approached Julie and Yogi in great desire for Julie's attention. A cry of "Julie, Julie, Julie" and "do it again" illuminated the parking lot at the Cincinnati arena.

Amazed by all of the attention, Yogi referenced Julie, "you're almost a famous as a pop star!" She smiled, "Julie, maybe you'll be on a cover of a magazine." Yogi added to the act reminding the crowd of the fact of Julie's MVP performance would be traveling down to San Antonio in about a week.

Needing to get to the bus, the twosome waved farewell to the fans and set out to rendezvous with the rest of the team. The excitement was almost too much for them to handle, since it was their first celebrity appearance. Arriving at the bus, Yogi got to tell everyone of Julie's fan club and how she was now a celebrity. The celebrity story gave the rest of the team something to chuckle at, but actual reality reflected Julie as a significant impact on the college basketball world, especially in the state of Louisiana.

One would expect the airplane ride back to Louisiana would be more than just satisfying, however superstar Julie had indifferences. In darkness of the aircraft, she suddenly experienced mild depression withdrawing from the interactions of others. Sorrowful expressions annexed her face, publishing uncomfortable feelings among the others, especially Yogi.

Yogi expressing concern, "Julie, what is wrong?" Looking deep into her facial expression, "you are a superstar, why do you experience sorrow and sadness?"

"I don't why I'm sad; I must be homesick or something." In the back of her mind she realized Schuyler's visit was finished and she might not encounter with him again.

On the bridge of tears, *"Schuyler, thank you for coming to my games. I'm sorry I didn't physically introduce myself to you, but I'm still interested in you dearly and watching every move you make."*

"Julie, I'm honored to have you with me, even if we are worlds apart we will always be together."

Her tears began to shed due to joy, not sorrow, as she observed the aircraft fly in the black of night in path that would ultimately take her to her campus home. Later in the comfort of her dormitory room, they reminisced about the tournament.

"Yogi, I'm sure glad we won the game." Julie prepared for bed. "I would have dreaded flying all the way back as the loser."

Bidding her good night, Yogi reminded, "Your performance was phenomenal, you played like you were in control of the whole court."

"Yogi, I couldn't do it without you!"

As Yogi sat on her bed, "Julie, I'm honored to not just be your teammate, but your friend."

"Maybe we'll sign some autographs tomorrow." Shutting her eyes in the dream of rest, she had no idea that a nightmare was waiting for in the near future.

Chapter 21

Settling down, back at school, and exhausted from a grueling Cincinnati trip, Julie set her sights on the San Antonio's river walk. She had heard about the beauty of the little river that flowed through downtown San Antonio, glamorizing the pageantry of the Final Four of Women's College Basketball. Hosting the Final Four, the Alamo Dome set the stage for one of the prestigious events in college athletics. South Eastern State had an invitation to this event, establishing precedence in school history as their very first trip into the semi-finals.

Schuyler was back to his junior college lessons, dreaming of some possibility to travel to Texas. Performing well in calculus and biology, he struggled in chemistry due to his telepathic tutor's inability to provide much assistance. Being a drama major, she never really experienced much chemistry-related subjects. She still was quite knowledgeable in calculus and biology, offering expertise in Schuyler's behalf.

Returning home from school on Monday, he had a message from Mrs. Garman of the hospital. Without haste, he notified her at her office and arranged a meeting with her the next day in the afternoon. Worried, his stomach became queasy from the thought of possible intervention with Mrs. Garman concerning pharmacy affairs. Due to possible complications, he dreaded his engagement with her.

Coach Jackson, back at the campus, was greatly satisfied with the team's accomplishments. Four straight upsets of highly talented teams, dramatic conclusions during each victory, and admittance into the semi-finals identified her as one of the exclusive coaches in the country.

It was long awaited, she had suffered for years in attempt to build a world-class program at the tiny Louisiana school; indeed the future was now!

Late in the afternoon on Monday, FF received an unwanted telephone call. The school's athletic director was notifying her of possible academic infractions concerning Flowers.

"This is ludicrous!" The coach responded back to athletic director. "She is an honor student due to graduate this semester."

"I don't have all of the details yet, but I will speak to Commissioner Tilley in greater detail tomorrow." The athletic director tried to ease her mind.

The finest day of Coach Jackson's life turned into the worst day of her life. Accepting an investigation of Julie's academic eligibility was a difficult pill to swallow, granting the news came from her athletic director, it seemed to possess no rhyme or reason. Without a word to anyone concerning the matter, she drove home to a lonely house in deep despair.

Schuyler, with early dismissal from class, took that long drive down that short road to encounter with Mrs. Garman. Recalling her glaring eyes and distinct voice inflection, he practiced his command voice in preparation of a highly classified conversation.

Mrs. Garman greeted in him with charming introduction. Ensuring his comfort, she sat down next to him on the couch. "After a bit of investigation of our pharmacy practice here at the hospital, I have discovered a disparity in medication accountability." She referred to a report, "it seems the pharmacy was ordering more pharmaceuticals than they were actually dispensing."

Pretending to be surprised, "Mrs. Garman, what do you mean?" Starting to get nervous, "how can you tell if drugs are missing?"

"Mr. Ballantine, you're from the Army. I'm sure you're familiar with drug utilization reports." She smiled, "is that the reason you wished to terminate your job so suddenly?"

"Am I in trouble too?"

Mrs. Garman disclosed an oath of statement form, "You are clear since the disparity continued even after you were terminated." Providing him the form, "you will have to write a statement for our investigation."

"Do I write it now?"

"You can either write one for me now, or wait and write one for the authorities later." She looked deeply into his eyes, "please help us with this."

Schuyler, being a good soldier, described the actions of his former pharmacy cohorts. He was reluctant at first, but he went ahead and provided the information.

As he left her office, *"Julie, what do you think?*

"Schuyler please don't get into trouble, I worry about you so much!"

An hour prior to Tuesday's practice, FF finally got the official word from Commissioner Tilley, via the athletic director, of the Flowers' investigation. In disbelief, FF read a summary of the academic inquiry of Flowers. The summary disclosed accusations of Julie not being academically eligible due to her drama curriculum. An undisclosed school was challenging the credibility of Julie's drama curriculum due to the non-traditional college credit earned during her performing arts schooling in New York.

Julie, who was summoned to the coach's office, was informed of the investigation. Suffering from the knee injury, she was not scheduled to practice anyway but endured skepticism from the recent turn of events. In despondency, she saw no reason for her ineligibility. Far from a sham school, her performing arts classes were provided to her in good faith and trust. Her entire basketball career was crashing before her eyes, not to mention her drama profession being in question.

"I'm sorry Julie, you can't practice or play for the team until allowance by the Commissioner." FF put her arm around her and proceeded to relinquish emotional tears along with her.

As the two of them consoled each other in the coach's office, a dark cloud had appeared over the athletic program at South Eastern State. No one would have thought a drama department's curriculum could decide the fate of a women's basketball tournament.

FF broke the news to the rest of the team at practice. She described the allegations pending against Julie's academic curriculum, explained her absence from the team until further notice, and urged the team to pull together in training for the San Antonio trip.

"Who is protesting her academics?" Heather stepped forward, "I'm sure their school as some form of field study."

Shaking her head, FF responded, "I'm not sure who is behind this." She reviewed her report, "It must be a disgruntle team, probably one we whipped-up on!"

"Is the decision final?" Yogi asked the coach, "Because I really want her to travel with us down in South Texas." "I've accepted no decision yet, I plan to fight the final verdict to the very end!" FF started to rant and rave, "even if she is ineligible, she still will be part of the team throughout the remainder of the tournament."

The team began practice, without their superstar sixth man, dreaming of a semi-final victory in honor of their fallen comrade.

Newspaper stories were smoking with the Flowers' investigation. Jealous media reporters, from certain localities, ridiculed her educational background. One sports article reported, "Cinderella Act Cancelled," scrutinizing her integrity as a student-athlete. Another article described, "Cinderella Acting Career Strikes Midnight." Overnight, she went from stardom to laughing stock. Her reputation was denounced through every sporting network from coast to coast. Indeed the shame that followed the investigation was immeasurable, sullying her self-esteem, self-confidence, and personal demeanor.

Eventually Schuyler got word of the investigation, *"Julie, say it isn't happening."* He pleaded with her. *"It can't be fair; you are a student of honor!"*

In pity for herself, *"I'm so depressed; I can't manufacture a single coherent thought."* She explained to Schuyler the circumstances generating the investigation against her drama curriculum.

He inquired if she might lose her MVP honors from the regional and if the team would have to forfeit the games won during the tournament.

"We know nothing yet, but I know my fate rests with the Commissioner's decision."

In my heart, I know you are right!

"Yes Schuyler, I understand what you are trying to say. Your mental telepathy transmits your valued opinion."

During this very stressful period, Julie kept in close contact with Schuyler in all accounts. He wanted to be the first to know any breaking news concerning her suspension.

A press conference awaited Coach Jackson's appearance. Julie's attendance was strongly requested also, but FF absolutely refused any interview with any member of the team besides her. She ensured all fire coming down range was aimed at her, alleviating any possible pressure placed upon her players, especially Julie. In route to the press conference, FF planed to remain cool, calm, and collective during the interview, a task that would be hard to do.

A sporting reporter, named RJ, had the honors to direct fire at the coach from the tournament's Cinderella Team, South Eastern State. Loud, offensive, and persistence described the reporter FF would have to face-off against. Like the battling among the Titans, FF would definitely have her hands full with RJ.

The press conference greeted Coach Jackson with open arms; RJ began the conversation by asking about the school's academic standards. "Coach, how do feel about the academic credibility of your school in the midst of this investigation?"

Biting her lip, she held back a bit. "We meet all standards under the Louisiana Board of Regents." Her facial expression challenged his ego.

"How long and often did Flowers attend performing arts schooling in New York?" He probed for feedback.

"Every summer she attended school there obtaining six semester hours of college credit each session." FF responded, wondering where this conversation was about to lead.

As he behaved very egotistical, "so she went to school in New York to receive college credit in Louisiana?"

"Yes, that was the schedule."

Like a Tiger about to pounce, he delivered the knockout punch. "Then how could the Board of Regents from Louisiana standardize Flowers' drama curriculum in another state such as New York?" He began to chuckle in support of his own comment.

Commencing to get a little hot underneath the collar, due to the last remark dealing with the Louisiana Board of Regents, FF looked the reporter in the eye and pointed at her crotch. "Right here, gotten it right here for ya!" With anger she added, "My players are all legitimate, our school's academic policies are to standard, and I don't think you have the nerve to admit it."

Astonished, he gave her respect. "Coach, your integrity to your school's loyalty cannot be broken." He tilted his head downward. "You are a tough interview, now I see why your team has challenged all of those favorite teams and came out victorious."

"I'm sorry for the outrage, but I cannot sit here and listen to such ridicule from an individual knowing very little about the subject matter." She crossed her legs, "I will never relinquish my struggle to clear the accusations."

In much due respect he concluded the interview with the coach, gaining knowledge of her fierce competitiveness as not just as a coach but as a person also. From the press conference, she earned much respect from the entire basketball community strengthening her supportive stand among her players and peers alike.

FF stormed out of the press conference, with a 100-yard stare, searching for another media spokesperson to retaliate upon. Unfortunately for Mr. Parsons, a heartfelt reporter, her heat rounds searched and found his grid coordinates.

"Coach Jackson, when do you expect a response back from Commissioner Tilley?" Sincerely he requested of her as he passed in the hallway, attempting to stimulate communicative contact with her.

"You don't ask me anything pertaining to the Commissioner, my team, or my school!" FF challenged the poor, unsuspecting reporter in the hallway.

"Yes ma'am! I retract my question." In defense of her wrath, Mr. Parsons felt her intimidation.

Her conscious influenced her behavior; she apologized to the meek reporter and proceeded to return to her office. The San Antonio strategic planning was a hot issue, directing her back to the war room to settle final arrangements prior to the team's voyage to San Antonio on Thursday morning, the following day. Expecting her fate, she was about to face the reality of not having Flowers' on her squad for the rest of the tournament.

Julie's packing for the trip included her basketball gear along with her personal clothing.

Expecting a positive verdict from the Commissioner, her heart was in good spirits; but lodged in the back of her mind, she feared the consequences of a disappointing decision. She hoped for the best, but expected the worse. The San Antonio vacation get-away did not look too fair-weathered. Thus, her stroll down the river walk was not expected to be as sunny as previous anticipated.

Thursday's flight soared in path aimed for San Antonio; a party of only twelve took the skies in search of story and reason. FF, with her eleven players, had accomplished so much in so short of time. In refusal to surrender to any top-ranked opponent, they captured the hearts of following devotees throughout the southland. Southern sports media praised the courage, candor, and commitment presented by the basketball program from South Eastern State. Under tremendous turmoil, Team FF faced obscurity and uncertainty as they flew into San Antonio's airport.

Expecting devastating reviews from the national media, FF avoided contact with any agencies outside of her own circle of followers. Ridiculed by numerous writers in the sporting realm, characterized as "The Sinderella Team" with fraudulent intentions, and humiliated by journalists on a continuous basis, FF deployed a previous unheard of women's basketball team into one of the biggest shows in college basketball. As The Final Four greeted their arrival, FF still held a stiff upper lip in process of guiding her team onto the stage of fame and fortune, a stage that may, or may not; highlight the act of Julie Crystal Flowers.

With no report back from Commissioner Tilley, FF was forced to segregate Julie from official team business. Julie was treated as a player with no team, like a queen in search of a throne, or a captain without a ship.

Set aside from the team, she ventured downtown to the river walk. It was a grand sight as business establishments flanked the river that flowed down the center of the city. Strolling along the river's walkway, wondering if her name's integrity would ever be restored, she dreamed of memories that attained her MVP status. Gazing at the sky above the Alamo Dome, where the rest of team was practicing, she could not suppress the heartbreaking passion of not belonging with the team. Four years of loyal commitments flashed before her eyes, joyful reminiscences sullied into remission, and feelings of worthlessness infected her mental well-being.

Later in the day, she encountered the historical site of The Alamo. Comprehending the bravery, valor, and honor of the Alamo's history, she strengthened courageous demeanor that energized her warrior spirit to accept the battlefield challenge of life itself. Even under direct fire from almost every media source in the land, she vowed to press on with her life and not allow any judgmental indifference take over her livelihood. As with names in the likes of Crocket, Travis, Bowie, and the rest of the defenders of The Alamo, she would accept no surrender in quest to reestablish her prominence as a student-athlete.

Friday turned-over a whole new day, but still no word from the Commissioner was forwarded to the South Eastern State Athletic Department. In disgust, FF submitted another inquiry of Flowers' status. In return, no verdict was still being reported. Due to the persistent outcome that negated Flowers' status, FF sought alternate avenues in search of the final answer. Taking the task upon herself, she researched the telephone number of the Commissioner's Office and placed a direct call in that direction.

After several hang-ups and line transfers, FF gave up trying to contact the commissioner. Instead of her calling in attempt to contact him, she had one of her players try a prank call.

"I understand what you want me to do coach," said Jamie Lee. "I'll call the number and pretend to be a dental office attempting to gain information of the Commissioner's whereabouts."

"Correct!" FF responded, "Maybe we can at least find out his location and activity."

Jamie Lee, in a sexy voice, made direct contact with the Commissioner's Office. She gave a phony statement about a missed dental appointment. "Sorry ma'am to disturb you on such a lovely day, but Mr. Tilley failed to show for his dental appointment today."

In surprise, she responded to the phony statement, "Mr. Tilley will not be in his office today."

She used her quick thinking. "Please ask Mr. Tilley to call the dental office back when he returns." Jamie Lee followed with another line.

"Due to a death in the family, he cannot return the call until tomorrow."

"Tomorrow will be too late; I need to talk with him today." She pleaded with her trying to get an answer concerning Julie's status before game time.

"I'm very sorry, but you'll have to call him tomorrow." She cut the line on Jamie Lee.

"Coach Jackson, the Commissioner is out of town with a death in the family." Jamie Lee shook her head. "We may not be able to get the final result of the investigation."

With lost hope, FF prepared her team for the evening's game against the Tornados. Without Julie on the bench, she would have to play the highly rated Tornados lacking the sensational sixth-man performance of Julie. It was quite a disappointing blow, not even receiving a final decision on the investigation.

Receiving the news from FF, Julie's spirit was broken. Little, if any, hope was left for reinstatement, a dejected Julie Crystal turned to her telepathic confidant. *"Schuyler, my basketball career looks bleak. The Commissioner didn't even return a final verdict on our appeal."*

Schuyler informed her of the information received from the news, and the news reported her ineligibility for the Tornado game. He apologized for not being able to attend the semi-final contest held in San Antonio, but his heart was with the team.

"I know you support the team's cause, I really miss your presence." She maneuvered to the team bus with Yogi, but this time as a spectator not as a player. Remorse was exemplified on her face, the lack of eye contact among her friends, and introvert behavior characterized the dethroned sixth man as she boarded the bus in route to the Alamo Dome.

Yogi sat beside Julie on the short road trip. "Julie, please do not reveal doubt on your face." She looked into Julie's eyes. "You hold your head high as a reigning queen, not a fallen warrior."

"You are correct Yogi; the worry only adds interest to the problem itself." She adjusted her hair, "I must keep the faith!"

As the bus crossed the interstate onto the street leading up to the Alamo Dome, Yogi and Julie noticed a crowd formulating throughout the courtyard in from of the main entrance. Nearing the main entrance, they became aware of a supporting cast for Julie. In amazement, over a hundred loyal South Eastern State fans had appeared early prior to the game to offer supportive assembly in favor of Flowers' reinstatement. Advertising their disapproval of Flowers' ineligibility, the Louisiana stronghold chanted, "Give us Julie, and let her play!" Displaying banners in support of Julie, the crowd formed a receiving line from the bus to the facility's entrance. Awaiting her dismount off the bus, they cheered the battle cry, "Julie, Julie, Julie!"

Julie was flattered from all of the attention. "Yogi, you go first." Julie asked her roommate.

Behind Patti and Marsha, Yogi stepped off the bus and waved to the crowd. "Following me is the best basketball player at the tournament!" She yelled to the fans in attempt to generate excitement.

In front of a partisan crowd, complimented by the fans, Julie charmed her admirers in classic fashion. Even under strict scrutiny from media throughout the country, her charismatic personality soared high as she gracefully strolled down the entire receiving line. Being the center of attention, she held her head high as she acknowledged deserving recognition from the hearts of the Louisiana devoted. Indeed the receiving line was her catwalk, instilling pride, honor, and gratification into the spirit of this proud warrior.

Heather and Brittney, walking behind Julie, watched the crowd cheer in favor of their MVP.

In the back of their minds, they realized the impact she placed upon not only their team, but also the state of Louisiana. Witnessing the event, the trailer park twins verified her widespread influence captivating her allies' endorsement.

Inside the Alamo Dome, it was lonely for the secluded Julie. Avoiding media attention, she kept a low profile. As the others suited for competition, she located an unused conference room and proceeded to watch local television. Alone with the local news, she quickly learned she was the talk of the town. In her support, a local sports reporter announced the unjust of the whole investigational process. Verifying Commissioner Tilley's incompetence of not returning a timely verdict, suggested violation of due process alarming the basketball community of the infringement of Flowers' lack to the right of a speedy trial.

As Julie sat comfortable in the conference room, Team FF was on full alert as if the enemy was about to penetrate the line. Tornado fever had struck FF, distributing an intense warning order to the players of her team. Even without the aid of their sixth man, FF was prepared to lead her troops into battle, a conflict to face the test of time. This semi-final game would not be just a Cinderella Team's storybook finish, or a monumental unexpected result, but a memorable game played in the heart of Texas without the services of one Julie Crystal Flowers, a lone star trapped in the shadows of the Alamo Dome.

"Schuyler, I'm here at the stadium but I'm not playing." Julie wiped the emotion from her eyes.

Too bad you're not playing; I'm getting ready to watch the game on television.

"I still have my knee injury, but I think I could play if they would only allow me to participate."

I feel really bad about the whole situation; I can only watch and hope.

"Maybe you can watch the game on television and provide our team with some feedback?"

"I know, but it's the best you can offer. Where are you now?" Julie asked as she continued to watch San Antonio's local news in the seclusion of the conference room.

Reporting his location and activity, Schuyler's selected a local sports bar as his observation post for the big game. The sports bar was near his former place of employment, the hospital. In reference to his employment status, he informed Julie of his lack of interest in job searching.

A few minutes before tip-off, Julie wandered back into the main arena and secured her reserved seat immediately behind SE State's bench. With hot, buttery popcorn and a Pepsi, she sat quietly watching her teammates draw closure to their pre-game basketball routines.

Prior to tip-off, FF received notification of the Flowers' appeal being upheld by Commissioner Tilley. Informed of Julie's clearance by the school's athletic director, FF ordered Julie to immediately suit-up for the second half.

"Coach, what took them so long on the appeal?" Julie gathered her uniform together.

"The Commissioner's Office faxed the notification to the wrong fax number." FF raised her arms in disgust. "Luckily, I had someone calling his office every ten minutes in attempt to get an update." She tried not to panic, but the incompetence of the whole process was getting her a little hot under the collar.

"Coach, so I'm cleared to play?" Julie applied her knee supporter in expectation of discomfort during action on the court.

"According to the fax I finally received, your status is clean and the team will not have to forfeit any previous games." She gave Julie a little congratulatory hug. "Everything is status quo, your records still stand, the team's victories stand, and we are going to go out there and kick some Tornado behind!"

"Schuyler, I'm cleared to play! She earnestly marched to courtside. *"The appeal's decision was mistakenly faxed to the wrong number.*

Schuyler ventured into the sports bar. As the clientele of the establishment recognized his air phenomena, he could feel a little uneasy. He couldn't pinpoint the strange feeling, but apprehensive sensations annexed his state of comfort. Watching the tip-off, he transmitted the vision of the televised game throughout the air phenomena network.

At the Alamo Dome, SE State's starting five struggled early with Tornado opposition. Relying mostly on trailer park twin shooting, they resisted Tornado advancement. Floor sergeant Yogi directed the offense maintaining striking distance within the early Tornado lead, but something was missing from both their offensive and defensive flow. With the lack of air phenomena presence, the team suffered a deficiency of togetherness.

In slow reaction to the flow of the game, both Yogi and Wicked Wanda exhibited poor judgment on several down-court passes during transitional offensive patterns. The team was definitely not the same without the services of Schuyler Ballantine.

Enjoying a beverage at the sports bar, Schuyler carefully watched the flow of the game trying to benefit the team as much as possible. *"Julie, can you follow the game better with me watching it on television?"*

"Schuyler, I'm sorry!" She watched Brittney shoot a free throw. *"The broadcast is a little behind actual real time; transmittance of the signal produces a slight delay in want you are seeing on television compared to what I'm currently watching at the present."*

In surprise, he could not accept her response. In attempt to persuade, he suggested the delay be so slight that it didn't create much of a factor.

In full knowledge of his inability to really provide much assistance to the team by watching the game on television, she pretended to concur with his suggestion. *"Affirmative, the delay is slight! Keep on watching the game as close as you can because the team is geared for your feedback."* She continued to watch her team fall further behind the Tornados as the first half lingered on.

Playing with virtually no bench experience, FF was forced to take frequent timeouts in order to rest her starting five. With Julie almost ready to report into the game, FF set her troops off the do battle, a confrontation in dire need of Julie's services as sixth man.

Sitting alone at the local sports bar, Schuyler attentively watched the game in waiting anxiously for his favorite team to generate a comeback. Nearing halftime, the Tornados had built a comfortable fifteen-point lead thwarting any possibility of SE State getting back into the contest.

Participating as a spectator, Julie sat patiently, resting her knee while watching her teammates struggle against the powerful Tornados. Due to her injury, she would sit out the entire first half. The Tornados, dressed in white with scarlet trim, featured the most dominating center in the nation. Michelle, the Tornado center, had led the nation in rebounding for the past two years. Matched against Monique in the first half, she virtually took command of the game at onset. Her offensive rebounding had produced ten points, complimented by her defensive rebounding that prevented second-chance points from the twins. Indeed, low post play would decide this game and Michelle would factor enormously for the Tornados.

The first half of the contest was all with the Tornados, but Team FF showed much promise. During the halftime break, after extensive stretching, Julie practiced shooting from her favorite perimeter spot. Indeed she was a little rusty, but even with a weak knee she was ready to play.

FF opened the second half, down by fifteen points, with Monique, Brittney, Heather, Yogi, and Julie. With Julie now in the game, FF hoped the 1-3-1 zone defense might stifle Michelle's play in the middle.

Excited about Julie's return to the basketball scene, Schuyler walked out to his car in the parking lot to retrieve some extra spending money.

Often, he had kept a little money stashed in the trunk for emergency situations, and with the game getting more exciting, he would for sure be persuaded to spend an extra bit of money at the bar.

Schuyler walked out to his car, noticing a flat tire; he frantically proceeded to take action to repair the flat tire. Before he could open the truck of the car in retrieval of a jack and tire tool, two strangers in a white car pulled up and asked him if he needed any assistance.

"No thanks, I can handle it." Schuyler told the two strangers as he initiated procedures to gather the materials necessary to change a flat tire. With one eye on the strangers in the white car and the other eye searching his trunk for the tools required for the task, he felt a sharp, devastating blow to the back of his neck. The blow was so severe; it rendered him into an unconscious state.

At the Alamo Dome, cease of Schuyler's air phenomena transmission caused extreme panic upon Julie. At first opportunity, she rendered the timeout signal to the referee.

"Why did you call timeout Julie?" FF asked, "I didn't signal for one."

"Coach, I needed a break; my head is spinning." A look of terror portrayed from her eyes.

In response to the situation, FF placed Wicked Wanda back into the game for Julie. Keeping Julie at her side, she tried to offer reassurance in effort to get Julie's mind back into the game. It was a difficult situation; Schuyler was for sure in some kind of trouble and Team FF needed Julie's leadership on the court. It was a tough decision, but FF refused to immediately put Julie back into the game under the circumstances.

In a frantic, Julie pleaded to Schuyler. *"Wake up sugar, you're not awake. What is happening? What hit you on the head?"* With tears pouring out her eyes, she went into distress as she sat next to FF on the bench.

"Please Julie, take control of yourself!" FF grabbed her arm. "What is wrong?" She tried to get Julie's attention, but failed.

"I don't know!" She continued to remain frighten under the uncertainty of Schuyler's condition.

With Team FF falling even further behind on the scoreboard in the second half, Schuyler remained unconscious in the back seat of the strange white car. The blow to the back of his neck was administered by a third individual who was stalking him the entire time while he was at the sports bar. While the two strangers in the white car distracted Schuyler, the third stranger delivered the knockout punch. As a helpless Schuyler was being transported in the getaway vehicle to an undisclosed site, a Louisianan basketball team was playing the biggest game of the school's history is an extreme state of shock.

Due to Yogi's fourth foul, FF put Julie back into game. Even though Julie's mind wasn't in the game, the team called for her entry. In almost a silent arena, the semi-final game progressed as the Tornados maintained a solid twenty-point advantage.

A traveling violation charged against Flowers, lifted FF out of her chair onto the edge of the court. In dispute, she challenged the young male referee's judgment. "Right here ref; got it right here for you!" She pointed at her crotch in effort of intimidation.

Alertly, the cocky referee signaled a technical foul against Coach Cheryl Jackson. Unlike past precedence, Coach Jackson was penalized for an intimidating display of her aggressive coaching style.

The technical foul inspired the team, stimulated the crowd, and applied cohesiveness amongst the team, but too much damage had been already been done by the Tornados. With less than five minutes remaining, South Eastern State trailed on the scoreboard 64–46. The inside play by Michelle created too much of a problem for Monique and the twins. Her rebounding dominance kept SE State's front line in check, allowing her offense to generate transitional advantages in route to numerous fast break baskets. Even though Brittney and Heather worked well together in order to get open for scoring opportunities, the backcourt didn't get the ball to them in a timely manner. Unlike the previous tournament games, a communication breakdown led to multiple turnovers limiting the number of scoring opportunities the twins could obtain. It was a difficult game for SE State, playing in handicap under the circumstances. The only moral victory was the Flowers' appeal being upheld by Commissioner Tilley, but still the victory was only short-lived as the team eventually crumbled apart down the stretch. It was a lesson learned, as history was made, because the little-heard-of school from Louisiana, South Eastern State, made its mark at the Alamo Dome. Similar to the siege of the Alamo, it was an overwhelming, devastating defeat; and similar to the defenders of the Alamo, it was the final stand of an elite few.

At closure of the semi-final game between the Tornados and South Eastern State, the scoreboard reported a lopsided victory in favor of the Tornados 76–52.

Preoccupied by external factors, Julie went through the motions at post-game team functions. With Schuyler's situation fixating her mind, she awaiting any source of news identifying his status. Currently his mental transmissions resembled dream patterns, exhibiting a possible prolonged unconscious state.

"Julie, are you ready to go watch the remaining semi-final game?" Yogi tugged at her arm leading her back into the arena.

At the sight of Julie, fans from Louisiana rushed to her in strong request of her attention. Calling for autographs, seeking a handshake of confidence, and soliciting a smile, dozens of admirers approached their idol in provision of strong support even in the midst of defeat.

Julie, timid to speak, offered gratification to the devoted followers. "Thank you very much, the pleasure is mine!" She began shaking hands, signing autographs, and mingling with the crowd. It was an honor to be treated in this manner, and her demonstration of respect and sense of duty publicized the perseverance that made her the champion she was.

In tears of happiness, a young girl beckoned her attentiveness. "Miss Julie, you will always be in our dreams." She blinked her eyes, gave Julie a hug, and whispered something in her ear. "Only you can save him." Backing down from Julie, she vanished into the crowd.

Puzzled from the little girl's expression, Julie attempted to satisfy her devotees in a compelling pace as she kept thinking about what the little girl whispered in her ear. The intense commotion captivated her attention, adding to characteristic attributes, as her engagement with the Louisianan faithful elevated her will and fortitude during a period of time mystified by air phenomena disruption.

"About finished with your fan club, Julie?" Signing a few autographs herself, Yogi interrupted. "When I'm with you Julie, I feel like a celebrity." Winking her eye, she smiled, "because you attract a crowd everywhere you go."

The roommates sat down together and watched the remaining semi-final game, reminiscing of the glorious season they had experienced. Featured by Julie's MVP performance during the regional, they both agreed their basketball careers at South Eastern State were much a success.

In fact, the entire original Fresh Five accomplished a great deal. Yogi, Wicked Wanda, Heather, Brittney, and Julie had all reported to SE State as unknowns to the basketball world, and after four years of hard work they blossomed into storybook history. Doubted from the very beginning, these five student-athletes accepted the battlefield challenge and fearlessly marched along the side of their beloved coach all the way to the Alamo Dome to face their final confrontation. Distracted by misleading confusion derived from external sources, The Fresh Five under the command of Cheryl Jackson gave everything they had in defense of their team. South Eastern State, sullied from academic defamation, failed to earn a victory at the Alamo Dome but earned something else of great value. They earned respect, and nothing more could honor a school more than how its basketball team handled the stressful situation placed in front of them. Noble recognition embraced Team FF, exhibiting the utmost mark of distinction of any organization. With all due respect to the other semi-final teams, SE State's colors of black and gold will fly high in the sky commending the school's fight to reestablish their reputation.

The entire week had been a very stressful period. The investigational crisis distracted the complete organization. FF spent more time defending university programs and policies than preparing her team for the Tornado game.

Also during the week of the Final Four, Julie occupied herself in condolence of sorrow from the suspension. Indeed her mind was not in the game, identifying shortcomings in reason for a disappointing performance.

In an isolated warehouse, Schuyler discovered himself imprisoned in a small room. Along with a head injury, he felt residual effects of an overdose of medication. To the best of his awareness, the perpetrators of the incident had injected into his arm a sedating drug to incapacitate for a few hours in effort to transport him to the secluded warehouse.

In response to his situation, *"Schuyler dear, you are locked in a room for what reason?"* A frantic Julie questioned as she immediately started to assemble her items in preparation for the trip back to Louisiana. Back at her hotel room, she beckoned a quick return home in order to gain access to her vehicle.

Alone in his cell, he informed Julie of his unknown status report. He knew nothing, but his current condition was poor. His cell inside of the warehouse contained a small window in view of the city. Identifying the city as Lexington, he believed to be somewhere on the west side in observation of an unidentified radio tower.

"I see the city Schuyler, but I don't recognize anything. I was there for the regional basketball games, but I only encountered the area between the hotel and the arena."

Schuyler looked out the window at the street below. It was far-fetched for him to escape via the window. Even though he could break through the glass, the leap to the ground would be too far.

Since the building containing the warehouse was a very high structure, the distance from the top of the warehouse to the ground was quite a distance. Nevertheless, Schuyler's cell window was too high up in the air to jump.

"Schuyler, I will notify the police of your situation!"

How can you do that?

"You are correct! The police will have no clue to what I would be reporting." She finished packing for the tomorrow's early morning trip back to Louisiana. *"How could I explain my findings?*

Yes, trying to explain our way of communication transmittance would grant you a visit to the mental treatment facility to verbalize with Doctor Walton.

"I don't know what to do yet, but by tomorrow afternoon I plan to be in Lexington!"

How will you get here so fast?

"I'll change my flight's destination from Baton Rouge to Lexington."

Will FF allow you to do that?

"I don't know, but I'll ask tomorrow.

It is late, get some rest and I'll try to get a Size, Activity, Location, Unit, Time, and Equipment report on the enemy by 0800 hours tomorrow morning.

"Schuyler, I love you so much!" Her heart increased activity. *"Watching you being enslaved hurts me so deeply."*

Only you can help me now. To the rest of the world I'm located in uncharted waters, vicinity unknown to the authorities.

Along with air phenomena, Schuyler would have to search for verification of his confinement. Believing to be alone inside of the warehouse, he patiently waited for a sign of supplementary inhabitants.

Peeking at his military watch, he noticed the hour getting late. Nearing midnight, he heard the ringing of a telephone. With little sight of the interior of the warehouse, he could not detect the exact location of the telephone station. His cell door did contain a small peephole but offered very little peripheral vision.

A strange voice communicated on the telephone within listening distance of Schuyler. "He has been quiet, probably still knocked out from the Demerol."

The stranger paused on the phone, "I hear he's the one who blew the whistle on our connection at the hospital in Richmond."

Schuyler remained silent and prepared to pretend to be still sedated if needed. His reason for imprisonment was about to be advertised.

"I will watch him here until tomorrow; then the Chief will take matters into his own hands." The stranger hung up the phone in the midst of silence.

In the corner of the room, Schuyler remained silent and waited for a future visit from the Chief, a visitation that could determine his future's outcome.

CHAPTER 22

The night spent in his isolated cubicle experienced him much discomfort. Even with his Army training, his appointment with the Chief established a frighten state of mind. Anxiety, fear, and despair took over his mental awareness encompassing thorough concentration of panic all the way through his body. Terror embraced all senses. He heard, saw, tasted, felt, and smelt horror throughout the entire night as he looked intently into the darkness of his musty cubicle of imprisonment. Help was far and scarce, but hope was just a brain wave away.

An emergency meeting at the Jupiter at 0500 hours, established organization of Morrison and Boyd in behalf of the detained subject. Under the extenuating circumstances, the Jupiter pair had erected a command and control center in defense of The Air.

Energizing the coffee machine, Morrison suggested immediate response to the condition. "I can't believe this is happening! He served in the Army for three years with minimal resistance and now he's locked-up somewhere in a warehouse."

Attempting the reassure his partner, "I'm sure his parents have reported him missing by now." Boyd rubbed his eyes in disbelief. "What can we do to help?"

Hardly waiting for his coffee to cool down, "We have to notify the authorities of his abduction!" Morrison looked out the window at the city. "He's vulnerable out there, he must be found."

"How can we address the situation to the police?" Boyd suggested difficulty with any possible course of action.

Morrison, under much pressure, responded to his partner's question. "I will submit an anonymous phone call to the police."

"Good idea, provide them with a description of the landscape and maybe they'll be able to find him." Boyd shared a cup of coffee with his partner. "Once daylight appears, I think we can search for him also."

In agreement, "we just need more intelligence from The Air himself." Morrison looked again out the window. "Besides informing the police, we must go out on the streets ourselves to locate the subject."

"I'll get an updated map of the city and we'll use his vision to lead us to him." Boyd prepared for his departure into the streets of Lexington.

"Excellent idea, I'll make a couple of phone calls and I'll rendezvous with you about 0800 hours." Morrison acknowledged his partner's exodus and proceeded to make contact with the local police.

Morrison and Boyd were analysts at a Think Tank, not detectives. Their quest to uncover the mysterious location of The Air was improbable, but at the moment it was all Schuyler had.

Heart-pounding tension kept Julie from sleeping throughout the night. Her paralyzed thought process prevented coherent reasoning. Hysterical visions rushed right through her mind, her mental capability was strained due to insecurity, and the uncertainties of Schuyler's safety threaten her sanity. Under extreme nervous tension, she convinced FF to allow her to alter her flight plans. Using the alibi of a family emergency, Julie persuaded her beloved coach to permit her to fly to Lexington. A hard sell, FF would only allow her to fly to Lexington via Baton Rouge.

Since the team's flight flew directly into Baton Rouge from San Antonio, Coach Jackson ensured Julie pursued the normal flight schedule. From Baton Rouge, Julie was on her on. With aid from FF, Julie got a connecting flight from Baton Rouge to Lexington by way of Atlanta. Thus in order to get to Lexington, she would have to fly from San Antonio through both Baton Rouge and Atlanta to land in Lexington. Yes it would be a long day for Julie Crystal Flowers on the airlines, but eventually she would reach her final destination before nightfall.

Alone in his cell, he peered out the tiny window at the scenery of what he thought was the city of Lexington. Daybreak had approached, providing him more clarity in his view. Checking his watch for the time of day, he noticed his watch contained a compass. Remembering instructions from SGT Canini, he shot an azimuth to a distant radio tower. By converting the azimuth to a back azimuth, via SGT C's method of adding or subtracting 180 degrees from the actual azimuth, he obtained his general location in proportion to the radio tower. Looking at the tower, he projected the distance as being comparable to a very long par-five golf hole. Utilizing his judgment, he estimated the tower's distance to be anywhere from 700 to 1000 yards from his exact location. Thus from his observation, he projected his location from the radio tower to be a back azimuth of 45 degrees with a distance of about 850 yards. Following the positioning from the radio tower, he spotted another tower farther in distance but in plain sight from his secluded window view. It resembled a water tower, but was of much greater distance than the radio tower. Firing an azimuth upon the general direction of the water tower, he calculated a back azimuth of 23 degrees with a distance of approximately two miles.

With the two back azimuths calculated, his location could be plotted on a topographical map by drawing straight lines from the known positions of the radio tower and water tower in the prescribed directions of their respective back azimuths. The point of intersection would approximate Schuyler's position. The estimated distances would be helpful in determining his location also, but the only hurdle to this entire process was the availability of a map. Locked inside the cell, Schuyler had no access to any map at all much less a topographical map. But with the back azimuths and estimated distance, help could be summoned.

Julie, knowing little about land navigation, recorded the information derived from Schuyler. After she hurried through her airport destinations, she would have valuable information to locate her telepathic lover. Traumatized from the abduction, she struggled to maintain her sanity as she began her quest to save her beloved Schuyler.

Searching for additional reference points, Schuyler looked closely at his terrain in attempt to recognize his surroundings. As he watched traffic below, he heard additional voices in the warehouse outside of his cell.

"Chief, he's ready for you to interrogate!" The guard spoke.

"Let me at him!" The Chief responded as the cell door was opened.

Terrified, Schuyler was allowed to exit the cell for interview with the Chief. The Chief, with his thug escort, demanded an explanation from Schuyler concerning the sudden investigations occurring at the hospital pharmacy. "What do you know about my pharmacy?"

Schuyler blinked his eyes, "which pharmacy are you talking about?" He remembered the Army's Code of Conduct, preparing to avoid questioning as much as possible and only provide general information such as name, rank, social security number, and date of birth. "I only have worked at the one hospital pharmacy with Victor Canon and Robert Bazano, terminating my job only due to conflicting schedules with my college work."

The Chief raised his voice, "don't act dumb with me!" He signaled for the thug to approach Schuyler.

"I'll take care of this one!" The thug struck Schuyler in the back of the knee with a baseball bat, inflicting great pain upon him.

Clutching his knee, "I'm sorry, I really don't know too much about it." He caught his breath and looked at the Chief. "I just know they ordered a lot of meds from some guy named Scratchy."

"Is there anything else?" The Chief commanded.

Pausing, Schuyler pretended to think very intensely. "No, I don't really remember anything too particular except they ordered a lot of medications for such a small pharmacy."

The Chief ordered, "put him back in his room until he remembers!" The thug shoved Schuyler back into the cell and secured the door.

Back inside his cubicle, he listened to the Chief, the thug, and the guard discussing his future; per their conversation, the Chief desired additional feedback than what he had previously been provided.

As he searched for additional benchmarks throughout the city, he quickly began collecting some more possible information to provide the Chief in order to buy some supplementary time.

Pressed for time, Julie was at the mercy of the airlines. Even with flight connections in Baton Rouge and Atlanta, she was only a few hours away from her dearly loved telepathic sweetheart.

Schuyler, remembering fond fantasizes of his golfing experiences with Julie, strolled down memory road with her. Describing his feelings, he reminded of her ability to strengthen his golf game by giving club selection advice. Prior to her involvement, he struggled as the sixth man of his school's golf team. As interaction persisted, an enrichment of his game derived from her blissful telepathic mentoring. His advancement to the High School Regional Tournament confirmed maturity in adulthood transformation; in concert with Julie Crystal Flowers, he achieved pinnacle levels of his beloved game of golf.

"I read you loud and clear, your transmission is received with great extent of confirmation!" Understanding she could easily arrive in Lexington, but have no idea where to search. *"Watching you play golf was a grand admiration I could only dream about."*

Affirming the transmission, he reminisced his old Army days and how she was an enormous factor in his successful career as an Army soldier. By virtue of her assistance, noteworthy basic training events such as the physical fitness test, the gas chamber, the obstacle course, the rifle range, and the road march illuminated leadership attributes in development of a true leader.

"In fact, your mentorship of Michael displayed tactical expertise only a real soldier could possess."

Schuyler dreamed about his experiences in Korea, restoring confidence due to widespread accomplishments. The SGT Canini influence as a member of the NBC team, the hazardous material panic while detailed with force protection duties, the softball championship, interaction with fellow students at University of Maryland, and Soldier of the Quarter achievements were all inspired from telepathic companionship during adulthood transformation.

"True, your character grew immensely during your overseas tour." She acknowledged his message. *"You were exemplary in almost every aspect of the military, identifying as a trustworthy soldier inheriting a vast amount of outstanding leadership traits along the way."*

In remembrance of educational benefits gained from her connection, he rendered much appreciation in behalf of her mathematical expertise. Not only was her time spent during homework hours recognized, but the ensuing romantic ventures that proceeded after the completed homework assignments.

"You have tapped my brain for quite a few pleasant memories, but you've provided much help in the advancement of my college basketball career."

Only from being a spectator!

"Don't sell yourself short, your presence at the regional tournament made an immeasurable difference!"

I was only enjoying the opportunity to watch my favorite basketball player perform at a level higher than anyone else.

"I love you so much Schuyler, I admire the way you are, and I wish nothing more than your complete safety."

The pain in his knee grew sharper, as he peered out the window into the unknown. Julie's comforting remarks was all he had to exist with. With uncertainty controlling his life, his will for safeguard exhibited his strength as a man. Even with his collegiate and military hardships, this incarceration would prove to be the deciding hurdle in any chance of adulthood transformation.

Morrison and Boyd, the Jupiter dynamic duo, in attempt to search for their subject braved the streets of Lexington. Knowing nothing about land navigation, the road map of the city provided little help. With Morrison driving and Boyd navigating, the duo was getting little accomplished.

"What do we have to go on?" Morrison asked as he commanded the search and rescue vehicle.

"The Vision is located in a warehouse approximately two miles west of a water tower and about 850 yards northwest of a radio tower."

"Before we go driving all over the city in search of a water tower, we need to do a bit more research." Morrison steered the vehicle off the main road in route to the local library. "John, a trip to library might be of some help!"

Boyd agreed there was little need for the two of them to drive aimlessly throughout the city of Lexington without the required information to locate their prized subject. The library, if anywhere, would have a map displaying man-made features such as water towers and radio towers. All they had to do was to find a radio tower west of a water tower with a distance of about one and one-half miles.

Julie had secured her flight out of Atlanta and was on her way to Lexington. She would shortly be getting there, but was clueless once she hit the streets of Lexington.

Schuyler, in the meantime, was served a box of chicken for his lunchtime meal. Even though the chicken was greasy, it was all he had to eat for quite some time. The tasty bird gave him subsistence, but offered no relief for the ailing pain in his leg. Awaiting his return appointment from the Chief, Schuyler continued to gaze out the window, not yet giving up hope for freedom.

With the Jupiter duo at the library, Julie on an airline in route to Lexington, another group was planning a rescue attempt. With no warning to Schuyler, in complete covertness, Brother Duncan was organizing a helicopter assault mission in attempt to secure his brother from the clutches of the Chief and his gang. Following the incident all along, Duncan was much more prepared to locate Schuyler than the others. The key to the assault was the element of surprise; at no time during the operation would Duncan render air transmission in communicating attempt of his brother. Duncan knew if Schuyler knew he was coming; then the Chief would know, therefore the mission would have to be as covert as possible.

The day was growing old as Duncan assembled his assault team. The team consisted of a helicopter pilot named Nick who flew medical evacuation flights for the hospital, a flight medic named Tim who had previous worked at The Office of The Surgeon General, and two former Special Forces' soldiers nicknamed "T" and "S". These four individuals would assist Duncan in the extraction and evacuation of his younger brother.

Utilization of an Army helicopter would be a huge obstacle to overtake. Being the assault occurring at night, the dispatch would have to be approved at higher headquarters. Luckily, Tim had the ear of some powerful Sergeant Majors and secured a dispatch for the helicopter.

As a medical asset, Nick was one of the best helicopter pilots on the entire post. Highly experienced in medical evacuations, his promise was vital to the mission. With the flight designated at night, expertise with air traffic controllers would pay huge dividends. During off-duty status, his charismatic style offered much entertainment to a wide variety of women.

Tim worked in the emergency room, but had prior experience as a flight medic. If Schuyler would need any emergency medical assistance, Tim would be the one to do it. With connections at the Army Surgeon General's Office, his influential demeanor guaranteed helicopter access for flight training even during the darkness of night. Appealing character of a successful politician, his networking abilities hurdled any logistical obstacle in their path.

The two helicopter assault soldiers, T and S, were selected to penetrate the warehouse in retrieval of Schuyler. With prior knowledge of their opposition's strength, from Schuyler's transmitted SALUTE report, the pair of assault soldiers should surely take by surprise any resistance orchestrated by the Chief.

Duncan, the only one with first-hand knowledge of the city of Lexington, would be available for additional assault firepower or assisting Tim with the evacuation of his brother.

The mission had been received, the warning order given, a preparatory plan devised, and movement was initiated for the covert operation of helicopter assault upon the targeted warehouse and precise extraction of Schuyler from his imprisonment.

Landing in Lexington, Julie departed the aircraft in direct route to the rental car agencies. Inquiring of any vehicle available, she secured access to a forest green sedan. With some knowledge of the city, from a prior basketball tournament, she endeavored onto the streets in search of the water tower benchmark. With strategy of purchasing a road map and requesting directions to the nearest water tower, she set her sights on tracking down her telepathic companion.

Achieving some success at the library, the Jupiter duo had a pretty good idea where both landmarks, the water tower and the radio tower, were situated. As they departed the library, the twosome appeared to be a bit better equipped to trace the undisclosed site of The Air.

With the others searching aimlessly in all directions for his unspecified locality, Duncan's aviation crew began their journey across the state. In possession of a valid dispatch and permission from air traffic control, this anonymous aircraft began their air assault mission.

Driving frantically within the dense urban traffic, Julie stopped several times at convenient stores and gas stations in quest of some useful directions to the either a water tower or a radio tower. Short-handed on luck, she received little assistance, but vowed to find her lost love.

The Jupiter duo had measured about a two-block radius of possible area containing The Air. In alignment of a radio tower and a water tower, they started searching for a chicken store that would match the brand of chicken served to The Air.

Hunting for the chicken place, Morrison and Boyd carefully followed the point of view of The Air in pursuit of future clues.

As the helicopter assault team occupied their Black Hawk in flight to rescue Duncan's brother, T and S precisely measured detailed targets on their topographical map. Remembering past helicopter assault missions that failed, the Black Hawk crew maintained awareness of their mission at all times. Duncan's handpicked crew planned strategic situations and alterative strategy in laying the groundwork for the undertaking.

Flying in darkness, Nick had cleared any warning directed from air traffic controllers. He estimated arrival into Lexington was expected at no later than thirty minutes. Knowing Schuyler would be looking out the window, Nick knew if he got close to his location then air phenomena would lead the aircraft to the site. Of course, Nick and the others were aware if they could detect themselves through the eyes of Schuyler, then the enemy would be able to detect them also.

Duncan's perspective was to expect the worse, but hope for the best. Currently only the single guard was at the warehouse, allowing an apparent rescue effort. Thus, if the situation remained the same then mission success was high.

Alerted by Mr. Ballantine, the city police was in eminent pursuit also. Bewildered due to the confusing information provided by Schuyler's father, law enforcement professionals traced any information in relationship to the missing person.

With the others closing in, actually the Jupiter duo was nearest to the prize. Morrison and Boyd had located the chicken outlet and were in fact only down the street from the warehouse itself. Unfortunately in reference to the window occupied by The Air, they were on the opposite side of the warehouse and could not discover exactly where The Air was located.

"Where are you Schuyler?" She continued to drive without direction, stopping every so often to ask directions.

I'm in a warehouse near a softball field.

"How can I find you?"

Darkness had come upon us. View the North Star in the sky; I believe I'm a little west of it.

"I wish I had paid more attention during your land navigation training, because I'm getting more lost quicker than I'm finding your unknown location." Julie searched the sky for the North Star as she drove the streets of Lexington.

With word of a nearby softball field, Nick had a good landing zone already. The crew was swiftly approaching their designation in anticipation of an excellent rallying point at a softball field.

In deep despondency, Schuyler suffered into the night. An ailing knee, hampered mobility, and darkness of night damaged a possible escape and evasion plan. At the moment, not much would prevent a probable escape since only the lone guard sat quietly in the warehouse.

The Jupiter duo was the first to determine his secret location. Due to the softball field clue, they finally maneuvered to the correct side of the building. The chicken clue had gotten them in the vicinity, but the softball field indication narrowed the possibilities down a bit. With their car park at the softball field, Morrison and Boyd could virtually see The Air looking out the window. Strange as it seemed, to all intents and purposes they could view themselves via air phenomena. When Schuyler gazed in their direction, the Jupiter couple could actually vision themselves.

Closing in on the radio tower, Julie kept pace. Even though she was a little behind the Jupiter twosome, she was heading in the right direction. As she was steering her rented vehicle in a western direction aligned with the North Star, she spotted an aircraft descending from the sky. With no prior knowledge of the mission, for some strange reason she began following the path of the aircraft. Continuing to drive in her westerly azimuth, she detected the aircraft being a medical evacuation helicopter. It seemed to be searching for a place to land.

As the chopper flew in search of the softball field, Schuyler began to watch the craft hover within the parameters of his air phenomena.

Once within sight of his brother, Duncan instantaneously discovered his brother's undisclosed location. Virtually in view of his captive brother's cell window, he without haste notified Nick of the possibility of using the rooftop of the warehouse.

Alertly, Nick banked the chopper at the warehouse and guided his craft immediately above the warehouse. Hovering as close to the roof as he dared, Nick allowed both T and S an excellent opportunity to repel down from the helicopter onto the roof.

Not a standard practice, repelling from a medical evacuation aircraft, T and S felt a little awkward as they climbed down a rope from the chopper. Since it was a short distance, they actually could almost jump from the aircraft, but utilized a bit of rope for safety reasons.

Admiring the entire feat, Morrison and Boyd watched the helicopter displace the two men and soar off away from the building only to land in a softball field nearby.

Almost at her destination, Julie traced the helicopter in attempt to rendezvous with them.

As Nick was landing the chopper with Tim and Duncan aboard, T and S were searching for a practical entrance into the warehouse. Utilizing rope, S was able to repel along the outside of the building in attempt to penetrate Schuyler's window. Sliding down the rope in view of Schuyler, S quickly noticed that the window was too small and retreated back up the rope onto the roof. Meanwhile, T had opened a window near the ceiling of the warehouse allowing easy access into the warehouse.

Approaching the warehouse, leaving only Nick in guard of the helicopter, Duncan and Tim advanced in opposite directions. Tim went around the back of the warehouse; Duncan strolled right up to the front door.

Entering the warehouse was no problem for T and S, but crawling down to the floor was an issue. Crawling along the rafters, in opposite directions, they maneuvered along the boundaries of the facility in approach of the lone guard.

Searching for an alternative entry into the building, Tim wandered aimlessly around the perimeter of the warehouse. Duncan, in comparison, was ready to try to enter the building through the front door. Prior to his entrance effort, Duncan directed Tim to wait outside of the building and to allow him to try to penetrate first.

With Morrison and Boyd in the parking lot of the softball field anticipating some firepower, Julie drove her vehicle toward the direction of the helicopter. *"Sugar, I'm here for you!"*

In Duncan's attempt to open the door, a rattling sound alarmed the guard. With caution, the guard approached the door. With little haste, T and S landed on the floor in strong effort to overpower the single guard. Armed with a revolver, the guard pulled his weapon in struggle to deliver deadly force, but T and S apprehended the armed guard without severe injury.

As T secured the guard, S opened the door to allow Duncan's safe entry. "Unlock the cell; get him out now!" Duncan requested.

Confronting Julie, Nick warned of the danger. She ignored his warning. "I'm a close friend of Schuyler, please allow me to help."

Suddenly, Nick noticed a strange car pulling up to the warehouse. Three men exited the strange car heading for the warehouse's entrance.

"Schuyler, the Chief and two henchmen are coming into the warehouse!" Julie warned in a hysterical tone.

Released from his imprisonment, Schuyler immediately ceased rejoicing and alerted the others of the Chief and his two henchmen.

In response to Schuyler's directives, T and S hid behind wooden beams awaiting entrance of the villains. Meanwhile, Duncan escorted a hobbling Schuyler toward a rear exit and Tim remained secure on the outside of the building.

The two henchmen, armed with revolvers, charged the front entrance but were extremely challenged by the surprise attack of T and S. Even armed and dangerous, the two villains were little match for the former Special Forces. Their hand-to-hand combat tactics eventually subdued the two henchmen. Putting up a terrific fight, and firing a few misdirected bullets, the Chief's two escorts landed themselves in the same cell as the guard. The muscle of T and S proved to be vital, capturing three of the Chief's organization in such a short time span. As the two former Special Forces comrades secured the three of them in Schuyler's former cell, Duncan aided Schuyler's escape out the back exit.

"Duncan, the Chief is coming around the other side of the building!" Tim aired in effort to alarm the Ballantine brothers.

"Oh no, it's too late! He is here; we are trapped." Schuyler informed as the Chief confronted he and his brother. *"What can we do?"*

"Halt!" The Chief ordered the two brothers to surrender. "Come with me." He pointed a revolver at Duncan.

"He can hardly walk." Pointing to his brother, Duncan explained to the armed Chief.

"Make him walk!" An angry Chief directed.

Leaving Julie at the helicopter, Nick approached the scene. He didn't know what he was exacting going to do, but he realized a bullet might breach his body.

Ensuring the three henchmen could not escape their cell; Tim secured the front of the building and remained out of sight of the Chief.

Guarding the helicopter, Julie ensured not to transmit signals to Schuyler in attempt to prevent telegraphing Nick's position.

Planning a counterattack against the Chief, T and S positioned themselves inside the rear portion of the warehouse. Even though T and S had possession of the henchmen's weapons, they were reluctant to use them because of possible harm to the Ballantine brothers in retaliation.

The Chief directed the brothers back inside the building. "Reverse your steps, we are going back inside!"

Hobbling along on a tortured leg, Schuyler followed Duncan back inside the warehouse. Under gunpoint, they were led by the Chief in route to the cell in effort to release his own recruits.

Following the others in the warehouse, Nick quietly infiltrated in through the back door. Failing to remain silent, his incursion was detected by the Chief.

In realization of the imminent danger, T and S promptly extinguished the lights trying to allow the others to evade.

As the warehouse went dark, bullets began to fly seemingly in all directions. Duncan pulled Schuyler to safety behind a wooden beam; Nick quickly exited the building, as the Chief fled for cover.

Under attack from interlocking fire from T and S, the Chief did manage to land a couple of shots in the direction of Duncan and Schuyler.

Applying suppressive fire, T and S eventually provided Duncan enough time to transport Schuyler out of the building's rear door onto the street's pavement. Bleeding profusely for a gunshot wound, Schuyler required immediate medical attention.

Running low on ammunition, rounds from Chief's revolver commenced to get sparse. Conserving unspent shells, he stayed concealed in high anticipation of any retaliatory attack.

Duncan, on the alert, noticed Nick preparing the helicopter for flight. Suffering from a gunshot wound to the shoulder, Duncan searched for a mode of transportation for his brother in route to the chopper.

Julie, driving up to the curb where Schuyler lay, requested to provide Schuyler's transportation to the helicopter. "Duncan, allow me to drive Schuyler to the medical evacuation helicopter!"

With little choice, Duncan accepted her offer. "Who are you?" He looked into her eyes with sincerity.

"I'm Schuyler's friend, Julie." She opened the back door of her vehicle. "Put him in the car!" She looked at the front seat, "you come with us!"

In agreement, Duncan secured Schuyler in the back seat. He looked back at the warehouse and yelled to T and S, "we're heading back!"

"Don't worry about us; take him back now!" T informed Duncan.

As Schuyler was being transported to the aircraft, Tim had prepared a litter for his patient. After delivery of his patient, he secured him onto a litter and commanded the loading of his patient, utilizing proper techniques, onto the helicopter.

After delivery of Schuyler, Julie drove back to the warehouse to aid T and S.

She was a little leery of returning to the warehouse, but could not leave the two Army soldiers behind. As she learned from Schuyler's Army training, no soldier should ever be left behind. In rendezvous with T and S, she watched the dust-off of the medical evacuation helicopter. With much confidence, she knew Schuyler was in goods hands with Duncan, Tim, and Nick; but with great worry she knew Schuyler was severely injured, to what extent she did not know.

Withstanding any residual fire from the Chief, T and S evaded injury and escaped easily out the rear door. Rallying with Julie, they departed the scene with only a few scratches. With the opportunity to capture the Chief along with his followers, they decided to disappear with Julie before the police appeared. With the gunfire, the local authorities were sure to investigate shortly.

Greeting the police, Morrison and Boyd explained the entire situation. Using the alibi of driving for chicken and noticing the commotion, they pretended not to be directly involved with the circumstances. Alerted earlier by the parents, the police understood a little bit of the occurring incident. Eventually after all of the turmoil, the authorities were tracking Nick's helicopter in effort to recover Schuyler. Since he was reported missing, it was still their duty to officially uncover him.

With Schuyler in route to the Army hospital via helicopter and Julie driving across the state in her rented car, Morrison and Boyd returned back to the Jupiter with much anticipation of the fate of The Air.

The valiant escape revealed courage. It did not contain just one person's bravery, but the ability of a cohesive team to unite principles in coming together to accomplish a common goal. Individual achievements such as Nick's piloting and Tim's medical expertise collaborated with battle drill tactical knowledge demonstrated by Duncan, T, and S. But among the gallantry in action, the measures taken by Julie Crystal Flowers made a mark on this covert operation. Without her initiative, timely decision-making, and attention to detail, the operation could have been a demoralizing failure. Of course she was not involved with the actual fighting, but her interactions via air transmittance provided much needed support in order for the others to accomplish their mission. For her interactions, Schuyler is flying safely back to the Army hospital for emergency care treatment. For Julie, all she could do is to pray for her beloved telepathic partner and hope for the best.

CHAPTER 23

Returning to their office, the Jupiter duo got down to business. Confident in the surgical expertise of military doctors, they expected their subject would pull through. But still the thought of losing The Air forever was a little too much for either one of them to swallow.

"He's still unconscious." Morrison's worry agitated Boyd.

Boyd responded, "I still detect brain activity, he's currently in a dream state similar if he was asleep."

"The medic must have sedated him, initiating medical treatment." Morrison waited for his hot coffee.

"The girl helped save his life, if not for her The Vision may not be." Boyd shared a cup of coffee with his partner.

The Jupiter twosome patiently waited, in the darkness of night, at their office for any clue possibly restoring The Air back to original form. It was a frustrating time, but they vowed to maintain optimism as The Air fought for his life.

In route, via rental car, Julie and two former Special Forces were flying low. Not a direct route, their trip would be a difficult one that would eventually lead them to the hospital admitting Schuyler as its patient.

The medical evacuation helicopter flew in a very direct route to their designation. Receiving air traffic control clearance, Nick steered the aircraft into the black of night as Tim treated his patient for a sucking chest wound. Positioning him on his injured side, fearing a possible damaged lung, Tim's medical know-how enabled Schuyler a solid fighting chance.

Injured also, Duncan's shoulder was in a sling. Wounded by an errant round from the Chief, he was limited in any aid afforded to Tim. Understanding Schuyler state of affairs, Duncan was merely powerless in his brother's defense.

Rain fell onto the night, impairing Julie's driving ability. Every sweep of the windshield wiper, every pound of her heart, and every blink of her eye exemplified the intense concentration beheld during this road trip. Even the silence of T and S, typified apprehensive dispositions of the two previous Special Force soldiers as their transportation pounded the wet pavement in route back to their desired designation.

Lying on the litter with an intravenous mixture in his arm, he gained consciousness. "Doc, how am I doing?" He directed in question to Tim.

"Just a nasty sucking chest wound." Tim reassured by patting him on the shoulder. "Be careful when you breathe; because there is a good chance that a lung could be damaged."

Duncan looked over at his brother, "we are going back to the hospital at the post."

Exhibiting his sling to Schuyler, "it looks like I took a bullet too."

Piloting the chopper, Nick prepared to descend upon the post. He had landed plenty of helicopters at the hospital's heliport; he radioed ahead alerting the emergency room of an incoming patient. Nick projected within ten minutes; his aircraft would be at the heliport.

In evident pain and much blood loss, Schuyler struggled to preserve his life. Experiencing continuous thinking of random thoughts, he could vision himself lying on some operating room table in the midst of surgery.

"Hold on, we are about to descend!" Informed by Nick, Tim broadcasted to Duncan and Schuyler. "In a matter of minutes we'll be transported from the heliport to the emergency room via ground ambulance.

Julie, in her mind, knew Schuyler was still holding onto his life, but still the expectancy of his arrival at the emergency room worried her to a great extent. Continuing to drive in a thundershower, she vowed to reach final destination as soon as possible.

As the helicopter prepared to land, Schuyler resisted the painful sensations directing from inside in chest cavity. Fighting off the effects of the bullet wound, he slipped back into shock.

Noticing something wrong with Schuyler, Julie exerted compelling effort to regain communicative connection. *"Schuyler, please respond to me!"* In emotional distress, *"I'm coming to be with you, I'll be there soon sugar!"*

Nick landed the chopper at the heliport, Tim and the emergency room medics removed Schuyler from the aircraft into the ground ambulance, and safely the emergency room staff admitted their newly arrived patient. In the trauma room, initial triage of Schuyler disclosed possible internal injuries in association with the sucking chest wound.

During stabilization in the trauma room, emergency room doctors placed their patient on respiratory support attempting to prevent further bleeding. Their patient had lost a lot of blood during the medical evacuation helicopter transport, along with various internal injuries. After initial stabilization, their patient was forwarded to the operating room.

As Schuyler was transferred to the operating room, Tim explained the details to Duncan and Nick. As an emergency room medic, his knowledge and expertise on the matter was very accommodating effectively familiarizing the urgency of the situation to the others.

As Duncan completed the admission papers, he displayed his brother's medical insurance card to the admission office. Explaining Schuyler's status, he informed of his prior military service. Since Schuyler was no longer active duty in the military, therefore he was not really entitled to medical care at military medical treatment facilities, but Tim's influence got him admitted into the facility due to the extreme circumstances. At conclusion of the admission paperwork, Duncan telephoned his parents in effort of notification.

Mr. and Mrs. Ballantine had been informed by the local police of the incident and were currently preparing an excursion of their own to the military post. Remaining quite calm during the entire ordeal, Schuyler's father arranged to initiate ground travel as soon as possible.

After termination of his conversation with his parents, Duncan returned back to the emergency room for treatment of his own. His shoulder, in severe pain due to his bullet wound, was much overdue for treatment. It was a significant night for the medical treatment facility; Sergeant Ballantine and former Specialist Ballantine were both being provided the utmost prestigious medical care that any hospital, military or civilian, could make available.

An operating room, full of activity, promptly put Schuyler under the knife. Skilled surgeons, nurses, and operating room technicians accepted the challenge as emergency surgery engaged Schuyler. Being under anesthesia, he could not transmit any information to the world in reference of his status.

Arriving to the hospital with T and S, Julie understood a long waiting process was presented before her. Again, she followed Schuyler's mental dreamlike frequency. His brain transmitted errant signals with little form or fashion. Failure to distinguish encouraging brain activity from pessimistic conditions, did not prevent her from devoting her psychosomatic interests from tearful attempt to communicate telepathically with him.

Watching nearly every stroke of the clock, Julie continuously tried to stimulate brain activity. *"Schuyler, remember who I am? I'm Julie, your dearest friend, math tutor, confidant, and lover. I came all the way from San Antonio to be with you now; my heart yearns for the day of togetherness."* She initiated tearful emotion as she sat in the waiting room dressed in damp clothing. Windblown hair, a hundred-yard stare, and wrinkled clothes described the prominent student-athlete as she watched her telepathic companion be transported from the operating room to the recovery room. As before, she tried to communicate telepathically, but received no concrete feedback of any coherent mental activity.

Tim informed the others of the success of the surgery, but reinforced the thought of his relentless struggle to survive. With the verdict still out, Schuyler's fate was still in limbo.

Using Duncan's telephone, Julie called her parents informing them of her whereabouts. Being so far away from Louisiana, it made if very difficult to explain her intentions. In conversation with her mother, she learned of an urgent message to return a telephone call to her basketball coach Cheryl Jackson.

After the telephone conversation with her parents, Julie was notified of Schuyler's admittance into the intensive care unit. "Tim, is this good news or what?"

Looking into her eyes, "he should be getting better," Tim reassured as he tried to persuade her outlook.

Carefully evaluating any recent progress in Schuyler's brain activity, she perceived little change, if any, in his current condition. "I'm going to check into a hotel, I expect to be staying here for a few days."

Duncan added to the conversation. "He'll be in on the ward for a couple of days." He issued his cell phone number, "gives us a call later in the day, Julie."

As Tim and Duncan acknowledged her departure, she returned to her rental car in search of a place to stay. It was mid-morning; she had little rest, needed a warm shower, and desperately needed to return a call back to Louisiana to get in touch with Coach Jackson.

At the hotel, Julie monitored Schuyler's condition through means of telepathic communication. Receiving no telepathic response, she feared the worse; detecting frequent dreaming, she alleged he would eventually regain consciousness. Desperately attempting to communicate with Coach Jackson, she began to speed-dial the phone. In utilization of her calling card, she finally reached FF on the telephone.

In concern of her prize performer, FF greatly requested her attention. "Julie, where are you?"

"I'm at an Army post along the border."

Not knowing what border she was talking about, FF went along with the vague location and proceeded to deliver the breaking news. "Even though we lost in the semi-finals at the Alamo Dome, I conversed with Commissioner Tilley."

"You mean the guy who couldn't even fax a vital message to the correct number." Julie cut into the conversation.

"Let me finish Julie, the Commissioner knows a talent scout who is interested in your acting prospects." FF paused in order to retrieve addition information. "In fact, you have a pending interview!"

"That's unbelievable!" Julie began to experience joyful tears of emotion as she tightly clutched the telephone. "How did he learn of my performing arts ambition?"

"Julie, your story is all over the news. The rise and fall of your empire during the National Tournament has been a tale told throughout the nation." FF sighed in relief as she continued to break the news. "Commissioner Tilley has virtually sealed a contract for your acting debut."

"It's a dream of a lifetime!" The newborn actress joyfully exclaimed in bliss. "What do I need to do?"

"I have the phone number for the Commissioner; you will have to contact him initially. Requesting to apologize for his incompetent actions, he wishes to speak with your personally and initiate the arrangements."

"I'll call him A.S.A.P.!"

FF exchanged the required information with Julie, inaugurating the process for stardom. Fitting as could be, Julie was going to benefit from all of the misunderstandings that occurred throughout the entire ordeal. Fate was on her side; her transformation from girl to woman would be attained through a window of opportunity in relationship to a career in performing arts. This former Louisiana basketball star's destiny was to travel west to California to embark on an acting career, a dream of lifetime.

"Schuyler, I've been asked to interview as an actress." Julie desperately made an effort to make contact with him. *"I just got the news from FF; I'm heading to California for pending auditions."* She waited for a response, *"please recover so I can deliver the good news."*

Schuyler, still in the intensive care unit, was under the careful eye of Captain Gore, the Chief Nurse of the ICU. Monitoring his vital signs, CPT Gore noticed signs of recovery. His patient perceived a slow response to the anesthesia, but had seemingly captured increasing strength. Reflex and pupil responses, along with improve breathing, revealed strong, evident signs of initiation of revitalization.

Prior to a restful nap, Julie observed improvement in his brain activity. In fact, she began to detect errant air phenomena transmissions transacting from the depth of mental expressions. As she fell asleep from a weary night, her heart experienced blissful sensations due to the remarkable development of Schuyler's condition.

While Julie slept, Schuyler exhibited extraordinary recuperation. Encouragement from the nursing staff fostered almost complete recovery.

"Welcome to the world, Schuyler," responded CPT Gore. "You had a rough time with the anesthesia, but you made it through."

Schuyler being too weak to talk nodded his head in acknowledgement. He looked around the room and recognized his brother's face.

"You're safe now brother," responded Duncan. "Mom and Dad will be here shortly."

Receiving a handshake from his brother, Schuyler tried to communicate. "Where is the girl?" He faintly spoke as gazed back at his brother. "Where are the others?"

"Tim and Nick are still here in the hospital, T and S are coming back later, and Julie went to a hotel for rest." Duncan watched the nurse prepare to change Schuyler's dressing.

As Schuyler received quality patient care from the ICU staff, Duncan conversed with Tim and Nick. The horrifying adventure was finally attaining closure. Schuyler's survival from the whole ordeal was appropriately obtained; the entire operation was a complete success. The rescue plan might have been a bit risky, but with the expertise of the players involved, the liberation of Schuyler Ballantine hailed as a heroic feat. In the safety of an Army hospital, a valued patient was in excellent hands in disposition as a patient admitted to the intensive care unit.

Later, he was transferred to another ward for a few days to allow for complete recovery. Being not an active-duty soldier, he did not warrant a lengthy stay in the hospital. After receiving quite a lot of fanfare from the hospital staff, his parents, his brother, and the others, he was ready to be discharged.

The only piece of the puzzle still missing was Julie. She never visited the hospital to pay respect to her beloved telepathic companion. Schuyler yearned dearly for her presence, but collected no reward.

Julie, after notifying Schuyler of her future acting plans, was afraid to make actual person-to-person contact with her telepathic lover. She was afraid of getting to close to the boy she admired, avoiding reality in their relationship. Even though she could read his mind in knowledge of his desire to compose an actual relationship, she understood her table was already set and establishing contact would make it more difficult to break away. Their worlds did not coincide, disparity between the telepathic couple was immense, and the thought of them together frighten her. Still a virgin, as well as Schuyler, she was fearful of a physical relationship.

Schuyler, on the other hand, telegraphed much craving for his dream girl. Even though his discharge from the hospital was that particular day, he felt as he had lost the battle. Even after an amazing rescue, surgery, and recuperation, his heart felt as empty as a vacuum. Understanding her outlook, he recognized the disparity. She was major league and he was little league. She was high-class and he was no-class. Her destiny was to be a famous actress and his was to observe her career at a distance. It was hard to accept, but it was reality. He could never measure up to her and it was evident.

In route to Louisiana to embark on her career, she suddenly reversed her direction and began driving back to the Army post. An abrupt change of heart steered her in the path of her telepathic companion. Realizing his true value, she could not walk away from a relationship that might provide her the companionship she had wished for her entire life.

The remembrance of his gift that allowed her to excel on the basketball court tantalized her thoughts. Questioning herself, she recognized the fact of his contribution placed upon her recent success. If not for his air phenomena, she would have only been a mediocre college basketball player, not capable of being the Regional Most Valuable Player.

As for his point of view, he needed her sensual telepathic touch to ease his tensions as he pursued in his dream life. In response to her telepathic interventions, he achieved greater than expected results during his high school golf career, mathematics study, basic training, Korea guard duty, and Soldier of the Month Board. Not to mention the countless times he and his telepathic lover experienced romantic togetherness. Without his beloved Julie Crystal Flowers, Schuyler would have never developed into the man he was.

In her drive back to rendezvous with her telepathic partner, she had second thoughts involving her future. It was evident the couple needed each other, and both had converted transformation from teen to adult, but she was hesitant in conversion from telepathic lover to physical lover. Wondering if a physical relationship was the only obstacle in her path, she shunned any negative aspects preventing her from meeting her one and only guy. Positive view of their relationship featured how she was there for him during both success and failure, along with his attention provided to her during crucial moments in her basketball career. Indeed, they were both each other's significant other.

Being discharged from the hospital was a big event for Schuyler, a wide-range of extended family members along with his parents prepared for his release from the hospital.

In good spirits, he received his discharge counseling from the pharmacist. Being a pharmacy technician himself, he fully comprehended the medication directions and advice from CPT Conrad, the pharmacy officer. The remaining task in the discharge procedure would be paying the bill. Mr. Ballantine took care of that cost, receiving his son in healthy condition was worth much more than a costly hospital bill.

At the Jupiter, Morrison and Boyd gladly accepted the end result. It was a close call with the gunshot wound, but The Air hung in there. The Jupiter had vested interest in their subject, evaluating metrics at various stages of his life. The Morrison and Boyd tandem had further research ahead of them through the eyes of their subject.

"I just hope the girl stays with him." Boyd expressed his wishful thinking. "I have fallen for her charismatic personality."

"The Air is the key; he will find success wherever he endeavors." Morrison reminded his partner. "Because he beholds the air phenomena and without him the phenomena dissolves."

Boyd terminated his computer for the day and began to exit the office with his partner. "The Vision is unique, he affects us all, and his air phenomenon is truly unlimited."

"John, we all learned a good lesson with this entire ordeal." Morrison opened the exit door for his partner. "We are the true phenomena because we are afforded the opportunity to witness the effect of The Air."

As the Jupiter duo walked to their parked vehicles, they agreed their research with air phenomena was indeed not a waste of time.

The idea of air phenomena occurring in their lifetime encouraged them both, allocating achievements beyond imagination. They believed air phenomena was their destiny and the destiny of air phenomena was their future; because without air phenomena they had no future and without their research air phenomena would have no past. Documenting air phenomena activity was their responsibility; an obligation the Jupiter duo took pleasure in.

In knowledge of Schuyler's discharge from the hospital being imminent, Julie realized her return arrival to the hospital would be too late to link with Schuyler. *"Schuyler, don't leave yet!"* She issued her warning order. *"I need to talk to you personally; I'm in route to your location."*

In full view of his parents, *"what is your estimated time of arrival?"* He prepared an alibi.

"I expect my E.T.A. will be in about thirty mikes." She initiated necessary movement to keep him stationary until she could arrive.

In comprehension of her arrival in about thirty minutes, Schuyler asked if he could visit the recreation center prior to departure. After obtaining permission from his parents of the recreation center trip, Duncan navigated the entire Ballantine family down the street to the recreation center. Fascinated with the assortment of video games, pool tables, and a variety of televised sporting events, Schuyler had selected the perfect spot to patiently wait for his telepathic companion.

Mr. Ballantine favored the center also; it offered the opportunity to watch both horse and car racing at the same time.

"I see that the recreation center is down the street from the hospital, I'll meet you there." She continued to drive her vehicle, not really knowing what she was going to say to him once they encountered. With perception of his shyness, she expected to assume command of the conversation. Preparing persuasive tact, she aspired to induce her telepathic lover in effort to arrange a cohesive bond among the two of them. She realized the cause and effect, balanced strengths and weaknesses, and most of all evaluated a futuristic prospective of a physical relationship.

Challenging his brother in a heated game of eight ball, Schuyler experienced rapid heartbeat, blurry vision, and sweating palms as he highly anticipated her arrival. He was so nervous, he scratched on his winning shot of the eight ball. After he lost three games in a row to his brother, he sensed his emotional state was undergoing involuntary conversions. His heartbeat grew stronger as the clock ticked; the most important engagement of his short lifetime was growing near. Knowing she was about to arrive, he still was unprepared to communicate.

Coming onto post was not as difficult as she feared; the same guards were on duty as before allowing easy access onto the military reservation. Careful not to exceed the speed limit, she eased her way past the repelling towers, the bowling alley, and slowly approached the eminent recreation center. *"Schuyler, I'm here in the parking lot! I'll meet you inside shortly."*

As nervous as could be, Schuyler immediately made a quick jaunt to the restroom. He was so panicky, he didn't know to urinate or vomit. With both a sensation to tinkle and throw-up, he did manage to expel a bit of urine. Breathing profusely, he deferred his nauseous condition as he prepared for the reception.

Extremely apprehensive herself; Julie Crystal Flowers had already entered the facility in search of her dream. Attracting the attention of several spectators, she suddenly took center stage. In reference to her basketball playing days, she was ready to encounter with him a center court.

Schuyler, in remembrance of his golfing past history, approached her as he was about to tee-off with her on the same hole.

In the quietness of the recreation center, one sixth man advanced toward the other sixth man as the Ballantine Family watched in extraordinary expectancy. Schuyler, the sixth man of his school's golf team, and Julie, the sixth man of her school's basketball team, faced each other heart-to-heart.

As Schuyler froze and could not utter a word, Julie initiated the conversation. Peering deep into his eyes, "Schuyler, I have dreamed about this day for an extremely long time." She took a deep breath, "the day I would finally talk to you in this manner."

Schuyler, in hesitance, attempted to express himself but faltered a bit. "When I watched you play basketball, I wanted to meet you but was too scared." His unsymmetrical voice inflection attracted her interest.

"I too was fearful, abstaining from any sort of physical contact." Her eyes were directed away for a moment, "I want to know if you feel the same way about me as I do about you."

In shyness he admired her beautiful smile, "worshiping every move you make on the basketball court and following every bit of news concerning your life has enchanted my strength of mind."

He added, "My compassionate tendencies belong to you *and only your compassion I crave."*

After a sensitive comment like the one he just transmitted, she delivered her knockout punch, "do you want to go to California with me and take a little convalescent leave?" Awaiting a response, but with only silence. She offered once more, "Schuyler, I want you to travel with me to LA and be my guest because I'm going out west to audition for roles as an actress."

"That's great, I'm very proud of you!" Delighted of the news, he almost forgot to ask his parents if he could travel with her. "But wait a minute; I need to gain clearance first."

"Just think about it." She presented additional information. "My agent, Mr. Barbor, has me scheduled for about six days worth of interviewing appointments; can you come along?"

In extreme exhilaration, Schuyler asked his parents if he could go to LA with her. Mr. Ballantine questioned circumstances involving his college attendance, but Julie convinced him of prompt return of his son.

In the midst of celebration from the union of the telepathic couple, Schuyler received counsel from his father. "Son, at first I was a little leery about you traveling out west; but go ahead." He put his hand on his shoulder. "I have watched your maturity from a member of the High School Golf Team, through intense Army activity, to being held hostage due to a pharmaceutical scam." He paused to regain his thoughts. "You have to make your own decisions now!"

Schuyler struggled to speak, "I really would like to visit with her."

"Son, from what you have been through, I have to greatly respect your resolution."

As the eventful day unfolded, Schuyler bid farewell to his parents and saluted Duncan goodbye. Exiting the post with Julie, instead of his parents, was quite an amendment to his plans. Optimistic and fulfilled, he proudly rode as passenger along side of the woman of his destiny.

As they drove carefully back to his residence, in route to her home, they planned their trip as if it was their honeymoon. Unlike a normal honeymoon, consummation was not forecasted.

Even though he was only a spectator in the grand career she had before her, he vowed to be by her side through any rough water she might encounter. He would stand by her side to the very end, illuminating her life to greatest extent. Her career was certain to be enlightened by his presence, for he brought air phenomena, a conception that had aided her previous basketball prominence. As the beholder of air phenomena, he glorified her introduction into a world never experiencing an existence of this sort. A new wave of communication would embark their final destination, with Schuyler by her side she would govern as inimitable focal point.

Transformation had been completed. The couple evolved into adulthood, being progressed from meek teenagers into mature young adults. Lack of support of one another would have impaired transformation; the strength and perseverance of their relationship escalated their progression.

She needed him, as he needed her. Through telepathic communication, the couple achieved their goals. Ambition in reference to golf, mathematics, the Army, or basketball was not the entire package to this telepathic arrangement. It was the transformation of two individuals, who lived apart, as they found themselves, their dreams, and their soul mates. It was no pot of gold at the end of a rainbow, but it was something special. The special something the two of them could share. Because she had the one who had telepathic vision, an attribute that only he possessed. He was her treasure as he treasured her, but the story's most significant outcome revealed the extraordinary significance of dreams. Julie Crystal Flowers had followed her dream throughout her life's story; but in the conclusion of her story, the dream followed her.

978-0-595-37250-8
0-595-37250-3

Printed in the United States
39739LVS00004B/58-84

9 780595 372508